MY
SISTER'S
KEEPER

Also by Jodi Picoult

Second Glance

Perfect Match

Salem Falls

Plain Truth

Keeping Faith

The Pact

Mercy

Picture Perfect

Harvesting the Heart

Songs of the Humpback Whale

MY SISTER'S KEEPER

A NOVEL

Jodi Picoult

ATRIA BOOKS

NEW YORK   LONDON   TORONTO   SYDNEY

**This Large Print Book carries the
Seal of Approval of N.A.V.H.**

ATRIA BOOKS
1230 Avenue of the Americas
New York, NY 10020

ISBN: 0-7434-8619-6

First Atria Books large-print hardcover edition May 2004

10   9   8   7   6   5   4   3   2   1

ATRIA B O O K S is a trademark of Simon & Schuster, Inc.

Manufactured in the United States of America

For information regarding special discounts for bulk
purchases, please contact Simon & Schuster Special Sales at
1-800-456-6798 or business@simonandschuster.com

To the Currans:

The best family members we're not

technically related to.

Thanks for being such a big part of our lives.

ACKNOWLEDGMENTS

As the mother of a child who had ten surgeries in three years, I would like to thank first the doctors and nurses who routinely take the hardest moments a family can experience and soften the edges: to Dr. Roland Eavey and the pediatric nursing staff at Mass. Eye and Ear— thank you for the real-life happy ending. In the course of writing **My Sister's Keeper**, as always, I was reminded of how very little I know, and how much I rely on the experience and the intellect of others. For allowing me to borrow from their lives personally and professionally, or for suggestions of pure writing genius: thank you, Jennifer Sternick, Sherry Fritzsche, Giancarlo Cicchetti, Greg Kachejian, Dr. Vincent Guarerra, Dr. Richard Stone, Dr. Farid Boulad, Dr. Eric Terman, Dr. James Umlas, Wyatt Fox, Andrea Greene and Dr. Michael Goldman, Lori Thompson, Synthia Follensbee, Robin Kall, Mary Ann McKenney, Harriet St. Laurent, April Murdoch, Aidan Curran,

Jane Picoult, and Jo-Ann Mapson. For making me "can man" for the night, and part of a bona fide firefighting team: thanks to Michael Clark, Dave Hautanemi, Richard "Pokey" Low, and Jim Belanger (who also gets a gold star for editing my mistakes). For throwing their considerable support behind me, thanks to Carolyn Reidy, Judith Curr, Camille McDuffie, Laura Mullen, Sarah Branham, Karen Mender, Shannon McKenna, Paolo Pepe, Seale Ballenger, Anne Harris, and the indomitable Atria sales force. For believing in me first, my pure gratitude to Laura Gross. For outstanding guidance and the freedom to spread my wings, my sincere appreciation to Emily Bestler. For Scott and Amanda MacLellan, and Dave Cranmer—who offered me insight into the triumphs and tragedies of living daily with a life-threatening disease—thank you for your generosity, and best wishes for a long and healthy future.

And, as always, thanks to Kyle, Jake, Sammy, and especially to Tim, for being what matters most.

PROLOGUE

No one starts a war—or rather, no one in his sense ought to do so—without first being clear in his mind what he intends to achieve by that war and how he intends to conduct it.

—CARL VON CLAUSEWITZ, Vom Kriege

In my first memory, I am three years old and I am trying to kill my sister. Sometimes the recollection is so clear I can remember the itch of the pillowcase under my hand, the sharp point of her nose pressing into my palm. She didn't stand a chance against me, of course, but it still didn't work. My father walked by, tucking in the house for the night, and saved her. He led me back to my own bed. "That," he told me, "never happened."

As we got older, I didn't seem to exist, except in relation to her. I would watch her sleep across the room from me, one long shadow linking our beds, and I would count the ways. Poison, sprinkled on her cereal. A wicked undertow off the beach. Lightning striking.

In the end, though, I did not kill my sister. She did it all on her own.

Or at least this is what I tell myself.

MONDAY

Brother, I am fire

Surging under ocean floor.

I shall never meet you, brother—

Not for years, anyhow;

Maybe thousands of years, brother.

Then I will warm you,

Hold you close, wrap you in circles,

Use you and change you—

Maybe thousands of years, brother.

—CARL SANDBURG, "Kin"

ANNA

WHEN I WAS LITTLE, the great mystery to me wasn't **how** babies were made, but **why**. The mechanics I understood—my older brother Jesse had filled me in—although at the time I was sure he'd heard half of it wrong. Other kids my age were busy looking up the words **penis** and **vagina** in the classroom dictionary when the teacher had her back turned, but I paid attention to different details. Like why some mothers only had one child, while other families seemed to multiply before your eyes. Or how the new girl in school, Sedona, told anyone who'd listen that she was named for the place where her parents were vacationing when they made her (**"Good thing they weren't staying in Jersey City,"** my father used to say).

Now that I am thirteen, these distinctions are

only more complicated: the eighth-grader who dropped out of school because she **got into trouble;** a neighbor who **got herself pregnant** in the hopes it would keep her husband from filing for divorce. I'm telling you, if aliens landed on earth today and took a good hard look at why babies get born, they'd conclude that most people have children by accident, or because they drink too much on a certain night, or because birth control isn't one hundred percent, or for a thousand other reasons that really aren't very flattering.

On the other hand, I was born for a very specific purpose. I wasn't the result of a cheap bottle of wine or a full moon or the heat of the moment. I was born because a scientist managed to hook up my mother's eggs and my father's sperm to create a specific combination of precious genetic material. In fact, when Jesse told me how babies get made and I, the great disbeliever, decided to ask my parents the truth, I got more than I bargained for. They sat me down and told me all the usual stuff, of course— but they also explained that they chose little embryonic me, specifically, because I could save my sister, Kate. "We loved you even more," my mother made sure to say, "because we knew what exactly we were getting."

It made me wonder, though, what would have happened if Kate had been healthy. Chances are, I'd still be floating up in Heaven or wherever, waiting to be attached to a body to spend some time on Earth. Certainly I would not be part of this family. See, unlike the rest of the free world, I didn't get here by accident. And if your parents have you for a reason, then that reason better exist. Because once it's gone, so are you.

Pawnshops may be full of junk, but they're also a breeding ground for stories, if you ask me, not that you did. What happened to make a person trade in the Never Before Worn Diamond Solitaire? Who needed money so badly they'd sell a teddy bear missing an eye? As I walk up to the counter, I wonder if someone will look at the locket I'm about to give up, and ask these same questions.

The man at the cash register has a nose the

shape of a turnip, and eyes sunk so deep I can't imagine how he sees well enough to go about his business. "Need something?" he asks.

It's all I can do to not turn around and walk out the door, pretend I've come in by mistake. The only thing that keeps me steady is knowing I am not the first person to stand in front of this counter holding the one item in the world I never thought I'd part with.

"I have something to sell," I tell him.

"Am I supposed to guess what it is?"

"Oh." Swallowing, I pull the locket out of the pocket of my jeans. The heart falls on the glass counter in a pool of its own chain. "It's fourteen-karat gold," I pitch. "Hardly ever worn." This is a lie; until this morning, I haven't taken it off in seven years. My father gave it to me when I was six after the bone marrow harvest, because he said anyone who was giving her sister such a major present deserved one of her own. Seeing it there, on the counter, my neck feels shivery and naked.

The owner puts a loupe up to his eye, which makes it seem almost normal size. "I'll give you twenty."

"Dollars?"

"No, pesos. What did you think?"

"It's worth five times that!" I'm guessing.

The owner shrugs. "I'm not the one who needs the money."

I pick up the locket, resigned to sealing the deal, and the strangest thing happens—my hand, it just clamps shut like the Jaws of Life. My face goes red with the effort to peel apart my fingers. It takes what seems like an hour for that locket to spill into the owner's outstretched palm. His eyes stay on my face, softer now. "Tell them you lost it," he offers, advice tossed in for free.

If Mr. Webster had decided to put the word **freak** in his dictionary, **Anna Fitzgerald** would be the best definition he could give. It's more than just the way I look: refugee-skinny with absolutely no chest to speak of, hair the color of dirt, connect-the-dot freckles on my cheeks that, let me tell you, do not fade with lemon juice or sunscreen or even, sadly, sandpaper. No, God was obviously in some kind of mood on my birthday, because he added to this fabulous physical combination the bigger picture—the household into which I was born.

My parents tried to make things normal, but that's a relative term. The truth is, I was never really a kid. To be honest, neither were Kate and Jesse. I guess maybe my brother had his moment in the sun for the four years he was alive before Kate got diagnosed, but ever since then, we've been too busy looking over our shoulders to run headlong into growing up. You know how most little kids think they're like cartoon characters—if an anvil drops on their heads they can peel themselves off the sidewalk and keep going? Well, I never once believed that. How could I, when we practically set a place for Death at the dinner table?

Kate has acute promyelocytic leukemia. Actually, that's not quite true—right now she doesn't have it, but it's hibernating under her skin like a bear, until it decides to roar again. She was diagnosed when she was two; she's sixteen now. **Molecular relapse** and **granulocyte** and **portacath**—these words are part of my vocabulary, even though I'll never find them on any SAT. I'm an allogeneic donor—a perfect sibling match. When Kate needs leukocytes or stem cells or bone marrow to fool her body into thinking it's healthy, I'm the one who provides them. Nearly every time Kate's hospitalized, I wind up there, too.

None of which means anything, except that you shouldn't believe what you hear about me, least of all that which I tell you myself.

As I am coming up the stairs, my mother comes out of her room wearing another ball gown. "Ah," she says, turning her back to me. "Just the girl I wanted to see."

I zip it up and watch her twirl. My mother could be beautiful, if she were parachuted into someone else's life. She has long dark hair and the fine collarbones of a princess, but the corners of her mouth turn down, like she's swallowed bitter news. She doesn't have much free time, since a calendar is something that can change drastically if my sister develops a bruise or a nosebleed, but what she does have she spends at Bluefly.com, ordering ridiculously fancy evening dresses for places she is never going to go. "What do you think?" she asks.

The gown is all the colors of a sunset, and made out of material that swishes when she moves. It's strapless, what a star might wear sashaying down a red carpet—totally not the dress code for a suburban house in Upper Darby, RI. My mother twists her hair into a knot and holds it in place. On her bed are three other dresses—one slinky and black, one bugle-beaded, one that seems impossibly small. "You look . . ."

Tired. The word bubbles right under my lips.

My mother goes perfectly still, and I wonder if I've said it without meaning to. She holds up a hand, shushing me, her ear cocked to the open doorway. "Did you hear that?"

"Hear what?"

"Kate."

"I didn't hear anything."

But she doesn't take my word for it, because when it comes to Kate she doesn't take anybody's word for it. She marches upstairs and opens up our bedroom door to find my sister hysterical on her bed, and just like that the world collapses again. My father, a closet astronomer, has tried to explain black holes to me, how they are so heavy they absorb everything, even light, right into their center. Moments like this are the same kind of vacuum; no matter what you cling to, you wind up being sucked in.

"Kate!" My mother sinks down to the floor, that stupid skirt a cloud around her. "Kate, honey, what hurts?"

Kate hugs a pillow to her stomach, and tears keep streaming down her face. Her pale hair is stuck to her face in damp streaks; her breathing's too tight. I stand frozen in the doorway of my own room, waiting for instructions: **Call Daddy. Call 911. Call Dr. Chance.** My mother goes so far as to shake a better explanation out of Kate. "It's Preston," she sobs. "He's leaving Serena for good."

That's when we notice the TV. On the screen, a blond hottie gives a longing look to a woman crying almost as hard as my sister, and then he slams the door. "But what hurts?" my mother asks, certain there has to be more to it than this.

"Oh my **God,**" Kate says, sniffling. "Do you have any idea how much Serena and Preston have been through? Do you?"

That fist inside me relaxes, now that I know

it's all right. Normal, in our house, is like a blanket too short for a bed—sometimes it covers you just fine, and other times it leaves you cold and shaking; and worst of all, you never know which of the two it's going to be. I sit down on the end of Kate's bed. Although I'm only thirteen, I'm taller than her and every now and then people mistakenly assume I'm the older sister. At different times this summer she has been crazy for Callahan, Wyatt, and Liam, the male leads on this soap. Now, I guess, it's all about Preston. "There was the kidnapping scare," I volunteer. I actually followed that story line; Kate made me tape the show during her dialysis sessions.

"And the time she almost married his twin by mistake," Kate adds.

"Don't forget when he died in the boat accident. For two months, anyway." My mother joins the conversation, and I remember that she used to watch this soap, too, sitting with Kate in the hospital.

For the first time, Kate seems to notice my mother's outfit. "What are you **wearing?**"

"Oh. Something I'm sending back." She

stands up in front of me so that I can undo her zipper. This mail-order compulsion, for any other mother, would be a wake-up call for therapy; for my mom, it would probably be considered a healthy break. I wonder if it's putting on someone else's skin for a while that she likes so much, or if it's the option of being able to send back a circumstance that just doesn't suit you. She looks at Kate, hard. "You're sure nothing hurts?"

After my mother leaves, Kate sinks a little. That's the only way to describe it—how fast color drains from her face, how she disappears against the pillows. As she gets sicker, she fades a little more, until I am afraid one day I will wake up and not be able to see her at all. "Move," Kate orders. "You're blocking the picture."

So I go to sit on my own bed. "It's only the coming attractions."

"Well, if I die tonight I want to know what I'm missing."

I fluff my pillows up under my head. Kate, as usual, has swapped so that she has all the funchy ones that don't feel like rocks under your neck. She's supposed to deserve this, because she's three years older than me or because she's sick or because the moon is in Aquarius—there's **always** a reason. I squint at the television, wishing I could flip through the stations, knowing I don't have a prayer. "Preston looks like he's made out of plastic."

"Then why did I hear you whispering his name last night into your pillow?"

"Shut up," I say.

"**You** shut up." Then Kate smiles at me. "He probably **is** gay, though. Quite a waste, considering the Fitzgerald sisters are—" Wincing, she breaks off mid-sentence, and I roll toward her.

"Kate?"

She rubs her lower back. "It's nothing."

It's her kidneys. "Want me to get Mom?"

"Not yet." She reaches between our beds, which are just far apart enough for us to touch each other if we both try. I hold out my hand, too. When we were little we'd make this bridge and try to see how many Barbies we could get to balance on it.

Lately, I have been having nightmares, where I'm cut into so many pieces that there isn't enough of me to be put back together.

• • •

My father says that a fire will burn itself out, unless you open a window and give it fuel. I suppose that's what I'm doing, when you get right down to it; but then again, my dad also says that when flames are licking at your heels you've got to break a wall or two if you want to escape. So when Kate falls asleep from her meds I take the leather binder I keep between my mattress and box spring and go into the bathroom for privacy. I know Kate's been snooping—I rigged up a red thread between the zipper's teeth to let me know who was prying into my stuff without my permission, but even though the thread's been torn there's nothing missing inside. I turn on the water in the bathtub so it sounds like I'm in there for a reason, and sit down on the floor to count.

If you add in the twenty dollars from the pawnshop, I have $136.87. It's not going to be enough, but there's got to be a way around that. Jesse didn't have $2,900 when he bought his beat-up Jeep, and the bank gave him some kind of loan. Of course, my parents had to sign the papers, too, and I doubt they're going to be willing to do that for me, given the circumstances. I count the money a second time, just in case the bills have miraculously reproduced, but math is math and the total stays the same. And then I read the newspaper clippings.

Campbell Alexander. It's a stupid name, in my opinion. It sounds like a bar drink that costs too much, or a brokerage firm. But you can't deny the man's track record.

To reach my brother's room, you actually have to leave the house, which is exactly the way he likes it. When Jesse turned sixteen he moved into the attic over the garage—a perfect arrangement, since he didn't want my parents to see what he was doing and my parents didn't really want to see. Blocking the stairs to his place are four snow tires, a small wall of cartons, and an oak desk tipped onto its side. Sometimes I think Jesse sets up these obstacles himself, just to make getting to him more of a challenge.

I crawl over the mess and up the stairs, which vibrate with the bass from Jesse's stereo. It takes nearly five whole minutes before he hears me knocking. "What?" he snaps, opening the door a crack.

"Can I come in?"

He thinks twice, then steps back to let me enter. The room is a sea of dirty clothes and magazines and leftover Chinese take-out cartons; it smells like the sweaty tongue of a hockey skate. The only neat spot is the shelf where Jesse keeps his special collection—a Jaguar's silver mascot, a Mercedes symbol, a Mustang's horse—hood ornaments that he told me he just found lying around, although I'm not dumb enough to believe him.

Don't get me wrong—it isn't that my parents don't care about Jesse or whatever trouble he's gotten himself mixed up in. It's just that they don't really have time to care about it, because it's a problem somewhere lower on the totem pole.

Jesse ignores me, going back to whatever he was doing on the far side of the mess. My attention is caught by a Crock-Pot—one that disappeared out of the kitchen a few months ago—which now sits on top of Jesse's TV with a copper tube threaded out of its lid and down through a plastic milk jug filled with ice, emptying into a glass Mason jar. Jesse may be a borderline delinquent, but he's brilliant. Just as I'm about to touch the contraption, Jesse turns around. "Hey!" He fairly flies over the couch to knock my hand away. "You'll screw up the condensing coil."

"Is this what I think it is?"

A nasty grin itches over his face. "Depends on what you think it is." He jimmies out the Mason jar, so that liquid drips onto the carpet. "Have a taste."

For a still made out of spit and glue, it produces pretty potent moonshine whiskey. An inferno races so fast through my belly and legs I fall back onto the couch. "Disgusting," I gasp.

Jesse laughs and takes a swig, too, although for him it goes down easier. "So what do you want from me?"

"How do you know I want something?"

"Because no one comes up here on a social call," he says, sitting on the arm of the couch. "And if it was something about Kate, you would've already told me."

"It **is** about Kate. Sort of." I press the newspaper clippings into my brother's hand; they'll do a better job explaining than I ever could. He scans them, then looks me right in the eye. His are the palest shade of silver, so surprising that sometimes when he stares at you, you can completely forget what you were planning to say.

"Don't mess with the system, Anna," he says bitterly. "We've all got our scripts down pat. Kate plays the Martyr. I'm the Lost Cause. And you, you're the Peacekeeper."

He thinks he knows me, but that goes both ways—and when it comes to friction, Jesse is an addict. I look right at him. "Says who?"

Jesse agrees to wait for me in the parking lot. It's one of the few times I can recall him doing anything I tell him to do. I walk around to the front of the building, which has two gargoyles guarding its entrance.

Campbell Alexander, Esquire's office is on the third floor. The walls are paneled with wood the color of a chestnut mare's coat, and when I step onto the thick Oriental rug on the floor, my sneakers sink an inch. The secretary is wearing black pumps so shiny I can see my own face in them. I glance down at my cutoffs and the Keds that I tattooed last week with Magic Markers when I was bored.

The secretary has perfect skin and perfect eyebrows and honeybee lips, and she's using them to scream bloody murder at whoever's on the other end of the phone. "You cannot expect me to tell a judge that. Just because **you** don't want to hear Kleman rant and rave doesn't mean that **I** have to . . . no, actually, that raise was for the exceptional job I do and the crap I put up with on a daily basis, and as a matter of fact, while we're on—" She holds the phone away from her ear; I can make out the buzz of disconnection. "Bastard," she mutters, and then seems to realize I'm standing three feet away. "Can I help you?"

She looks me over from head to toe, rating me on a general scale of first impressions, and finding me severely lacking. I lift my chin and pretend to be far more cool than I actually am. "I have an appointment with Mr. Alexander. At four o'clock."

"Your voice," she says. "On the phone, you didn't sound quite so . . ."

Young?

She smiles uncomfortably. "We don't try juvenile cases, as a rule. If you'd like I can offer you the names of some practicing attorneys who—"

I take a deep breath. "Actually," I interrupt, "you're wrong. Smith v. Whately, Edmunds v. Womens and Infants Hospital, and Jerome v. the Diocese of Providence all involved litigants under the age of eighteen. All three resulted in verdicts for Mr. Alexander's clients. And those were just in the past **year.**"

The secretary blinks at me. Then a slow smile toasts her face, as if she's decided she just might like me after all. "Come to think of it, why don't you just wait in his office?" she suggests, and she stands up to show me the way.

Even if I spend every minute of the rest of my life reading, I do not believe that I will ever manage to consume the sheer number of words routed high and low on the walls of Campbell Alexander, Esquire's office. I do the math—if there are 400 words or so on every page, and each of those legal books are 400 pages, and there are twenty on a shelf and six shelves per bookcase—why, you're pushing nineteen million words, and that's only part-way across the room.

I'm alone in the office long enough to note that his desk is so neat, you could play Chinese football on the blotter; that there is not a single photo of a wife or a kid or even himself; and that in spite of the fact that the room is spotless, there's a mug full of water sitting on the floor.

I find myself making up explanations: it's a swimming pool for an army of ants. It's some kind of primitive humidifier. It's a mirage.

I've nearly convinced myself about that last one, and am leaning over to touch it to see if it's real, when the door bursts open. I practically fall out of my chair and that puts me eye to eye with an incoming German shepherd, which spears me with a look and then marches over to the mug and starts to drink.

Campbell Alexander comes in, too. He's got black hair and he's at least as tall as my dad—six feet—with a right-angle jaw and eyes that look frozen over. He shrugs out of a suit jacket and hangs it neatly on the back of the door, then yanks a file out of a cabinet before moving to his desk. He never makes eye contact with me, but he starts talking all the same. "I don't want any Girl Scout cookies," Campbell Alexander says. "Although you do get Brownie points for tenacity. Ha." He smiles at his own joke.

"I'm not selling anything."

He glances at me curiously, then pushes a button on his phone. "Kerri," he says when the secretary answers. "What is this doing in my office?"

"I'm here to retain you," I say.

The lawyer releases the intercom button. "I don't think so."

"You don't even know if I have a case."

I take a step forward; so does the dog. For the first time I realize it's wearing one of those vests with a red cross on it, like a St. Bernard that might carry rum up a snowy mountain. I automatically reach out to pet him. "Don't," Alexander says. "Judge is a service dog."

My hand goes back to my side. "But you aren't blind."

"Thank you for pointing that out to me."

"So what's the matter with you?"

The minute I say it, I want to take it back. Haven't I watched Kate field this question from hundreds of rude people?

"I have an iron lung," Campbell Alexander says curtly, "and the dog keeps me from getting too close to magnets. Now, if you'd do me the exalted honor of leaving, my secretary can find you the name of someone who—"

But I can't go yet. "Did you really sue God?" I take out all the newspaper clippings, smooth them on the bare desk.

A muscle tics in his cheek, and then he picks up the article lying on top. "I sued the Diocese of Providence, on behalf of a kid in one of their orphanages who needed an experimental treatment involving fetal tissue, which they felt violated Vatican II. However, it makes a much better headline to say that a nine-year-old is suing God for being stuck with the short end of the straw in life." I just stare at him. "Dylan Jerome," the lawyer admits, "wanted to sue God for not caring enough about him."

A rainbow might as well have cracked down the middle of that big mahogany desk. "Mr. Alexander," I say, "my sister has leukemia."

"I'm sorry to hear that. But even if I were willing to litigate against God again, which I'm not, you can't bring a lawsuit on someone else's behalf."

There is way too much to explain—my own blood seeping into my sister's veins; the nurses holding me down to stick me for white cells Kate might borrow; the doctor saying they didn't get enough the first time around. The bruises and the deep bone ache after I gave up my marrow; the shots that sparked more stem cells in me, so that there'd be extra for my sister. The fact that I'm not sick, but I might as well be. The fact that the only reason I was born was as a harvest crop for Kate. The fact that even now, a major decision about me is being made, and no one's bothered to ask the one person who most deserves it to speak her opinion.

There's way too much to explain, and so I do the best I can. "It's not God. Just my parents," I say. "I want to sue them for the rights to my own body."

CAMPBELL

WHEN YOU ONLY HAVE a hammer, everything looks like a nail.

This is something my father, the first Campbell Alexander, used to say; it is also in my opinion the cornerstone of the American civil justice system. Simply put, people who have been backed into a corner will do anything to fight their way to the center again. For some, this means throwing punches. For others, it means instigating a lawsuit. And for that, I'm especially grateful.

On the periphery of my desk Kerri has arranged my messages the way I prefer—urgent ones written on green Post-its, less pressing matters on yellow ones, lined up in neat columns like a double game of solitaire. One phone number catches my eye, and I frown, moving the green Post-it to the yellow side instead. **Your mother called four times!!!** Kerri has written. On second thought, I rip the Post-it in half and send it sailing into the trash.

The girl sitting across from me waits for an answer, one I'm deliberately withholding. She says she wants to sue her parents, like every other teenager on the planet. But **she** wants to sue for the rights to her own body. It is exactly the kind of case I avoid like the Black Plague—one which requires far too much effort and client baby-sitting. With a sigh, I get up. "What did you say your name was?"

"I didn't." She sits a little straighter. "It's Anna Fitzgerald."

I open the door and bellow for my secretary. "Kerri! Can you get the Planned Parenthood number for Ms. Fitzgerald?"

"**What?**" When I turn around, the kid is standing. "Planned **Parenthood?**"

"Look, Anna, here's a little advice. Instigating a lawsuit because your parents won't let you get birth control pills or go to an abortion clinic is like using a sledgehammer to kill a mosquito. You can save your allowance money and go to Planned Parenthood; they're far better equipped to deal with your problem."

For the first time since I've entered my office, I really, truly look at her. Anger glows around this kid like electricity. "My sister is dying, and my mother wants me to donate one of my kidneys to her," she says hotly. "Somehow I don't think a handful of free condoms is going to take care of that."

You know how every now and then, you have a moment where your whole life stretches out ahead of you like a forked road, and even as you choose one gritty path you've got your eyes on the other the whole time, certain that you're making a mistake? Kerri approaches, holding out a strip of paper with the number I've asked for, but I close the door without taking it and walk back to my desk. "No one can make you donate an organ if you don't want to."

"Oh, really?" She leans forward, counting off on her fingers. "The first time I gave something to my sister, it was cord blood, and I was a newborn. She has leukemia—APL—and my cells put her into remission. The next time she relapsed, I was five and I had lymphocytes drawn from me, three times over, because the doctors never seemed to get enough of them the first time around. When that stopped working, they took bone marrow for a transplant. When Kate got infections, I had to donate granulocytes. When she relapsed again, I had to donate peripheral blood stem cells."

This girl's medical vocabulary would put some of my paid experts to shame. I pull a legal pad out of a drawer. "Obviously, you've agreed to be a donor for your sister before."

She hesitates, then shakes her head. "Nobody ever asked."

"Did you tell your parents you don't want to donate a kidney?"

"They don't listen to me."

"They might, if you mentioned this."

She looks down, so that her hair covers her face. "They don't really pay attention to me, except when they need my blood or something. I wouldn't even be alive, if it wasn't for Kate being sick."

An heir and a spare: this was a custom that went back to my ancestors in England. It sounded callous—having a subsequent child just in case the first one happens to die—yet it had been eminently practical once. Being an afterthought might not sit well with this kid, but the truth is that children are conceived for less than admirable reasons every single day: to glue a bad marriage together; to keep the family name alive; to mold in a parent's own image. "They had me so that I could save Kate," the girl explains. "They went to special doctors and everything, and picked the embryo that would be a perfect genetic match."

There had been ethics courses in law school, but they were generally regarded as either a gut or an oxymoron, and I usually skipped them. Still, anyone who tuned in periodically to CNN would know about the controversies of stem cell research. Spare-parts babies, designer infants, the science of tomorrow to save the children of today.

I tap my pen on the desk, and Judge—my dog—sidles closer. "What happens if you don't give your sister a kidney?"

"She'll die."

"And you're okay with that?"

Anna's mouth sets in a thin line. "I'm here, aren't I?"

"Yes, you are. I'm just trying to figure out

what made you want to put your foot down, after all this time."

She looks over at the bookshelf. "Because," she says simply, "it never stops."

Suddenly, something seems to jog her memory. She reaches into her pocket and puts a wad of crumpled bills and change onto my desk. "You don't have to worry about getting paid, either. That's $136.87. I know it's not enough, but I'll figure out a way to get more."

"I charge two hundred an hour."

"**Dollars?**"

"Wampum doesn't fit in the ATM deposit slot," I say.

"Maybe I could walk your dog, or something."

"Service dogs get walked by their owners." I shrug. "We'll work something out."

"You can't be my lawyer for free," she insists.

"Fine, then. You can polish my doorknobs." It's not that I'm a particularly charitable man, but rather that legally, this case is a lock: she doesn't want to give a kidney; no court in its right mind would force her to give up a kidney; I don't have to do any legal research; the parents will cave in before we go to trial, and that will be that. Plus, the case will generate a ton of publicity for me, and will jack up my pro bono for the whole damn decade. "I'm going to file a petition for you in family court: legal emancipation for medical purposes," I say.

"Then what?"

"There will be a hearing, and the judge will appoint a guardian ad litem, which is—"

"—a person trained to work with kids in the family court, who determines what's in the child's best interests," Anna recites. "Or in other words, just another grown-up deciding what happens to me."

"Well, that's the way the law works, and you can't get around it. But a GAL is theoretically only looking out for **you,** not your sister or your parents."

She watches me take out a legal pad and scrawl a few notes. "Does it bother you that your name is backward?"

"What?" I stop writing, and stare at her.

"Campbell Alexander. Your last name is a first name, and your first name is a last name." She pauses. "Or a soup."

"And how does that have any bearing on your case?"

"It doesn't," Anna admits, "except that it was a pretty bad decision your parents made for **you**."

I reach across my desk to hand her a card. "If you have any questions, call me."

She takes it, and runs her fingers over the raised lettering of my name. My **backward** name. For the love of God. Then she leans across the desk, grabs my pad, and tears the bottom off the page. Borrowing my pen, she writes something down and hands it back to me. I glance down at the note in my hand:

Anna 555-3211   ♥

"If **you** have any questions," she says.

When I walk out to the reception area, Anna is gone and Kerri sits at her desk, a catalog spread-eagled across it. "Did you know they used to use those L. L. Bean canvas bags to carry ice?"

"Yeah." And vodka and Bloody Mary mix. Toted from the cottage to the beach every Saturday morning. Which reminds me, my mother called.

Kerri has an aunt who makes her living as a psychic, and every now and then this genetic predisposition rears its head. Or maybe she's just been working for me long enough to know most of my secrets. At any rate, she knows what I am thinking. "She says your father's taken up with a seventeen-year-old and that discretion isn't in his vocabulary and that she's checking herself into The Pines unless you call her by . . ." Kerri glances at her watch. "Oops."

"How many times has she threatened to commit herself this week?"

"Only three," Kerri says.

"We're still way below average." I lean over the desk and close the catalog. "Time to earn a living, Ms. Donatelli."

"What's going on?"

"That girl, Anna Fitzgerald—"

"Planned Parenthood?"

"Not quite," I say. "We're representing her. I need to dictate a petition for medical emancipation, so that you can file it with the family court by tomorrow."

"Get **out**! You're representing her?"

I put a hand over my heart. "I'm wounded that you think so little of me."

"Actually, I was thinking about your wallet. Do her parents know?"

"They will by tomorrow."

"Are you a complete idiot?"

"Excuse me?"

Kerri shakes her head. "Where's she going to live?"

The comment stops me. In fact, I hadn't really considered it. But a girl who brings a lawsuit against her parents will not be particularly comfortable residing under the same roof, once the papers are served.

Suddenly Judge is at my side, pushing against my thigh with his nose. I shake my head, annoyed. Timing is everything. "Give me fifteen minutes," I tell Kerri. "I'll call you when I'm ready."

"Campbell," Kerri presses, relentless, "you can't expect a kid to fend for herself."

I head back into my office. Judge follows, pausing just inside the threshold. "It's not my problem," I say; and then I close the door, lock it securely, and wait.

SARA

1990

THE BRUISE IS THE SIZE AND SHAPE of a four-leaf clover, and sits square between Kate's shoulder blades. Jesse is the one to find it, while they are both in the bathtub. "Mommy," he asks, "does that mean she's lucky?"

I try to rub it off first, assuming it's dirt, without success. Kate, two, the subject of scrutiny, stares up at me with her china blue eyes. "Does it hurt?" I ask her, and she shakes her head.

Somewhere in the hallway behind me, Brian is telling me about his day. He smells faintly of smoke. "So the guy bought a case of expensive cigars," he says, "and had them insured against fire for $15,000. Next thing you know, the insurance company gets a claim, saying all the cigars were lost in a series of small fires."

"He **smoked** them?" I say, washing the soap out of Jesse's hair.

Brian leans against the threshold of the door. "Yeah. But the judge ruled that the company guaranteed the cigars as insurable against fire, without defining **acceptable** fire."

"Hey, Kate, does it hurt now?" Jesse says, and he presses his thumb, hard, against the bruise on his sister's spine.

Kate howls, lurches, and spills bathwater all over me. I lift her out of the water, slick as a fish, and pass her over to Brian. Pale towheads bent together, they are a matched set. Jesse looks more like me—skinny, dark, cerebral. Brian says this is how we know our family is complete: we each have our clone. "You get yourself out of the tub this minute," I tell Jesse.

He stands up, a sluice of four-year-old boy, and manages to trip as he navigates the wide lip of the tub. He smacks his knee hard, and bursts into tears.

I gather Jesse into a towel, soothing him as I try to continue my conversation with my husband. This is the language of a marriage: Morse code, punctuated by baths and dinners and stories before bed. "So who subpoenaed you?" I ask Brian. "The defendant?"

"The prosecution. The insurance company paid out the money, and then had him arrested for twenty-four counts of arson. I got to be their expert."

Brian, a career firefighter, can walk into a blackened structure and find the spot where the flames began: a charred cigarette butt, an exposed wire. Every holocaust starts with an ember. You just have to know what to look for.

"The judge threw out the case, right?"

"The judge sentenced him to twenty-four consecutive one-year terms," Brian says. He puts Kate down on the floor and begins to pull her pajamas over her head.

In my previous life, I was a civil attorney. At one point I truly believed that was what I wanted to be—but that was before I'd been handed a fistful of crushed violets from a toddler. Before I understood that the smile of a child is a tattoo: indelible art.

It drives my sister Suzanne crazy. She's a finance whiz who decimated the glass ceiling at the Bank of Boston, and according to her, I am a waste of cerebral evolution. But I think half the battle is figuring out what works for you, and I am much better at being a mother than I ever would have been as a lawyer. I sometimes wonder if it is just me, or if there are other women who figure out where they are supposed to be by going nowhere.

I look up from drying Jesse off, and find Brian staring at me. "Do you miss it, Sara?" he asks quietly.

I wrap our son in the towel and kiss him on the crown of his head. "Like I'd miss a root canal," I say.

By the time I wake up the next morning, Brian has already left for work. He's on two days, then two nights, and then off for four, before the cycle repeats again. Glancing at the clock, I realize I've slept past nine. More amazingly, my children have not woken me up. In my bathrobe, I run downstairs, where I find Jesse playing on the floor with blocks. "I eated breakfast," he informs me. "I made some for you, too."

Sure enough, there is cereal spilled all over the kitchen table, and a frighteningly precarious chair poised beneath the cabinet that holds the corn flakes. A trail of milk leads from the refrigerator to the bowl. "Where's Kate?"

"Sleeping," Jesse says. "I tried poking her and everything."

My children are a natural alarm clock; the thought of Kate sleeping so late makes me remember that she's been sniffling lately, and then wonder if that's why she was so tired last night. I walk upstairs, calling her name loud. In her bedroom, she rolls toward me, swimming up from the dark to focus on my face.

"Rise and shine." I pull up her shades, let the sun spill over her blankets. I sit her up and rub her back. "Let's get you dressed," I say, and I peel her pajama top over her head.

Trailing her spine, like a line of small blue jewels, are a string of bruises.

"Anemia, right?" I ask the pediatrician. "Kids her age don't get mono, do they?"

Dr. Wayne pulls his stethoscope away from Kate's narrow chest and tugs down her pink shirt. "It could be a virus. I'd like to draw some blood and run a few tests."

Jesse, who has been patiently playing with a GI Joe that has no head, perks up at this news. "You know how they draw blood, Kate?"

"Crayons?"

"With **needles**. Great big long ones that they stick in like a shot—"

"Jesse," I warn.

"Shot?" Kate shrieks. "Ouch?"

My daughter, who trusts me to tell her when it's safe to cross the street, to cut her meat into tiny pieces, and to protect her from all sorts of horrible things like large dogs and darkness and loud firecrackers, stares at me with great expectation. "Only a small one," I promise.

When the pediatric nurse comes in with her tray, her syringe, her vials, and her rubber tourniquet, Kate starts to scream. I take a deep breath. "Kate, look at me." Her cries bubble down to small hiccups. "It's just going to be a tiny pinch."

"Liar," Jesse whispers under his breath.

Kate relaxes, just the slightest bit. The nurse lays her down on the examination table and asks me to hold down her shoulders. I watch the needle break the white skin of her arm; I hear the sudden scream—but there isn't any blood flowing. "Sorry, sugar," the nurse says. "I'm going to have to try again." She removes the needle, and sticks Kate again, who howls even louder.

Kate struggles in earnest through the first and second vials. By the third, she has gone completely limp. I don't know which is worse.

We wait for the results of the blood test. Jesse lies on his belly on the waiting room rug, picking up God knows what sorts of germs from all the sick children who pass through this office. What I want is for the pediatrician to come out, tell me to get Kate home and make her drink lots of orange juice, and wave a prescription for Ceclor in front of us like a magic wand.

It is an hour before Dr. Wayne summons us to his office again. "Kate's tests were a little problematic," he says. "Specifically, her white cell count. It's much lower than normal."

"What does that mean?" In that moment, I curse myself for going to law school, and not med school. I try to remember what white cells even do.

"She may have some sort of autoimmune deficiency. Or it might just be a lab error." He touches Kate's hair. "I think, just to be safe, I'm going to send you up to a hematologist at the hospital, to repeat the test."

I am thinking: **You must be kidding.** But instead, I watch my hand move of its own accord to take the piece of paper Dr. Wayne offers. Not a prescription, as I'd hoped, but a name. **Ileana Farquad, Providence Hospital, Hematology/Oncology.**

"Oncology." I shake my head. "But that's cancer." I wait for Dr. Wayne to assure me it's only part of the physician's title, to explain that the blood lab and the cancer ward simply share a physical location, and nothing more.

He doesn't.

The dispatcher at the fire station tells me that Brian is on a medical call. He left with the rescue truck twenty minutes ago. I hesitate, and look down at Kate, who's slumped in one of the plastic seats in the hospital waiting room. A medical call.

I think there are crossroads in our lives when we make grand, sweeping decisions without even realizing it. Like scanning the newspaper headline at a red light, and therefore missing the rogue van that jumps the line of traffic and causes an accident. Entering a coffee shop on a whim and meeting the man you will marry one day, while he's digging for change at the counter. Or this one: instructing your husband to meet you, when for hours you have been convincing yourself this is nothing important at all.

"Radio him," I say. "Tell him we're at the hospital."

There is a comfort to having Brian beside me, as if we are now a pair of sentries, a double line of defense. We have been at Providence Hospital for three hours, and with every passing minute it gets more difficult to deceive myself into believing that Dr. Wayne made a mistake. Jesse is asleep in a plastic chair. Kate has undergone another traumatic blood draw, and a chest X ray, because I mentioned that she has a cold.

"Five months," Brian says carefully to the resident sitting in front of him with a clipboard. Then he looks at me. "Isn't that when she rolled over?"

"I think so." By now the doctor has asked us everything from what we were wearing the night Kate was conceived to when she first mastered holding a spoon.

"Her first word?" he asks.

Brian smiles. "Dada."

"I meant **when**."

"Oh." He frowns. "I think she was just shy of one."

"Excuse me," I say. "Can you tell me why any of this is important?"

"It's just a medical history, Mrs. Fitzgerald. We want to know everything we can about your daughter, so that we can understand what's wrong with her."

"Mr. and Mrs. Fitzgerald?" A young woman approaches, wearing a lab coat. "I'm a phlebotomist. Dr. Farquad wants me to do a coag panel on Kate."

At the sound of her name, Kate blinks up from my lap. She takes one look at the white coat and slides her arms inside the sleeves of her own shirt.

"Can't you do a finger stick?"

"No, this is really the easiest way."

Suddenly I remember how, when I was pregnant with Kate, she would get the hiccups. For hours at a time, my stomach would twitch. Every move she made, even ones that small, forced me to do something I could not control.

"Do you think," I say quietly, "that's what I want to hear? When you go down to the cafeteria and ask for coffee, would you like it if someone gave you Coke, because it's easier to reach? When you go to pay by credit card, would you like it if you were told that's too much hassle, so you'd better break out your cash?"

"Sara." Brian's voice is a distant wind.

"Do you think that it's easy for me to be sitting here with my child and not have any idea what's going on or why you're doing all these tests? Do you think it's easy for **her**? Since when does anyone get the option to do what's **easiest**?"

"Sara." It is only when Brian's hand falls onto my shoulder that I realize how hard I am shaking.

One more moment, and then the woman storms away, her clogs striking the tile floor. The minute she is out of sight I wilt.

"Sara," Brian says. "What's the matter with you?"

"What's the matter with **me**? I don't know, Brian, because no one is coming to tell us what's wrong with—"

He wraps me in his arms, Kate caught between us like a gasp. "Ssh," he says. He tells me it's going to be all right, and for the first time in my life I don't believe him.

Suddenly Dr. Farquad, whom we have not seen for hours, comes into the room. "I hear there was a little problem with the coagulopathy panel." She pulls up a chair in front of us. "Kate's complete blood count had some abnormal results. Her white blood count is very low—1.3. Her hemoglobin is 7.5, her hematocrit is 18.4, her platelets are 81,000, and her neutrophils are 0.6. Numbers like that sometimes indicate an autoimmune disease. But Kate's also presenting with twelve percent promyelocytes, and five percent blasts, and that suggests a leukemic syndrome."

"Leukemic," I repeat. The word is runny, slippery, like the white of an egg.

Dr. Farquad nods. "Leukemia is a blood cancer."

Brian only stares at her, his eyes fixed. "What does that mean?"

"Think of bone marrow as a childcare center for developing cells. Healthy bodies make blood cells that stay in the marrow until they're mature enough to go out and fight disease or clot or carry oxygen or whatever it is that they're supposed to do. In a person with leukemia, the childcare-center doors are opened too early. Immature blood cells wind up circulating, unable to do their job. It's not always odd to see promyelocytes in a CBC, but when we checked Kate's under a microscope, we could see abnormalities." She looks in turn at each of us. "I'll need to do a bone marrow aspiration to confirm this, but it seems that Kate has acute promyelocytic leukemia."

My tongue is pinned by the weight of the question that, a moment later, Brian forces out of his own throat: "Is she . . . is she going to die?"

I want to shake Dr. Farquad. I want to tell her I will draw the blood for the coag panel myself from Kate's arms if it means she will take back what she said. "APL is a very rare subgroup of myeloid leukemia. Only about twelve hundred people a year are diagnosed with it. The rate of survival for APL patients is twenty to thirty percent, if treatment starts immediately."

I push the numbers out of my head and instead sink my teeth into the rest of her sentence. "There's a treatment," I repeat.

"Yes. With aggressive treatment, myeloid leukemias carry a survival prognosis of nine months to three years."

Last week, I had stood in the doorway of Kate's bedroom, watching her clutch a satin security blanket in her sleep, a shred of fabric she was rarely without. **You mark my words,** I had whispered to Brian. **She'll never give that up. I'm going to have to sew it into the lining of her wedding dress.**

"We'll need to do that bone marrow aspiration. We'll sedate her with a light general anesthetic. And we can draw the coag panel while she's asleep." The doctor leans forward, sympathetic. "You need to know that kids beat the odds. Every single day."

"Okay," Brian says. He claps his hands together, as if he is gearing up for a football game. "Okay."

Kate pulls her head away from my shirt. Her cheeks are flushed, her expression wary.

This is a mistake. This is someone else's unfortunate vial of blood that the doctor has analyzed. Look at my child, at the shine of her flyaway curls and the butterfly flight of her smile—this is not the face of someone dying by degrees.

I have only known her for two years. But if you took every memory, every moment, if you stretched them end to end—they'd reach forever.

They roll up a sheet and tuck it under Kate's belly. They tape her down to the examination table, two long strips. One nurse strokes Kate's hand, even after the anesthesia has kicked in and she's asleep. Her lower back is bared for the long needle that will go into her iliac crest to extract marrow.

When they gently turn Kate's face to the other side, the tissue paper beneath her cheek is damp. I learn from my own daughter that you don't have to be awake to cry.

• • •

Driving home, I am struck by the sudden thought that the world is inflatable—trees and grass and houses ready to collapse with the single prick of a pin. I have the sense that if I veer the car to the left, smash through the picket fence and the Little Tykes playground, it will bounce us back like a rubber bumper.

We pass a truck. **Batchelder Casket Company**, it reads on the side. **Drive Safely.** Isn't that a conflict of interest?

Kate sits in her car seat, eating animal crackers. "Play," she commands.

In the rearview mirror, her face is luminous. **Objects are closer than they appear.** I watch her hold up the first cracker. "What does the tiger say?" I manage.

"**Rrrroar.**" She bites off its head, then waves another cracker.

"What does the elephant say?"

Kate giggles, then trumpets through her nose.

I wonder if it will happen in her sleep. Or if

she will cry. If there will be some kind nurse who gives her something for the pain. I envision my child dying, while she is happy and laughing two feet behind me.

"Giraffe say?" Kate asks. "Giraffe?"

Her voice, it's so full of the future. "Giraffes don't say anything," I answer.

"Why?"

"Because that's how they're born," I tell her, and then my throat swells shut.

The phone rings just as I come in from the neighbor's house, having arranged for her to take care of Jesse while we take care of Kate. We have no protocol for this situation. Our only baby-sitters are still in high school; all four grandparents are deceased; we've never dealt with day care providers—taking care of the children is my job.

By the time I come into the kitchen, Brian is well into conversation with the caller. The phone cord is wrapped around his knees, an umbilicus. "Yeah," he says, "hard to believe. I haven't made it into a single game this season . . . no point, now that they've traded him." His eyes meet mine as I put on the kettle for tea. "Oh, Sara's great. And the kids, uh-huh, they're fine. Right. You give my best to Lucy. Thanks for calling, Don." He hangs up. "Don Thurman," he explains. "From the fire academy, remember? Nice guy."

As he stares at me, the genial smile sloughs off his face. The teakettle starts to whistle, but neither of us makes a motion to move it off the burner. I look at Brian, cross my arms.

"I couldn't," he says quietly. "Sara, I just couldn't."

In bed that night, Brian is an obelisk, another shape breaking the darkness. Although we have not spoken for hours, I know that he is every bit as awake as I am.

This is happening to us because I yelled at Jesse last week, yesterday, moments ago. This is happening because I didn't buy Kate the M&Ms she wanted at the grocery store. This is happening because once, for a split second, I wondered what my life would have been like if I'd never had children. This is happening because I did not realize how good I have it.

"Do you think we did it to her?" Brian asks.

"Did it to her?" I turn to him. "How?"

"Like, our genes. You know."

I don't respond.

"Providence Hospital doesn't know anything," he says fiercely. "Do you remember when the chief's son broke his left arm, and they put a cast on the right one?"

I stare at the ceiling again. "Just so you know," I say, more loudly than I've intended, "I'm not going to let Kate die."

There is an awful sound beside me—an animal wounded, a drowning gasp. Then Brian presses his face against my shoulder, sobs into my skin. He wraps his arms around me and holds on as if he's losing his balance. "I'm not," I repeat, but even to myself, it sounds like I am trying too hard.

BRIAN

FOR EVERY NINETEEN DEGREES HOTTER a fire burns, it doubles in size. This is what I am thinking while I watch sparks shoot out of the incinerator chimney, a thousand new stars. The dean of Brown University's medical school wrings his hands beside me. In my heavy coat, I am sweating.

We've brought an engine, a ladder, and a rescue truck. We have assessed all four sides of the building. We've confirmed that no one is inside. Well, except for the body that got stuck in the incinerator, and caused this.

"He was a large man," the dean says. "This is what we always do with the subjects when the anatomy classes are through."

"Hey, Cap," Paulie yells. Today, he is my main pump operator. "Red's got the hydrant dressed. You want me to charge a line?"

I am not certain, yet, that I will take a hose up. This furnace was designed to consume remains at 1,600 degrees Fahrenheit. There is fire above and below the body.

"Well?" the dean says. "Aren't you going to do something?"

It is the biggest mistake rookies make: the assumption that fighting a fire means rushing in with a stream of water. Sometimes, that makes it worse. In this case, it would spread biohazardous waste all over the place. I'm thinking we need to keep the furnace closed, and make sure the fire doesn't get out of the chimney. A fire can't burn forever. Eventually, it consumes itself.

"Yes," I tell him. "I'm going to wait and see."

When I work the night shift, I eat dinner twice. The first meal is early, an accommodation made by my family so that we can all sit around a table together. Tonight, Sara makes a roast beef. It sits on the table like a sleeping infant as she calls us for supper.

Kate is the first to slip into her seat. "Hey baby," I say, squeezing her hand. When she smiles at me, it doesn't reach her eyes. "What have you been up to?"

She pushes her beans around her plate. "Saving Third World countries, splitting a few atoms, and finishing up the Great American Novel. In between dialysis, of course."

"Of course."

Sara turns around, brandishing a knife. "Whatever I did," I say, shrinking away, "I'm sorry."

She ignores me. "Carve the roast, will you?"

I take the carving utensils and slice into the roast beef just as Jesse sloughs into the kitchen. We allow him to live over the garage, but he is required to eat with us; it's part of the bargain. His eyes are devil-red; his clothes are ringed with sweet smoke. "Look at that," Sara sighs, but when I turn, she is staring at the roast. "It's too rare." She picks the pan up with her bare hands, as if her skin is coated with asbestos. She sticks the beef back into the oven.

Jesse reaches for a bowl of mashed potatoes and begins to heap them onto his plate. More, and more, and more again.

"You reek," Kate says, waving her hand in front of her face.

Jesse ignores her, taking a bite of his potatoes. I wonder what it says about me, that I am
actually thrilled I can identify pot running through
his system, as opposed to some of the others—
Ecstasy, heroin, and God knows what else—
which leave less of a trace.

"Not all of us enjoy Eau de Stoned," Kate
mutters.

"Not all of us can get our drugs through a portacath," Jesse answers.

Sara holds up her hands. "Please. Could we
just . . . not?"

"Where's Anna?" Kate asks.

"Wasn't she in your room?"

"Not since this morning."

Sara sticks her head through the kitchen door.
"Anna! Dinner!"

"Look at what I bought today," Kate says,
plucking at her T-shirt. It is a psychedelic tie-dye,
with a crab on the front, and the word Cancer.
"Get it?"

"You're a Leo." Sara looks like she is on the
verge of tears.

"How's that roast coming?" I ask, to distract her.

Just then, Anna enters the kitchen. She

throws herself into her chair and ducks her head. "Where have you been?" Kate says.

"Around." Anna looks down at her plate, but makes no effort to serve herself.

This is not Anna. I am used to struggling with Jesse, to lightening Kate's load; but Anna is our family's constant. Anna comes in with a smile. Anna tells us about the robin she found with a broken wing and a blush on its cheek; or about the mother she saw at Wal-Mart with not one but two sets of twins. Anna gives us a backbeat, and seeing her sitting there unresponsive makes me realize that silence has a sound.

"Something happen today?" I ask.

She looks up at Kate, assuming the question has been put to her sister, and then startles when she realizes I am talking to her. "No."

"You feel okay?"

Again, Anna does a double take; this is a question we usually reserve for Kate. "Fine."

"Because you're, you know, not eating."

Anna looks down on her plate, notices that it's empty, and then heaps it high with food. She shovels green beans into her mouth, two forkfuls.

Out of the blue I remember when the kids

were little, crammed into the back of the car like cigars wedged in a box, and I would sing to them. **Anna anna bo banna, banana fanna fo fanna, me my mo manna . . . Anna.** ("Chuck," Jesse would yell out. "Do Chuck!")

"Hey." Kate points to Anna's neck. "Your locket's missing."

It's the one I gave her, years ago. Anna's hand comes up to her collarbone. "Did you lose it?" I ask.

She shrugs. "Maybe I'm just not in the mood to wear it."

She's never taken it off, far as I know. Sara pulls the roast out of the oven and sets it on the table. As she picks up the knife to carve, she looks over at Kate. "Speaking of things we're not in the mood to wear," she says, "go put on another shirt."

"Why?"

"Because I said so."

"That's not a reason."

Sara spears the roast with the knife. "Because I find it offensive at the dinner table."

"It's not any more offensive than Jesse's metalhead shirts. What's the one you had on yesterday? Alabama Thunder Pussy?"

Jesse rolls his eyes toward her. It's an expression I've seen before: the horse in a spaghetti Western, gone lame, the moment before it's shot for mercy.

Sara saws through the meat. Pink before, now it is an overcooked log. "Now look," she says. "It's ruined."

"It's fine." I take the one piece she has managed to dissect from the rest and cut a smaller bite. I might as well be chewing leather. "Delicious. I'm just gonna run down to the station and get a blowtorch so that we can serve everyone else."

Sara blinks, and then a laugh bubbles out of her. Kate giggles. Even Jesse cracks a smile.

This is when I realize that Anna has already left the table, and more importantly, that nobody noticed.

Back at the station, the four of us sit upstairs in the kitchen. Red's got some kind of sauce going on the stove; Paulie reads the **ProJo**, and Caesar's writing a letter to this week's object of lust. Watching him, Red shakes his head. "You ought to just keep that filed on disk and print multiple copies at a time."

Caesar's just a nickname. Paulie coined it years ago, because he's always roamin'. "Well, this one's different," Caesar says.

"Yeah. She's lasted **two** whole days." Red pours the pasta into the colander in the sink, steam rising up around his face. "Fitz, give the boy some pointers, will you?"

"Why me?"

Paulie glances up over the rim of the paper. "Default," he says, and it's true. Paulie's wife left him two years ago for a cellist who'd swung through Providence on a symphony tour; Red's such a confirmed bachelor he wouldn't know what a lady was if she came up and bit him. On the other hand, Sara and I have been married twenty years.

Red sets a plate down in front of me as I start to talk. "A woman," I say, "isn't all that different from a bonfire."

Paulie tosses down the paper and hoots. "Here we go: the Tao of Captain Fitzgerald."

I ignore him. "A fire's a beautiful thing, right? Something you can't take your eyes off, when it's burning. If you can keep it contained, it'll throw light and heat for you. It's only when it gets out of control that you have to go on the offensive."

"What Cap is trying to tell you," Paulie says, "is that you need to keep your date away from crosswinds. Hey, Red, you got any Parmesan?"

We sit down to my second dinner, which usually means that the bells will ring within minutes. Firefighting is a world of Murphy's Law; it is when you can least afford a crisis that one crops up.

"Hey, Fitz, do you remember the last dead guy who got stuck?" Paulie asks. "Back when we were vollies?"

God, yes. A fellow who weighed five hundred pounds if he weighed an ounce, who'd died of heart failure in his bed. The fire department had been called in on that one by the funeral home, which couldn't get the body downstairs. "Ropes and pulleys," I recall out loud.

"And he was supposed to be cremated, but he was too big . . ." Paulie grins. "Swear to God, as my mother's up in Heaven, they had to take him to a vet instead."

Caesar blinks up at him. "What for?"

"How do you think they get rid of a dead horse, Einstein?"

Putting two and two together, Caesar's eyes widen. "No kidding," he says, and on second thought, pushes away Red's pasta Bolognese.

"Who do you think they'll ask to clean out the med school chimney?" Red says.

"The poor OSHA bastards," Paulie answers.

"Ten bucks says they call here and tell us it's our job."

"There won't be any call," I say, "because there won't be anything left to clean out. That fire was burning too hot."

"Well, at least we know this one wasn't arson," Paulie mutters.

In the past month, we have had a rash of fires set intentionally. You can always tell—there will be splash patterns of flammable liquid, or multiple points of origin, or smoke that burns black, or an unusual concentration of fire in one spot. Whoever is doing this is smart, too—at several structures the combustibles have been put beneath stairs, to cut off our access to the flames. Arson fires are dangerous because they don't follow the science we use to combat them. Arson fires are the structures most likely to collapse around you while you're inside fighting them.

Caesar snorts. "Maybe it was. Maybe the fat guy was really a suicide arsonist. He crawled up into the chimney and lit himself on fire."

"Maybe he was just desperate to lose weight," Paulie adds, and the other guys crack up.

"Enough," I say.

"Aw, Fitz, you gotta admit it's pretty funny—"

"Not to that man's parents. Not to his family."

There is that uncomfortable silence as the other men grasp at words. Finally Paulie, who has known me the longest, speaks. "Something going on with Kate again, Fitz?"

There is always something going on with my eldest daughter; the problem is, it never seems to end. I push away from the table and set my plate in the sink. "I'm going up to the roof."

We all have our hobbies—Caesar's got his girls, Paulie his bagpipes, Red his cooking, and me, I have my telescope. I mounted it years ago to the roof of the fire station, where I can get the best view of the night sky.

If I weren't a fireman, I'd be an astronomer. It takes too much math for my brain, I know that, but there's always been something about charting the stars that appeals to me. On a really dark night, you can see between 1,000 and 1,500 stars, and there are millions more that haven't been discovered. It is so easy to think that the world revolves around you, but all you have to do is stare up at the sky to realize it isn't that way at all.

Anna's real name is Andromeda. It's on her birth certificate, honest to God. The constellation she's named after tells the story of a princess, who was shackled to a rock as a sacrifice to a sea monster—punishment for her mother Casseopeia, who had bragged to Poseidon about her own beauty. Perseus, flying by, fell in love with Andromeda and saved her. In the sky, she's pictured with her arms outstretched and her hands chained.

The way I saw it, the story had a happy ending. Who wouldn't want that for a child?

When Kate was born, I used to imagine how beautiful she would be on her wedding day. Then she was diagnosed with APL, and instead, I'd imagine her walking across a stage to get her high school diploma. When she relapsed, all this went out the window: I pictured her making it to her fifth birthday party. Nowadays, I don't have expectations, and this way she beats them all.

Kate is going to die. It took me a long time to be able to say that. We all are going to die, when you get down to it, but it's not supposed to be like this. Kate ought to be the one who has to say good-bye to **me**.

It almost seems like a cheat that after all these years of defying the odds, it won't be the leukemia that kills her. Then again, Dr. Chance told us a long time ago that this was how it usually worked—a patient's body just gets worn down, from all the fighting. Little by little, pieces of them start to give up. In Kate's case, it is her kidneys.

I turn my telescope to Barnard's Loop and M42, glowing in Orion's sword. Stars are fires that burn for thousands of years. Some of them burn slow and long, like red dwarfs. Others—blue giants— burn their fuel so fast they shine across great distances, and are easy to see. As they start to run out of fuel, they burn helium, grow even hotter, and explode in a supernova. Supernovas, they're brighter than the brightest galaxies. They die, but everyone watches them go.

• • •

Earlier, after we ate, I helped Sara clean up in the kitchen. "You think something's going on with Anna?" I asked, moving the ketchup back into the fridge.

"Because she took off her necklace?"

"No." I shrugged. "Just in general."

"Compared to Kate's kidneys and Jesse's sociopathy, I'd say she's doing fine."

"She wanted dinner over before it started."

Sara turned around at the sink. "What do you think it is?"

"Uh . . . a guy?"

Sara glanced at me. "She's not dating any-one."

Thank God. "Maybe one of her friends said something to upset her." Why was Sara asking **me?** What the hell did I know about the mood swings of thirteen-year-old girls?

Sara wiped her hands on a towel and turned on the dishwasher. "Maybe she's just being a teenager."

I tried to think back to what Kate was like when she was thirteen, but all I could remember was the relapse and the stem cell transplant she had. Kate's ordinary life had a way of fading into the background, overshadowed by the times she was sick.

"I have to take Kate to dialysis tomorrow," Sara said. "When will you get home?"

"By eight. But I'm on call, and I wouldn't be surprised if our arsonist struck again."

"Brian?" she asked. "How did Kate look to you?"

Better than Anna did, I thought, but this was not what she was asking. She wanted me to measure the yellow cast of Kate's skin against yesterday; she wanted me to read into the way she leaned her elbows on the table, too tired to hold her body upright.

"Kate looks great," I lied, because this is what we do for each other.

"Don't forget to say good night to them before you leave," Sara said, and she turned to gather the pills Kate takes at bedtime.

It's quiet, tonight. Weeks have rhythms all their own, and the craziness of a Friday or Saturday night shift stands in direct contrast to a dull Sunday or Monday. I can already tell: this will be one of those nights where I bunk down and actually get to sleep.

"Daddy?" The hatch to the roof opens, and Anna crawls out. "Red told me you were up here."

Immediately, I freeze. It is ten o'clock at night. "What's wrong?"

"Nothing. I just . . . wanted to visit."

When the kids were small, Sara would stop by with them all the time. They'd play in the bays around the sleeping giant engines; they'd fall asleep upstairs in my bunk. Sometimes, in the warmest part of the summer, Sara would bring along an old blanket and we would spread it here on the roof, lie down with the kids between us, and watch the night rise.

"Mom know where you are?"

"She dropped me off." Anna tiptoes across the roof. She's never been all that great with heights, and there is only a three-inch lip around the concrete. Squinting, she bends to the telescope. "What can you see?"

"Vega," I tell her. I take a good look at Anna, something I haven't done in some time. She's not stick-straight anymore; she's got the begin-nings of curves. Even her motions—tucking her hair behind her ear, peering into the telescope—have a sort of grace I associate with full-grown women. "Got something you want to talk about?"

Her teeth snag on her bottom lip, and she looks down at her sneakers. "Maybe instead **you** could talk to **me,**" Anna suggests.

So I sit her down on my jacket and point to the stars. I tell her that Vega is a part of Lyra, the lyre that belonged to Orpheus. I am not one for stories, but I remember the ones that match up with the constellations. I tell her about this son of the sun god, whose music charmed animals and softened boulders. A man who loved his wife, Eurydice, so much that he wouldn't let Death take her away.

By the time I finish, we are lying flat on our backs. "Can I stay here with you?" Anna asks.

I kiss the top of her head. "You bet."

"Daddy," Anna whispers, when I think for sure she has fallen asleep, "did it work?"

It takes me a moment to understand she is talking about Orpheus and Eurydice.

"No," I admit.

She lets loose a sigh. "Figures," she says.

TUESDAY

My candle burns at both ends;

It will not last the night;

But ah, my foes, and oh, my friends—

It gives a lovely light!

—EDNA ST. VINCENT MILLAY,
"First Fig," **A Few Figs from
Thistles**

ANNA

I USED TO PRETEND that I was just passing through this family on my way to my real one. It isn't too much of a stretch, really—there's Kate, the spitting image of my dad; and Jesse, the spitting image of my mom; and then there's me, a collection of recessive genes that came out of left field. In the hospital cafeteria, eating rubberized French fries and red Jell-O, I'd glance around from table to table, thinking my bona fide parents might be just a tray away. They'd sob with sheer joy to find me, and whisk me off to our castle in Monaco or Romania and give me a maid that smelled like fresh sheets, and my own Bernese mountain dog, and a private phone line. The thing is, the first person I'd have called to crow over my new fortune would be Kate.

Kate's dialysis sessions run three times a week, for two hours at a time. She has a Mahhukar catheter, which looks just like her central line used to look and protrudes from the same spot on her chest. This gets hooked up to a machine that does the work her kidneys aren't doing. Kate's blood (well, it's my blood if you want to get technical about it) leaves her body through one needle, gets cleaned, and then goes into her body again through a second needle. She says it doesn't hurt. Mostly, it's just boring. Kate usually brings a book or her CD player and headphones. Sometimes we play games. "Go out into the hall and tell me about the first gorgeous guy you find," Kate'll instruct, or, "Sneak up on the janitor who surfs the Net and see whose naked pictures he's downloading." When she is tied to the bed, I am her eyes and her ears.

Today, she is reading **Allure** magazine. I wonder if she even knows that every V-necked model she comes across she touches at the breastbone, in the same place where she has a catheter and they don't. "Well," my mother announces out of the blue, "this is interesting."

She waves a pamphlet she's taken from the bulletin board outside Kate's room: **You and Your New Kidney.** "Did you know that they don't take out the old kidney? They just transplant the new one into you and hook it up."

"That creeps me out," Kate says. "Imagine the coroner who cuts you open and sees you've got three instead of two."

"I think the point of a transplant is so that the coroner **won't** be cutting you open anytime soon," my mother replies. This fictional kidney she's discussing resides right now in my own body.

I've read that pamphlet, too.

Kidney donation is considered relatively safe surgery, but if you ask me, the writer must have been comparing it to something like a heart-lung transplant, or some brain tumor removal. In my opinion, safe surgery is the kind where you go into the doctor's office and you're awake the whole time and the procedure is finished in five minutes—like when you have a wart removed or a cavity drilled. On the other hand, when you donate a kidney, you spend the night before the operation fasting and taking laxatives. You're given anesthesia, the risks of which can include stroke, heart attack, and lung problems. The four-hour surgery isn't a walk in the park, either—you have a 1 in 3,000 chance of dying on the operating table. If you don't, you are hospitalized for four to seven days, although it takes four to six weeks to fully recover. And that doesn't even include the long-term effects: an increased chance of high blood pressure, a risk of complications with pregnancy, a recommendation to refrain from activities where your lone remaining kidney might be damaged.

Then again, when you get a wart removed or a cavity drilled, the only person who benefits in the long run is yourself.

There is a knock on the door, and a familiar face peeks in. Vern Stackhouse is a sheriff, and therefore a member of the same public servant community as my father. He used to come over to our house every now and then to say hi or leave off Christmas presents for us; more recently, he's saved Jesse's butt by bringing him home from a scrape, rather than letting the justice system deal with him. When you're part of the family with the dying daughter, people cut you slack.

Vern's face is like a soufflé, caving in at the most unexpected places. He doesn't seem to know whether it's all right for him to enter the room. "Uh," he says. "Hi, Sara."

"Vern!" My mother gets to her feet. "What are you doing at the hospital? Everything all right?"

"Oh yeah, fine. I'm just here on business."

"Serving papers, I suppose."

"Um-hmm." Vern shuffles his feet and stuffs his hand inside his jacket, like Napoleon. "I'm real sorry about this, Sara," he says, and then he holds out a document.

Just like Kate, all the blood leaves my body. I couldn't move if I wanted to.

"What the . . . Vern, am I being sued?" My mother's voice is far too quiet.

"Look, I don't read them. I just serve them. And your name, it was right there on my list. If, uh, there's anything I . . . " He doesn't even finish his sentence. With his hat in his hands, he ducks back out the door.

"Mom?" Kate asks. "What's going on?"

"I have no idea." She unfolds the papers. I'm close enough to read them over her shoulder. THE STATE OF RHODE ISLAND AND PROVIDENCE PLANTATIONS, it says right across the top, official as can be. FAMILY COURT FOR PROVIDENCE COUNTY. IN RE: ANNA FITZGERALD, A.K.A. JANE DOE.

PETITION FOR MEDICAL EMANCIPATION.

Oh shit, I think. My cheeks are on fire; my heart starts to pound. I feel like I did the time the principal sent home a disciplinary notice because I drew a sketch of Mrs. Toohey and her colossal butt in the margin of my math textbook. No, actually, scratch that—it's a million times worse.

That she gets to make all future medical decisions.

That she not be forced to submit to medical treatment which is not in her best interests or for her benefit.

That she not be required to undergo any more treatment for the benefit of her sister, Kate.

My mother lifts her face to mine. "Anna," she whispers, "what the hell is this?"

It feels like a fist in my gut, now that it's here and happening. I shake my head. What can I possibly tell her?

"Anna!" She takes a step toward me.

Behind her, Kate cries out. "Mom, ow, Mom . . . something hurts, get the nurse!"

My mother turns halfway. Kate is curled onto her side, her hair spilling over her face. I think that through the fall of it, she's looking at me, but I cannot be sure. "Mommy," she moans, "please."

For a moment, my mother is caught between us, a soap bubble. She looks from Kate to me and back again.

My sister's in pain, and I'm relieved. What does **that** say about me?

The last thing I see as I run out of the room is my mother pushing the nurse's call button over and over, as if it's the trigger to a bomb.

I can't hide in the cafeteria, or the lobby, or anywhere else that they will expect me to go. So I take the stairs to the sixth floor, the maternity ward. In the lounge, there is only one phone, and it is being used. "Six pounds eleven ounces," the man says, smiling so hard I think his face might splinter. "She's perfect."

Did my parents do this when I came along? Did my father send out smoke signals; did he count my fingers and toes, sure he'd come up with the finest number in the universe? Did my mother kiss the top of my head and refuse to let the nurse take me away to be cleaned up? Or did they simply hand me away, since the real prize had been clamped between my belly and the placenta?

The new father finally hangs up the phone, laughing at absolutely nothing. "Congratulations," I say, when what I really want to tell him is to pick up that baby of his and hold her tight, to set the moon on the edge of her crib and to hang her name up in stars so that she never, ever does to him what I have done to my parents.

I call Jesse collect. Twenty minutes later, he pulls up to the front entrance. By now, Deputy Stackhouse has been notified that I've gone missing; he's waiting at the door when I exit. "Anna, your mom's awfully worried about you.

She's paged your dad. He's got the whole hospital being turned inside out."

I take a deep breath. "Then you better go tell her I'm okay," I say, and I jump into the passenger door that Jesse's opened for me.

He peels away from the curb and lights a Merit, although I know for a fact he told my mother he stopped smoking. He cranks up his music, hitting the flat of his hand on the edge of the steering wheel. It isn't until he pulls off the highway at the exit for Upper Darby that he shuts the radio off and slows down. "So. Did she blow a gasket?"

"She paged Dad away from work."

In our family, it is a cardinal sin to page my father away. Since his job is emergencies, what crisis could we possibly have that compares? "Last time she paged Dad," Jesse informs me, "Kate was getting diagnosed."

"Great." I cross my arms. "That makes me feel infinitely better."

Jesse just smiles. He blows a smoke ring. "Sis," he says, "welcome to the Dark Side."

• • •

They come in like a hurricane. Kate barely manages to look at me before my father sends her upstairs to our room. My mother whacks her purse down, then her car keys, and then advances on me. "All right," she says, her voice so tight it might snap. "What's going on?"

I clear my throat. "I got a lawyer."

"Evidently." My mother grabs the portable phone and hands it to me. "Now get rid of him."

It takes enormous effort, but I manage to shake my head and drop the phone into the cushions of the couch.

"Anna, so help me—"

"Sara." My father's voice is an ax. It comes between us, and sends us both spinning. "I think we need to give Anna a chance to explain. We **agreed** to give her a chance to explain, right?"

I duck my head. "I don't want to do it any-more."

That ignites my mother. "Well, you know Anna, neither do I. In fact, neither does Kate. But it's not something we have a choice about."

The thing is, I **do** have a choice. Which is exactly why I have to be the one to do this.

My mother stands over me. "You went to a

lawyer and made him think this is all about you—and it's not. It's about **us. All** of us—"

My father's hands curl around her shoulders and squeeze. As he crouches down in front of me, I smell smoke. He's come from someone else's fire right into the middle of this one, and for this and nothing else, I'm embarrassed. "Anna, honey, we know you think you were doing something you needed to do—"

"**I** don't think that," my mother interrupts.

My father closes his eyes. "Sara. Dammit, shut up." Then he looks at me again. "Can we talk, just us three, without a lawyer having to do it for us?"

What he says makes my eyes fill up. But I knew this was coming. So I lift my chin and let the tears go at the same time. "Daddy, I can't."

"For God's sake, Anna," my mother says. "Do you even realize what the consequences would be?"

My throat closes like the shutter of a camera, so that any air or excuses must move through a tunnel as thin as a pin. **I'm invisible,** I think, and realize too late I have spoken out loud.

My mother moves so fast I do not even see it

coming. But she slaps my face hard enough to make my head snap backward. She leaves a print that stains me long after it's faded. Just so you know: shame is five-fingered.

Once, when Kate was eight and I was five, we had a fight and decided we no longer wanted to share a room. Given the size of our house, though, and the fact that Jesse lived in the other spare bedroom, we didn't have anywhere else to go. So Kate, being older and wiser, decided to split our space in half. "Which side do you want?" she asked diplomatically. "I'll even let you pick."

Well, I wanted the part with my bed in it. Besides, if you divided the room in two, the half with my bed would also, by default, have the box that held all our Barbie dolls and the shelves where we kept our arts and crafts supplies. Kate went to reach for a marker there, but I stopped her. "That's on **my** side," I pointed out.

"Then give me one," she demanded, so I handed her the red. She climbed up onto the desk, reaching as high as she could toward the ceiling. "Once we do this," she said, "you stay on your side, and I stay on my side, right?" I nodded, just as committed to keeping up this bargain as she was. After all, I had all the good toys. Kate would be begging me for a visit long before I'd be begging her.

"Swear it?" she asked, and we made a pinky promise.

She drew a jagged line from the ceiling, over the desk, across the tan carpet, and back up over the nightstand up the opposite wall. Then she handed me the marker. "Don't forget," she said. "Only cheats go back on a promise."

I sat on the floor on my side of the room, removing every single Barbie we owned, dressing and undressing them, making a big fuss out of the fact that I had them and Kate didn't. She perched on her bed with her knees drawn up, watching me. She didn't react at all. Until, that is, my mother called us down for lunch.

Then Kate smiled at me, and walked out the door of the bedroom—which was on **her** side.

I went up to the line she had drawn on the carpet, kicking at it with my toes. I didn't want to be a cheat. But I didn't want to spend the rest of my life in my room, either.

I do not know how long it took my mother to wonder why I wasn't coming to the kitchen for lunch, but when you are five, even a second can last forever. She stood in the doorway, staring at the line of marker on the walls and carpet, and closed her eyes for patience. She walked into our room and picked me up, which was when I started fighting her. "Don't," I cried. "I won't ever get back in!"

A minute later she left, and returned with pot holders, dishtowels, and throw pillows. She placed these at odd distances, all along Kate's side of the room. "Come on," she urged, but I did not move. So she came and sat down beside me on my bed. "It may be Kate's pond," she said, "but these are **my** lily pads." Standing, she jumped onto a dishtowel, and from there, onto a pillow. She glanced over her shoulder, until I climbed onto the dishtowel. From the dishtowel, to the pillow, to a pot holder Jesse had made in first grade, all the way across Kate's side of the room. Following my mother's footsteps was the surest way out.

• • •

I am taking a shower when Kate jimmies the lock and comes into the bathroom. "I want to talk to you," she says.

I poke my head out from the side of the plastic curtain. "When I'm finished," I say, trying to buy time for the conversation I don't really want to have.

"No, now." She sits down on the lid of the toilet and sighs. "Anna . . . what you're doing—"

"It's already done," I say.

"You can undo it, you know, if you want."

I am grateful for all the steam between us, because I couldn't bear the thought of her being able to see my face right now. "I know," I whisper.

For a long time, Kate is silent. Her mind is running in circles, like a gerbil on a wheel, the same way mine is. Chase every rung of possibility, and you still get absolutely nowhere.

After a while, I peek my head out again. Kate wipes her eyes and looks up at me. "You do realize," she says, "that you're the only friend I've got?"

"That's not true," I immediately reply, but we both know I'm lying. Kate has spent too much time out of organized school to find a group she fits into. Most of the friends she has made during her long stretch of remission have disappeared—a mutual thing. It turned out to be too hard for an average kid to know how to act around someone on the verge of dying; and it was equally as difficult for Kate to get honestly excited about things like homecoming and SATs, when there was no guarantee she'd be around to experience them. She's got a few acquaintances, sure, but mostly when they come over they look like they're serving out a sentence, and sit on the edge of Kate's bed counting down the minutes until they can leave and thank God this didn't happen to them.

A real friend isn't capable of feeling sorry for you.

"I'm not your friend," I say, yanking the curtain back into place. "I'm your sister." **And doing a damn lousy job at that,** I think. I push my face into the shower spray, so that she cannot tell I'm crying, too.

Suddenly, the curtain whips aside, leaving me totally bare. "That's what I wanted to talk about," Kate says. "If you don't want to be my sister anymore, that's one thing. But I don't think I could stand to lose you as a friend."

She pulls the curtain back into place, and the steam rises around me. A moment later I hear the door open and close, and the knife-slice of cold air that comes on its heels.

I can't stand the thought of losing her, either.

That night, once Kate falls asleep, I crawl out of my bed and stand beside hers. When I hold my palm up under her nose to see if she's breathing, a mouthful of air presses against my hand. I could push down, now, over that nose and mouth, hold her when she fights. How would that really be any different than what I am already doing?

The sound of footsteps in the hallway has me diving underneath the cave of my covers. I turn onto my side, away from the door, just in case my eyelids are still flickering by the time my parents enter the room. "I can't believe this," my mother whispers. "I just can't believe she's done this."

My father is so quiet that I wonder if maybe I

have been mistaken, if maybe he isn't here at all.

"This is Jesse, all over again," my mother adds. "She's doing it for the attention." I can feel her looking down at me, like I'm some kind of creature she's never seen before. "Maybe we need to take her somewhere, alone. Go to a movie, or shopping, so she doesn't feel left out. Make her see that she doesn't have to do something crazy to get us to notice her. What do you think?"

My father takes his time answering. "Well," he says quietly, "maybe this isn't crazy."

You know how silence can push in at your eardrums in the dark, make you deaf? That's what happens, so that I almost miss my mother's answer. "For God's sake, Brian . . . whose side are you on?"

And my father: "Who said there were sides?"

But even I could answer that for him. There are always sides. There is always a winner, and a loser. For every person who gets, there's someone who must give.

A few seconds later, the door closes, and the hall light that has been dancing on the ceiling disappears. Blinking, I roll onto my back—and find my mother still standing beside my bed. "I thought you were gone," I whisper.

She sits down on the foot of my bed and I inch away. But she puts her hand on my calf before I move too far. "What else do you think, Anna?"

My stomach squeezes tight. "I think . . . I think you must hate me."

Even in the dark, I can see the shine of her eyes. "Oh, Anna," my mother sighs, "how can you not know how much I love you?"

She holds out her arms and I crawl into them, as if I'm small again and I fit there. I press my face hard into her shoulder. What I want, more than anything, is to turn back time a little. To become the kid I used to be, who believed whatever my mother said was one hundred percent true and right without looking hard enough to see the hairline cracks.

My mother holds me tighter. "We'll talk to the judge and explain it. We can fix this," she says. "We can fix everything." And because those words are really all I've ever wanted to hear, I nod.

SARA

1990

THERE IS AN UNEXPECTED COMFORT to being at the oncology wing of the hospital, a sense that I am a member of the club. From the kindhearted parking attendant who asks us if it's our first time, to the legions of children with pink emesis basins tucked beneath their arms like teddy bears—these people have all been here before us, and there's safety in numbers.

We take the elevator to the third floor, to the office of Dr. Harrison Chance. His name alone has put me off. Why not Dr. Victor? "He's late," I say to Brian, as I check my watch for the twentieth time. A spider plant languishes, brown, on a windowsill. I hope he is better with people.

To amuse Kate, who is starting to lose it, I

inflate a rubber glove and knot it into a cox-comb balloon. On the glove dispenser near the sink is a prominent sign, warning parents not to do this very thing. We bat it back and forth, playing volleyball, until Dr. Chance himself comes in without a single apology for his delay.

"Mr. and Mrs. Fitzgerald." He is tall and rail-thin, with snapping blue eyes magnified by thick glasses, and a tightly set mouth. He catches Kate's makeshift balloon in one hand and frowns at it. "Well, I can see there's already a problem."

Brian and I exchange a glance. Is this coldhearted man the one who will lead us through this war, our general, our white knight? Before we can even backpedal with explanations, Dr. Chance takes a Sharpie marker and draws a face on the latex, com-plete with a set of wire-rimmed glasses to match his own. "There," he says, and with a smile that changes him, he hands it back to Kate.

• • •

I only see my sister Suzanne once or twice a year. She lives less than an hour and several thousand philosophical convictions away.

As far as I can tell, Suzanne gets paid a lot of money to boss people around. Which means, theoretically, that she did her career training with me. Our father died while mowing the lawn on his forty-ninth birthday; our mother never quite sewed herself together in the aftermath. Suzanne, ten years my senior, took up the slack. She made sure I did my homework and filled out law school applications and dreamed big. She was smart and beautiful and always knew what to say at any given moment. She could take any catastrophe and find the logical antidote to cure it, which is what made her such a success at her job. She was just as comfortable in a boardroom as she was jogging along the Charles. She made it all look easy. Who **wouldn't** want a role model like that?

My first strike was marrying a guy without a college degree. My second and third were getting pregnant. I suppose that when I didn't go on to become the next Gloria

Allred, she was justified in counting me a failure. And I suppose that until now, I was justified in thinking that I **wasn't** one.

Don't get me wrong, she loves her niece and nephew. She sends them carvings from Africa, shells from Bali, chocolates from Switzerland. Jesse wants a glass office like hers when he grows up. "We can't all be Aunt Zanne," I tell him, when what I mean is that **I** can't be her.

I don't remember which of us stopped returning phone calls first, but it was easier that way. There's nothing worse than silence, strung like heavy beads on too delicate a conversation. So it takes me a full week before I pick up the phone. I dial direct. "Suzanne Crofton's line," a man says.

"Yes." I hesitate. "Is she available?"

"She's in a meeting."

"Please . . ." I take a deep breath. "Please tell her it's her sister calling."

A moment later that smooth, cool voice falls into my ear. "Sara. It's been a while."

She is the person I ran to when I got my period; the one who helped me knit back together my first broken heart; the hand I would reach for in the middle of the night when I could no longer remember which side our father parted his hair on, or what it sounded like when our mother laughed. No matter what she is now, before all that, she was my built-in best friend. "Zanne?" I say. "How are you?"

Thirty-six hours after Kate is officially diagnosed with APL, Brian and I are given an opportunity to ask questions. Kate messes with glitter glue with a child-life specialist while we meet with a team of doctors, nurses, and psychiatrists. The nurses, I have already learned, are the ones who give us the answers we're desperate for. Unlike the doctors, who fidget like they need to be somewhere else, the nurses patiently answer us as if we are the first set of parents to ever have this kind of meeting with them, instead of the thousandth. "The thing about leukemia," one nurse explains, "is that we haven't even inserted a needle for the first treatment when we're already thinking three treatments down the line. This particular illness carries a pretty poor prognosis, so we need to be thinking ahead to what happens next. What makes APL a little trickier is that it's a chemoresistant disease."

"What's that?" Brian asks.

"Normally, with myelogenous leukemias, as long as the organs hold up, you can potentially reinduce the patient into remission every time there's a relapse. You're exhausting their body, but you know it will respond to treatment over and over. However, with APL, once you've offered a given therapy, you usually can't rely upon it again. And to date, there's only so much we can do."

"Are you saying," Brian swallows. "Are you saying she's going to die?"

"I'm saying there are no guarantees."

"So what do you do?"

A different nurse answers. "Kate will start a week of chemotherapy, in the hopes that we can kill off the diseased cells and put her into remission. She'll most likely have nausea and vomiting, which we'll try to keep to a minimum with antiemetics. She'll lose her hair."

At this, a tiny cry escapes from me. This is such a small thing, and yet it's the banner that will let others know what's wrong with Kate. Only six months ago, she had her first haircut; the gold ringlets curled like coins on the floor of the SuperCuts.

"She may develop diarrhea. There's a very good chance that, with her own immune system laid low, she will get an infection that will require hospitalization. Chemo may cause developmental delays, as well. She'll have a course of consolidation chemotherapy about two weeks after that, and then a few courses of maintenance therapy. The exact number will depend on the results we get from periodic bone marrow aspirations."

"Then what?" Brian asks.

"Then we watch her," Dr. Chance replies. "With APL, you'll want to be vigilant for signs of relapse. She'll have to come into the ER if she has any hemorrhaging, fever, cough, or infection. And as far as further treatment, she'll have some options. The idea is to get Kate's body producing healthy bone marrow. In the unlikely event that we achieve molecular remission with chemo, we can retrieve Kate's own cells and reinstill them—an autologous harvest. If she relapses, we may try to transplant someone else's marrow into Kate to produce blood cells. Does Kate have any siblings?"

"A brother," I say. A thought dawns, a horrible one. "Could he have this, too?"

"It's very unlikely. But he may wind up being a match for an allogeneic transplant. If not, we'll put Kate on the national registry for MUD—a matched, unrelated donor. However, getting a transplant from a stranger who's a match is much more dangerous than getting one from a relative—the risk of mortality greatly increases."

The information is endless, a series of darts thrown so fast I cannot feel them sting anymore. We are told: **Do not think; just give your child up to us, because otherwise she's going to die.** For every answer they give us, we have another question.

Will her hair grow back?

Will she ever go to school?

Can she play with friends?

Did this happen because of where we live?

Did this happen because of who we are?

"What will it be like," I hear myself ask, "if she dies?"

Dr. Chance looks at me. "It depends on what she succumbs to," he explains. "If it's infection, she'll be in respiratory distress and on a ventilator. If it's hemorrhage, she'll bleed out after losing consciousness. If it's organ failure, the characteristics will vary depending on the system in distress. Often there's a combination of all of these."

"Will she know what's happening," I ask, when what I really mean is, **How will I survive this?**

"Mrs. Fitzgerald," he says, as if he has heard my unspoken question, "of the twenty children here today, ten will be dead in a few years. I don't know which group Kate will be in."

• • •

To save Kate's life, part of her has to die. That's the purpose of chemotherapy—to wipe out all the leukemic cells. To this end, a central line has been placed beneath Kate's collarbone, a three-pronged port that will be the entry point for multiple medication administrations, IV fluids, and blood draws. I look at the tubes sprouting from her thin chest and think of science fiction movies.

She has already had a baseline EKG, to make sure her heart can withstand chemo. She's had dexamethasone ophthalmic drops, because one of the drugs causes conjunctivitis. She's had blood drawn from her central line, to test for renal and liver function.

The nurse hangs the infusion bags on the IV pole and smoothes Kate's hair. "Will she feel it?" I ask.

"Nope. Hey, Kate, look here." She points to the bag of Daunorubicin, covered with a dark bag to protect it from light. Spotting it are brightly colored stickers she's helped Kate make while we were waiting. I saw one teenager with a Post-it note on his: **Jesus saves. Chemo scores.**

This is what starts coursing through her veins: the Daunorubicin, 50 mg in 25 ccs of D5W; Cytarabine, 46 mg in a D5W infusion, a continuous twenty-four-hour IV; Allopurinol, 92 mg IV. Or in other words, poison. I imagine a great battle going on inside her. I picture shining armies, casualties that evaporate through her pores.

They tell us Kate will most likely get sick within a few days, but it takes only two hours before she starts throwing up. Brian pushes the call button, and a nurse comes into the room. "We'll get her some Reglan," she says, and she disappears.

When Kate isn't vomiting, she's crying. I sit on the edge of the bed, holding her half on my lap. The nurses do not have time to nurse. Short-staffed, they administer antiemetics in the IV; they stay for a few moments to see how Kate responds—but inevitably they are called elsewhere to another emergency and the rest falls to us. Brian, who has to leave the room if one of our children gets a stomach virus, is a model of efficiency: wiping her forehead, holding her thin shoulders, dabbing tissues around her mouth. "You can get through this," he murmurs to her each time she spits up, but he may only be talking to himself.

And I, too, am surprising myself. With grim resolve I make a ballet out of rinsing the emesis basin and bringing it back. If you focus on sandbagging the beachhead, you can ignore the tsunami that's approaching.

Try it any other way, and you'll go crazy.

Brian brings Jesse to the hospital for his blood test: a simple finger stick. He needs to be restrained by Brian and two male residents; he screams down the hospital. I stand back, and cross my arms, and inadvertently think of Kate, who stopped crying over procedures two days ago.

Some doctor will look at this sample of blood, and will be able to analyze six proteins, floating invisibly. If these six proteins are the same as Kate's, then Jesse will be an HLA match—a potential donor for bone marrow for his sister. **How bad can the odds be, I think, to match six times over?**

As bad as getting leukemia in the first place.

The phlebotomist goes off with her blood sample, and Brian and the doctors release Jesse. He bolts off the table into my arms. "Mommy, they stuck me." He holds up his finger, festooned with a Rugrats Band-Aid. His damp, bright face is hot against my skin.

I hold him close. I say all the right things. But it is so, so hard to make myself feel sorry for him.

"Unfortunately," Dr. Chance says, "your son isn't a match."

My eyes focus on the houseplant, which still sits withered and brown on the sill. Someone ought to get rid of that thing. Someone ought to replace it with orchids, with birds-of-paradise, and other unlikely blooms.

"It's possible that an unrelated donor will crop up on the national marrow registry."

Brian leans forward, stiff and tense. "But you said a transplant from an unrelated donor was dangerous."

"Yes, I did," Dr. Chance says. "But sometimes it's all we've got."

I glance up. "What if you can't find a match in the registry?"

"Well." The oncologist rubs his forehead. "Then we try to keep her going until research catches up to her."

He is talking about my little girl as if she were some kind of machine: a car with a faulty carburetor, a plane whose landing gear is stuck. Rather than face this, I turn away just in time to see one of the misbegotten leaves on the plant make its suicide plunge to the carpet. Without an explanation I get to my feet and pick up the planter. I walk out of Dr. Chance's office, past the receptionist and the other shell-shocked parents waiting with their sick children. At the first trash receptacle I find, I dump the plant and all its desiccated soil. I stare at the terra-cotta pot in my hand, and I am just thinking about smashing it down on the tile floor when I hear a voice behind me.

"Sara," Dr. Chance says. "You all right?"

I turn around slowly, tears springing to my eyes. "I'm fine. I'm healthy. I'm going to live a long, long life."

Handing him the planter, I apologize. He nods, and offers me a handkerchief from his own pocket.

"I thought it might be Jesse who could save her. I wanted it to be Jesse."

"We all did," Dr. Chance answers. "Listen. Twenty years ago, the survival rate was even smaller. And I've known lots of families where one sibling isn't a match, but another sibling turns out to be just right."

We only have those two, I start to say, and then I realize that Dr. Chance is talking about a family I haven't yet had, of children I never intended. I turn to him, a question on my lips.

"Brian will wonder where we've gone." He

starts to walk toward his office, holding up the pot. "What plants," he asks conversationally, "would I be least likely to kill?"

It is so easy to presume that while your own world has ground to an absolute halt, so has everyone else's. But the trash collector has taken our garbage and left the cans in the road, just like always. There is a bill from the oil truck tucked into the front door. Neatly stacked on the counter is a week's worth of mail. Amazingly, life has gone on.

Kate is released from the hospital a full week after her admission for induction chemotherapy. The central line still snaking from her chest bells out her blouse. The nurses give me a pep talk for encouragement, and a long list of instructions to follow: when to and when not to call the emergency room, when we are expected back for more chemotherapy, how to be careful during Kate's period of immunosuppression.

At six the next morning, the door to our bedroom opens. Kate tiptoes toward the bed, although Brian and I have come awake in an instant. "What is it, honey?" Brian asks.

She doesn't speak, just lifts her hand to her head and threads her fingers through her hair. It comes out in a thick clump, drifts down to the carpet like a small blizzard.

"All done," Kate announces a few nights later at dinner. Her plate is still full; she hasn't touched her beans or her meat loaf. She dances off to the living room to play.

"Me too." Jesse pushes back from the table. "Can I be excused?"

Brian spears another mouthful with his fork. "Not until you finish everything green."

"I hate beans."

"They're not too crazy about you, either."

Jesse looks at Kate's plate. "**She** gets to be finished. That's not fair."

Brian sets his fork down on the side of his plate. "Fair?" he answers, his voice too quiet. "You want to be fair? All right, Jess. The next time Kate has a bone marrow aspiration, we'll let you get one, too. When we flush her central line, we'll make sure you go through something equally as painful. And next time she gets chemo, we'll—"

"Brian!" I interrupt.

He stops as abruptly as he's started, and passes a shaking hand over his eyes. Then his gaze lands on Jesse, who has taken refuge under my arm. "I . . . I'm sorry, Jess. I don't . . ." But whatever he is about to say vanishes, as Brian walks out of the kitchen.

For a long moment we sit in silence. Then Jesse turns to me. "Is Daddy sick, too?"

I think hard before I answer. "We're all going to be fine," I reply.

On the one-week anniversary of our return home, we are awakened in the middle of the night by a crash. Brian and I race each other to Kate's room. She lies in bed, shaking so hard that she's knocked a lamp off her nightstand. "She's burning up," I tell Brian, when I lay my hand against her forehead.

I have wondered how I will decide whether or not to call the doctor, should Kate develop any strange symptoms. I look at her now and cannot believe I would ever be so stupid to believe that I wouldn't know, immediately, what **Sick** looks like. "We're going to the ER," I announce, although Brian is already wrapping Kate's blankets around her and lifting her out of her crib. We bustle her to the car and start the engine and then remember that we cannot leave Jesse home alone.

"You go with her," Brian answers, reading my mind. "I'll stay here." But he doesn't take his eyes off Kate.

Minutes later, we are speeding toward the hospital, Jesse in the backseat next to his sister, asking why we need to get up, when the sun hasn't.

In the ER, Jesse sleeps on a nest of our coats. Brian and I watch the doctors hover over Kate's feverish body, bees over a field of flowers, drawing what they can from her. She is pan-cultured and given a spinal tap to try to isolate the cause of the infection and rule out meningitis. A radiologist brings in a portable X-ray machine to take a film of her chest, to see if this infection lives in her lungs.

Afterward, he places the chest film on the light panel outside the door. Kate's ribs seem as thin as matchsticks, and there is a large gray blot just off center. My knees go weak, and I find myself grabbing on to Brian's arm. "It's a tumor. The cancer's metastasized."

The doctor puts his hand on my shoulder. "Mrs. Fitzgerald," he says, "that's Kate's heart."

Pancytopenia is a fancy word that means there is nothing in Kate's body protecting her against infection. It means, Dr. Chance says, that the chemo worked—that a great majority of white blood cells in Kate's body have been wiped out. It also means that nadir sepsis—a post-chemo infection—is not a likelihood, but a given.

She is dosed with Tylenol to reduce her fever. She has blood, urine, and respiratory secretion cultures taken, so that the appropriate antibiotics can be administered. It takes six hours before she is free of the rigors—a round of violent shaking so fierce that she is in danger of shimmying off the bed.

The nurse—a woman who braided Kate's hair in silky cornrows one afternoon a few weeks back, to make her smile—takes Kate's temperature and then turns to me. "Sara," she says gently, "you can breathe now."

Kate's face looks as tiny and white as those distant moons that Brian likes to spot in his telescope—still, remote, cold. She looks like a corpse . . . and even worse, this is a relief, compared to watching her suffer.

"Hey." Brian touches the crown of my head. He juggles Jesse in his other arm. It is nearly noon, and we are all still in pajamas; we never thought to take a change of clothes. "I'm gonna take him down to the cafeteria; get some lunch. You want something?"

I shake my head. Scooting my chair closer to Kate's bed, I smooth the covers over her legs. I take her hand, and measure it against my own.

Her eyes slit open. For a moment she struggles, unsure of where she is. "Kate," I whisper. "I'm right here." As she turns her head and focuses on me, I lift her palm to my mouth, press a kiss in its center. "You are so brave," I tell her, and then I smile. "When I grow up, I want to be just like you."

To my surprise, Kate shakes her head hard. Her voice is a feather, a thread. "No Mommy," she says. "You'd be sick."

In my first dream, the IV fluid is dripping too quickly into Kate's central line. The saline pumps her up from the inside out, a balloon to be inflated. I try to pull the infusion, but it's held fast in the central line. As I watch, Kate's features smooth, blur, obliterate, until her face is a white oval that could be anyone at all.

In my second dream, I am in a maternity ward, giving birth. My body tunnels in, my heart pulses low in my belly. There is a rush of pressure, and then the baby arrives in a lightning rush and flow. "It's a girl," the nurse beams, and she hands me the newborn.

I pull the pink blanket from her face, then stop. "This isn't Kate," I say.

"Of course not," the nurse agrees. "But she's still yours."

The angel that arrives is wearing Armani and barking into a cell phone as she enters the hospital room. "Sell it," my sister orders. "I don't care if you have to set up a lemonade stand in Fanueil Hall and give the shares away, Peter. I said **sell**." She pushes a button and holds out her arms to me. "Hey," Zanne soothes when I burst into tears. "Did you really think I'd listen to you when you told me not to come?"

"But—"

"Faxes. Phones. I can work from your home. Who else is going to watch Jesse?"

Brian and I look at each other; we haven't thought that far. In response, Brian stands up, hugs Zanne awkwardly. Jesse runs toward her at full tilt. "Who's that kid you adopted,

Sara . . . because Jesse can't possibly be that big . . ." She disengages Jesse from her knees and leans down over the hospital bed, where Kate is sleeping. "I bet you don't remember me," Zanne says, her eyes bright. "But I remember you."

It comes so easy—letting her take charge. Zanne gets Jesse involved in a game of tic-tac-toe and bullies a Chinese restaurant that doesn't deliver into bringing up lunch. I sit beside Kate, basking in my sister's competence. I let myself pretend she can fix the things I can't.

After Zanne takes Jesse home for the night, Brian and I become bookends in the dark, bracketing Kate. "Brian," I whisper. "I've been thinking."

He shifts in his seat. "What about?"

I lean forward, so that I catch his eye. "Having a baby."

Brian's eyes narrow. "Jesus, Sara." He gets to his feet, turns his back to me. "Jesus."

I stand up, too. "It's not what you think."

When he faces me, pain draws every line of his features tight. "We can't just replace Kate if she dies," he says.

In the hospital bed, Kate shifts, rustling the sheets. I force myself to imagine her at age four, wearing a Halloween costume; age twelve, trying out lip gloss; age twenty, dancing around a dorm room. "I know. So we have to make sure that she doesn't."

WEDNESDAY

I will read ashes for you, if you ask me.

I will look in the fire and tell you from
the gray lashes

And out of the red and black tongues
and stripes,

I will tell how fire comes

And how fire runs as far as the sea.

—CARL SANDBURG,
"Fire Pages"

CAMPBELL

WE ARE ALL, I SUPPOSE, beholden to our parents—the question is, how much? This is what runs through my mind while my mother jabbers on about my father's latest affair. Not for the first time, I wish for siblings—if only so that I would receive sunrise phone calls like this only once or twice a week, instead of seven.

"Mother," I interrupt, "I doubt that she's actually sixteen."

"You underestimate your father, Campbell."

Maybe, but I also know that he's a federal judge. He may leer after schoolgirls, but he'd never do anything illegal. "Mom, I'm late for court. I'll check back in with you later," I say, and I hang up before she can protest.

I am not going to court, but still. Taking a deep breath, I shake my head and find Judge staring at me. "Reason number 106 why dogs are smarter than humans," I say. "Once you leave the litter, you sever contact with your mothers."

I walk into the kitchen as I am knotting my tie. My apartment, it is a work of art. Sleek and minimalist, but what is there is the best that money can buy—a one-of-a-kind black leather couch; a flat screen television hanging on the wall; a locked glass case filled with signed first editions from authors like Hemingway and Hawthorne. My coffeemaker comes imported from Italy; my refrigerator is sub-zero. I open it and find a single onion, a bottle of ketchup, and three rolls of black-and-white film.

This, too, is no surprise—I rarely eat at home. Judge is so used to restaurant food he wouldn't recognize kibble if it slid its way down his throat. "What do you think?" I ask him. "Rosie's sound good?"

He barks as I fasten his service-dog harness. Judge and I have been together for seven years. I bought him from a breeder of police dogs, but he was specially trained with me in mind. As for his name, well, what attorney wouldn't want to be able to put a Judge in a crate every now and then?

Rosie's is what Starbucks wishes it was: eclectic and funky, crammed with patrons who at any time might be reading Russian lit in its original tongue or balancing a company's budget on a laptop or writing a screenplay while mainlining caffeine. Judge and I usually walk there and sit at our usual table, in the back. We order a double espresso and two chocolate croissants, and we flirt shamelessly with Ophelia, the twenty-year-old waitress. But today, when we walk inside, Ophelia is nowhere to be found and there is a woman sitting at **our** table, feeding a toddler in a stroller a bagel. This throws me for such a loop that Judge needs to tug me to the only spot that's free, a stool at the counter that looks out on the street.

Seven-thirty A.M., and already this day is a bust.

A heroin-thin boy with enough rings in his eyebrows to resemble a shower curtain rod approaches with a pad. He sees Judge at my feet. "Sorry, dude. No dogs allowed."

"This is a service dog," I explain. "Where's Ophelia?"

"She's gone, man. Eloped, last night."

Eloped? People still **do** that? "With whom?" I ask, though it's none of my business.

"Some performance artist who sculpts dog crap into busts of world leaders. It's supposed to be a **statement.**"

I feel a momentary pang for poor Ophelia. Take it from me: love has all the lasting permanence of a rainbow—beautiful while it's there, and just as likely to have disappeared by the time you blink.

The waiter reaches into his back pocket and hands me a plastic card. "Here's the Braille menu."

"I want a double espresso and two croissants, and I'm not blind."

"Then what's Fido for?"

"I have SARS," I say. "He's tallying the people I infect."

The waiter can't seem to figure out if I am joking. He backs away, unsure, to get my coffee.

Unlike my normal table, this one has a view of the street. I watch an elderly lady narrowly avoid the swipe of a taxi; a boy dances past with a radio three times the size of his head balanced on his shoulder. Twins in parochial school uniforms giggle behind the pages of a teen magazine. And a woman with a running river of black hair spills coffee on her skirt, dropping the paper cup on the pavement.

Inside me, everything stops. I wait for her to lift her face—to see if this could possibly be who I think it is—but she turns away from me, blotting the fabric with a napkin. A bus cuts the world in half, and my cell phone begins to ring.

I glance down at the incoming number: no surprise there. Turning off the power button without bothering to take my mother's call, I glance back at the woman outside the window, but by then the bus is gone and so is she.

I open the door of the office, already barking orders for Kerri. "Call Osterlitz and ask him whether he's available to testify during the Weiland trial; get a list of other complainants who've gone up against New England Power in the past five years; make me a copy of the Melbourne deposition; and phone Jerry at the court and ask who the judge is going to be for the Fitzgerald kid's hearing."

She glances up at me as the phone begins to ring. "Speaking of." She jerks her head in the direction of the door to my inner sanctum. Anna Fitzgerald stands on the threshold with a spray can of industrial cleaner and a chamois cloth, polishing the doorknob.

"What are you doing?" I ask.

"What you told me to." She looks down at the dog. "Hey, Judge."

"Line two for you," Kerri interrupts. I give her a measured look—why she even let this kid in here is beyond me—and try to get into my office, but whatever Anna has put on the hardware makes it too greasy to turn. I struggle for a moment, until she grips the knob with the cloth and opens the door for me.

Judge circles the floor, finding the most comfortable spot. I punch the blinking light on the call row. "Campbell Alexander."

"Mr. Alexander, this is Sara Fitzgerald. Anna Fitzgerald's mother." I let this information settle. I stare at her daughter, polishing a mere five feet away.

"Mrs. Fitzgerald," I answer, and as expected, Anna stops in her tracks.

"I'm calling because . . . well, you see, this is all a misunderstanding."

"Have you filed a response to the petition?"

"That isn't going to be necessary. I spoke to

Anna last night, and she isn't going to continue with her case. She wants to do anything she can to help Kate."

"Is that so." My voice falls flat. "Unfortunately, if my client is planning to call off her lawsuit, I'll need to hear it directly from her." I raise a brow, catch Anna's gaze. "You wouldn't happen to know where she is?"

"She went out for a run," Sara Fitzgerald says. "But we're going to come down to the courthouse this afternoon. We'll talk to the judge, and get this straightened out."

"I suppose I'll see you then." I hang up the phone and cross my arms, look at Anna. "Is there something you'd like to tell me?"

She shrugs. "Not really."

"That's not what your mother seems to think. Then again, she's also under the impression that you're out playing Flo Jo."

Anna glances out into the reception area, where Kerri, naturally, is hanging on our words like a cat on a rope. She closes the door and walks up to my desk. "I couldn't tell her I was coming here, not after last night."

"What happened last night?" When Anna

goes mute, I lose my patience. "Listen. If you're not going to go through with a lawsuit . . . if this is a colossal waste of my time . . . then I'd appreciate it if you had the honesty to tell me now, rather than later. Because I'm not a family therapist or your best buddy; I'm your attorney. And for me to be your attorney there actually has to be a case. So I will ask you one more time: have you changed your mind about this lawsuit?"

I expect this tirade to put an end to the litigation, to reduce Anna to a wavering puddle of indecision. But to my surprise, she looks right at me, cool and collected. "Are you still willing to represent me?" she asks.

Against my better judgment, I say yes.

"Then no," she says, "I haven't changed my mind."

The first time I sailed in a yacht club race with my father I was fourteen, and he was dead set against it. I wasn't old enough; I wasn't mature enough; the weather was too iffy. What he really was saying was that having me crew for him was more likely to lose him the cup than to win it. In my father's eyes, if you weren't perfect, you simply **weren't**.

His boat was a USA-1 class, a marvel of mahogany and teak, one he'd bought from the keyboard player J. Geils up in Marblehead. In other words: a dream, a status symbol, and a rite of passage, all wrapped up in a gleaming white sail and a honey-colored hull.

We hit the start dead-on, crossing the line at full sail just as the cannon shot off. I did my best to be a step ahead of where my father needed me to be—guiding the rudder before he even gave the order, jibing and tacking until my muscles burned with effort. And maybe this even would have had a happy ending, but then a storm blew in from the north, bringing sheets of rain and swells that stretched ten feet high, pitching us from height to gulley.

I watched my father move in his yellow slicker. He didn't seem to notice it was raining; he certainly didn't want to crawl into a hole and clutch his sick stomach and die, like I did. "Campbell," he bellowed, "come about."

But to turn into the wind meant to ride

another roller coaster up and down. "Campbell," my father repeated, **"now."**

A trough opened up in front of us; the boat dipped so sharply I lost my footing. My father lunged past me, grabbing for the rudder. For one blessed moment, the sails went still. Then the boom whipped across, and the boat tacked along an opposite course.

"I need coordinates," my father ordered.

Navigating meant going down into the hull where the charts were, and doing the math to figure out what heading we had to be on to reach the next race buoy. But being below, away from the fresh air, only made it worse. I opened a map just in time to throw up all over it.

My father found me by default, because I hadn't returned with an answer. He poked his head down and saw me sitting in a puddle of my own vomit. "For Christ's sake," he muttered, and left me.

It took all the strength I had to pull myself up after him. He jerked the wheel and yanked at the rudder. He pretended I was not there. And when he jibed, he did not call it. The sail whizzed across the boat, ripping the seam of the sky. The boom flew, clipped me on the back of the head, and knocked me out.

I came to just as my father was stealing the wind of another boat, mere feet from the finish line. The rain had mellowed to a mist, and as he put our craft between the airstream and our closest competitor, the other boat fell back. We won by seconds.

I was told to clean up my mess and take the taxi in, while my father sailed the dory to the yacht club to celebrate. It was an hour later when I finally arrived, and by then he was in high spirits, drinking scotch from the crystal cup he had won. "Here comes your crew, Cam," a friend called out. My father lifted the victory cup in salute, drank deeply, and then slammed it down so hard on the bar that its handle shattered.

"Oh," said another sailor. "That's a shame."

My father never took his eyes off me. "Isn't it, though," he said.

On the rear bumper of practically every third car in Rhode Island you'll find a red-and-white sticker celebrating the victims of some of the bigger criminal cases in the state: **My Friend Katy DeCubellis Was Killed by a Drunk Driver. My Friend John Sisson Was Killed by a Drunk Driver.** These are given out at school fairs and fund-raisers and hair salons, and it doesn't matter if you never knew the kid who got killed; you put them on your vehicle out of solidarity and secret joy that this tragedy did not happen to you.

Last year, there were red-and-white stickers with a new victim's name: Dena DeSalvo. Unlike the other victims, this was one I knew marginally. She was the twelve-year-old daughter of a judge, who reportedly broke down during a custody trial held shortly after the funeral and took a three-month leave of absence to deal with his grief. The same judge, incidentally, who has been assigned to Anna Fitzgerald's case.

As I make my way into the Garrahy Complex, where the family court is housed, I wonder if a man carrying around so much baggage will be able to try a case where a winning outcome for my client will precipitate the death of her teenage sister.

There is a new bailiff at the entrance, a man with a neck as thick as a redwood and most likely the brainpower to match. "Sorry," he says. "No pets."

"This is a service dog."

Confused, the bailiff leans forward and peers into my eyes. I do the same, right back at him. "I'm nearsighted. He helps me read the road signs." Stepping around the guy, Judge and I head down the hall to the courtroom.

Inside, the clerk is being taken down a peg by Anna Fitzgerald's mother. That's my assumption, at least, because in actuality the woman looks nothing like her daughter, who stands beside her. "I'm quite sure that in this case, the judge would understand," Sara Fitzgerald argues. Her husband waits a few feet behind her, apart.

When Anna notices me, a wash of relief rushes over her features. I turn to the clerk of the court. "I'm Campbell Alexander," I say. "Is there a problem?"

"I've been trying to explain to Mrs. Fitzgerald, here, that we only allow attorneys into chambers."

"Well, I'm here on behalf on Anna," I reply.

The clerk turns to Sara Fitzgerald. "Who's representing your party?"

Anna's mother is stricken for a moment. She

turns to her husband. "It's like riding a bicycle," she says quietly.

Her husband shakes his head. "Are you sure you want to do this?"

"I **don't** want to do this. I **have** to do this."

The words fall into place like cogs. "Hang on," I say. "You're a **lawyer?**"

Sara turns. "Well, yes."

I glance down at Anna, incredulous. "And you neglected to mention this?"

"You never asked," she whispers.

The clerk gives us each an Entry of Appearance form, and summons the sheriff.

"Vern." Sara smiles. "Good to see you again."

Oh, this just keeps getting better.

"Hey!" The sheriff kisses her cheek, shakes hands with the husband. "Brian."

So not only is she an attorney; she also has all the public servants in the palm of her hand. "Are we finished with Old Home Day?" I ask, and Sara Fitzgerald rolls her eyes at the sheriff: **The guy's a jerk, but what are you gonna do?** "Stay here," I tell Anna, and I follow her mother back toward chambers.

Judge DeSalvo is a short man with a mono-brow and a fondness for coffee milk. "Good morning," he says, waving us toward our seats. "What's with the dog?"

"He's a service dog, Your Honor." Before he can say anything else, I leap into the genial conversation that heralds every meeting in chambers in Rhode Island. We are a small state, smaller still in the legal community. It is not only conceivable that your paralegal is the niece or sister-in-law of the judge with whom you're meeting; it's downright likely. As we chat, I glance over at Sara, who needs to understand which of us is part of this game, and which of us isn't. Maybe she was an attorney, but not in the ten years I've been one.

She is nervous, pleating the bottom of her blouse. Judge DeSalvo notices. "I didn't know you were practicing law again."

"I wasn't planning to, Your Honor, but the complainant is my daughter."

At that, the judge turns to me. "Well, what's this all about, Counselor?"

"Mrs. Fitzgerald's youngest daughter is seeking medical emancipation from her parents."

Sara shakes her head. "That's not true, Judge." Hearing his name, my dog glances up. "I spoke to

Anna, and she assured me she really doesn't want to do this. She had a bad day, and wanted a little extra attention." Sara lifts a shoulder. "You know how thirteen-year-olds can be."

The room grows so quiet, I can hear my own pulse. Judge DeSalvo doesn't know how thirteen-year-olds can be. His daughter died when she was twelve.

Sara's face flames red. Like the rest of this state, she knows about Dena DeSalvo. For all I know, she's got one of the bumper stickers on her minivan. "Oh God, I'm sorry. I didn't mean—"

The judge looks away. "Mr. Alexander, when was the last time you spoke with your client?"

"Yesterday morning, Your Honor. She was in my office when her mother called me to say it was a misunderstanding."

Predictably, Sara's jaw drops. "She couldn't have been. She was jogging."

I look at her. "You sure about that?"

"She was **supposed** to be jogging . . ."

"Your Honor," I say, "this is precisely my point, and the reason Anna Fitzgerald's petition has merit. Her own mother isn't aware of where she is on any given morning; medical decisions regarding Anna are made with the same haphazard—"

"Counselor, can it." The judge turns to Sara. "Your daughter told you she wanted to call off the lawsuit?"

"Yes."

He glances at me. "And she told you that she wanted to continue?"

"That's right."

"Then I'd better talk directly to Anna."

When the judge gets up and walks out of chambers, we follow. Anna is sitting on a bench in the hall with her father. One of her sneakers is untied. "I spy something green," I hear her say, and then she looks up.

"Anna," I say, at the exact same moment as Sara Fitzgerald.

It is my responsibility to explain to Anna that Judge DeSalvo wants a few minutes in private. I need to coach her, so that she says the right things, so that the judge doesn't throw the case out before she gets what she wants. She is my client; by definition, she is supposed to follow my counsel.

But when I call her name, she turns toward her mother.

ANNA

I DON'T THINK anyone would come to my funeral. My parents, I guess, and Aunt Zanne and maybe Mr. Ollincott, the social studies teacher. I picture the same cemetery we went to for my grandmother's funeral, although that was in Chicago so it doesn't really make any sense. There would be rolling hills that look like green velvet, and statues of gods and lesser angels, and that big brown hole in the ground like a split seam, waiting to swallow the body that used to be me.

I imagine my mom in a black-veiled Jackie O hat, sobbing. My dad holding on to her. Kate and Jesse staring at the shine of the coffin and trying to plea-bargain with God for all the times they did something mean to me. It is possible that some of the guys from my hockey team would come, clutching lilies and their composure. "That Anna," they'd say, and they wouldn't cry but they'd want to.

There would be an obituary on page twenty-four of the paper, and maybe Kyle McFee would see it and come to the funeral, his beautiful face twisted up with the **what-ifs** of the girlfriend he never got to have. I think there would be flowers, sweet peas and snapdragons and blue balls of hydrangea. I hope someone would sing "Amazing Grace," not just the famous first verse but all of them. And afterward, when the leaves turned and the snow came, every now and then I would rise in everyone's minds like a tide.

At Kate's funeral, everyone will come. There will be nurses from the hospital who've gotten to be our friends, and other cancer patients still counting their lucky stars, and townspeople who helped raise money for her treatments. They will have to turn mourners away at the cemetery gates. There will be so many lush funeral baskets that some will be donated to charity. The newspaper will run a story of her short and tragic life.

Mark my words, it will be on the front page.

• • •

Judge DeSalvo's wearing flip-flops, the kind soccer players wear when they take off their cleats. I don't know why, but this makes me feel a little better. I mean, it's bad enough I'm here in this courthouse, being led toward his private room in the back; there's something nice about knowing that I'm not the only one who doesn't quite fit the part.

He takes a can from a dwarf fridge and asks me what I'd like to drink. "Coke would be great," I say.

The judge opens the can. "Did you know that if you leave a baby tooth in a glass of Coke, in a few weeks it'll completely disappear? Carbonic acid." He smiles at me. "My brother is a dentist in Warwick. Does that trick every year for the kindergartners."

I take a sip of the Coke, and imagine my insides dissolving. Judge DeSalvo doesn't sit down behind his desk, but instead takes a chair right next to me. "Here's the problem, Anna," he says. "Your mom is telling me you want to do one thing. And your lawyer is telling me you want to do another. Now, under normal circumstances, I'd expect your mother to know you better than some guy you met two days ago. But you never would have met this guy if you hadn't sought him out for his services. And that makes me think that I need to hear what you think about all this."

"Can I ask you something?"

"Sure," he says.

"Does there have to be a trial?"

"Well . . . your parents can just agree to medical emancipation, and that would be that," the judge says.

Like **that** would ever happen.

"On the other hand, once someone files a petition—like you have—then the respondent—your parents—have to go to court. If your parents really believe you're not ready to make these kinds of decisions by yourself, they have to present their reasons to me, or else risk having me find in your favor by default."

I nod. I have told myself that no matter what, I'm going to keep cool. If I fall apart at the seams, there's no way this judge will think

I'm capable of deciding **anything**. I have all these brilliant intentions, but I get sidetracked by the sight of the judge, lifting his can of apple juice.

Not too long ago, when Kate was in the hospital to get her kidneys checked out, a new nurse handed her a cup and asked for a urine sample. "It better be ready when I come back for it," she said. Kate—who isn't a fan of snotty demands—decided the nurse needed to be taken down a peg. She sent me out on a mission to the vending machines, to get the very juice that the judge is drinking now. She poured this into the specimen cup, and when the nurse came back, held it up to the light. "Huh," Kate said. "Looks a little cloudy. Better filter it through again." And then she lifted it to her lips and drank it down.

The nurse turned white and flew out of the room. Kate and I, we laughed until our stomachs cramped. For the rest of that day, all we had to do was catch each other's eye and we'd dissolve.

Like a tooth, and then there's nothing left.

"Anna?" Judge DeSalvo prompts, and then

he sets that stupid can of Mott's down on the table between us and I burst into tears.

"I can't give a kidney to my sister. I just can't."

Without a word, Judge DeSalvo hands me a box of Kleenex. I wad some into a ball, wipe at my eyes and my nose. For a while, he's quiet, letting me catch my breath. When I look up I find him waiting. "Anna, no hospital in this country will take an organ from an unwilling donor."

"Who do you think signs off on it?" I ask. "Not the little kid getting wheeled into the OR—her **parents.**"

"You're not a little kid; you could certainly make your objections known," he says.

"Oh, right," I say, tearing up again. "When you complain because someone's sticking a needle into you for the tenth time, it's considered standard operating procedure. All the adults look around with fake smiles and tell each other that no one voluntarily **asks** for more needles." I blow my nose into a Kleenex. "The kidney—that's just today. Tomorrow it'll be something else. It's always something else."

"Your mother told me you want to drop the lawsuit," he says. "Did she lie to me?"

"No." I swallow hard.

"Then . . . why did you lie to **her?**"

There are a thousand answers for that; I choose the easy one. "Because I love her," I say, and the tears come all over again. "I'm sorry. I'm really sorry."

He stares at me hard. "You know what, Anna? I'm going to appoint someone who's going to help your lawyer tell me what's best for you. How does that sound?"

My hair's fallen all over the place; I tuck it behind my ear. My face is so red it feels swollen. "Okay," I answer.

"Okay." He presses an intercom button, and asks to have everyone else sent back.

My mother comes into the room first and starts to make her way over to me, until Campbell and his dog cut her off. He raises his brows and gives me a thumbs-up sign, but it's a question. "I'm not sure what's going on," Judge DeSalvo says, "so I'm appointing a guardian ad litem to spend two weeks with her. Needless to say, I expect full cooperation on both of your parts. I want the guardian ad litem's report back, and then we'll have a hearing. If there's anything more I need to know at that time, bring it with you."

"Two weeks . . ." my mother says. I know what she's thinking. "Your Honor, with all due respect, two weeks is a very long time, given the severity of my other daughter's illness."

She looks like someone I do not recognize. I have seen her before be a tiger, fighting a medical system that isn't moving fast enough for her. I have seen her be a rock, giving the rest of us something to cling to. I have seen her be a boxer, coming up swinging before the next punch can be thrown by Fate. But I have never seen her be a lawyer before.

Judge DeSalvo nods. "All right. We'll have a hearing next Monday, then. In the meantime I want Kate's medical records brought to—"

"Your Honor," Campbell Alexander interrupts. "As you're well aware, due to the strange circumstances of this case, my client is living with opposing counsel. That's a flagrant breach of justice."

My mother sucks in her breath. "You are **not**

suggesting my child be taken away from me."

Taken away? Where would I **go?**

"I can't be sure that opposing counsel won't try to use her living arrangements to her best advantage, Your Honor, and possibly pressure my client." Campbell stares right at the judge, unblinking.

"Mr. Alexander, there is no way I am pulling this child out of her home," Judge DeSalvo says, but then he turns to my mother. "However, Mrs. Fitzgerald, you cannot talk about this case with your daughter unless her attorney is present. If you can't agree to that, or if I hear of any breach in that domestic Chinese wall, I may have to take more drastic action."

"Understood, Your Honor," my mother says.

"Well." Judge DeSalvo stands up. "I'll see you all next week." He walks out of the room, his flip-flops making small sucking slaps on the tile floor.

The minute he is gone, I turn to my mother. **I can explain,** I want to say, but it never makes its way out loud. Suddenly a wet nose pokes into my hand. Judge. It makes my heart, that runaway train, slow down.

"I need to speak to my client," Campbell says.

"Right now she's my daughter," my mother says, and she takes my hand and yanks me out of my chair. At the threshold of the door, I manage to look back. Campbell's fuming. I could have told him it would wind up like this. **Daughter** trumps everything, no matter what the game.

World War III begins immediately, not with an assassinated archduke or a crazy dictator but with a missed left turn. "Brian," my mother says, craning her neck. "That was North Park Street."

My father blinks out of his fog. "You could have told me **before** I passed it."

"I did."

Before I can even weigh the costs and benefits of entering someone else's battle again, I say, **"I** didn't hear you."

My mother's head whips around. "Anna, right now, you are the **last** person whose input I need or want."

"I just—"

She holds up her hand like the privacy partition in a cab. She shakes her head.

On the backseat, I slide sideways and curl my feet up, facing to the rear, so that all I see is black.

"Brian," my mother says. "You missed it **again.**"

When we walk in, my mother steams past Kate, who opened the door for us, and past Jesse, who is watching what looks like the scrambled Playboy channel on TV. In the kitchen, she opens cabinets and bangs them shut. She takes food from the refrigerator and smacks it onto the table.

"Hey," my father says to Kate. "How're you feeling?"

She ignores him, pushing into the kitchen. "What happened?"

"What **happened**. Well." My mother pins me with a gaze. "Why don't you ask your sister what happened?"

Kate turns to me, all eyes.

"Amazing how quiet you are now, when a judge isn't listening," my mother says.

Jesse turns off the television. "She made you talk to a judge? Damn, Anna."

My mother closes her eyes. "Jesse, you know, now would be a good time for you to leave."

"You don't have to ask me twice," he says, his voice full of broken glass. We hear the front door open and shut, a whole story.

"Sara." My father steps into the room. "We all need to cool off a little."

"I have one child who's just signed her sister's death sentence, and I'm supposed to cool off?"

The kitchen gets so silent we can hear the refrigerator whispering. My mother's words hang like too-ripe fruit, and when they fall on the floor and burst, she shudders into motion. "Kate," she says, hurrying toward my sister, her arms already outstretched. "Kate, I shouldn't have said that. It's not what I meant."

In my family, we seem to have a tortured history of not saying what we ought to and not meaning what we do. Kate covers her mouth with her hand. She backs out of the kitchen door, bumping into my father, who fumbles but cannot catch her as she scrambles upstairs. I hear the door to our room slam shut. My mother, of course, goes after her.

So I do what I do best. I move in the opposite direction.

Is there any place on earth that smells better than a Laundromat? It's like a rainy Sunday when you don't have to get out from under your covers, or like lying back on the grass your father's just mowed—comfort food for your nose. When I was little my mom would take hot clothes out of the dryer and dump them on top of me where I was sitting on the couch. I used to pretend they were a single skin, that I was curled tight beneath them like one large heart.

The other thing I like is that Laundromats draw lonely people like metal to magnets. There's a guy passed out on a bank of chairs in the back, with army boots and a T-shirt that says **Nostradamus Was an Optimist.** A woman at the folding table sifts through a heap of men's button-down shirts, sniffing back tears. Put ten people together in a Laundromat and chances are you won't be the one who's worst off.

I sit down across from a bank of washers and try to match up the clothes with the people waiting. The pink panties and lace nightgown belong to the girl who is reading a romance novel. The woolly red socks and checkered shirt are the skanky sleeping student. The soccer jerseys and kiddie overalls come from the toddler who keeps handing filmy white dryer sheets to her mom, oblivious on a cell phone. What kind of person can afford a cell phone, but not her own washer and dryer?

I play a game with myself, sometimes, and try to imagine what it would be like to be the person whose clothes are spinning in front of me. If I were washing those carpenter jeans, maybe I'd be a roofer in Phoenix, my arms strong and my back tan. If I had those flowered sheets, I might be on break from Harvard, studying criminal profiling. If I owned that satin cape, I might have season tickets to the ballet. And then I try to picture myself doing any of these things and I can't. All I can ever see is me, being a donor for Kate, each time stretching to the next.

Kate and I are Siamese twins; you just can't see the spot where we're connected. Which makes separation that much more difficult.

When I look up the girl who works the Laundromat is standing over me, with her lip ring and blue streaked dreadlocks. "You need change?" she asks.

To tell you the truth, I'm afraid to hear my own answer.

JESSE

I AM THE KID WHO PLAYED with matches. I used to steal them from the shelf above the refrigerator, take them into my parents' bathroom. Jean Naté Bath Splash ignites, did you know that? Spill it, strike, and you can set fire to the floor. It burns blue, and when the alcohol is gone, it stops.

Once, Anna walked in on me when I was in the bathroom. "Hey," I said. "Check this out." I dribbled some Jean Naté on the floor, her initials. Then I torched them. I figured she'd run screaming like a tattletale, but instead she sat right down on the edge of the bathtub. She reached for the bottle of Jean Naté, made some loopy design on the tiles, and told me to do it again.

Anna is the only proof I have that I was born

into this family, instead of dropped off on the doorstep by some Bonnie and Clyde couple that ran off into the night. On the surface, we're polar opposites. Under the skin, though, we're the same: people think they know what they're getting, and they're always wrong.

Fuck them all. I ought to have that tattooed on my forehead, for all the times I've thought it. Usually I am in transit, speeding in my Jeep until my lungs give out. Today, I'm driving ninety-five down 95. I weave in and out of traffic, sewing up a scar. People yell at me behind their closed windows. I give them the finger.

It would solve a thousand problems if I rolled the Jeep over an embankment. It's not like I haven't thought about it, you know. On my license, it says I'm an organ donor, but the truth is I'd consider being an organ **martyr**. I'm sure I'm worth a lot more dead than alive—the sum of the parts equals more than the whole. I wonder who might wind up walking around with my liver, my lungs, even my eyeballs. I wonder what poor asshole would get stuck with whatever it is in me that passes for a heart.

To my dismay, though, I get all the way to the exit without a scratch. I peel off the ramp and tool along Allens Avenue. There's an underpass there where I know I'll find Duracell Dan. He's a homeless dude, Vietnam vet, who spends most of his time collecting batteries that people toss into the trash. What the hell he does with them, I don't know. He opens them up, I know that much. He says the CIA hides messages for all its operatives in Energizer double-As, that the FBI sticks to Evereadys.

Dan and I have a deal: I bring him a McDonald's Value Meal a few times a week, and in return, he watches over my stuff. I find him huddled over the astrology book that he considers his manifesto. "Dan," I say, getting out of the car and handing him his Big Mac. "What's up?"

He squints at me. "The moon's in freaking Aquarius." He stuffs a fry into his mouth. "I never should have gotten out of bed."

If Dan has a bed, it's news to me. "Sorry about that," I say. "Got my stuff?"

He jerks his head to the barrels behind the

concrete pylon where he keeps my things. The perchloric acid filched from the chemistry lab at the high school is intact; in another barrel is the sawdust. I hike the stuffed pillowcase under my arm and haul it to the car. I find him waiting at the door. "Thanks."

He leans against the car, won't let me get inside. "They gave me a message for you."

Even though everything that comes out of Dan's mouth is total bullshit, my stomach rolls over. "Who did?"

He looks down the road, then back at me. "You know." Leaning closer, he whispers, "Think twice."

"That was the message?"

Dan nods. "Yeah. It was that, or **Drink** twice. I can't be sure."

"**That** advice I might actually listen to." I shove him a little, so that I can get into the car. He is lighter than you'd think, like whatever was inside him was used up long ago. With that reasoning, it's a wonder I don't float off into the sky. "Later," I tell him, and then I drive toward the warehouse I've been watching.

I look for places like me: big, hollow, forgotten by most everyone. This one's in the Olneyville area. At one time, it was used as a storage facility for an export business. Now, it's pretty much just home to an extended family of rats. I park far enough away that no one would think twice about my car. I stuff the pillowcase of sawdust under my jacket and take off.

It turns out that I learned something from my dear old dad after all: firemen are experts at getting into places they shouldn't be. It doesn't take much to pick the lock, and then it's just a matter of figuring out where I want to start. I cut a hole in the bottom of the pillowcase and let the sawdust draw three fat initials, JBF. Then I take the acid and dribble it over the letters.

This is the first time I've done it in the middle of the day.

I take a pack of Merits out of my pocket and tamp them down, then stick one into my mouth. My Zippo's almost out of lighter fluid; I need to remember to get some. When I'm finished, I get to my feet, take one last drag, and toss the cigarette into the sawdust. I know this one's going to move fast, so I'm already running when the wall of fire rises behind me.

Like all the others, they will look for clues. But this cigarette and my initials will have long been gone. The whole floor underneath them will melt. The walls will buckle and give.

The first engine reaches the scene just as I get back to my car and pull the binoculars out of my trunk. By then, the fire's done what it wants to—escape. Glass has blown out of windows; smoke rises black, an eclipse.

The first time I saw my mother cry I was five. She was standing at the kitchen window, pretending that she wasn't. The sun was just coming up, a swollen knot. "What are you doing?" I asked. It was not until years later that I realized I had heard her answer all wrong. That when she said **mourning,** she had not been talking about the time of day.

The sky, now, is thick and dark with smoke. Sparks shower as the roof falls in. A second crew of firefighters arrives, the ones who have been called in from their dinner tables and showers and living rooms. With the binoculars, I can make out his name, winking on the back of his turnout coat like it's spelled in diamonds. Fitzgerald. My father lays hands on a

charged line, and I get into my car and drive
away.

At home, my mother is having a nervous
breakdown. She flies out the door as soon as I
pull into my parking spot. "Thank God," she
says. "I need your help."

She doesn't even look back to see if I'm following her inside, and that is how I know it's
Kate. The door to my sisters' room has been
kicked in, the wooden frame around it splintered. My sister lies still on her bed. Then all of
a sudden she bursts to life, jerking up like a
tire jack and puking blood. A stain spreads over
her shirt and onto her flowered comforter, red
poppies where there weren't any before.

My mother gets down beside her, holding
back her hair and pressing a towel up to her
mouth when Kate vomits again, another gush
of blood. "Jesse," she says matter-of-factly,
"your father's out on a call, and I can't reach
him. I need you to drive us to the hospital, so
that I can sit in the back with Kate."

Kate's lips are slick as cherries. I pick her

up in my arms. She's nothing but bones, poking sharp through the skin of her T-shirt.

"When Anna ran off, Kate wouldn't let me into her room," my mother says, hurrying beside me. "I gave her a little while to calm down. And then I heard her coughing. I had to get in there."

So you kicked it down, I think, and it doesn't surprise me. We reach the car, and she opens the door so that I can slide Kate inside. I pull out of the driveway and speed even faster than normal through town, onto the highway, toward the hospital.

Today, when my parents were at court with Anna, Kate and I watched TV. She wanted to put on her soap and I told her fuck off and put on the scrambled Playboy channel instead. Now, as I run through red lights, I'm wishing that I'd let her watch that retarded soap. I'm trying not to look at her little white coin of a face in the rearview mirror. You'd think, with all the time I've had to get used to it, that moments like this wouldn't come as such a shock. The question we cannot ask pushes through my veins with each beat: **Is this it? Is this it? Is this it?**

The minute we hit the ER driveway, my mother's out of the car, hurrying me to get Kate. We are quite a picture walking through the automatic doors, me with Kate bleeding in my arms, and my mother grabbing the first nurse who walks by. "She needs platelets," my mother orders.

They take her away from me, and for a few moments, even after the ER team and my mother have disappeared with Kate behind closed curtains, I stand with my arms buoyed, trying to get used to the fact that there's no longer anything in them.

Dr. Chance, the oncologist I know, and Dr. Nguyen, some expert I don't, tell us what we've already figured out: these are the death throes of end-stage kidney disease. My mother stands next to the bed, her hand tight around Kate's IV pole. "Can you still do a transplant?" she asks, as if Anna never started her lawsuit, as if it means absolutely nothing.

"Kate's in a pretty grave clinical state," Dr. Chance tells her. "I told you before I didn't know if she was strong enough to survive that level of surgery; the odds are even slighter now."

"But if there was a donor," she says, "would you do it?"

"Wait." You'd think my throat had just been paved with straw. "Would mine work?"

Dr. Chance shakes his head. "A kidney donor doesn't have to be a perfect match, in an ordinary case. But your sister isn't an ordinary case."

When the doctors leave, I can feel my mother staring at me. "Jesse," she says.

"It wasn't like I was volunteering. I just wanted to, you know, **know.**" But inside, I'm burning just as hot as I was when that fire caught at the warehouse. What made me believe I might be worth something, even now? What made me think I could save my sister, when I can't even save myself?

Kate's eyes open, so that she's staring right at me. She licks her lips—they're still caked with blood—and it makes her look like a vampire. The undead. If only.

I lean closer, because she doesn't have enough in her right now to make the words creep across the air between us. **Tell,** she mouths, so that my mother won't look up.

I answer, just as silent. **Tell?** I want to make sure I've got it right.

Tell Anna.

But the door to the room bursts open and my father fills the room with smoke. His hair and clothes and skin reek of it, so much so that I look up, expecting the sprinklers to go off. "What happened?" he asks, going right to the bed.

I slip out of the room, because nobody needs me there anymore. In the elevator, in front of the NO SMOKING sign, I light a cigarette.

Tell Anna what?

SARA

1990–1991

BY PURE CHANCE, or maybe karmic distribution, all three clients at the hair salon are pregnant. We sit under the dryers, hands folded over our bellies like a row of Buddhas. "My top choices are Freedom, Low, and Jack," says the girl next to me, who is getting her hair dyed pink.

"What if it's not a boy?" asks the woman sitting on my other side.

"Oh, those are meant to be for **either.**"

I hide a smile. "I vote for Jack."

The girl squints, looking out the window at the rotten weather. "**Sleet** is nice," she says absently, and then tries it on for size. "Sleet, pick up your toys. Sleet, honey, come on, or we're gonna be late for the Uncle Tupelo concert." She digs a piece of paper and a pencil stub out of her maternity overalls and scribbles down the name.

The woman on my left grins at me. "Is this your first?"

"My third."

"Mine too. I have two boys. I'm keeping my fingers crossed."

"I have a boy and a girl," I tell her. "Five and three."

"Do you know what you're having this time?"

I know everything about this baby, from her sex to the very placement of her chromosomes, including the ones that make her a perfect match for Kate. I know exactly what I am having: a miracle. "It's a girl," I answer.

"Ooh, I'm so jealous! My husband and I, we didn't find out at the ultrasound. I thought if I heard it was another boy, I might never finish out the last five months." She shuts off her hair dryer and pushes it back. "You have any names picked?"

It strikes me that I don't. Although I am nine months pregnant, although I have had plenty of time to dream, I have not really considered the specifics of this child. I have thought of this daughter only in terms of what she will be able to do for the daughter I already have. I haven't admitted this even to Brian, who lies at night with his head on my considerable belly, waiting for the twitches that herald—he thinks—the first female placekicker for the Patriots. Then again, my dreams for her are no less exalted; I plan for her to save her sister's life.

"We're waiting," I tell the woman.

Sometimes I think it is all we ever do.

There was a moment, after Kate's three months of chemotherapy last year, that I was stupid enough to believe we had beaten the odds. Dr. Chance said that she seemed to be in remission, and that we would just keep an eye on what came next. And for a little while, my life even got back to normal: chauffeuring Jesse to soccer practice and helping out in Kate's preschool class and even taking a hot bath to relax.

And yet, there was a part of me that knew the other shoe was bound to drop. This part scoured Kate's pillow every morning, even after her hair started to grow back with its frizzy, burned ends, just in case it started falling out again. This part went to the geneticist recommended by Dr. Chance. Engineered an embryo given the thumbs-up by scientists to be a perfect match for Kate. Took the hormones for IVF and conceived that embryo, just in case.

It was during a routine bone marrow aspiration that we learned Kate was in molecular relapse. On the outside, she looked like any other three-year-old girl. On the inside, the cancer had surged through her system again, steamrolling the progress that had been made with chemo.

Now, in the backseat with Jesse, Kate's kicking her feet and playing with a toy phone. Jesse sits next to her, staring out the window. "Mom? Do buses ever fall on people?"

"Like out of trees?"

"No. Like . . . just over." He makes a flipping motion with his hand.

"Only if the weather's really bad, or if the driver's going too fast."

He nods, accepting my explanation for his safety in this universe. Then: "Mom? Do you have a favorite number?"

"Thirty-one," I tell him. This is my due date. "How about you?"

"Nine. Because it can be a number, or how old you are, or a six standing on its head." He pauses only long enough to take a breath. "Mom? Do we have special scissors to cut meat?"

"We do." I take a right and drive past a cemetery, headstones canted forward and back like a set of yellowed teeth.

"Mom?" Jesse asks, "is that where Kate will go?"

The question, just as innocent as any of the others Jesse would ask, makes my legs go weak. I pull the car over and put on my hazard lights. Then I unbuckle my seat belt and turn around. "No, Jess," I tell him. "She's staying with us."

"Mr. and Mrs. Fitzgerald?" the producer says. "This is where we'll put you."

We sit down on the set at the TV studio. We've been invited here because of our baby's unorthodox conception. Somehow, in an effort to keep Kate healthy, we've unwittingly become the poster children for scientific debate.

Brian reaches for my hand as we are approached by Nadya Carter, the reporter for the newsmagazine. "We're just about ready. I've already taped an intro about Kate. All I'm going to do is ask you a few questions, and we'll be finished before you know it."

Just before the camera starts rolling, Brian wipes his cheeks on the sleeve of his shirt. The makeup artist, standing behind the lights, moans. "Well, for God's sake," he whispers to me. "I'm not going on national TV wearing blush."

The camera comes to life with far less ceremony than I've expected, just a little hum that runs up my arms and legs.

"Mr. Fitzgerald," Nadya says, "can you explain to us why you chose to visit a geneticist in the first place?"

Brian looks at me. "Our three-year-old

daughter has a very aggressive form of leukemia. Her oncologist suggested we find a bone marrow donor—but our oldest son wasn't a genetic match. There's a national registry, but by the time the right donor comes along for Kate, she might not . . . be around. So we thought it might be a good idea to see if another sibling of Kate's matched up."

"A sibling," Nadya says, "who doesn't exist."

"Not yet," Brian replies.

"What made you turn to a geneticist?"

"Time constraints," I say bluntly. "We couldn't keep having babies year after year until one was a match for Kate. The doctor was able to screen several embryos to see which one, if any, would be the ideal donor for Kate. We were lucky enough to have one out of four—and it was implanted through IVF."

Nadya looks down at her notes. "You've received hate mail, haven't you?"

Brian nods. "People seem to think that we're trying to make a designer baby."

"Aren't you?"

"We didn't ask for a baby with blue eyes, or

one that would grow to be six feet tall, or one that would have an IQ of two hundred. Sure, we asked for specific characteristics—but they're not anything anyone would ever consider to be model human traits. They're just **Kate's** traits. We don't want a superbaby; we just want to save our daughter's life."

I squeeze Brian's hand. God, I love him.

"Mrs. Fitzgerald, what will you tell this baby when she grows up?" Nadya asks.

"With any luck," I say, "I'll be able to tell her to stop bugging her sister."

I go into labor on New Year's Eve. The nurse taking care of me tries to distract me from my contractions by talking about the signs of the sun. "This one, she's gonna be a Capricorn," Emelda says as she rubs my shoulders.

"Is that good?"

"Oh, Capricorns, they get the job done."

Inhale, exhale. "Good . . . to . . . know," I tell her.

There are two other babies being born. One

woman, Emelda says, has her legs crossed. She's trying to make it to 1991. The New Year's Baby is entitled to packs of free diapers and a $100 savings bond from Citizens Bank for that distant college education.

When Emelda goes out to the nurse's desk, leaving us alone, Brian reaches for my hand. "You okay?"

I grimace my way through another contraction. "I'd be better if this was over."

He smiles at me. To a paramedic/firefighter, a routine hospital delivery is something to shrug at. If my water had broken during a train wreck, or if I was laboring in the back of a taxi—

"I know what you're thinking," he interrupts, although I haven't said a word out loud, "and you're wrong." He lifts my hand, kisses the knuckles.

Suddenly an anchor unspools inside me. The chain, thick as a fist, twists in my abdomen. "Brian," I gasp, "get the doctor."

My OB comes in and holds his hand between my legs. He glances up at the clock. "If you can hold on a minute, this kid's gonna be born famous," he says, but I shake my head.

"Get it out," I tell him. "**Now.**"

The doctor looks at Brian. "Tax deduction?" he guesses.

I am thinking of saving, but it has nothing to do with the IRS. The baby's head slips through the seal of my skin. The doctor's hand holds her, slides that gorgeous cord free of her neck, delivers her shoulder by shoulder.

I struggle to my elbows to watch what is going on below. "The umbilical cord," I remind him. "Be careful." He cuts it, beautiful blood, and hurries it out of the room to a place where it will be cryogenically preserved until Kate is ready for it.

Day Zero of Kate's pre-transplant regimen starts the morning after Anna is born. I come down from the maternity ward and meet Kate in Radiology. We are both wearing yellow isolation gowns, and this makes her laugh. "Mommy," she says, "we match."

She has been given a pediatric cocktail for sedation, and under any other circumstance, this would be funny. Kate can't find her own feet. Every time she stands up, she collapses. It strikes me that this is how Kate will look when she gets drunk on peach schnapps for the first time in high school or college; and then I quickly remind myself that Kate might never be that old.

When the therapist comes to take her into the RT suite, Kate latches on to my leg. "Honey," Brian says, "it's gonna be fine."

She shakes her head and burrows closer. When I crouch down, she throws herself into my arms. "I won't take my eyes off you," I promise.

The room is large, with jungle murals painted on the walls. The linear accelerators are built into the ceiling and a pit below the treatment table, which is little more than a canvas cot covered with a sheet. The radiation therapist places thick lead pieces shaped like beans onto Kate's chest and tells her not to move. She promises that when it's all over, Kate can have a sticker.

I stare at Kate through the protective glass wall. Gamma rays, leukemia, parenthood. It is the things you cannot see coming that are strong enough to kill you.

There is a Murphy's Law to oncology, one which is not written anywhere but held in widespread belief: if you don't get sick, you won't get well. Therefore, if your chemo makes you violently ill, if radiation sears your skin—it's all good. On the other hand, if you sail through therapy quickly with only negligible nausea or pain, chances are the drugs have somehow been excreted by your body and aren't doing their job.

By this criterion, Kate should surely be cured by now. Unlike last year's chemo, this course of treatment has taken a little girl who didn't even have a runny nose and has turned her into a physical wreck. Three days of radiation has caused constant diarrhea, and put her back into a diaper. At first, this embarrassed her; now she is so sick she doesn't care. The following five days of chemo have lined her throat with mucus, which keeps her clutching at a suction tube as if it is a life preserver. When she is awake, all she does is cry.

Since Day Six, when Kate's white blood cell and neutrophil counts began to plummet, she has been in reverse isolation. Any germ in the world might kill her now; for this reason, the world is made to keep its distance. Visitors to her room are restricted, and those who are allowed in look like spacemen, gowned and masked. Kate has to read picture books while wearing rubber gloves. No plants or flowers are permitted, because they carry bacteria that could kill her. Any toy given to her must be scrubbed down with antiseptic solution first. She sleeps with her teddy bear, sealed in a Ziploc bag, which rustles all night and sometimes wakes her up.

Brian and I sit outside the anteroom, waiting. While Kate sleeps, I practice giving injections to an orange. After the transplant Kate will need growth factor shots, and the chore will fall to me. I prick the syringe under the thick skin of the fruit, until I feel the soft give of tissue underneath. The drug I will be giving

is subcutaneous, injected just under the skin.
I need to make sure the angle is right and that
I am giving the proper amount of pressure.
The speed with which you push the needle
down can cause more or less pain. The
orange, of course, doesn't cry when I make a
mistake. But the nurses still tell me that
injecting Kate won't feel much different.

Brian picks up a second orange and begins
to peel it. "Put that down!"

"I'm hungry." He nods at the fruit in my
hands. "And you've already got a patient."

"For all you know that was someone else's.
God knows what it's doped up with."

Suddenly Dr. Chance turns the corner and
approaches us. Donna, an oncology nurse,
walks behind him, brandishing an IV bag
filled with crimson liquid. "Drum roll," she
says.

I put down my orange, follow them into
the anteroom, and suit up so that I can come
within ten feet of my daughter. Within minutes Donna attaches the bag to a pole, and
connects the drip to Kate's central line. It is so
anticlimactic that Kate doesn't even wake up.

I stand on one side, as Brian goes to the other. I hold my breath. I stare down at Kate's hips, the iliac crest, where bone marrow is made. Through some miracle, these stem cells of Anna's will go into Kate's bloodstream in her chest, but will find their way to the right spot.

"Well," Dr. Chance says, and we all watch the cord blood slowly slide through the tubing, a Crazy Straw of possibility.

JULIA

AFTER TWO HOURS OF LIVING with my sister again, I'm finding it hard to believe we ever comfortably shared a womb. Isobel has already organized my CDs by year of release, swept under the couch, and tossed out half the food in my refrigerator. "Dates are our friend, Julia." She sighs. "You have yogurt in here from when Democrats ruled the White House."

I slam the door shut and count to ten. But when Izzy moves toward the gas oven and starts looking for the cleaning controls, I lose my cool. "Sylvia doesn't need cleaning."

"That's another thing: Sylvia the oven. Smilla the Fridge. Do we really need to name our kitchen appliances?"

My kitchen appliances. **Mine,** not **ours,**

goddammit. "I'm totally getting why Janet broke up with you," I mutter.

At that, Izzy looks up, stricken. "You are horrible," she says. "You are horrible and after I was born I should have sewed Mom shut." She runs to the bathroom in tears.

Isobel is three minutes older than me, but I've always been the one who takes care of her. I'm her nuclear bomb: when there's something upsetting her, I go in and lay waste to it, whether that's one of our six older brothers teasing her or the evil Janet, who decided she wasn't gay after seven years into a committed relationship with Izzy. Growing up, Izzy was the Goody Two-shoes and I was the one who came up fighting—swinging my fists or shaving my head to get a rise out of our parents or wearing combat boots with my high school uniform. Yet now that we're thirty-two, I'm a card-carrying member of the Rat Race; while Izzy is a lesbian who builds jewelry out of paper clips and bolts. Go figure.

The door to the bathroom doesn't lock, but Izzy doesn't know that yet. So I walk in and wait till she finishes splashing cold water on her face, and I hand her a towel. "Iz. I didn't mean it."

"I know." She looks at me in the mirror. Most people can't tell us apart now that I have a real job that requires conventional hair and conventional clothes. "At least you **had** a relationship," I point out. "The last time I had a date was when I bought that yogurt."

Izzy's lips curve, and she turns to me. "Does the toilet have a name?"

"I was thinking of **Janet,**" I say, and my sister cracks up.

The telephone rings, and I go into the living room to answer it. "Julia? This is Judge DeSalvo calling. I've got a case that needs a guardian ad litem, and I'm hoping you might be able to help me out."

I became a guardian ad litem a year ago, when I realized that nonprofit work wasn't covering my rent. A GAL is appointed by a court to be a child's advocate during legal proceedings that involve a minor. You don't have to be a lawyer to be trained as a GAL, but you do have to have a moral compass and a heart. Which, actually, probably renders most lawyers unqualified for the job.

"Julia? Are you there?"

I would turn cartwheels for Judge DeSalvo; he pulled strings to get me a job when I first became a GAL. "Whatever you need," I promise. "What's going on?"

He gives me background information—phrases like **medical emancipation** and **thirteen** and **mother with legal background** float by me. Only two items stick fast: the word **urgent,** and the name of the attorney.

God, I can't do this.

"I can be there in an hour," I say.

"Good. Because I think this kid needs someone in her corner."

"Who was that?" Izzy asks. She is unpacking the box that holds her work supplies: tools and wire and little containers of metal bits that sound like teeth gnashing when she sets them down.

"A judge," I reply. "There's a girl who needs help."

What I don't tell my sister is that I'm talking about me.

Nobody's home at the Fitzgerald house. I ring the doorbell twice, certain this must be a mistake. From what Judge DeSalvo's led me to believe, this is a family in crisis. But I find myself standing in front of a well-kept Cape, with carefully tended flower gardens lining the walk.

When I turn around to go back to my car, I see the girl. She still has that knobby, calf-like look of preteens; she jumps over every sidewalk crack. "Hi," I say, when she is close enough to hear me. "Are you Anna?"

Her chin snaps up. "Maybe."

"I'm Julia Romano. Judge DeSalvo asked me to be your guardian ad litem. Did he explain to you what that is?"

Anna narrows her eyes. "There was a girl in Brockton who got kidnapped by someone who said they'd been asked by her mom to pick her up and drive her to the place where her mom worked."

I rummage in my purse and pull out my driver's license, and a stack of papers. "Here," I say. "Be my guest." She glances at me, and then at the god-awful picture on my license; she reads through the copy of the emancipation petition I picked up at the family court before I came here. If I am a psychotic killer, then I have done my homework well. But there is a part of me already giving Anna credit for being wary: this is not a child who rushes headlong into situations. If she's thinking long and hard about going off with me, presumably she must have thought long and hard about untangling herself from the net of her family.

She hands back everything I've given her. "Where is everyone?" she asks.

"I don't know. I thought you could tell me."

Anna's gaze slides to the front door, nervous. "I hope nothing happened to Kate."

I tilt my head, considering this girl, who has already managed to surprise me. "Do you have time to talk?" I ask.

• • •

The zebras are the first stop in the Roger Williams Zoo. Of all the animals in the Africa section, these have always been my favorite. I can give or take elephants; I never can find the cheetah—but the zebras captivate me. They'd be one of the few things that would fit if we were lucky enough to live in a world that's black or white.

We pass blue duikers, bongos, and something called a naked mole rat that doesn't come out of its cave. I often take kids to the zoo when I'm assigned to their cases. Unlike when we sit down face-to-face in the courthouse, or even at Dunkin' Donuts, at the zoo they are more likely to open up to me. They'll watch the gibbons swinging around like Olympic gymnasts and just start talking about what happens at home, without even realizing what they are doing.

Anna, though, is older than all of the kids I've worked with, and less than thrilled to be here. In retrospect, I realize this was a bad choice. I should have taken her to a mall, to a movie.

We walk through the winding trails of the zoo, Anna talking only when forced to respond. She answers me politely when I ask her questions about her sister's health. She says that her mother is, indeed, the opposing attorney. She thanks me when I buy her an ice cream.

"Tell me what you like to do," I say. "For fun."

"Play hockey," Anna says. "I used to be a goaltender."

"Used to be?"

"The older you get, the less the coach forgives you if you miss a game." She shrugs. "I don't like letting a whole team down."

Interesting way to put it, I think. "Do your friends still play hockey?"

"Friends?" She shakes her head. "You can't really have anyone over to your house when your sister needs to be resting. You don't get invited back for sleepovers when your mom comes to pick you up at two in the morning to go to the hospital. It's probably been a while since you've been in middle school, but most people think freakhood is contagious."

"So who **do** you talk to?"

She looks at me. "Kate," she says. Then she asks if I have a cell phone.

I take one out of my pocketbook and watch her dial the hospital's number by heart. "I'm looking for a patient," Anna says to the operator. "Kate Fitzgerald?" She glances up at me. "Thanks anyway." Punching the buttons, she hands the phone back to me. "Kate isn't registered."

"That's good, right?"

"It could just mean that the paperwork hasn't caught up to the operator yet. Sometimes it takes a few hours."

I lean against a railing near the elephants. "You seem pretty worried about your sister right now," I point out. "Are you sure you're ready to face what's going to happen if you stop being a donor?"

"I know what's going to happen." Anna's voice is low. "I never said I **liked** it." She raises her face to mine, challenging me to find fault with her.

For a minute I look at her. What would **I** do, if I found out that Izzy needed a kidney, or part of my liver, or marrow? The answer isn't even questionable—I would ask how quickly we could go to the hospital and have it done.

But then, it would have been **my** choice, **my** decision.

"Have your parents ever asked you if you want to be a donor for your sister?"

Anna shrugs. "Kind of. The way parents ask questions that they already have answered in their heads. **You weren't the reason that the whole second grade stayed in for recess, were you?** Or, **You want some broccoli, right?**"

"Did you ever tell your parents that you weren't comfortable with the choice they'd made for you?"

Anna pushes away from the elephants and begins to trudge up the hill. "I might have complained a couple of times. But they're Kate's parents, too."

Small tumblers in this puzzle begin to hitch for me. Traditionally, parents make decisions for a child, because presumably they are looking out for his or her best interests. But if they are blinded, instead, by the best interests of another one of their children, the system breaks down. And somewhere, underneath all the rubble, are casualties like Anna.

The question is, did she instigate this lawsuit because she truly feels that she can make better choices about her own medical care than her parents can, or because she wants her parents to hear her for once when she cries?

We wind up in front of the polar bears, Trixie and Norton. For the first time since we've gotten here, Anna's face lights up. She watches Kobe, Trixie's cub—the newest addition to the zoo. He swats at his mother as she lies on the rocks, trying to get her to play. "The last time there was a polar bear baby," Anna says, "they gave it to another zoo."

She is right; memories of the articles in the **ProJo** swim into my mind. It was a big public relations move for Rhode Island.

"Do you think he wonders what he did to get himself sent away?"

We are trained, as guardians ad litem, to see the signs of depression. We know how to read body language, and flat affect, and mood swings. Anna's hands are clenched around the metal railing. Her eyes go dull as old gold.

Either this girl loses her sister, I think, **or she's going to lose herself.**

"Julia," she asks, "would it be okay if we went home?"

The closer we get to her house, Anna distances herself from me. A pretty nifty trick, given that the physical space between us remains unaltered. She shrinks against the window of my car, staring at the streets that bleed by. "What happens next?"

"I'm going to talk to everyone else. Your mom and dad, your brother and sister. Your lawyer."

Now a dilapidated Jeep is parked in the driveway, and the front door of the house is open. I turn off the ignition, but Anna makes no move to release her seat belt. "Will you walk me in?"

"Why?"

"Because my mother's going to kill me."

This Anna—genuinely skittish—bears little resemblance to the one I've spent the past hour with. I wonder how a girl might be both brave enough to instigate a lawsuit, and afraid to face her own mother. "How come?"

"I sort of left today without telling her where I was going."

"You do that a lot?"

Anna shakes her head. "Usually I do whatever I'm told."

Well, I am going to have to speak to Sara Fitzgerald sooner or later. I get out of the car, and wait for Anna to do the same. We walk up the front path, past the groomed flower beds, and through the front door.

She is not the foe I've built her up to be. For one thing, Anna's mother is shorter than I am, and slighter. She has dark hair and haunted eyes and is pacing. The moment it creaks open, she runs to Anna. "For God's sake," she cries, shaking her daughter by the shoulders, "where have you been? Do you have any idea—"

"Excuse me, Mrs. Fitzgerald. I'd like to introduce myself." I step forward, extending my hand. "I'm Julia Romano, the guardian ad litem appointed by the court."

She slides her arm around Anna, a stiff show of tenderness. "Thank you for bringing Anna home. I'm sure you have lots to discuss with her, but right now—"

"Actually, I was hoping I could speak to **you**. I've been asked by the court to present my findings in less than a week, so if you've got a few minutes—"

"I don't," Sara says abruptly. "Now isn't really a good time. My other daughter has just been readmitted to the hospital." She looks at Anna, still standing in the doorway of the kitchen: **I hope you're happy.**

"I'm sorry to hear that."

"I am too." Sara clears her throat. "I appreciate you coming by to talk to Anna. And I know you're just doing your job. But this is all going to work itself out, really. It's a misunderstanding. I'm sure Judge DeSalvo will be telling you that in a day or so."

She takes a step backward, challenging me—and Anna—to say otherwise. I glance at Anna, who catches my eye and shakes her head almost imperceptibly, a plea to just let this go for now.

Who is she protecting—her mother, or herself?

A red flag unravels across my mind: **Anna is thirteen. Anna lives with her mother. Anna's mother is opposing counsel. How can Anna possibly live in the same home and not be swayed by Sara Fitzgerald?**

"Anna, I'll call you tomorrow." Then without saying good-bye to Sara Fitzgerald, I leave her house, headed for the one place on earth I never wanted to go.

The law offices of Campbell Alexander look exactly the way I've pictured them: at the top of a building cast in black glass, at the end of a hallway lined with a Persian runner, through two heavy mahogany doors that keep out the riffraff. Sitting at the massive receptionist's desk is a girl with porcelain features and a telephone earpiece hidden under the mane of her hair. I ignore her and walk toward the only closed door. "Hey!" she yells. "You can't go in there!"

"He'll be expecting me," I say.

Campbell doesn't look up from whatever he's writing with great fury. His shirtsleeves are rolled up to the elbow. He needs a haircut. "Kerri," he says, "see if you can find some Jenny Jones transcript about identical twins who don't know that they—"

"Hello, Campbell."

First, he stops writing. Then he lifts his head. "Julia." He gets to his feet, a schoolboy caught in an indecent act.

I step inside and close the door behind me. "I'm the guardian ad litem assigned to Anna Fitzgerald's case."

A dog that I haven't noticed till now takes its place by Campbell's side. "I'd heard that you went to law school."

Harvard. On full scholarship.

"Providence is a pretty tight place . . . I kept expecting . . ." His voice trails off, and he shakes his head. "Well, I thought for sure we'd run into each other before now."

He smiles at me, and I suddenly am seventeen again—the year I realized love doesn't follow the rules, the year I understood that nothing is worth having so much as something unattainable. "It's not all that hard to avoid someone, when you want to," I answer coolly. "You of all people should know."

CAMPBELL

I'M REMARKABLY CALM, really, until the principal of Ponaganset High School starts to give me a telephone lecture on political correctness. "For God's sake," he sputters. "What kind of message does it send when a group of Native American students names their intramural basketball league 'The Whiteys'?"

"I imagine it sends the same message that you did when you picked the Chieftains as your school mascot."

"We've been the Ponaganset Chieftains since 1970," the principal argues.

"Yes, and they've been members of the Narragansett tribe since they were born."

"It's derogatory. And politically incorrect."

"Unfortunately," I point out, "you can't sue a person for political incorrectness, or clearly you would have been handed a summons years ago. However, on the flip side, the Constitution does protect various individual rights to Americans, including Native Americans—one for assembly, and one for free speech, which suggest that the Whiteys would be granted permission to convene even if your ridiculous threat of a lawsuit managed to make its way to court. For that matter, you may want to consider a class action against humanity in general, since surely you'd also like to stifle the inherent racism implicit in the White House, the White Mountains, and the White Pages." There is dead silence on the other end of the phone. "Shall I assume, then, that I can tell my client you don't plan to litigate after all?"

After he hangs up on me, I push the intercom button. "Kerri, call Ernie Fishkiller, and tell him he's got nothing to worry about."

As I settle down to the mountain of work on my desk, Judge lets out a sigh. He's asleep, curled like a braided rug to the left of my desk. His paw twitches.

That's the life, she said to me, as we watched a puppy chase its own tail. That's what I want to be next.

I had laughed. You would wind up as a cat, I told her. They don't need anyone else.

I need you, she replied.

Well, I said. Maybe I'll come back as catnip.

I press my thumbs into the balls of my eyes. Clearly I am not getting enough sleep; first there was that moment at the coffee shop, now this. I scowl at Judge, as if it is his fault, and then focus my attention on some notes I've made on a legal pad. New client—a drug dealer caught by the prosecution on videotape. There's no way out of a conviction on this one, unless the guy has an identical twin his mother kept secret.

Which, come to think of it . . .

The door opens, and without glancing up I fire a directive at Kerri. "See if you can find some Jenny Jones transcript about identical twins who don't know that they—"

"Hello, Campbell."

I am going crazy; I am definitely going crazy. Because not five feet away from me is Julia Romano, whom I have not seen in fifteen years. Her hair is longer now, and fine lines bracket her mouth, parentheses around a lifetime of words I was not around to hear. "Julia," I manage.

She closes the door, and at the sound, Judge jumps to his feet. "I'm the guardian ad litem assigned to Anna Fitzgerald's case," she says.

"Providence is a pretty tight place . . . I kept expecting . . . Well, I thought for sure we'd run into each other before now."

"It's not all that hard to avoid someone, when you want to," she answers. "You of all people should know." Then, all of a sudden, the anger seems to steam out of her. "I'm sorry. That was totally uncalled for."

"It's been a long time," I reply, when what I really want to do is ask her what she's been doing for the past fifteen years. If she still drinks tea with milk **and** lemon. If she's happy. "Your hair isn't pink anymore," I say, because I am an idiot.

"No, it's not," she replies. "Is that a problem?"

I shrug. "It's just. Well . . ." Where are words, when you need them? "I liked the pink," I confess.

"It tends to take away from my authority in a courtroom," Julia admits.

This makes me smile. "Since when do you care what people think of you?"

She doesn't respond, but something changes. The temperature of the room, or maybe the wall that comes up in her eyes. "Maybe instead of dragging up the past, we should talk about Anna," she suggests diplomatically.

I nod. But it feels like we are sitting on the tight bench of a bus with a stranger between us, one that neither of us is willing to admit to or mention, and so we find ourselves talking around him and through him and sneaking glances when the other one isn't looking. How am I supposed to think about Anna Fitzgerald when I'm wondering whether Julia has ever woken up in someone's arms and for just a moment, before the sleep cleared from her mind, thought maybe it was me?

Sensing tension, Judge gets up and stands beside me. Julia seems to notice for the first time that we are not alone in the room. "Your partner?"

"Only an associate," I say. "But he made **Law Review.**" Her fingers scratch Judge behind the ear—goddamn lucky bastard—and grimacing,

I ask her to stop. "He's a service dog. He isn't supposed to be petted."

Julia looks up, surprised. But before she can ask, I turn the conversation. "So. Anna." Judge pushes his nose into my palm.

She folds her arms. "I went to see her."

"And?"

"Thirteen-year-olds are heavily influenced by their parents. And Anna's mother seems convinced that this trial isn't going to happen. I have a feeling she might be trying to convince Anna of that, too."

"I can take care of that," I say.

She looks up, suspicious. "How?"

"I'll get Sara Fitzgerald removed from the house."

Her jaw drops. "You're kidding, right?"

By now, Judge has started pulling my clothes in earnest. When I don't respond, he barks twice. "Well, I certainly don't think my client ought to be the one to move out. **She** hasn't violated the judge's orders. I'll get a temporary restraining order keeping Sara Fitzgerald from having any contact with her."

"Campbell, that's her mother!"

"This week, she's opposing counsel, and if she's prejudicing my client in any way she needs to be ordered not to do so."

"Your **client** has a name, and an age, and a world that's falling apart—the last thing she needs is more instability in her life. Have you even bothered to get to know her?"

"Of course I have," I lie, as Judge begins to whine at my feet.

Julia glances down at him. "Is something wrong with your dog?"

"He's fine. Look. My job is to protect Anna's legal rights and win the case, and that's exactly what I'm going to do."

"Of course you are. Not necessarily because it's in **Anna's** best interests . . . but because it's in **yours**. How ironic is it that a kid who wants to stop being used for another person's benefit winds up picking **your** name out of the Yellow Pages?"

"You don't know anything about me," I say, my jaw tightening.

"Well, whose fault is **that**?"

So much for not bringing up the past. A shudder runs the length of me, and I grab Judge by the collar. "Excuse me," I say, and I walk out the office door, leaving Julia for the second time in my life.

When you get right down to it, The Wheeler School was a factory, pumping out debutantes and future investment bankers. We all looked alike and talked alike. To us, summer was a verb.

There were students, of course, who broke that mold. Like the scholarship kids, who wore their collars up and learned to row, never realizing that all along we were well aware they weren't one of us. There were the stars, like Tommy Boudreaux, who was drafted by the Detroit Redwings in his junior year. Or the head cases, who tried to slit their wrists or mix booze and Valium and then left campus just as silently as they had once wandered around it.

I was a sixth-former the year that Julia Romano came to Wheeler. She wore army boots and a Cheap Trick T-shirt under her school blazer; she was able to memorize entire sonnets without breaking a sweat. During free periods, while the rest of us were copping smokes behind the headmaster's back, she climbed the stairs to the ceiling of the gymnasium and sat with her back against a heating duct, reading books by Henry Miller and Nietzsche. Unlike the other girls in school, with their smooth waterfalls of yellow hair caught up in a headband like ribbon candy, hers was an absolute tornado of black curls, and she never wore makeup—just those sharp features, take it or leave it. She had the thinnest hoop I'd ever seen, a silver filament, through her left eyebrow. She smelled like fresh dough rising.

There were rumors about her: that she'd been booted out of a girl's reform school; that she was some whiz kid with a perfect PSAT score; that she was two years younger than everyone else in our grade; that she had a tattoo. Nobody quite knew what to make of her. They called her Freak, because she wasn't one of us.

One day Julia Romano arrived at school

with short pink hair. We all assumed she'd be suspended, but it turned out that in the litany of rules about what one had to wear at Wheeler, coiffure was conspicuously absent. It made me wonder why there wasn't a single guy in the school with dreadlocks, and I realized it wasn't because we couldn't stand out; it's because we didn't want to.

At lunch that day she passed the table where I was sitting with a bunch of guys on the sailing team and some of their girlfriends.

"Hey," one girl said, "did it hurt?"

Julia slowed down. "Did what hurt?"

"Falling into the cotton candy machine?"

She didn't even blink. "Sorry, I can't afford to get my hair done at Wash, Cut and Blow Jobs 'R' Us." Then she walked off to the corner of the cafeteria where she always ate by herself, playing solitaire with a deck of cards that had pictures of patron saints on the backs.

"Shit," one of my friends said, "that's one girl I wouldn't mess with."

I laughed, because everyone else did.

But I also watched her sit down, push the tray of food away from her, and begin to lay out her cards. I wondered what it would be like to not give a damn about what people thought of you.

One afternoon, I went AWOL from the sailing team where I was captain, and followed her. I made sure to stay far enough behind that she wouldn't realize I was there. She headed down Blackstone Boulevard, turned into Swan Point Cemetery, and climbed to the highest point. She opened her knapsack, took out her textbooks and binder, and spread herself in front of a grave. "You might as well come out," she said then, and I nearly swallowed my tongue, expecting a ghost, until I realized she was talking to me. "If you pay an extra quarter, you can even stare up close."

I stepped out from behind a big oak, my hands dug into my pockets. Now that I was there, I had no idea why I'd come. I nodded toward the grave. "That a relative?"

She looked over her shoulder. "Yeah. My grandma had the seat right next to him on the Mayflower." She stared at me, all right angles and edges. "Don't you have some cricket match to go to?"

"Polo," I said, breaking a smile. "I'm just waiting for my horse to get here."

She didn't get the joke . . . or maybe she didn't find it funny. "What do you want?"

I couldn't admit that I was following her. "Help," I said. "Homework."

In truth I had not looked over our English assignment. I grabbed a paper on top of her binder and read aloud: You come across a horrible four-car accident. There are people moaning in pain, and bodies strewn all over the place. Do you have an obligation to stop?

"Why should I help?" she said.

"Well, legally, you shouldn't. If you pull someone out and hurt them more, you could get sued."

"I meant why should I help you."

The paper floated to the ground. "You don't think very much of me, do you?"

"I don't think about any of you, period. You're a bunch of superficial idiots who wouldn't be caught dead with someone who's different from you."

"Isn't that what you're doing, too?"

She stared at me for a long second. Then she started stuffing her backpack. "You've got a trust fund, right? If you need help, go pay a tutor."

I put my foot down on top of a textbook. "Would you do it?"

"Tutor you? No way."

"Stop. At the car accident."

Her hands quieted. "Yeah. Because even if the law says that no one is responsible for anyone else, helping someone who needs it is the right thing to do."

I sat down beside her, close enough that the skin of her arm hummed right next to mine. "You really believe that?"

She looked down at her lap. "Yeah."

"Then how," I asked, "can you walk away from me?"

Afterward, I wipe my face with paper towels from the dispenser and fix my tie. Judge pads in tight circles beside me, the way he always does. "You did good," I tell him, patting the thick ruff of his neck.

When I get back into my office, Julia is gone. Kerri sits at the computer in a rare moment of productivity, typing. "She said that if you needed her, you could damn well come find her. Her words, not mine. And she asked for all the medical records." Kerri glances over her shoulder at me. "You look like shit."

"Thanks." An orange Post-it on her desk catches my attention. "Is this where she wants the records sent?"

"Yeah."

I slip the address into my pocket. "I'll take care of it," I say.

A week later, in front of the same grave, I unlaced Julia Romano's combat boots. I peeled away her camouflage jacket. Her feet were narrow and as pink as the inside of a tulip. Her collarbone was a mystery. "I knew you were beautiful under there," I said, and this was the first spot on her that I kissed.

• • •

The Fitzgeralds live in Upper Darby, in a house that could belong to any typical American family. Two-car garage; aluminum siding; Totfinder stickers in the windows for the fire department. By the time I get there, the sun is setting behind the roofline.

The whole drive over, I've tried to convince myself that what Julia said has absolutely no bearing on why I've decided to visit my client. That I was always planning to take this little detour before I headed home for the night.

But the truth is, in all the years I've been practicing, this is the first time I've paid a house call.

Anna opens the door when I ring the bell. "What are you doing here?"

"Checking up on you."

"Does that cost extra?"

"No," I say dryly. "It's part of a special promotion I'm doing this month."

"Oh." She crosses her arms. "Have you talked to my mother?"

"I'm trying my best **not** to. I assume she's not home?"

Anna shakes her head. "She's at the hospital. Kate got admitted again. I thought you might have gone over there."

"Kate's not my client."

This actually seems to disappoint her. She tucks her hair behind her ears. "Did you, like, want to come in?"

I follow her into the living room and sit down on the couch, a palette of cheery blue stripes. Judge sniffs the edges of the furniture. "I heard you met the guardian ad litem."

"Julia. She took me to the zoo. She seems all right." Her eyes dart to mine. "Did she say something about me?"

"She's worried that your mother might be talking to you about this case."

"Other than Kate," Anna says, "what else is there to talk about?"

We stare at each other for a moment. Beyond a client-attorney relationship, I am at a loss.

I could ask to see her room, except that there's no way in hell any male defense attorney would ever go upstairs alone with a thirteen-year-old girl. I could take her out to dinner, but I doubt she'd appreciate Café Nuovo, one of my favorite haunts, and I don't think I could stomach a Whopper. I could ask her about school, but it isn't in session.

"Do you have kids?" Anna asks.

I laugh. "What do you think?"

"It's probably a good thing," she admits. "No offense, but you don't exactly look like a parent."

That fascinates me. "What do parents look like?"

She seems to think about this. "You know how the tightrope guy at the circus wants everyone to believe his act is an art, but deep down you can see that he's really just hoping he makes it all the way across? Like **that**." She glances at me. "You can relax, you know. I'm not going to tie you up and make you listen to gangsta rap."

"Oh, well," I joke. "In that case." I loosen my tie and sit back on the pillows.

It makes a smile dart briefly across her face. "You don't have to pretend to be my friend or anything."

"I don't want to pretend." I run my hand through my hair. "The thing is, this is new to me."

"What is?"

I gesture around the living room. "Visiting a client. Shooting the breeze. Not leaving a case at the office at the end of the day."

"Well, this is new to me, too," Anna confesses. "What is?"

She twists a strand of hair around her pinky. "Hoping," she says.

The part of town where Julia's apartment is located is an upscale area with a reputation for divorced bachelors, a point that irritates me the whole time I am trying to find a parking spot. Then the doorman takes one look at Judge and bars my path. "No dogs allowed," he says. "Sorry."

"This is a service dog." When that doesn't seem to ring a bell, I spell it out for him. "You know. Like Seeing Eye."

"You don't **look** blind."

"I'm a recovering alcoholic," I tell him. "The dog gets between me and a beer."

Julia's apartment is on the seventh floor. I knock on her door and then see an eye checking me out through the peephole. She opens it a crack, but leaves the chain in place. She has a kerchief wrapped around her head, and she looks like she's been crying.

"Hi," I say. "Can we start over?"

She wipes her nose. "Who the hell are you?"

"Okay. Maybe I deserve that." I glance at the chain. "Let me in, will you?"

She gives me a look, like I'm crazy or something. "Are you on **crack?**"

There is a scuffle, and another voice, and then the door opens wide and stupidly I think: **There are two of her.** "Campbell," the real Julia says, "what are you doing here?"

I hold up the medical records, still getting over the shock. How the hell is it that she never managed to mention, that entire year at Wheeler, having a twin?

"Izzy, this is Campbell Alexander. Campbell, this is my sister."

"Campbell . . ." I watch Izzy turn my name over on her tongue. At second glance, she really looks nothing like Julia at all. Her nose is a bit longer, her complexion not nearly the same shade of gold. Not to mention the fact that watching her mouth move doesn't make me hard. "Not **the** Campbell?" she says, turning to Julia. "From . . ."

"Yeah," she sighs.

Izzy's gaze narrows. "I **knew** I shouldn't let him in."

"It's fine," Julia insists, and she takes the files from me. "Thanks for bringing these."

Izzy waggles her fingers. "You can leave now."

"Stop." Julia swats her sister's arm. "Campbell is the attorney I'm working with this week."

"But wasn't he the guy who—"

"Yes, thanks, I have a fully functioning memory."

"So!" I interrupt. "I stopped off at Anna's house."

Julia turns to me. "And?"

"Earth to Julia," Izzy says. "This is self-destructive behavior."

"Not when it involves a paycheck, Izzy. We have a case together, that's it. Okay? And I really don't feel like being lectured by **you** about self-destructive behavior. Who called Janet for a mercy fuck the night after she dumped you?"

"Hey." I turn to Judge. "How about those Red Sox?"

Izzy stamps down the hall. "It's your suicide," she yells, and then I hear a door slam.

"I think she really likes me," I say, but Julia doesn't crack a smile.

"Thanks for the medical records. Bye."

"Julia—"

"Hey, I'm just saving you the trouble. It must've been hard training a dog to drag you out of a room when you need rescuing from some emotionally volatile situation, like an old girlfriend who's telling the truth. How does it work, Campbell? Hand signals? Word commands? A high-pitched whistle?"

I look wistfully down the empty hallway. "Can I have Izzy back instead?"

Julia tries to push me out the door.

"All right. I'm sorry. I didn't mean to cut you off today in the office. But . . . it was an emergency."

She stares at me. "What did you say the dog's for?"

"I didn't." When she turns, Judge and I follow her deeper into the apartment, closing the door behind us. "So I went to see Anna Fitzgerald. You were right—before I took out a restraining order against her mother, I needed to talk to her."

"And?"

I think back to the two of us, sitting on that striped couch, stretching a web of trust between us. "I think we're on the same page." Julia doesn't respond, just picks up a glass of white wine on the kitchen counter. "Why yes, I'd love some," I say.

She shrugs. "It's in Smilla."

The fridge, of course. For its sense of snow. When I walk there and take out the bottle, I can feel her trying not to smile. "You forget that I know you."

"Knew," she corrects.

"Then educate me. What have you been doing for fifteen years?" I nod down the hallway toward Izzy's room. "I mean, other than cloning yourself." A thought occurs to me, and before I can even voice it Julia answers.

"My brothers all became builders and chefs and plumbers. My parents wanted their girls to go to college, and figured attending Wheeler senior year might stack the odds. I had good enough grades to get a partial scholarship there;

Izzy didn't. My parents could only afford to send one of us to private school."

"Did she go to college?"

"RISD," Julia says. "She's a jewelry designer."

"A **hostile** jewelry designer."

"Having your heart broken can do that." Our eyes meet, and Julia realizes what she's said. "She just moved in today."

My eyes canvass the apartment, looking for a hockey stick, a **Sports Illustrated** magazine, a La-Z-Boy chair, anything telltale and male. "Is it hard getting used to a roommate?"

"I was living alone before, Campbell, if that's what you're asking." She looks at me over the edge of her wine glass. "How about you?"

"I have six wives, fifteen children, and an assortment of sheep."

Her lips curve. "People like you always make me feel like I'm underachieving."

"Oh yeah, you're a real waste of space on the planet. Harvard undergrad, Harvard Law, a bleeding heart guardian ad litem—"

"How'd you know where I went to law school?"

"Judge DeSalvo," I lie, and she buys it.

I wonder if Julia feels like it has been moments, not years, since we've been together. If sitting at this counter with me feels as effortless for her as it does for me. It's like picking up an unfamiliar piece of sheet music and starting to stumble through it, only to realize it is a melody you'd once learned by heart, one you can play without even trying.

"I didn't think you'd become a guardian ad litem," I admit.

"Neither did I." Julia smiles. "I still have moments where I fantasize about standing on a soapbox in Boston Common, railing against a patriarchal society. Unfortunately, you can't pay a landlord in dogma." She glances at me. "Of course, I also mistakenly believed you'd be President of the United States by now."

"I inhaled," I confess. "Had to set my sights a little lower. And you—well, actually, I figured you'd be living in the suburbs, doing the soccer mom thing with a bunch of kids and some lucky guy."

Julia shakes her head. "I think you're confusing me with Muffy or Bitsie or Toto or whatever the hell the names of the girls in Wheeler were."

"No. I just thought that . . . that I might be the guy."

There is a thick, viscous silence. "You didn't want to be that guy," Julia says finally. "You made that pretty clear."

That's not true, I want to argue. But how else would it look to her, when afterward, I wanted nothing to do with her. When, afterward, I acted just like everyone else. "Do you remember—" I begin.

"I remember everything, Campbell," she interrupts. "If I didn't, this wouldn't be so hard."

My pulse jumps so high that Judge gets to his feet and pushes his snout into my hip, alarmed. I had believed back then that nothing could hurt Julia, who seemed to be so free. I had hoped that I could be as lucky.

I was mistaken on both counts.

Anna

IN OUR LIVING ROOM we have a whole shelf devoted to the visual history of our family. Everyone's baby pictures are there, and some school head shots, and then various photos from vacations and birthdays and holidays. They make me think of notches on a belt or scratches on a prison wall—proof that time's passed, that we haven't all just been swimming in limbo.

There are double frames, singles, 8 x 10s, 4 x 6s. They are made of blond wood and inlaid wood and one very fancy glass mosaic. I pick up one of Jesse—he's about two, in a cowboy costume. Looking at it, you'd never know what was coming down the pike.

There is Kate with hair and Kate all bald; one of Kate as a baby sitting on Jesse's lap; one of my mother holding each of them on the edge of a pool. There are pictures of me, too, but not many. I go from infant to about ten years old in one fell swoop.

Maybe it's because I was the third child, and they were sick and tired of keeping a catalog of life. Maybe it's because they forgot.

It's nobody's fault, and it's not a big deal, but it's a little depressing all the same. A photo says, **You were happy, and I wanted to catch that.** A photo says, **You were so important to me that I put down everything else to come watch.**

My father calls at eleven o'clock to ask if I want him to come get me. "Mom's going to stay at the hospital," he explains. "But if you don't want to be alone in the house, you can sleep at the station."

"No, it's okay," I tell him. "I can always get Jesse if I need something."

"Right," my father says. "Jesse." We both pretend that this is a reliable backup plan.

"How's Kate?" I ask.

"Still pretty out of it. They've got her drugged up." I hear him drag in a breath. "You know,

Anna," he begins, but then there is a shrill bell in the background. "Honey, I've got to go." He leaves me with an earful of dead air.

For a second I just hold the phone, picturing my dad stepping into his boots and pulling up the puddle of pants by their suspenders. I imagine the door of the station yawning like Aladdin's cave, and the engine screaming out, my father in the front passenger seat. Every time he goes to work, he has to put out fires.

It's just the encouragement I need. Grabbing a sweater, I leave the house and head for the garage.

There was this kid in my school, Jimmy Stredboe, who used to be a total loser. He got zits on top of his zits; he had a pet rat named Orphan Annie; and once in science class he puked into the fish tank. No one ever talked to him, in case dorkhood was contagious. But then one summer he was diagnosed with MS. After that, no one was mean to Jimmy anymore. If you passed him in the hall, you smiled. If he sat next to you at the lunch table, you nodded hello. It was as if being a walking tragedy canceled out ever having been a geek.

From the moment I was born, I have been the girl with the sick sister. All my life bank tellers have given me extra lollipops; principals have known me by name. No one is ever outright mean to me.

It makes me wonder how I'd be treated if I were like everyone else. Maybe I'm a pretty rotten person, not that anyone would ever have the guts to tell me this to my face. Maybe everyone thinks I'm rude or ugly or stupid but they have to be nice because it could be the circumstances of my life that make me that way.

It makes me wonder if what I'm doing now is just my true nature.

The headlights of another car bounce off the rearview mirror, lighting up like green goggles around Jesse's eyes. He drives with one wrist on the wheel, lazy. He needs a haircut, in a big way. "Your car smells like smoke," I say.

"Yeah. But it covers the aroma of spilled

whiskey." His teeth flash in the dark. "Why? Is it bothering you?"

"Kind of."

Jesse reaches across my body to the glove compartment. He takes out a pack of Merits and a Zippo, lights up, and blows smoke in my direction. "Sorry," he says, though he isn't.

"Can I have one?"

"One what?"

"A cigarette." They are so white they seem to glow.

"You want a cigarette?" Jesse cracks up.

"I'm not joking," I say.

Jesse raises one brow, and then turns the wheel so sharply I think he might roll the Jeep. We wind up in a huff of road dust on the shoulder. Jesse turns on the interior lights and shakes the pack so that one cigarette shimmies out.

It feels too delicate between my fingers, like the fine bone of a bird. I hold it the way I think a drama queen ought to, between the vise of my second and middle fingers. I put it up to my lips.

"You have to light it first." Jesse laughs, and he sparks up the Zippo.

There is no freaking way I'm leaning into a

flame; chances are I'll set my hair on fire instead of the cigarette. "You do it for me," I say.

"Nope. If you're gonna learn, you're gonna learn it all." He flicks the lighter again.

I touch the cigarette to the burn, suck in hard the way I have seen Jesse do. It makes my chest explode, and I cough so forcefully that for a minute I actually believe I can taste my lung at the base of my throat, pink and spongy. Jesse goes to pieces and plucks the cigarette out of my hand before I drop it. He takes two long drags and then tosses it out the window.

"Nice try," he says.

My voice is a sandpit. "It's like licking a barbecue."

While I work on remembering how to breathe, Jesse pulls into the road again. "What made you want to?"

I shrug. "I figured I might as well."

"If you'd like a checklist of depravity, I can make one up for you." When I don't reply, he glances over at me. "Anna," he says, "you're not doing the wrong thing."

By now he's pulled into the hospital's parking lot. "I'm not doing the right thing, either," I point out.

He turns off the ignition but doesn't make an attempt to leave the car. "Have you thought about the dragon guarding the cave?"

I narrow my eyes. "Speak English."

"Well, I'm guessing Mom's asleep about five feet away from Kate."

Oh, shit. It is not that I think my mother would throw me out, but she certainly won't leave me alone with Kate, and right now that's what I want more than anything. Jesse looks at me. "Seeing Kate isn't going to make you feel better."

There's really no way to explain why I need to know that she's okay, at least now, even though I have taken steps that will put an end to that.

For once, though, someone seems to understand. Jesse stares out the window of the car. "Leave it to me," he says.

We were eleven and fourteen, and we were training for the **Guinness Book of World Records**. Surely there had never been two sisters who did simultaneous headstands for so long that their cheeks went hard as plums and their eyes saw nothing but red. Kate had the shape of a pixie, all noodle arms and legs; and when she bent to the ground and kicked up her feet, it looked as delicate as a spider walking a wall. Me, I sort of defied gravity with a thud.

We balanced in silence for a few seconds. "I wish my head was flatter," I said, as I felt my eyebrows scrunch down. "Do you think there's a man who'll come to the house to time us? Or do we just mail a videotape?"

"I guess they'll let us know." Kate folded her arms along the carpet.

"Do you think we'll be famous?"

"We might get on the **Today** show. They had that eleven-year-old kid who could play the piano with his feet." She thought for a second. "Mom knew someone who got killed by a piano falling out a window."

"That's not true. Why would anyone push a piano out a window?"

"It is true. You ask her. And they weren't taking it out, they were putting it **in.**" She crossed her legs against the wall, so that it looked like she was just sitting upside down. "What do you think is the best way to die?"

"I don't want to talk about this," I said.

"Why? I'm dying. **You're** dying." When I frowned, she said, "Well, you **are.**" Then she grinned. "I just happen to be more gifted at it than you are."

"This is a stupid conversation." Already, it was making my skin itch in places I knew I would never be able to scratch.

"Maybe an airplane crash," Kate mused. "It would suck, you know, when you realized you were going down . . . but then it happens and you're just powder. How come people get vaporized, but they still manage to find clothes in trees, and those black boxes?"

By now my head was starting to pound. "Shut up, Kate."

She crawled down the wall and sat up, flushed. "There's just sleeping through it as you croak, but that's kind of boring."

"Shut **up,**" I repeated, angry that we had only lasted about twenty-two seconds, angry that now we were going to have to try for a record all over again. I tipped myself sunnyside up again and tried to clear the knot of hair out of my face. "You know, normal people don't sit around thinking about dying."

"Liar. Everyone thinks about dying."

"Everyone thinks about **you** dying," I said.

The room went so still that I wondered if we ought to go for a different record—how long can two sisters hold their breath?

Then a twitchy smile crossed her face. "Well," Kate said. "At least now you're telling the truth."

Jesse gives me a twenty-dollar bill for cab fare home; because that's the only hitch in his plan—once we go through with this, he isn't going to be driving back. We take the stairs up to the eighth floor instead of the elevator, because they let us out behind the nurse's station, not in front of it. Then he tucks me inside a linen closet filled with plastic pillows and sheets stamped with the hospital's name. "Wait," I blurt out, when he's about to leave me. "How am I going to know when it's time?"

He starts to laugh. "You'll know, trust me."

He takes a silver flask out of his pocket—it's one my father got from the chief and thinks he lost three years ago—screws off the cap, and pours whiskey all over the front of his shirt. Then he starts to walk down the hall. Well, **walk** would be a loose approximation—Jesse slams like a billiard ball into the walls and knocks over an entire cleaning cart. "Ma?" he yells out. "Ma, where are you?"

He isn't drunk, but he sure as hell can do a great imitation. It makes me wonder about the times I have looked out my bedroom window in the middle of the night and seen him puking into the rhododendrons—maybe that was all for show, too.

The nurses swarm out from their hive of a desk, trying to subdue a boy half their age and three times as strong, who at that very moment grabs the uppermost tier of a linen rack and pulls it forward, making a crash so loud it rings in my ears. Call buttons start ringing like an operator's switchboard behind the nurse's desk, but all three of the night-duty ladies are doing their best to hold Jesse down while he kicks and flails.

The door to Kate's room opens, and bleary-eyed, my mother steps out. She takes a look at Jesse, and for a second her whole face is frozen with the realization that, in fact, things **can** get worse. Jesse swings his head toward her, a great big bull, and his features melt. "Hiya, Mom," he greets, and he smiles loosely up at her.

"I am so sorry," my mother says to the nurses. She closes her eyes as Jesse stumbles upright and throws his sloppy arms around her.

"There's coffee in the cafeteria," one nurse suggests, and my mother is too embarrassed to even answer her. She just moves toward the elevator banks with Jesse attached to her like a mussel on a crusty hull, and pushes the down button over and over in the fruitless hope that it will actually make the doors open faster.

When they leave, it is almost too easy. Some of the nurses hurry off to check on the patients who've rung in; others settle back behind their desk, trading hushed commentary about Jesse and my poor mother like it's some card game. They never look my way as I sneak out of the linen closet, tiptoe down the hall, and let myself into my sister's hospital room.

• • •

One Thanksgiving when Kate was not in the hospital, we actually pretended to be a regular family. We watched the parade on TV, where a giant balloon fell prey to a freak wind and wound up wrapped around a NYC traffic light. We made our own gravy. My mother brought the turkey's wishbone out to the table, and we fought over who would be granted the right to snap it. Kate and I were given the honors. Before I got a good grip, my mother leaned close and whispered into my ear, "You **know** what to wish for." So I shut my eyes tight and thought hard of remission for Kate, even though I had been planning to ask for a personal CD player, and got a nasty satisfaction out of the fact that I did not win the tug-of-war.

After we ate, my father took us outside for a game of two-on-two touch football while my mother was washing the dishes. She came outside when Jesse and I had already scored twice. "Tell me," she said, "that I am hallucinating." She didn't have to say anything else—we'd all seen Kate tumble like an ordinary kid and wind up bleeding uncontrollably like a sick one.

"Aw, Sara." My dad turned up the wattage on his smile. "Kate's on my team. I won't let her get sacked."

He swaggered over to my mother, and kissed her so long and slow that my own cheeks started to burn, because I was sure the neighbors would see. When he lifted his head, my mother's eyes were a color I had never seen before and don't think I have ever seen again. "Trust me," he said, and then he threw the football to Kate.

What I remember about that day was the way the ground bit back when you sat on it— the first hint of winter. I remember being tackled by my father, who always braced himself in a push-up so that I got none of the weight and all of his heat. I remember my mother, cheering equally for both teams.

And I remember throwing the ball to Jesse, but Kate getting in the way—an expression of absolute shock on her face as it landed in the cradle of her arms and Dad yelled her on to the touchdown. She sprinted, and nearly had it, but then Jesse took a running leap and slammed her to the ground, crushing her underneath him.

In that moment everything stopped. Kate lay with her arms and legs splayed, unmoving. My father was there in a breath, shoving at Jesse. "What the hell is the matter with you!"

"I forgot!"

My mother: "Where does it hurt? Can you sit up?"

But when Kate rolled over, she was smiling. "It doesn't hurt. It feels great."

My parents looked at each other. Neither of them understood like I did, like Jesse did—that no matter who you are, there is some part of you that always wishes you were someone else—and when, for a millisecond, you **get** that wish, it's a miracle. "He forgot," Kate said to nobody, and she lay on her back, beaming up at the cold hawkeye sun.

Hospital rooms never get completely dark; there is always some glowing panel behind the bed in the case of catastrophe, a runway strip so that the nurses and doctors can find their way. I have seen Kate a hundred times in beds like this one, although the tubes and wires change.

She always looks smaller than I remember.

I sit down as gently as I can. The veins on Kate's neck and chest are a road map, highways that don't go anywhere. I trick myself into believing that I can see those rogue leukemia cells moving like a rumor through her system.

When she opens her eyes, I nearly fall off the bed; it's an **Exorcist** moment. "Anna?" she says, staring right at me. I have not seen her look this scared since we were little, and Jesse convinced us that an old Indian ghost had come back to claim the bones buried by mistake under our house.

If you have a sister and she dies, do you stop saying you have one? Or are you always a sister, even when the other half of the equation is gone?

I crawl onto the bed, which is narrow, but still big enough for both of us. I rest my head on her chest, so close to her central line that I can see the liquid dripping into her. Jesse is wrong—I didn't come to see Kate because it would make me feel better. I came because without her, it's hard to remember who I am.

THURSDAY

You, if you were sensible,

When I tell you the stars flash signals, each one dreadful,

You would not turn and answer me

"The night is wonderful."

—D. H. LAWRENCE,
"Under the Oak"

BRIAN

WE NEVER KNOW, AT FIRST, if we are headed into a cooker or a smudge. At 2:46 A.M. last night, the lights went on upstairs. The bells went off, too, but I can't say that I ever really hear them. In ten seconds, I was dressed and walking out the door of my room at the station. In twenty, I was stepping into my turnout gear, pulling up the long elastic suspenders, and shrugging into the turtle-shell of my coat. By the time two minutes passed, Caesar was driving the engine onto the streets of Upper Darby; Paulie and Red were the can man and the hydrant man, riding behind.

Sometime after that, consciousness came in small bright flashes: we remembered to check our breathing apparatus; we slid on our gloves; dispatch called to tell us that the house was on

Hoddington Drive; that it appeared to be either a structure fire or a room and contents fire. "Turn left here," I told Caesar. Hoddington was only eight blocks away from where I lived.

The house looked like the mouth of a dragon. Caesar drove around as far as he could, trying to get me a view of three sides. Then we all piled out of the engine and stared for a moment, four Davids against a Goliath. "Charge a two-and-a-half inch line," I told Caesar, to-night's motor pump operator. A woman in a nightgown ran toward me, sobbing, three children holding her skirt. **"Mija,"** she screamed, pointing. **"¡Mija!"**

"¿Dónde está?" I got right in front of her, so that she couldn't see anything but my face. **"¿Cuantos años tiene?"**

She pointed to a window on the second floor. **"Tres,"** she cried.

"Cap," Caesar yelled, "we're ready over here."

I heard the approaching whine of a second engine, the reserve guys coming to back us up. "Red, vent the northeast corner of the roof; Paulie, put the wet stuff on the red stuff and push it out when it's got somewhere to go.

We've got a kid on the second floor. I'm going in to see if I can get her."

It was not, like in the movies, a slam dunk—a scene for the hero to go win his Oscar. If I got in there, and the stairs had gone . . . if the structure threatened to collapse . . . if the temperature of the space had gotten so hot that everything was combustible and ripe for flashover—I would have backed out and told my men to back out with me. The safety of the rescuer is of a higher priority than the safety of the victim.

Always.

I'm a coward. There are times when my shift is over that I'll stay and roll hose, or put on a fresh pot of coffee for the crew coming in, instead of heading straight to my house. I have often wondered why I get more rest in a place where, for the most part, I'm roused out of bed two or three times a night. I think it is because in a firehouse, I don't have to worry about emergencies happening—they're supposed to. The minute I walk through the door at home, I'm worrying about what might come next.

Once, in second grade, Kate drew a picture of a firefighter with a halo above his helmet. She told her class that I would only be allowed to go to Heaven, because if I went to Hell, I'd put out all the fires.

I still have that picture.

In a bowl, I crack a dozen eggs and start to whip them into a frenzy. The bacon's already spitting on the stove; the griddle's heating for pancakes. Firemen eat together—or at least we try to, before the bells ring. This breakfast will be a treat for my guys, who are still showering away the memories of last night from their skin. Behind me, I hear the fall of footsteps. "Pull up a chair," I call over my shoulder. "It's almost ready."

"Oh, thanks, but no," says a female voice. "I wouldn't want to impose."

I turn around, brandishing my spatula. The sound of a woman here is surprising; one who's shown up just shy of seven A.M. is even more remarkable. She is small, with wild hair that makes me think of a forest fire. Her hands are covered with winking silver rings. "Captain Fitzgerald, I'm Julia Romano. I'm the guardian ad litem assigned to Anna's case."

Sara's told me about her—the woman the judge will listen to, when push comes to shove.

"Smells great," she says, smiling. She walks up and takes the spatula out of my hand. "I can't watch someone cook without helping. It's a genetic abnormality." I watch her reach into the fridge, rummaging around. Of all things, she comes back with a jar of horseradish. "I was hoping you might have a few minutes to talk."

"Sure." Horseradish?

She adds a good wad of the stuff to the eggs, and then pulls orange zest off the spice rack, along with some chili powder, and sprinkles this on as well. "How's Kate doing?"

I pour a circle of batter on the griddle, watch it come to a bubble. When I flip it, it's an even, creamy brown. I've already spoken to Sara this morning. Kate's night was uneventful; Sara's wasn't. But that's because of Jesse.

There is a moment during a structure fire when you know you are either going to get the upper hand, or that it's going to get the upper hand on you. You notice the ceiling patch about to fall and the staircase eating itself alive and the synthetic carpet glued to the soles of your boots.

The sum of the parts overwhelms, and that's when you back out and force yourself to remember that every fire will burn itself out, even without your help.

These days, I'm fighting fire on six sides. I look in front of me and see Kate sick. I look behind me and see Anna with her lawyer. The only time Jesse isn't drinking like a fish, he's strung out on drugs; Sara's grasping at straws. And me, I've got my gear on, safe. I'm holding dozens of hooks and irons and poles—all tools that are meant to destroy, when what I need is something to rope us together.

"Captain Fitzgerald . . . **Brian!**" Julia Romano's voice knocks me out of my own head, into a kitchen that's rapidly filling with smoke. She reaches past me and shoves the pancake that's burning off the griddle.

"Jesus!" I drop the charcoal disk that used to be a pancake into the sink, where it hisses at me. "I'm sorry."

Like **open sesame,** those two simple words change the landscape.

"Good thing we've got the eggs," Julia Romano says.

• • •

In a burning house, your sixth sense kicks in. You can't see, because of the smoke. You can't hear, because fire roars loud. You can't touch, because it will be the end of you.

In front of me, Paulie manned the nozzle. A line of firefighters backed him up; a charged hose was a thick, dead weight. We worked our way up the stairs, still intact, intent on shoving this fire out the hole Red had put in the roof. Like anything that's confined, fire has a natural instinct to escape.

I got down on my hands and knees and started to crawl through the hallway. The mother said it was the third door on the left. The fire rolled along the other side of the ceiling, racing to the vent. As the spray attacked, white steam swallowed the other firefighters.

The door to the child's room was open. I crawled in calling her name. A larger shape at the window drew me like a magnet, but it turned out to be an oversized stuffed animal. I checked the closets and under the bed, too, but nobody was there.

I backed into the hallway again and nearly tripped over the hose, fist-thick. A human could think; a fire couldn't. A fire would follow a specific path; a child might not. Where would I have gone if I were terrified?

Moving fast, I started poking my head into doorways. One was pink, a baby's room. Another had Matchbox cars all over the floor and bunk beds. One was not a room at all, but a closet. The master bedroom was on the far side of the staircase.

If I were a kid, I'd want my mother.

Unlike the other bedrooms, this one was leaking thick, black smoke. Fire had burned a seam at the bottom of the door. I opened it, knowing I was going to let in air, knowing it was the wrong thing to do and the only choice I had.

Predictably, the smoldering line ignited, flame filling the doorway. I charged through it like a bull, feeling embers rain down the back of my helmet and coat. "Luisa!" I yelled out. I felt my way around the perimeter of the room, found the closet. I knocked hard and called again.

It was faint, but there was definitely a knock back.

• • •

"We've been lucky," I tell Julia Romano, quite possibly the last words she'd ever expect to hear me say. "Sara's sister watches the kids if it's going to be a long haul. For shorter runs, we swap off—you know, Sara stays with Kate one night at the hospital, and I go home to the other kids, or vice versa. It's easier now. They're old enough to take care of themselves."

She writes something down in her little book when I say that, and it makes me squirm in my seat. Anna's only thirteen—is that too young to stay alone in a house? Social Services might say so, but Anna's different. Anna grew up years ago.

"Do you think Anna's doing okay?" Julia asks.

"I don't think she would have filed a lawsuit if she was." I hesitate. "Sara says she wants attention."

"What do **you** think?"

To buy time, I take a forkful of eggs. The horseradish turned out to be surprisingly good. It brings out the orange. I tell Julia Romano this.

She folds her napkin next to her own plate. "You didn't answer my question, Mr. Fitzgerald."

"I don't think it's that simple." I very carefully set my silverware down. "Do you have brothers or sisters?"

"Both. Six older brothers and a twin sister."

I whistle. "Your parents must have a hell of a lot of patience."

She shrugs. "Good Catholics. I don't know how they did it, either, but none of us fell through the cracks."

"Did you always think so?" I ask. "Did you ever feel, when you were a kid, that maybe they were playing favorites?" Her face tightens, just the tiniest bit, and I feel bad about putting her on the spot. "We all know you're supposed to love your kids equal, but that's not always how it works out." I get to my feet. "You got a little extra time? There's someone I'd like you to meet."

Last winter we got an ambulance call in the dead of winter for a guy who lived up a rural road. The contractor he hired to plow his driveway had found him and called 911; apparently the guy had gotten out of his car the night before, slipped, and froze right to the gravel; the contractor nearly ran over him, thinking he was a drift.

When we got to the scene, he'd been outside for nearly eight hours, and he was nothing more than an ice cube with no pulse. His knees were bent; I remember this, because when we finally pried him out and set him on a backboard, there they were, sticking straight up in the air. We got the heat cranked in the ambulance and brought him inside, starting to cut off his clothes. By the time we had our paperwork in order for the hospital transport, the guy was sitting up and talking to us.

I tell you this to show you that in spite of what you'd think, miracles happen.

It's a cliché, but the reason I became a firefighter in the first place was because I wanted to save people. So the moment I emerged from the fiery arched doorway with Luisa in my arms, when her mother first saw us and fell to her knees, I knew I had done my job and done it well. She swooped down beside the EMT from the second crew who got a line into the girl's arm and put her on oxygen. The kid was coughing, frightened, but she would be fine.

The fire was all but out; the boys were inside doing salvage and overhaul. Smoke drew a veil over the night sky; I couldn't make out a single star in the constellation Scorpio. I took off my gloves and wiped my hands across my eyes, which would sting for hours. "Good work," I said to Red, as he packed up the hose.

"Good save, Cap," he called back.

It would have been better, of course, if Luisa had been in her own room, as her mother expected. But kids don't stay where they're supposed to. You turn around and find her not in the bedroom but hiding in a closet; you turn around and see she's not three but thirteen. Parenting is really just a matter of tracking, of hoping your kids do not get so far ahead you can no longer see their next moves.

I took off my helmet and stretched the muscles of my neck. I looked up at the structure that was once a home. Suddenly I felt fingers wrap around my hand. The woman who lived here stood with tears in her eyes. Her youngest was still in her arms; the other kids were sitting in the fire truck under Red's supervision. Silently she raised my knuckles to her lips. A streak of soot came off my jacket to stripe her cheek. "You're welcome," I said.

On our way back to the station I directed Caesar the long way, so that we passed right down the street where I live. Jesse's Jeep sat in my driveway; the lights in the house were all off. I pictured Anna with the covers pulled up to her chin, like usual; Kate's bed empty.

"We all set, Fitz?" Caesar asked. The truck was barely crawling, almost stopped directly in front of my driveway.

"Yeah, we're set," I said. "Let's take it on home."

I became a firefighter because I wanted to save people. But I should have been more specific. I should have named names.

JULIA

BRIAN FITZGERALD'S CAR is filled with stars. There are charts on the passenger seat and tables jammed into the console between us; the backseat is a palette for Xerox copies of nebulae and planets. "Sorry," he says, reddening. "I wasn't expecting company."

I help him clear off a space for me, and in the process pick up a map made of pinpricks. "What's this?" I ask.

"A sky atlas." He shrugs. "It's kind of a hobby."

"When I was little, I once tried to name every star in the sky after one of my relatives. The scary part is I hadn't run out of names by the time I fell asleep."

"Anna's named after a galaxy," Brian says.

"That's much cooler than being named after a patron saint," I muse. "Once, I asked my mom why stars shine. She said they were night-lights, so the angels could find their way around in Heaven. But when I asked my dad, he started talking about gas, and somehow I put it all together and figured that the food God served caused multiple trips to the bathroom in the middle of the night."

Brian laughs out loud. "And here I was trying to explain atomic fusion to my kids."

"Did it work?"

He considers for a moment. "They could all probably find the Big Dipper with their eyes closed."

"That's impressive. Stars all look the same to me."

"It's not that hard. You spot a piece of a constellation—like Orion's belt—and suddenly it's easier to find Rigel in his foot and Betelgeuse in his shoulder." He hesitates. "But ninety percent of the universe is made of stuff we can't even see."

"Then how do you know it's there?"

He slows to a stop at a red light. "Dark matter has a gravitational effect on other objects. You can't see it, you can't feel it, but you can watch something being pulled in its direction."

Ten seconds after Campbell left last night, Izzy walked into the living room where I was just on the cusp of having one of those bone-cleansing cries a woman should treat herself to at least once during a lunar cycle. "Yeah," she said dryly. "I can see this is a totally professional relationship."

I scowled at her. "Were you eavesdropping?"

"Pardon me if you and Romeo were having your little tête-à-tête through a thin wall."

"If you've got something to say," I suggested, "say it."

"Me?" Izzy frowned. "Hey, it's none of my business, is it?"

"No, it's not."

"Right. So I'll just keep my opinion to myself."

I rolled my eyes. "Out with it, Isobel."

"Thought you'd never ask." She sat down beside me on the couch. "You know, Julia, the first time a bug sees that big purple zapper light, it looks like God. The second time, he runs in the other direction."

"First, don't compare me to a mosquito. Second, he'd **fly** in the other direction, not run. Third, there **is** no second time. The bug's dead."

Izzy smirked. "You are **such** a lawyer."

"I am not letting Campbell zap me."

"Then request a transfer."

"This isn't the Navy." I hugged one of the throw pillows from the couch. "And I can't do that, not now. It'll make him think that I'm such a wimp I can't balance my professional life with some stupid, silly, adolescent . . . incident."

"You **can't.**" Izzy shook her head. "He's an egotistical dickhead who's going to chew you up and spit you out; and you have a really awful history of falling for assholes that you ought to run screaming from; and I don't feel like sitting around listening to you try to convince yourself you don't still feel something for Campbell Alexander when, in fact, you've spent the past fifteen years trying to fill in the hole he made inside you."

I stared at her. "Wow."

She shrugged. "Guess I had a lot to get off my chest, after all."

"Do you hate **all** men, or just Campbell?"

Izzy seemed to think about that for a while. "Just Campbell," she said finally.

What I wanted, at that moment, was to be alone in my living room so that I could throw things, like the TV remote or the glass vase or preferably my sister. But I couldn't order Izzy out of a house she'd moved into just hours before. I stood up and plucked my house keys off the counter. "I'm going out," I told her. "Don't wait up."

I'm not much of a party girl, which explains why I hadn't frequented Shakespeare's Cat before, although it was a mere four blocks from my condo. The bar was dark and crowded and smelled of patchouli and cloves. I pushed my way inside, hopped up on a stool, and smiled at the man sitting next to me.

I was in the mood to make out in the back row of the movie theater with someone who did not know my first name. I wanted three guys to fight for the honor of buying me a drink.

I wanted to show Campbell Alexander what he'd been missing.

The man beside me had sky-eyes, a black ponytail, and a Cary Grant grin. He nodded politely at me, then turned away and began to kiss a white-haired gentleman flush on the mouth. I looked around and saw what I had missed on my entrance: the bar was filled with single men—but they were dancing, flirting, hooking up with each other.

"What can I get you?" The bartender had fuchsia porcupine hair and an oxen ring pierced through his nose.

"This is a gay bar?"

"No, it's the officers' club at West Point.

You want a drink or not?" I pointed over his shoulder to the bottle of tequila, and he reached for a shot glass.

I rummaged in my purse and pulled out a fifty-dollar bill. "The whole thing." Glancing down at the bottle, I frowned. "I bet Shakespeare didn't even **have** a cat."

"Who peed in your coffee?" the bartender asked.

Narrowing my eyes, I stared at him. "You're not gay."

"Sure I am."

"Based on my track record, if you were gay, I'd probably find you attractive. As it is . . ." I looked at the busy couple beside me, and then shrugged at the bartender. He blanched, then handed me back my fifty. I tucked it back into my wallet. "Who says you can't buy friends," I murmured.

Three hours later, I was the only person still there, unless you counted Seven, which was what the bartender had rechristened himself last August after deciding to jettison whatever sort of label the name Neil suggested. Seven stood for absolutely nothing, he had told me, which was exactly the way he liked it.

"Maybe I should be Six," I told him, when I'd made my way to the bottom of the tequila bottle, "and you could be Nine."

Seven finished stacking the clean glasses. "That's it. You're cut off."

"He used to call me Jewel," I said, and that was enough to make me start crying.

A jewel's just a rock put under enormous heat and pressure. Extraordinary things are always hiding in places people never think to look.

But Campbell had looked. And then he'd left me, reminding me that whatever he'd seen wasn't worth the time or effort.

"I used to have pink hair," I told Seven.

"I used to have a real job," he answered.

"What happened?"

He shrugged. "I dyed my hair pink. What happened to you?"

"I let mine grow out," I answered.

Seven wiped up a spill I'd made without noticing. "Nobody ever wants what they've got," he said.

• • •

Anna sits at the kitchen table by herself, eating a bowl of Golden Grahams. Her eyes
widen, as she is surprised to see me with her
father, but that's as much as she'll reveal.
"Fire last night, huh?" she says, sniffing.

Brian crosses the kitchen and gives her a
hug. "Big one."

"The arsonist?" she asks.

"Doubt it. He goes for empty buildings
and this one had a kid in it."

"Who you saved," Anna guesses.

"You bet." He glances at me. "I thought
I'd take Julia up to the hospital. Want to
come?"

She looks down at her bowl. "I don't
know."

"Hey." Brian lifts her chin. "No one's
going to keep you from seeing Kate."

"No one's going to be too thrilled to see me
there, either," she says.

The telephone rings, and he picks it up.
He listens for a moment, and then smiles.
"That's great. That's so great. Yeah, of course

I'm coming in." He hands the phone to Anna. "Mom wants to talk to you," he says, and he excuses himself to change clothes.

Anna hesitates, then curls her hand around the receiver. Her shoulders hunch, a small cubicle of personal privacy. "Hello?" And then, softly: "Really? She did?"

A few moments later, she hangs up. She sits down and takes another spoonful of cereal, then pushes away her bowl. "Was that your mom?" I ask, sitting down across from her.

"Yeah. Kate's awake," Anna says.

"That's good news."

"I guess."

I put my elbows on the table. "Why **wouldn't** it be good news?"

But Anna doesn't answer my question. "She asked where I was."

"Your mother?"

"Kate."

"Have you talked to her about your lawsuit, Anna?"

Ignoring me, she grabs the cereal box and begins to roll down the plastic insert.

"It's stale," she says. "No one ever gets all the air out, or closes the top right."

"Has **anyone** told Kate what's going on?"

Anna pushes on the box top to get the cardboard tab into its slot, to no avail. "I don't even **like** Golden Grahams." When she tries again, the box falls out of her arms and spills its contents all over the floor. **"Shoot!"** She crawls under the table, trying to scoop up the cereal with her hands.

I get on the floor with Anna and watch her shove fistfuls into the liner. She won't look in my direction. "We can always buy Kate some more before she gets home," I say gently.

Anna stops and glances up. Without the veil of that secret, she looks much younger. "Julia? What if she hates me?"

I tuck a strand of hair behind Anna's ear. "What if she doesn't?"

"The bottom line," Seven explained last night, "is that we never fall for the people we're supposed to."

I glanced at him, intrigued enough to muster the effort to raise my face from where it was plastered on the bar. "It's not just me?"

"Hell, no." He set down a stack of clean glasses. "Think about it: Romeo and Juliet bucked the system, and look where it got them. Superman has the hots for Lois Lane, when the better match, of course, would be with Wonder Woman. Dawson and Joey—need I say more? And don't even get me started on Charlie Brown and the little redheaded girl."

"What about you?" I asked.

He shrugged. "Like I said, it happens to everyone." Leaning his elbows on the counter, he came close enough that I could see the dark roots beneath his magenta hair. "For me, it was Linden."

"I'd break up with someone who was named for a tree, too," I sympathized. "Guy or girl?"

He smirked. "I'll never tell."

"So what made her wrong for you?"

Seven sighed. "Well, she—"

"Ha! You said she!"

He rolled his eyes. "Yes, Detective Julia. You've outed me at this gay establishment. Happy?"

"Not particularly."

"I sent Linden back to New Zealand. Green card ran out. It was that, or get married."

"What was wrong with her?"

"Absolutely nothing," Seven confessed. "She cleaned like a banshee; she never let me wash a dish; she listened to everything I had to say; she was a hurricane in bed. She was crazy about me, and believe it or not, I was the one for her. It was, like, ninety-eight percent perfect."

"What about the other two percent?"

"You tell me." He started stacking the clean glasses on the far side of the bar. "Something was missing. I couldn't tell you what it was, if you asked, but it was off. And if you think of a relationship as a living entity, I guess it's one thing if the missing two percent is, like, a fingernail. But when it's the heart, that's a whole different ball of wax." He turned to me. "I didn't cry when she got on the plane. She lived with me for four years, and when she walked away, I didn't feel much of anything at all."

"Well, I had the other problem," I told him. "I had the heart of the relationship, and no body to grow it in."

"What happened then?"

"What else," I said. "It broke."

The ridiculous irony is that Campbell was attracted to me because I stood apart from everyone else at The Wheeler School; and I was attracted to Campbell because I desperately wanted a connection with someone. There were comments, I knew, and stares sent our way as his friends tried to figure out why Campbell was wasting his time with someone like me. No doubt, they thought I was an easy lay.

But we weren't doing that. We met after school at the cemetery. Sometimes we would speak poetry to each other. Once, we tried to have an entire conversation without the letter "s." We sat back to back, and tried to think each other's thoughts—pretending clairvoyance, when it only made sense that his whole mind would be full of me and mine would be full of him.

I loved the way he smelled whenever his head dipped close to hear what I was saying—like the sun striking the cheek of a tomato, or soap drying on the hood of a car. I loved the way his hand felt on my spine. I loved.

"What if," I said one night, stealing breath from the edge of his lips, "we did it?"

He was lying on his back, watching the moon rock back and forth on a hammock of stars. One hand was tossed up over his head, the other anchored me against his chest. "Did what?"

I didn't answer, just got up on one elbow and kissed him so deep that the ground gave way. "Oh," Campbell said, hoarse. "That."

"Have you ever?" I asked.

He just grinned. I thought that he'd probably fucked Muffy or Buffy or Puffy or all three in the baseball dugout at Wheeler, or after a party at one of their homes when they both still smelled of Daddy's bourbon. I wondered why, then, he wasn't trying to sleep with me. I assumed that it was because I wasn't Muffy or Buffy or Puffy, but just Julia Romano, which wasn't good enough.

"Don't you want to?" I asked.

It was one of those moments where I knew we were not having the conversation that we needed to be having. And since I didn't really know what to say, never having crossed this particular bridge between thought and deed before, I pressed my hand up against the thick ridge in his pants. He backed away from me.

"Jewel," he said, "I don't want you to think that's why I'm here."

Let me tell you this: if you meet a loner, no matter what they tell you, it's not because they enjoy solitude. It's because they have tried to blend into the world before, and people continue to disappoint them. "Then why **are** you here?"

"Because you know all the words to

'American Pie,' " Campbell said. "Because when you smile, I can almost see that tooth on the side that's crooked." He stared at me. "Because you're not like anyone I've ever met."

"Do you love me?" I whispered.

"Didn't I just say that?"

This time, when I reached for the buttons of his jeans, he didn't move away. In my palm he was so hot I imagined he would leave a scar. Unlike me, he knew what to do. He kissed and slipped, pushed, cracked me wide. Then he went perfectly still. "You didn't say you were a virgin," he said.

"You didn't ask."

But he'd assumed. He shuddered and began to move inside me, a poetry of limbs. I reached up to hold on to the gravestone behind me, words I could see in my mind's eye: Nora Deane, b. 1832, d. 1838.

"Jewel," he whispered, when it was over. "I thought . . ."

"I know what you thought." I wondered what happened when you offered yourself to someone, and they opened you, only to discover you were not the gift they expected and they had to smile and nod and say thank you all the same.

I blame Campbell Alexander entirely for my bad luck with relationships. It is embarrassing to admit, but I have only had sex with three and a half other men, and none of those were any great improvement on my first experience.

"Let me guess," Seven said last night. "The first was a rebound. The second was married."

"How'd you know?"

He laughed. "Because you're a cliché."

I swirled my pinky in my martini. It was an optical illusion, making the finger look split and crooked. "The other one was from Club Med, a windsurfing instructor."

"That must have been worthwhile," Seven said.

"He was absolutely gorgeous," I answered. "And had a dick the size of a cocktail frank."

"Ouch."

"Actually," I mused, "you couldn't feel it at all."

Seven grinned. "So he was the half?"

I turned beet red. "No, that was some other guy. I don't know his name," I admitted. "I sort of woke up with him on top of me, after a night like this one."

"You," Seven pronounced, "are a train wreck of sexual history."

But this is inaccurate. A runaway train is an accident. Me, I'll jump in front of the tracks. I'll even tie myself down in front of the speeding engine. There's some illogical part of me that still believes if you want Superman to show up, first there's got to be someone worth saving.

Kate Fitzgerald is a ghost just waiting to happen. Her skin is nearly translucent, her hair so fair it bleeds into the pillowcase. "How are you doing, baby?" Brian murmurs, and he leans down to kiss her on the forehead.

"I think I might have to blow off the Ironman competition," Kate jokes.

Anna is hovering at the door in front of me; Sara holds out her hand. It is all the encouragement Anna needs to crawl up on Kate's mattress, and in my mind I mark off this small gesture from mother to child. Then Sara sees me standing at the threshold. "Brian," she says, "what is she doing here?"

I wait for Brian to explain, but he doesn't seem inclined to utter a word. So I paste a smile on my face and step forward. "I heard Kate was feeling better today, and I thought it might be a good time to talk to her."

Kate struggles to her elbows. "Who are you?"

I expect a fight from Sara, but it is Anna who speaks up. "I don't think it's such a good idea," she says, although she knows this is the very reason I've come here. "I mean, Kate's still pretty sick."

It takes me a moment, but then I understand: in Anna's life, everyone who ever talks to Kate takes Kate's side. She is doing what she can to keep me from defecting.

"You know, Anna's right," Sara hastily adds. "Kate's only just turned a corner."

I place my hand on Anna's shoulder. "Don't worry." Then I turn to her mother. "It's my understanding that you wanted this hearing—"

Sara cuts me off. "Ms. Romano, could we have a word outside?"

We step into the hallway, and Sara waits for a nurse to pass with a Styrofoam tray of needles. "I know what you think of me," she says.

"Mrs. Fitzgerald—"

She shakes her head. "You're sticking up for Anna, and you **should.** I practiced law once, and I understand. It's your job, and part of that is figuring out what makes us **us.**" She rubs her forehead with one fist. **"My** job is to take care of my daughters. One of them is extremely ill, and the other one's extremely unhappy. And I may not have it all figured out yet, but . . . I do know that Kate won't get better any quicker if she finds out that the reason you're here is because Anna hasn't withdrawn her lawsuit yet. So I'm asking you not to tell her, either. Please."

I nod slowly, and Sara turns to go back into Kate's room. With her hand on the door, she hesitates. "I love **both** of them," she says, an equation I am supposed to be able to solve.

I told Seven the Bartender that true love is felonious.

"Not if they're over eighteen," he said, shutting the till of the cash register.

By then the bar itself had become an appendage, a second torso holding up my first. "You **take** someone's breath away," I stressed. "You **rob** them of the ability to utter a single word." I tipped the neck of the empty liquor bottle toward him. "You **steal** a heart."

He wiped up in front of me with a dishrag. "Any judge would toss that case out on its ass."

"You'd be surprised."

Seven spread the rag out on the brass bar to dry. "Sounds like a misdemeanor, if you ask me."

I rested my cheek on the cool, damp wood. "No way," I said. "Once you're in, it's for life."

Brian and Sara take Anna down to the cafeteria. It leaves me alone with Kate, who is eminently curious. I imagine that the number of times her mother has willingly left her side is something she can count on two hands. I explain that I'm helping the family make some decisions about her health care.

"Ethics committee?" Kate guesses. "Or are you from the hospital's legal department? You look like a lawyer."

"What does a lawyer look like?"

"Kind of like a doctor, when he doesn't want to tell you what your labs say."

I pull up a chair. "Well, I'm glad to hear you're doing better today."

"Yeah. Apparently yesterday I was pretty out of it," Kate says. "Doped up enough to make Ozzy and Sharon look like Ozzie and Harriet."

"Do you know where you stand, medically, right now?"

Kate nods. "After my BMT, I got graft-versus-host disease—which is sort of good, because it kicks the leukemia's butt, but it also does some funky stuff to your skin and organs. The doctors gave me steroids and cyclosporine to control it, and that worked, but it also managed to break down my kidneys, which is the emergency flavor of the month. That's pretty much the way it goes—fix one leak in the dike just in time to watch another one start spouting. Something is always falling apart in me."

She says this matter-of-factly, as if I've grilled her about the weather or what's on the hospital menu. I could ask her if she has talked to the nephrologists about a kidney transplant, if she has any particular feelings about undergoing so many different, painful treatments. But this is exactly what Kate is expecting me to ask, which is probably why the question that comes out of my mouth is completely different. "What do you want to be when you grow up?"

"No one **ever** asks me that." She eyes me carefully. "What makes you think I'm going to grow up?"

"What makes you think that you're not? Isn't that why you're doing all this?"

Just when I think she isn't going to answer me, she speaks. "I always wanted to be a ballerina." Her arm goes up, a weak arabesque. "You know what ballerinas have?"

Eating disorders, I think.

"Absolute control. When it comes to their bodies, they know exactly what's going to happen, and when." Kate shrugs, coming back to this moment, this hospital room. "Anyway," she says.

"Tell me about your brother."

Kate starts to laugh. "You haven't had the pleasure of meeting him yet, I guess."

"Not yet."

"You can pretty much form an opinion about Jesse in the first thirty seconds you spend with him. He gets into a lot of bad stuff he shouldn't."

"You mean drugs, alcohol?"

"Keep going," Kate says.

"Has that been hard for your family to deal with?"

"Well, yeah. But I don't really think it's something he does on purpose. It's the way he gets noticed, you know? I mean, imagine what it would be like if you were a squirrel living in the elephant cage at the zoo. Does anyone ever go there and say, **Hey, check out that squirrel?** No, because there's something so much bigger you notice first." Kate runs her fingers up and down one of the tubes sprouting out of her chest. "Sometimes it's shoplifting, and sometimes it's getting drunk. Last year, it was an anthrax hoax. That's the kind of stuff Jesse does."

"And Anna?"

Kate starts to pleat the blanket in folds on her lap. "There was one year when every single holiday, and I mean even like Memorial Day, I was in the hospital. It wasn't anything planned, of course, but that's the way it happened. We had a tree in my room for Christmas, and an Easter egg hunt in the cafeteria, and we trick-or-treated on the orthopedic ward. Anna was around six years old, and she threw a total fit because she couldn't bring sparklers into the hospital on the Fourth of July—all the oxygen tents." Kate looks up at me. "She ran away. Not far, or anything—I think she got to the lobby before someone nabbed her. She was going to find herself another family, she told me. Like I said, she was only six, and no one really took it seriously. But I used to wonder what it would be like to be normal. So I totally understood why she'd wonder about it, too."

"When you're not sick, do you and Anna get along pretty well?"

"We're like any pair of sisters, I guess. We fight over who gets to put on whose CDs; we talk about cute guys; we steal each other's good nail polish. She gets into my stuff and I yell; I get into her stuff and she cries down the house. Sometimes she's great. And other times I wish she'd never been born."

That sounds so patently familiar that I

grin. "I have a twin sister. Every time I used to say that, my mother would ask me if I could really, truly picture being an only child."

"Could you?"

I laugh. "Oh . . . there were definitely times I could imagine life without her."

Kate doesn't crack a smile. "See," she says, "my sister's the one who's always had to imagine life without me."

SARA

1996

AT EIGHT, KATE IS A LONG TANGLE of arms and legs, sometimes resembling a creature made of sunlight and pipe cleaners more than she does a little girl. I stick my head into her room for the third time that morning, to find her in yet a different outfit. This one is a dress, white with red cherries printed across it. "You're going to be late for your own birthday party," I tell her.

Thrashing her way out of the halter top, Kate strips off the dress. "I look like an ice cream sundae."

"There are worse things," I point out.

"If you were me, would you wear the pink skirt or the striped one?"

I look at them both, puddles on the floor. "The pink one."

"You don't like the stripes?"

"Then wear that one."

"I'm going to wear the cherries," she decides, and she turns around to grab it. On the back of her thigh is a bruise the size of a half-dollar, a cherry that has stained its way through the fabric.

"Kate," I ask, "what's that?"

Twisting around, she looks at the spot where I point. "I guess I banged it."

For five years, Kate has been in remission. At first, when the cord blood transplant seemed to be working, I kept waiting for someone to tell me this was all a mistake. When Kate complained that her feet hurt, I rushed her to Dr. Chance, certain this was the bony pain of recurrence, only to find out that she'd outgrown her sneakers. When she fell down, instead of kissing her scrapes, I'd ask her if her platelets were good.

A bruise is created when there is bleeding in tissues beneath the skin, usually—but not always—the result of a trauma.

It has been five whole years, did I mention that?

Anna sticks her head into the room. "Daddy says the first car just pulled up and if Kate wants to come down wearing a flour sack he doesn't care. What's a flour sack?"

Kate finishes hiking the sundress over her head, then pulls up the hem and rubs the bruise. "Huh," she says.

Downstairs, there are twenty-five second-graders, a cake in the shape of a unicorn, and a local college kid hired to make swords and bears and crowns out of balloons. Kate opens her presents—necklaces made of glittery beads, craft kits, Barbie paraphernalia. She saves the biggest box for last—the one Brian and I have gotten her. Inside a glass bowl swims a fantail goldfish.

Kate has wanted a pet forever. But Brian is allergic to cats, and dogs require a lot of attention, which led us to this. Kate could not be happier. She carries him around for the rest of the party. She names him Hercules.

After the party, when we are cleaning up, I find myself staring at the goldfish. Bright as a penny, he swims in circles, happy to be going nowhere.

• • •

It takes only thirty seconds to realize that you will be canceling all your plans, erasing whatever you had been cocky enough to schedule on your calendar. It takes sixty seconds to understand that even if you'd been fooled into thinking so, you do not have an ordinary life.

A routine bone marrow aspiration—one we'd scheduled long before I ever saw that bruise—has come back with some abnormal promyelocytes floating around. Then a polymerase chain reaction test—one that allows the study of DNA—showed that in Kate, the 15 and 17 chromosomes were translocated.

All of this means that Kate is in molecular relapse now, and clinical symptoms can't be that far behind. Maybe she won't present with blasts for a month. Maybe we won't find blood in her urine or stools for a year. But inevitably, it will happen.

They say that word, **relapse**, like they might say **birthday** or **tax deadline**, something that happens so routinely it has become part of your internal calendar, whether you want it to or not.

Dr. Chance has explained that this is one of the great debates for oncologists—do you fix a wheel that isn't broken, or do you wait until the cart collapses? He recommends that we put Kate on ALL-TRANS Retinoic Acid. It comes in a pill half the size of my thumb, and was basically stolen from ancient Chinese medics who'd been using it for years. Unlike chemotherapies, which go in and kill every-thing in their path, ATRA heads right for chromosome 17. Since the translocation of chromosomes 15 and 17 is in part what keeps promyelocyte maturation from happening correctly, ATRA helps uncoil the genes that have bound themselves together . . . and stops the abnormalities from going further.

Dr. Chance says the ATRA may put Kate back into remission.

Then again, she might develop a resis-tance to it.

"Mom?" Jesse comes into the living room, where I am sitting on the couch. I've been there for hours now. I can't seem to make myself get up and do any of the things I am supposed to, because what is the point of packing school lunches or hemming a pair of pants or even paying the heating bill?

"Mom," Jesse says again. "You didn't forget, did you?"

I look at him as if he is speaking Greek. "What?"

"You said you'd take me to buy new cleats after we go to the orthodontist. You **promised**."

Yes, I did. Because soccer starts two days from now, and Jesse's outgrown his old pair. But now I do not know if I can drag myself to the orthodontist's, where the receptionist will smile at Kate and tell me, like she always does, how beautiful my children are. And there is something about the thought of going to Sports Authority that seems downright obscene.

"I'm canceling the orthodontist appointment," I say.

"Cool!" He smiles, his silver mouth glinting. "Can we just go get the cleats?"

"Now is not a good time."

"But—"

"Jesse. Let. It. Go."

"I can't play if I don't get new shoes. And you're not even **doing** anything. You're just sitting here."

"Your sister," I say evenly, "is incredibly sick. I'm sorry if that interferes with your dentist's appointment or your plan to go buy a pair of cleats. But those don't rate quite as high in the grand scheme of things right now. I'd think that since you're ten, you might be able to grow up enough to realize that the whole world doesn't always revolve around you."

Jesse looks out the window, where Kate straddles the arm of an oak tree, coaching Anna in how to climb up. "Yeah, **right**, she's sick," he says. "Why don't **you** grow up? Why don't you figure out that the world doesn't revolve around **her**?"

For the first time in my life I begin to understand how a parent might hit a child—it's because you can look into their eyes and see a reflection of yourself that you wish you hadn't. Jesse runs upstairs to slam the door to his bedroom.

I close my eyes, take a few deep breaths.

And it strikes me: not everyone dies of old age. People get run over by cars. People crash in airplanes. People choke on peanuts. There are no guarantees about anything, least of all one's future.

With a sigh I walk upstairs, knock on my son's door. He has just recently discovered music; it throbs through the thin line of light at the base of the door. As Jesse turns down the stereo the notes flatten abruptly. **"What."**

"I'd like to talk to you. I'd like to apologize."

There is a scuffle on the other side of the door, and then it swings open. Blood covers Jesse's mouth, a vampire's lipstick; bits of wire stick out like a seamstress's pins. I notice the fork he is holding, and realize this is what he has used to pull off his braces. "Now you never have to take me anywhere," he says.

Two weeks go by with Kate on ATRA. "Did you know," Jesse says one day, while I am getting her pill ready, "a giant tortoise can live for 177 years?" He is on a **Ripley's Believe It or Not** kick. "An Arctic clam can live for 220 years."

Anna sits at the counter, eating peanut butter with a spoon. "What's an Arctic clam?"

"Who cares?" Jesse says. "A parrot can live for eighty years. A cat can live for thirty."

"How about Hercules?" Kate asks.

"It says in my book that with good care, a goldfish can live for seven years."

Jesse watches Kate put the pill on her tongue, take a swig of water to swallow it. "If you were Hercules," he says, "you'd already be dead."

Brian and I slide into our respective chairs in Dr. Chance's office. Five years have passed, but the seats fit like an old baseball glove. Even the photographs on the oncologist's desk have not changed—his wife is wearing the same broad-brimmed hat on a rocky Newport jetty; his son is frozen at age six, holding a speckled trout—contributing to the feeling that in spite of what I believed, we never really left here.

The ATRA worked. For a month, Kate reverted to molecular remission. And then a CBC turned up more promyelocytes in her blood.

"We can keep pulsing her with ATRA," Dr. Chance says, "but I think that its failure already tells us she's maxed out that course."

"What about a bone marrow transplant?"

"That's a risky call—particularly for a child who still isn't showing symptoms of a full-blown clinical relapse." Dr. Chance looks at us. "There's something else we can try first. It's called a donor lymphocyte infusion—a DLI. Sometimes a transfusion of white blood cells from a matched donor can help the original clone of cord blood cells fight the leukemia cells. Think of them as a relief army, supporting the front line."

"Will it put her into remission?" Brian asks.

Dr. Chance shakes his head. "It's a stop-gap measure—Kate will, in all probability, have a full-fledged relapse—but it buys time to build up her defenses before we have to rush into a more aggressive treatment."

"And how long will it take to get the lymphocytes here?" I ask.

Dr. Chance turns to me. "That depends. How soon can you bring in Anna?"

• • •

When the elevator doors open there is only one other person inside it, a homeless man with electric blue sunglasses and six plastic grocery bags filled with rags. "Close the doors, dammit," he yells as soon as we step inside. "Can't you see I'm blind?"

I push the button for the lobby. "I can take Anna in after school. Kindergarten gets out at noon tomorrow."

"Don't touch my bag," the homeless man growls.

"I didn't," I answer, distant and polite.

"I don't think you should," Brian says.

"I'm nowhere near him!"

"Sara, I meant the DLI. I don't think you should take Anna in to donate blood."

For no reason at all, the elevator stops on the eleventh floor, then closes again.

The homeless man begins to rummage in his plastic bags. "When we had Anna," I remind Brian, "we knew that she was going to be a donor for Kate."

"Once. And she doesn't have any memory of us doing that to her."

I wait until he looks at me. "Would you give blood for Kate?"

"Jesus, Sara, what kind of question—"

"I would, too. I'd give her half my heart, for God's sake, if it helped. You do whatever you have to, when it comes to people you love, right?" Brian ducks his head, nods. "What makes you think that Anna would feel any different?"

The elevator doors open, but Brian and I remain inside, staring at each other. From the back, the homeless man shoves between us, his bounty rustling in his arms. "Stop yelling," he shouts, though we stand in utter silence. "Can't you tell that I'm deaf?"

To Anna, it is a holiday. Her mother and father are spending time with her, alone. She gets to hold both of our hands the whole way across the parking lot. So what if we're going to a hospital?

I have explained to her that Kate isn't feeling good, and that the doctors need to take something from Anna and give it to Kate to make her feel better. I figured that was more than enough information.

We wait in the examination room, coloring line drawings of pterodactyls and **T-Rexes**. "Today at snack Ethan said that the dinosaurs all died because they got a cold," Anna says, "but no one believed him."

Brian grins. "Why do you think they died?"

"Because, duh, they were a million years old." She looks up at him. "Did they have birthday parties back then?"

The door opens, and the hematologist comes in. "Hello, gang. Mom, you want to hold her on your lap?"

So I crawl onto the table and settle Anna in my arms. Brian gets stationed behind us, so that he can grab Anna's shoulder and elbow and keep it immobilized. "You ready?" the doctor asks Anna, who is still smiling.

And then she holds up a syringe.

"It's only a little stick," the doctor promises, exactly the wrong words, and Anna starts thrashing. Her arms clip me in the face, the belly. Brian cannot grab hold of her.

Over her screams, he yells at me. "I thought you **told** her!"

The doctor, who's left the room without me even noticing, returns with several nurses in tow. "Kids and phlebotomy never mix well," she says, as the nurses slide Anna off my lap and soothe her with their soft hands and softer words. "Don't worry; we're pros."

It is a déjà vu, just like the day Kate was diagnosed. **Be careful what you wish for,** I think. Anna **is** just like her sister.

I'm vacuuming the girls' room when the handle of the Electrolux smacks Hercules' bowl and sends the fish flying. No glass breaks, but it takes me a moment to find him, thrashing himself dry on the carpet beneath Kate's desk.

"Hang on, buddy," I whisper, and I flip him into the bowl. I fill it with water from the bathroom sink.

He floats to the top. **Don't,** I think. **Please.**

I sit down on the edge of the bed. How can I possibly tell Kate I've killed her fish? Will she notice if I run to the pet store and get a replacement?

Suddenly Anna is next to me, home from morning kindergarten. "Mommy? How come Hercules isn't moving?"

I open my mouth, a confession melting on my tongue. But at that moment the goldfish shudders sideways, dives, and starts to swim again. "There," I say. "He's fine."

When five thousand lymphocytes don't seem to be enough, Dr. Chance calls for ten thousand. Anna's appointment for a second donor lymphocyte draw falls in the middle of the gymnastics birthday party of a girl in her class. I agree to let her go for a little while, and then drive to the hospital from the gym.

The girl is a sugar-spun princess with fairy-white hair, a tiny replica of her mother. As I slip off my shoes to trek across the padded floor, I try desperately to remember their names. The child is . . . Mallory. And the mother is . . . Monica? Margaret?

I spot Anna right away, sitting on the trampoline as an instructor bounces them up and down like popcorn. The mother comes over to me, a smile strung on her face like a row of Christmas lights. "You must be Anna's mom. I'm Mittie," she says. "I'm so sorry she has to leave, but of course, we understand. It must be amazing, going somewhere no one else ever gets to go."

The hospital? "Well, just hope you never have to do the same."

"Oh, I know. I get dizzy going up an elevator." She turns to the trampoline. "Anna, honey! Your mother's here!"

Anna barrels across the padded floor. This is exactly what I'd wanted to do to my living room when the kids were all small: cushion the walls and floor and ceiling for protection. And yet it turned out that I could have rolled Kate in bubble wrap, the danger for her was already under the skin.

"What do you say?" I prompt, and Anna thanks Mallory's mother.

"Oh, you're welcome." She hands Anna a small bag of treats. "Now, have your husband call us anytime. We'd be happy to take Anna while you're in Texas."

Anna hesitates in the middle of a shoelace knot. "Mittie?" I ask, "what exactly did Anna tell you?"

"That she had to leave early so your whole family could take you to the airport. Because once training starts in Houston, you won't see them until after the flight."

"The flight?"

"On the space shuttle . . . ?"

For a moment I am stunned—that Anna would make up such a ridiculous story, that this woman would believe it. "I'm not an astronaut," I confess. "I don't know why Anna would even say something like that."

I pull Anna to her feet, one shoelace still untied. Dragging her out of the gymnasium, we reach the car before I say a word. "Why did you lie to her?"

Anna scowls. "Why did I have to leave the party?"

Because your sister is more important than cake and ice cream; because I cannot do this for her; because I said so.

I'm so angry that I have to try twice before I can unlock the van. "Stop acting like a five-year-old," I accuse, and then I remember that's exactly what she is.

"It was so hot," Brian says, "a silver tea set melted. Pencils were bent in half."

I look up from the newspaper. "How did it start?"

"Cat and dog chasing each other, when the owners were on vacation. They turned on a Jenn-Air range." He peels his jeans down, winces. "I got second-degree burns just kneeling on the roof."

His skin is raw, blistered. I watch him apply Neosporin and gauze. He keeps talking, telling me something about a rookie nicknamed Caesar who just joined their company. But my eyes are drawn to the advice column in the newspaper:

Dear Abby,
    Every time my mother-in-law visits, she insists on cleaning out the refrigera-

tor. My husband says she's just trying to help, but it makes me feel like I'm being judged. She's made my life a wreck. How do I make this woman stop without ruining my marriage?

Sincerely,

Past My Expiration Date, Seattle

What sort of woman considers this to be her biggest problem? I picture her scrawling out a note to Dear Abby on linen-blend stationery. I wonder if she's ever felt a baby turn inside her, tiny hands and feet walking in slow circles, as if the inside of a mother is a place to be carefully mapped.

"What are you glued to?" Brian asks, coming to read the column over my shoulder.

I shake my head in disbelief. "A woman whose life is being ruined by rings from jelly jars."

"Cream gone bad," Brian adds, chuckling.

"Slimy lettuce. Oh my God, how can she stand to be alive?" We both start laughing then. Contagious, all we have to do is look at each other to laugh even harder.

And then just as suddenly as all this was funny, it isn't anymore. Not all of us live in a world where our refrigerator contents are the barometer for our personal happiness. Some of us work in buildings that are burning down around us. Some of us have little girls who are dying. "Slimy fucking lettuce," I say, my voice hitching. "It's not fair."

Brian is across the room in an instant; he folds me into his embrace. "It never is, baby," he answers.

One month later, we go back for a third lymphocyte donation. Anna and I take our seats in the doctor's office, waiting to be called. After a few minutes, she tugs on my sleeve. "Mommy," she says.

I glance down at her. Anna is swinging her feet. On her fingernails is Kate's mood-changing nail polish. "What?"

She smiles up at me. "In case I forget to tell

you after, it wasn't as bad as I thought it was going to be."

One day my sister arrives unannounced, and with Brian's permission, spirits me away to a penthouse suite at the Ritz Carlton in Boston. "We can do anything you want," she tells me. "Art museums, Freedom Trail walks, dinners out on the Harbor." But what I really want to do is just **forget**, and so three hours later I am sitting on the floor beside her, finishing our second $100 bottle of wine.

I lift the bottle by its neck. "I could have bought a dress with this."

Zanne snorts. "At Filene's Basement, maybe." Her feet are on a brocade chair; her body is sprawled on the white carpet. On the TV, Oprah counsels us to minimize our lives. "Plus, when you zip up a great Pinot Noir, you never look fat."

I look over at her, suddenly feeling sorry for myself.

"No. You're not doing the crying thing. Crying is not included in the room rate."

But suddenly all I can think of is how stupid the women on Oprah sound, with their stuffed Filofaxes and crammed closets. I wonder what Brian made for dinner. If Kate's all right. "I'm going to call home."

She comes up on an elbow. "You are allowed to take a break, you know. No one has to be a martyr twenty-four/seven."

But I hear her wrong. "I think once you sign on to be a mother, that's the only shift they offer."

"I said **martyr**," Zanne laughs. "Not **mother**."

I smile a little. "Is there a difference?"

She takes the telephone receiver out of my hand. "Did you want to get your crown of thorns out of the suitcase first? Listen to yourself, Sara, and stop being such a drama queen. Yes, you drew a bad lot of fate. Yes, it sucks to be you."

Bright color rises on my cheeks. "You have no idea what my life is like."

"Neither do you," Zanne says. "You're not living, Sara. You're waiting for Kate to die."

"I am not—" I begin, but then I stop. The thing is, I **am**.

Zanne strokes my hair and lets me cry. "It is so hard sometimes," I confess, words I have not said to anyone, not even Brian.

"As long as it's not **all** the time," Zanne says. "Honey, Kate is not going to die sooner because you have one more glass of wine, or because you stay overnight in a hotel, or because you let yourself crack up at a bad joke. So sit your ass back down and turn up the volume and act like you're a normal person."

I look around at the opulence of the room, at our decadent sprawl of wine bottles and chocolate strawberries. "Zanne," I say, wiping my eyes, "this is not what normal people do."

She follows my gaze. "You're absolutely right." She picks up the remote control, flipping channels until she finds Jerry Springer. "That better?"

I start to laugh, and then she starts to laugh, and soon the room is spinning around me and we are lying on our backs, staring up at the crown molding edging the ceiling. I suddenly remember how, when we were kids, Zanne used to always walk ahead of me to the bus stop. I could have run and caught up—but I never did. I only wanted to follow her.

Laughter rises like steam, swims through the windows. After three days of a torrential downpour, the kids are delighted to be outside, kicking around a soccer ball with Brian. When life is normal, it is **so** normal.

I duck into Jesse's room, trying to navigate strewn LEGO pieces and comic books so that I can set his clean clothes down on the bed. Then I go into Kate and Anna's room, and separate their folded laundry.

When I place Kate's T-shirts on her dresser I see it: Hercules is swimming upside down. I reach into the bowl and turn him, holding his tail; he wafts for a few strokes and then floats slowly to the surface, white-bellied and gasping.

I remember Jesse saying that with good care, a fish might live seven years. This has only been seven months.

After carrying the fishbowl into my bedroom, I pick up the phone and dial Information. "Petco," I say.

When I'm connected, I ask a clerk about Hercules. "Do you, like, want to buy a new fish?" she asks.

"No, I want to save this one."

"Ma'am," the girl says, "we're talking about a **goldfish**, right?"

So I call three vets, none of whom treat fish. I watch Hercules in his death throes for another minute, and then ring the oceanography department at URI, asking for any professor that's available.

Dr. Orestes studies tide pools, he tells me. Mollusks and shellfish and sea urchins, not goldfish. But I find myself telling him about my daughter, who has APL. About Hercules, who survived once against all odds.

The marine biologist is silent for a moment. "Have you changed his water?"

"This morning."

"You get a lot of rain down there the past couple of days?"

"Yes."

"Got a well?"

What does that have to do with anything?

"Yes . . ."

"It's just a hunch, but with runoff, your water might have too many minerals in it. Fill the bowl with bottled water, and maybe he'll perk up."

So I empty out Hercules' bowl, scrub it, and add a half-gallon of Poland Spring. It takes twenty minutes, but then Hercules begins to swim around. He navigates between the lobes of the fake plant. He nibbles at food.

Kate finds me watching him a half hour later. "You didn't have to change the water. I did it this morning."

"Oh, I didn't know," I lie.

She presses her face up to the glass bowl, her smile magnified. "Jesse says goldfish can only pay attention for nine seconds," Kate says, "but I think Hercules knows exactly who I am."

I touch her hair. And wonder if I have used up my miracle.

Anna

IF YOU LISTEN to enough infomercials you start to believe some crazy things: that Brazilian honey can be used as leg wax, that knives can cut metal, that the power of positive thinking can work like a pair of wings to get you where you need to be. Thanks to a little bout of insomnia and way too many doses of Tony Robbins, I decided one day to force myself into imagining what it would be like after Kate died. That way, or so Tony vowed, when it **really** happened, I'd be ready.

I kept at it for weeks. It is harder than you think to keep yourself in the future, especially when my sister was walking around at the time being her usual pain-in-the-butt self. My way of dealing with this was to pretend Kate was already haunting me. When I stopped talking to her, she figured she'd done something wrong, which she probably **had,** anyway. There were entire days where I did nothing but cry; others where I felt like I'd swallowed a lead plate; some more where I worked really hard at going through the motions of getting dressed and making my bed and studying my vocab words because it was easier than doing anything else.

But then, there were times when I let the veil lift a little, and other ideas would pop up. Like what it would be like to study oceanography at the University of Hawaii. Or try skydiving. Or move to Prague. Or any of a million other pipe dreams. I'd try to stuff myself into one of these scenarios, but it was like wearing a size five sneaker when your foot is a seven— you can get by for a few steps, and then you sit down and pull off the shoe because it just plain hurts too much. I am convinced that there is a censor sitting on my brain with a red stamp, reminding me what I am not supposed to even **think** about, no matter how seductive it might be.

It's probably a good thing. I have a feeling that

if I really try to figure out who I am without Kate in the equation, I'm not going to like who I see.

My parents and I are sitting together at a table in the hospital cafeteria, although I use the word **together** loosely. It's more like we're astronauts, each wearing a separate helmet, each sustained by our own private source of air. My mother has the little rectangular container of sugar packets in front of her. She is organizing them with ruthlessness, the Equal and then the Sweet 'n Low and then the nubbly brown natural crystals. She looks up at me. "Honey."

Why are terms of endearment always foods? **Honey, cookie, sugar, pumpkin**. It's not like caring about someone is enough to actually sustain you.

"I understand what you're trying to do here," my mother continues. "And I agree that maybe your father and I need to listen to you a little bit more. But Anna, we don't need a judge to help us do this."

My heart is a soft sponge at the base of my throat. "You mean it's okay to stop?"

When she smiles, it feels like the first warm day of March—after an eternity of snow, when you suddenly remember how summer feels on the backs of your bare calves and in the part of your hair. "That's **exactly** what I mean," my mother says.

No more blood draws. No granulocytes or lymphocytes or stem cells or kidney. "If you want, I'll tell Kate," I offer. "So you don't have to."

"That's all right. Once Judge DeSalvo knows, we can pretend it never happened."

In the back of my mind, a hammer trips. "But . . . won't Kate ask why I'm not her donor anymore?"

My mother goes very still. "When I said **stop,** I meant the lawsuit."

I shake my head hard, as much to give her an answer as to dislodge the knot of words tangled in my gut.

"My God, Anna," my mother says, stunned. "What have we done to you to deserve this?"

"It's not what you've done to me."

"It's what we **haven't** done, right?"

"You aren't listening to me!" I yell, and at

that very moment, Vern Stackhouse walks up to our table.

The deputy looks from me to my mother to my father and forces a smile. "Guess this isn't the best time to interrupt," he says. "I'm real sorry about this, Sara. Brian." He hands my mother an envelope, nods, and walks off.

She pulls out the paper inside and reads it, then turns to me. "What did you say to him?" she demands.

"To who?"

My father picks up the notice. It is full of legal language, which might as well be Greek. "What's this?"

"A motion for a temporary restraining order." She grabs it from my father. "Do you realize you're asking to have me kicked out of the house, and to have no contact with you? Is that really what you want?"

Kick her out? I can't breathe. "I never asked for that."

"Well, an attorney wouldn't have filed it on his own behalf, Anna."

Do you know how sometimes—when you are riding your bike and you start skidding across sand, or when you miss a step and start tumbling down the stairs—you have those long, long seconds to know that you are going to be hurt, and badly? "I don't know what's going on," I say.

"Then how can you think you're qualified to make decisions for yourself?" My mother stands so abruptly her chair clatters to the cafeteria floor. "If this is what you want, Anna, we can start right now." Her voice, it's thick and rough as rope the moment before she leaves me.

About three months ago, I borrowed Kate's makeup. Okay, so borrowed wouldn't be the right word, exactly: stole. I didn't have any of my own; I wasn't supposed to be allowed to wear it until I turned fifteen. But a miracle had happened, and Kate wasn't around to ask, and desperate times call for desperate measures.

The miracle was five-eight, with hair the color of Silver Queen corn silk and a smile that made me feel like I'd been spinning in circles. His name was Kyle and he'd moved from Idaho, right into the homeroom seat behind mine. He didn't know anything about me or my family, so when he asked me if I wanted to go to a movie with him I knew it wasn't because he felt sorry for me. We saw the new **Spider-Man** movie, or at least he did. I spent all my time trying to figure out how electricity could leap the tiny space between my arm and his.

When I came home, I still was walking about six inches above the ground, which is why Kate was able to blindside me. She knocked me onto my bed, pinned me by my shoulders. "You thief," she accused. "You went into my bathroom drawer without asking."

"You take my things all the time. You borrowed my blue sweatshirt two days ago."

"That's totally different. You can **wash** a sweatshirt."

"How come it's okay to have my germs floating around your arteries, but not on your freaking Max Factor Cherry Bomb lip gloss?" I shoved a little harder, and managed to roll us, so that now I had the upper hand.

Her eyes lit up. "Who was it?"

"What are you talking about?"

"If you're wearing makeup, Anna, there must have been a reason."

"Get lost," I said.

"Fuck off." Kate smiled at me. Then she reached one free hand under my arm and tickled me, taking me by surprise so much that I let go of her. A minute later we had wrestled off the bed, each of us trying to get the other to cry uncle. "Anna, stop already," Kate gasped. "You're killing me."

Those words, they were all it took. My hands fell off her as if I'd been burned. We lay shoulder to shoulder between our beds, staring up at the ceiling and breathing hard, both of us pretending that what she'd said had not cut quite so close to the bone.

In the car, my parents fight. **Maybe we should hire a real lawyer,** my father says, and my mother replies, **I** am **one.**

But Sara, my father says, **if this isn't going to go away, all I'm saying is—**

What are **you saying, Brian?** she challenges. **What are you really saying? That some man in**

a suit whom you've never met would be able to explain Anna better than her own mother? And then my father drives the rest of the way in silence.

To my shock, there are TV cameras waiting on the steps of the Garrahy building. I'm sure they're here for something really big, so imagine my surprise when a microphone gets stuck into my face, and a reporter with helmet hair asks me why I am suing my parents. My mother pushes the woman away. "My daughter has no comment," she says, over and over; and when one guy asks if I'm aware that I am Rhode Island's first designer baby, I think for a minute she might actually deck him.

I've known since I was seven how I was conceived, and it wasn't that huge a deal. First off, my parents told me when the thought of them having sex was far more disgusting than the thought of creation in a petri dish. Second, by then tons of people were having fertility drugs and septuplets and my story wasn't really all that original anymore. But a designer baby? Yeah, **right**. If my parents were going to go to all that trouble, you'd think they'd have made sure to implant the genes for obedience, humility, and gratitude.

My father sits next to me on a bench, his hands knotted between his knees. Inside the judge's chambers, my mother and Campbell Alexander are verbally slugging it out. Here in the hallway, we're unnaturally quiet, as if they've taken all possible words with them and left us with nothing.

I hear a woman curse, and then Julia rounds the bend. "Anna. Sorry I'm late; I couldn't get past the media. Are you all right?"

I nod, and then I shake my head.

Julia kneels down in front of me. "Do you want your mother to leave the house?"

"No!" To my utter embarrassment, my eyes get glassy with tears. "I've changed my mind. I don't want to do this anymore. None of it."

She looks at me for a long moment, then nods. "Let me go in and talk to the judge."

When she leaves, I concentrate on getting air into my lungs. There are so many things I have to work hard at now, that I used to be able to carry out instinctively—draw in oxygen, keep my silence, do the right thing. The weight of my father's eyes on me makes me turn. "Did you mean it?" he asks. "About not wanting to do this anymore?"

I don't answer. I don't move a fraction of an inch.

"Because if you're still not sure, maybe it's not such a bad idea, having some breathing space. I mean, I've got that extra bed in my room at the station." He rubs the back of his neck. "It wouldn't be like we were moving out, or anything. Just . . ." He looks at me.

". . . breathing," I finish, and do just that.

My father stands up and holds out his hand. We walk out of the Garrahy Complex, side by side. The reporters come on like wolves, but this time, their questions bounce right off me. My chest feels full of glitter and helium, the way it used to when I was little and riding my father's shoulders at twilight, when I knew that if I held up my hands and spread my fingers like a net, I could catch the coming stars.

CAMPBELL

THERE MAY BE a special corner of Hell for attorneys who are shamelessly self-aggrandizing, but you can bet we all are ready for our close-ups. When I arrive at the family court to find a horde of reporters on parade, I offer around sound bites as if they are candy, and make sure that the cameras are on me. I say the appropriate things about how this case is unorthodox, but ultimately painful for everyone involved. I hint that the judge's ruling may affect the rights of minors nationwide, as well as stem cell research. Then I smooth the jacket of my Armani suit, tug on Judge's leash, and explain that I really must go speak to my client.

Inside, Vern Stackhouse catches my eye and gives me a thumbs-up. I'd run into the deputy earlier, and very innocently asked whether his sister, a reporter for the **ProJo,** would be coming down today. "I can't really say anything," I hinted, "but the hearing . . . it's going to be pretty big."

In that special corner of Hell, there's probably a throne for those of us who try to capitalize off our pro bono work.

Minutes later, we are in chambers. "Mr. Alexander." Judge DeSalvo lifts up the motion for a restraining order. "Would you like to tell me why you've filed this, when I explicitly addressed the issue yesterday?"

"I had my initial meeting with the guardian ad litem, Judge," I reply. "While Ms. Romano was present, Sara Fitzgerald told my client the lawsuit was a misunderstanding that would work itself out." I slide my glance toward Sara, who shows no emotion but a tightening of her jaw. "This is a direct violation of your order, Your Honor. Although this court tried to fashion conditions that would keep the family together, I don't think it's going to work until Mrs. Fitzgerald finds it possible to mentally separate her role as parent from her role as opposing counsel. Until then, a physical separation is necessary."

Judge DeSalvo taps his fingers on the desk. "Mrs. Fitzgerald? Did you say those things to Anna?"

"Well, of course I did!" Sara explodes. "I'm trying to get to the bottom of this!"

The admission is a circus tent collapsing, leaving all of us in utter silence. Julia chooses that moment to burst through the door. "Sorry I'm late," she says, breathless.

"Ms. Romano," the judge asks, "have you had a chance to speak to Anna today?"

"Yes, just now." She looks at me, and then at Sara. "I think she's very confused."

"What's your opinion of the motion Mr. Alexander's filed?"

She tucks an errant coil of hair behind one ear. "I don't think I have enough information to make a formal decision, but my gut feeling says it would be a mistake for Anna's mother to be removed from the house."

Immediately, I tense. Reacting, the dog gets to his feet. "Judge, Mrs. Fitzgerald just admitted that she violated the court's order. At the very least she should be reported to the bar for ethical violations, and—"

"Mr. Alexander, there is more to this case than the letter of the law." Judge DeSalvo turns to Sara. "Mrs. Fitzgerald, I strongly recommend you look into hiring an independent attorney to represent you and your husband in this petition. I am not going to grant the restraining order today, but I will warn you once again not to talk with your child about this case until the hearing next week. If it comes to my attention at some future date that you have ignored this directive once again, I will report you to the bar myself and personally escort you from your home." He smacks the file folder shut and gets up. "Do **not** bother me again until Monday, Mr. Alexander."

"I need to see my client," I announce, and I hurry out to the hallway where I know Anna is waiting with her father.

Sara Fitzgerald, predictably, is right at my heels. Following her—intent on keeping the peace, no doubt—is Julia. All three of us come to an abrupt stop at the sight of Vern

Stackhouse, dozing on the bench where Anna was sitting. "Vern?" I say.

He immediately leaps to his feet, clearing his throat defensively. "It's a lumbar problem. Gotta sit down every now and then to take the pressure off."

"You know where Anna Fitzgerald went?"

He jerks his head toward the front door of the building. "She and her dad took off a while ago."

From the look on Sara's face, this is news to her, too. "Do you need a ride back to the hospital?" Julia asks.

She shakes her head and peers through the glass doors, where the reporters have rallied. "Is there a back way out?"

At my side, Judge begins to stick his muzzle into my hand. **Damn.**

Julia steers Sara Fitzgerald toward the rear of the building. "I need to talk to you," she calls over her shoulder to me.

I wait for her to turn her back. Then I promptly grab Judge's harness and haul him down a corridor.

"Hey!" A moment later, Julia's heels strike

the tile behind me. "I **said** I wanted to talk to you!"

For a minute I seriously consider ducking out a window. Then I stop abruptly, turn, and offer up my most engaging smile. "Technically speaking, you said you **needed** to talk to me. If you'd said you **wanted** to talk to me, I might have waited around." Judge sinks his teeth into the corner of my suit, my **expensive** Armani suit, and tugs. "Right now, though, I have a meeting to get to."

"What the hell is wrong with you?" she says. "You told me you talked to Anna about her mother and that we were all on the same page."

"I **did,** and we **were**—Sara was coercing her, and Anna wanted that to stop. I explained the alternatives."

"Alternatives? She's a **thirteen-year-old girl**. Do you know how many kids I see whose take on a trial is completely different from their parents'? A mother comes in and promises that her child will testify against a child molester, because she wants the perp put away for life. But the child doesn't care what happens to the perp, as long as he never has to be in the same room as the guy again. Or he thinks that maybe the perp should get another chance, just like **his** parents give him when **he's** bad. You can't expect Anna to be like a normal adult client. She doesn't have the emotional capability to make decisions independent of her home situation."

"Well, that's the point of this whole petition," I say.

"As a matter of fact, Anna told me, not a half hour ago, that she's changed her mind about this whole petition." Julia raises a brow. "Didn't know that, did you?"

"She hasn't talked to me about it."

"That's because you're talking about the wrong things. You had a conversation with her about a legal way to keep her from being pressured to call off the lawsuit. Of **course** she jumped all over that. But do you really think she was considering what it might truly mean—that there would be one less parent home to cook or drive or help her with homework, that she wouldn't be able to kiss her mother good night, that the rest of her family would most likely be very upset with her? All she heard, when you talked, were the words **no pressure**. She never heard **separation**."

Judge begins to whine in earnest. "I have to go."

She follows me. "Where?"

"I told you, I have an **appointment**." The corridor is lined with rooms, all locked. Finally I find a knob that turns in my hand. I walk inside and bolt the door behind me. "Gentlemen," I say heartily.

Julia rattles the knob. She bangs on the smoky postage-stamp square of glass. I feel sweat break out on my forehead. "You're not getting away this time," she yells through the door at me. "I'm still waiting right here."

"I'm still busy," I yell back. When Judge pushes his snout in front of me, I sink my fingers into the thick fur at his neck. "It's okay," I tell him, and then I turn around to face the empty room.

JESSE

EVERY NOW AND THEN I have to contradict myself and believe in God, such as at this very moment when I come home to find a bodacious babe on my doorstep, one who gets to her feet and asks me if I know Jesse Fitzgerald.

"Who's asking?" I say.

"Me."

I give her my most charming smile. "Then here I am."

Let me just step back for a moment and tell you that she's older than me, but with every glance that makes less and less of a difference—she's got hair I could get lost in, and a mouth so soft and full I have a hard time tearing my eyes away to check out the rest of her. I'm itching to get my hands on her skin—even the ordinary parts—just to see if it feels as smooth as it looks.

"I'm Julia Romano," she says. "I'm a guardian ad litem."

All the violins soaring in my veins screech to a stop. "Is that like a cop?"

"No, I'm an attorney, and I'm working with a judge to help your sister."

"You mean Kate?"

Something in her face tightens. "I mean Anna. She filed a lawsuit for medical emancipation from your parents."

"Oh, yeah. I know about that."

"Really?" This seems to surprise her, as if defiance is something Anna's cornered the market on. "Do you happen to know where she is?"

I glance at the house, dark and empty. "Am I my sister's keeper?" I say. Then I grin at her. "If you feel like waiting, you can come up and see my etchings."

To my shock, she agrees. "Actually, that's not a bad idea. I'd like to talk to you."

I lean against the door again and cross my arms, so that my biceps flex. I give her the grin that's stopped half the female population of Roger Williams University in their tracks. "You got plans for tonight?"

She stares at me like I've just spoken Greek. No, damn, she'd probably understand Greek. Martian. Or freaking Vulcan. "Are you asking me out on a **date?**"

"I'm sure as hell trying," I say.

"You're sure as hell failing," she responds flatly. "I'm old enough to be your mother."

"You have the most fantastic eyes." By **eyes,** I mean **tits**, but whatever.

Julia Romano chooses that moment to button her suit jacket, which makes me laugh out loud. "Why don't we just talk here?"

"Whatever," I say, and I lead her up to my apartment.

Given what it usually looks like, the place isn't so bad. The dishes on the counter are only a day or two old; and spilled cereal isn't nearly as bad to come home to after a full day as spilled milk. On the middle of the floor is a bucket and rag and container of gas; I'm working up some firesticks. There are clothes all over the floor, some artfully arranged to minimize the effect of a leak in my moonshine still.

"What do you think?" I smile at her. "Martha Stewart would love it, huh?"

"Martha Stewart would make you her life project," Julia murmurs. She sits down on the couch, leaps up, and removes a handful of potato chips that have, holy God, already left a grease print in the shape of a heart on her sweet ass.

"You want a drink?" Don't let it be said my mother never taught me manners.

She glances around, then shakes her head. "I'll pass."

Shrugging, I pull a Labatt's out of the fridge. "So there's been a little fallout along the home front?"

"Wouldn't you know?"

"I try not to."

"How come?"

"Because it's what I do best." Grinning, I take a nice long pull of my beer. "Although this is one blowout I would've loved to see."

"Tell me about Kate and Anna."

"What am I supposed to tell you?" I swing

down next to her on the couch, way too close. On purpose.

"How do you get along with them?"

I lean forward. "Why, Ms. Romano. Are you asking me if I play nice?" When she doesn't as much as blink, I knock off the act. "They survive me," I answer. "Like everyone else."

This answer must interest her, because she writes something down on her little white pad. "What was it like, growing up in this family?"

A dozen flip responses work their way up my throat, but the one that comes out is a totally dark horse. "When I was twelve, there was this time Kate got sick—not even big sick, just an infection, but she couldn't seem to get rid of it by herself. So they took Anna in to give granulocytes—white blood cells. It wasn't like Kate planned it or anything, but it happened to be Christmas Eve. We were supposed to all go out as a family, you know, and get a tree." I pull a pack of smokes from my pocket. "You mind?" I ask, but I never give her a chance to answer before I light up. "I was shuttled over to some neighbor's house last minute, which sucked, because they were having a nice Christmas Eve with their relatives and kept whispering about me like I was a charity case and deaf to boot. Anyway, that all got lame pretty fast, so I said I had to pee and I snuck out. I walked home and took one of my dad's axes and a handsaw and chopped down this little spruce in the middle of the front yard. By the time the neighbor figured out I was gone, I had the whole thing set up in our living room in the tree stand, garland, ornaments, you name it."

In my mind, I can still see those lights—red and blue and yellow, blinking over and over on a tree as overdressed as an Eskimo in Bali. "So Christmas morning, my parents come to the neighbors to collect me. They look like hell, the both of them, but when they bring me home there are presents under the tree. I'm all excited and I find one with my name on it, and it turns out to be this little windup car—something that would have been great for a three-year-old, but not me, and that I happened to know was for sale in the hospital gift shop. As was every single other present I got that year. Go freaking figure." I stab my cigarette butt out on the thigh of my jeans. "They never even said anything about the tree," I tell her. "That's what it's like growing up in this family."

"Do you think it's the same for Anna?"

"No. Anna's on their radar, because she plays into their grand plan for Kate."

"How do your parents decide when Anna will help Kate medically?" she asks.

"You make it sound like there's some process involved. Like there's actually a **choice.**"

She lifts her head. "Isn't there?"

I ignore her, because that's a rhetorical question if I've ever heard one, and stare out the window. In the front yard, you can still see the stump from that spruce. No one in this family ever covers up their mistakes.

When I was seven I got it in my head to dig to China. How hard could it be, I figured—a straight shot, a tunnel? I took a shovel out of the garage and I started a hole just wide enough for me to slip into. Every night I would drag the old plastic sandbox cover across it, just in case of rain. For four weeks I worked at this, as the rocks bit into my arms to make battle scars, and roots grabbed at my ankles.

What I didn't count on were the tall walls that grew around me, or the belly of the planet, hot under my sneakers. Digging straight down, I'd gotten hopelessly lost. In a tunnel, you have to light your own way, and I've never been very good at that.

When I yelled out, my father found me in seconds, although I'm sure I waited through several lives. He crawled into the pit, torn between my hard work and my stupidity. "This could have collapsed on you!" he said, and lifted me onto solid ground.

From that point of view, I realized that my hole was not miles deep after all. My father, in fact, could stand on the bottom and it only reached up to his chest.

Darkness, you know, is relative.

BRIAN

IT TAKES ANNA less than ten minutes to move into my room at the station. While she puts her clothes into a drawer and sets her hairbrush next to mine on the dresser, I go out to the kitchen where Paulie is chefing up dinner. The guys are all waiting for an explanation.

"She's going to stay with me here for a while," I say. "We're working some things out."

Caesar looks up from a magazine. "Is she gonna ride with us?"

I haven't thought of this. Maybe it will take her mind off things, to feel like she's an apprentice of sorts. "You know, she just might."

Paulie turns around. He's making fajitas tonight, beef. "Everything okay, Cap?"

"Yeah, Paulie, thanks for asking."

"If there's anyone upsetting her," Red says,

"they'll have to go through all four of us now."

The others nod. I wonder what they would think if I told them that the people upsetting Anna are Sara and me.

I leave the guys finishing up dinner preparations and go back to my room, where Anna sits on the second twin bed with her feet pretzeled beneath her. "Hey," I say, but she doesn't respond. It takes me a moment to see that she's wearing headphones, blasting God knows what into her ears.

She sees me and shuts off the music, pulling the phones to rest on her neck like a choker. "Hey."

I sit down on the edge of the bed and look at her. "So. You, uh, want to do something?"

"Like what?"

I shrug. "I don't know. Play cards?"

"You mean like poker?"

"Poker, Go Fish. Whatever."

She looks at me carefully. "Go **Fish?**"

"Want to braid your hair?"

"Dad," Anna asks, "are you feeling all right?"

I am more comfortable rushing into a building that is going to pieces around me than I am trying to make her feel at ease. "I just—I want you to know you can do anything you want here."

"Is it okay to leave a box of tampons in the bathroom?"

Immediately, my face goes red, and as if it's catching, so does Anna's. There is only one female firefighter, a part-timer, and the women's room is on the lower level of the station. But still.

Anna's hair swings over her face. "I didn't mean . . . I can just keep them—"

"You can put them in the bathroom," I announce. Then I add with authority, "If anyone complains, we'll say they're mine."

"I'm not sure they'll believe you, Dad."

I wrap an arm around her. "I may not do this right at first. I've never bunked with a thirteen-year-old girl."

"I don't shack up with forty-two-year-old guys too often, either."

"Good, because I'd have to kill them."

Her smile is a stamp against my neck. Maybe this will not be as hard as I think. Maybe I can convince myself that this move will ultimately keep my family together, even though the first step involves breaking it apart.

"Dad?"

"Hmm?"

"Just so you know: no one plays Go Fish after they're potty-trained."

She hugs me extra tight, the way she used to when she was small. I remember, in that instant, the last time I carried Anna. We were hiking across a field, the five of us—and the cat-tails and wild daisies were taller than her head. I swung her up into my arms, and together we parted a sea of reeds. But for the first time we both noticed how far down her legs dangled, how she was too big to sit on my hip, and before long she was struggling to get down and walk on her own.

Goldfish get big enough only for the bowl you put them in. Bonsai trees twist in miniature. I would have given anything to keep her little. They outgrow us so much faster than we out-grow them.

It seems remarkable that while one of our daughters is leading us into a legal crisis, the other is in the throes of a medical one—but then again, we have known for quite some time that Kate's at the end stages of renal failure. It is Anna, this time, who's thrown us for a loop. And yet—like always—you figure it out; you manage to deal with both. The human capacity for burden is like bamboo—far more flexible than you'd ever believe at first glance.

While Anna was packing up her things that afternoon, I went to the hospital. Kate was having her dialysis done when I came into the room. She was asleep with her CD headphones on; Sara rose from a chair with one finger pressed to her lips, a warning.

She led me into the hallway. "How's Kate?" I asked.

"About the same," she answered. "How's Anna?"

We traded the status of our children like baseball cards that we'd flash for a peek, but didn't want to give up just yet. I looked at Sara, wondering how I was supposed to tell her what I'd done.

"Where did you two run off to while I was fending off the judge?" she said.

Well. If you sit around and think about how hot the fire's going to be, you'll never get into the thick of it. "I took Anna to the station."

"Something going on at work?"

I took a deep breath and leaped off the cliff that my marriage had become. "No. Anna's going to stay with me there for a few days. I think maybe she needs a little time by herself."

Sara stared at me. "But Anna's **not** going to be by herself. She's going to be with **you**."

The hallway seemed too bright and too wide all of a sudden. "Is that a bad thing?"

"Yes," she said. "Do you really think that buying into Anna's tantrum is going to help her any in the long run?"

"I'm not buying into her tantrum; I'm giving her space to come to the right conclusions by herself. You're not the one who's been sitting outside with her while you're in the judge's chambers. I'm worried about her."

"Well, that's where we're different," Sara argued. "I'm worried about both our daughters."

I looked at her, and for just a splinter of a minute saw the woman she used to be—one who knew where to find her smile, instead of having to rummage for it; one who always messed up punch lines and still got a laugh; one who could reel me in without even trying. I put my hands on her cheeks. **Oh,** there **you are,** I thought, and I leaned down to kiss her on the forehead. "You know where to find us," I said, and walked away.

Shortly after midnight we get an ambulance call. Anna blinks from her bed as the bells go off and light automatically floods the room. "You can stay," I tell her, but she's already up and putting on her shoes.

I've given her old turnout gear from our part-time female firefighter: a pair of boots, a hard hat. She shrugs into the coat and climbs into the rear of the ambulance, strapping herself to the rear-facing seat behind Red, who's driving.

We scream down the streets of Upper Darby to the Sunshine Gates Nursing Home, an anteroom for meeting St. Peter. Red grabs the stretcher from the ambulance while I carry in the paramedic's bag. A nurse meets us at the front doors. "She fell down and lost consciousness for a while. And she's got an altered mental state."

We are led to one of the rooms. Inside, an

elderly woman lies on the floor, tiny and fine-boned as a bird, blood oozing from the top of her head. It smells like she's lost control of her bowels. "Hi, hon," I say, leaning down immediately. I reach for her hand, the skin thin as crepe. "Can you squeeze my fingers?" And to the nurse: "What's her name?"

"Eldie Briggs. She's eighty-seven."

"Eldie, we're going to help you," I say, continuing to assess her. "She's got a lac on the occipital area. I'm going to need the backboard." While Red runs out to the ambulance to get it, I take Eldie's blood pressure and pulse—irregular. "Do you have any pain in your chest?" The woman moans, but shakes her head and then winces. "I'm going to have to put you in a collar, hon, all right? It looks like you hit your head pretty hard." Red returns, bearing the board. Lifting my head, I look at the nurse again. "Do we know if her change in consciousness was the result of the fall, or did it cause the fall?"

She shakes her head. "No one saw it happen."

"Of course," I mutter under my breath. "I need a blanket."

The hand that offers it is tiny and shaking. Until that moment, I've completely forgotten Anna is with us. "Thanks, baby," I say, taking the time to smile at her. "You want to help me here? Can you get down to Mrs. Briggs's feet?"

She nods, white-faced, and crouches down. Red aligns the backboard. "We're going to roll you, Eldie . . . on three . . ." We count, shift, strap her on. The motion makes her scalp wound gush again.

We load her into the ambulance. Red hauls off to the hospital as I move around the cramped quarters of the cabin, hooking up the oxygen tank, ministering. "Anna, grab me an IV start kit?" I begin to cut Eldie's clothes off her. "You still with us, Mrs. Briggs? Little needle stick coming," I say. I position her arm and try to get a vein, but they are like the faintest tracings of pencil, blueprint shadings. Sweat beads on my forehead. "I can't get in with a twenty. Anna, can you find a twenty-two?"

It doesn't help that the patient is moaning, crying. That the ambulance is swaying back and forth, turning corners, braking, as I try to insert the smaller needle. "Dammit," I say, throwing the second line on the floor.

I do a quick cardiac strip and then pick up the radio and dial into the hospital to tell them we're incoming. "Eighty-seven-year-old patient, had a fall. She's alert and answering questions, BP 136 over 83, pulse 130 and irregular. I tried to get IV access for you but haven't had a lot of luck with that. She does have a lac on the back of her head but it's pretty well controlled by now. I've got her on oxygen. Any questions?"

In the beam of an approaching truck, I see Anna's face. The truck turns, the light falls, and I realize that my daughter is holding this stranger's hand.

At the emergency entrance of the hospital, we pull the stretcher out of the cabin and wheel into the automatic doors. A team of doctors and nurses is already waiting. "She's still talking to us," I say.

A male nurse taps her thin wrists. "Jesus."

"Yeah, that's why I couldn't get a line. I needed pedi cuffs to get her pressure."

Suddenly I remember Anna, who's standing wide-eyed in the doorway. "Daddy? Is that lady going to die?"

"I think she might have had a stroke . . . but she's going to make it. Listen, why don't you just go wait over there, in a chair? I'll be out in five minutes, tops."

"Dad?" she says, and I pause at the threshold. "Wouldn't it be cool if they were all that way?"

She doesn't see it the way I do—that Eldie Briggs is a paramedic's nightmare, that her veins are shot and her condition's waffling and that this has not been a good call at all. What Anna means is that whatever is wrong with Eldie Briggs can be fixed.

I go inside and continue to feed information to the ER staff as needed. About ten minutes later, I finish up my Run Form and look for my daughter in the waiting area, but she's gone missing. I find Red smoothing fresh sheets onto the stretcher, strapping a pillow under its belt. "Where's Anna?"

"I figured she was with you."

Glancing down one hallway and then the other, all I see are weary physicians, other paramedics, small scatterings of dazed people sipping coffee and hoping for the best. "I'll be right back."

Compared to the frenzy of the ER, the eighth floor is all tucked tight. The nurses all greet me by name as I head for Kate's room and gently push open the door.

Anna is too big for Sara's lap, but that's where she's sitting. She and Kate are both asleep. Over the crown of Anna's head, Sara watches me approach.

I kneel in front of my wife and brush Anna's hair off her temples. "Baby," I whisper, "it's time to go home."

Anna sits up slowly. She lets me take her hand and draw her upright, Sara's palm trailing down her spine. "It's not home," Anna says, but she follows me out of the room all the same.

Past midnight, I lean down beside Anna and balance my words on the edge of her ear. "Come see this," I coax. She sits up, grabs a sweatshirt, stuffs her feet into her sneakers. Together, we climb to the station's roof.

The night is falling down around us. Meteors rain like fireworks, quick rips in the seam of the dark. "Oh!" Anna exclaims, and she lies down so that she can see better.

"It's the Perseids," I tell her. "A meteor shower."

"It's incredible."

Shooting stars are not stars at all. They're just rocks that enter the atmosphere and catch fire under friction. What we wish on, when we see one, is only a trail of debris.

In the upper left quadrant of the sky, a radiant bursts in a new stream of sparks. "Is it like this every night, while we're asleep?" Anna asks.

It is a remarkable question—**Do all the wonderful things happen when we are not aware of them?** I shake my head. Technically, the earth's path crosses this comet's gritty tail once a year. But a show as dynamic as this one might be once in a lifetime.

"Wouldn't it be cool if a star landed in the backyard? If we could find it when the sun came up and put it into a fishbowl and use it as a night-light or a camping lantern?" I can almost see her doing it, combing the lawn for the mark of burned grass. "Do you think Kate can see these, out her window?"

"I'm not sure." I come up on an elbow and look at her carefully.

But Anna keeps her eyes glued to the

upended bowl of the heavens. "I know you want to ask me why I'm doing all this."

"You don't have to say anything if you don't want to."

Anna lies down, her head pillowed against my shoulder. Every second, another streak of silver glows: parentheses, exclamation points, commas—a whole grammar made of light, for words too hard to speak.

Friday

Doubt thou that the stars are fire;

Doubt thou that the sun doth move;

Doubt truth to be a liar;

But never doubt that I love.

—WILLIAM SHAKESPEARE,
Hamlet

CAMPBELL

THE MINUTE I WALK into the hospital with Judge at my side, I know I'm in trouble. A security officer—think Hitler in drag with a very bad perm—crosses her arms and blocks my entry at the elevator bank. "No dogs," she orders.

"This is a service dog."

"You're not blind."

"I have an irregular heartbeat and he's CPR certified."

I head up to the office of Dr. Peter Bergen, a psychiatrist who happens to be the chairman of the medical ethics board at Providence Hospital. I'm here by default: I can't seem to find my client, who may or may not still be pursuing her lawsuit. Frankly, after the hearing yesterday I was pissed off—I wanted **her** to come to **me**. When she didn't, I went so far as to sit on her doorstep last night for an hour, but no one showed up at her home; this morning, assuming Anna was with her sister, I came to the hospital—only to be told I couldn't go in to see Kate. I can't find Julia, either, although I fully expected to see her still waiting yesterday on the other side of the door when Judge and I left after the incident at the courthouse. I asked her sister for a cell number, at least, but something tells me that 401-GO2-HELL is out of service.

So, because I have nothing better to do, I'm going to work on my case on the off chance that it still exists.

Bergen's secretary looks like the kind of woman whose bra size ranks higher than her IQ. "Ooh, a puppy!" she squeals. She reaches out to pat Judge.

"Please. Don't." I start to come up with one of my ready replies, but why waste it on her? Then I head for the door in the back.

There I find a small, squat man with a stars-and-stripes bandanna over his graying curls, wearing yoga gear and doing Tai Chi. "Busy," Bergen grunts.

"Something we have in common, Doctor. I'm

Campbell Alexander, the attorney who asked for the charts on the Fitzgerald girl."

Arms extended forward, the psychiatrist exhales. "I sent them over."

"You sent Kate Fitzgerald's records. I need Anna Fitzgerald's."

"You know," he replies, "now is not a very good time for me . . ."

"Don't let me interrupt your workout." I sit down, and Judge lies at my feet. "As I was saying—Anna Fitzgerald? Do you have any notes from the ethics committee about her?"

"The ethics committee has never convened on Anna Fitzgerald's behalf. It's her sister who's the patient."

I watch him arch his back, then hunch forward. "Do you have any idea how many times Anna's been both an outpatient and an inpatient in this hospital?"

"No," Bergen says.

"I'm counting eight."

"But those procedures wouldn't necessarily come before the ethics committee. When the physicians agree with what the patients want, and vice versa, there's no conflict. No reason for us to even **hear** about it." Dr. Bergen lowers the foot he has raised in the air and reaches for a towel to mop under his arms. "We all have full-time jobs, Mr. Alexander. We're psychiatrists and nurses and doctors and scientists and chaplains. We don't go looking for problems."

Julia and I leaned against my locker, having an argument about the Virgin Mary. I had been fingering her miraculous medal—well, actually, it was her collarbone I was after, and the medal had gotten in the way. "What if," I said, "she was just some kid who got herself in trouble, and came up with an ingenious way out of it?"

Julia nearly choked. "I think they can even throw you out of the Episcopal Church for that one, Campbell."

"Think about it—you're thirteen, or however old they were back then when they were shacking up—and you have a nice little roll in the hay with Joseph, and before you know it your EPT is coming up positive. You can either face your father's wrath, or you can spin a good story. Who's going to contradict you if you say God's the one who knocked you up? Don't you think Mary's dad was thinking, 'I could ground her . . . but what if that causes a plague?' "

Just then I jacked open my locker and a hundred condoms spilled out. A bunch of guys from the sailing team morphed out of their hiding spots, laughing like hyenas. "Figured you could use a new supply," one of them said.

Well, what was I supposed to do? I smiled.

Before I knew it Julia had taken off. For a girl, she ran goddamn fast. I didn't catch up to her until the school was a distant smudge behind us. "Jewel," I said, although I didn't know what should come after that. It was not the first time I had made a girl cry, but it was the first time it hurt me to do it. "Should I have decked them all? Is that what you want?"

She rounded on me. "What do you tell them about us when you're in the locker room?"

"I don't tell them anything."

"What do you tell your parents about us?"

"I don't," I admitted.

"Fuck you," she said, and she started running again.

The elevator doors open on the third floor, and there's Julia Romano. We stare at each other for a moment, and then Judge gets up and starts wagging his tail. "Going down?"

She steps inside and pushes the button for the lobby, already lit. But it makes her lean across me, so that I can smell her hair—vanilla and cinnamon. "What are you doing here?" she asks.

"Becoming supremely disappointed in the state of American health care. How about you?"

"Meeting with Kate's oncologist, Dr. Chance."

"I assume that means we still have a lawsuit?"

Julia shakes her head. "I don't know. No one in that family's returning my calls, except for Jesse, and that's strictly hormonal."

"Did you go up to—"

"Kate's room? Yeah. They wouldn't let me in. Something about dialysis."

"They said the same thing to me," I tell her.

"Well, if you talk to her—"

"Look," I interrupt. "I have to assume we still have a hearing in three days until Anna tells me otherwise. If that's the case, you and I really need to sit down and figure out what the hell is going on in this kid's life. Do you want to grab a cup of coffee?"

"No," Julia says, and she starts to leave.

"Stop." When I grasp her arm, she freezes. "I know this is uncomfortable for you. It's uncomfortable for me, too. But just because you and I can't seem to grow up doesn't mean Anna shouldn't have a chance to." This is accompanied by a particularly hangdog look.

Julia folds her arms. "Did you want to write that one down, so you can use it again?"

I burst out laughing. "Jesus, you're tough—"

"Oh, stuff it, Campbell. You're so glib you probably oil your lips every morning."

That conjures all sorts of images for me, but they involve **her** body parts.

"You're right," she says then.

"Now **that** I want to write down . . ." When she starts walking away this time, Judge and I follow.

She heads out of the hospital and down a side street, an alley, and past a tenement before we break into the sunshine again on Mineral Spring Avenue in North Providence. By that time, I'm grateful that my left hand is wrapped tight to the leash of a dog with an excessive amount of teeth. "Chance told me that there's nothing left to do for Kate," Julia tells me.

"You mean other than the kidney transplant."

"No. Here's the incredible thing." She stops walking, plants herself in front of me. "Dr. Chance doesn't think Kate's strong enough."

"And Sara Fitzgerald's pushing for it," I say.

"When you think about it, Campbell, you can't blame her logic. If Kate's going to die without the transplant anyway, why not go for it?"

We step delicately around a homeless man and his collection of bottles. "Because the transplant involves major surgery for her other daughter," I point out. "And putting Anna's health at risk for a procedure that's not necessary for her seems a little cavalier."

Suddenly Julia comes to a halt in front of a

small shack with a hand-painted sign, Luigi Ravioli. It looks like the sort of place they keep dark, so that you don't notice the rats. "Isn't there a Starbucks nearby?" I ask, just as an enormous bald man in a white apron opens the door and nearly knocks Julia over.

"Isobella!" he cries, kissing her on both cheeks.

"No, Uncle Luigi, it's Julia."

"Julia?" He pulls back and frowns. "You sure? You ought to cut your hair or something, give us a break."

"You used to get on my case about my hair when it was short."

"We got on your case about your hair because it was **pink**." He looks at me. "You hungry?"

"We were hoping for some coffee, and a quiet table."

He grins. "A quiet table?"

Julia sighs. "Not **that** kind of quiet table."

"Right, right, everything's a big secret. Come in, I'll give you the room in the back." He glances down at Judge. "Dog stays here."

"Dog comes," I respond.

"Not in my restaurant," Luigi insists.

"He's a service dog, he can't stay outside."

Luigi leans close, a couple of inches away from my face. "You're blind?"

"Color-blind," I reply. "He tells me when the traffic lights change."

Julia's uncle's mouth turns down at the corners. "Everyone's a wiseass today," he says, and then he leads the way.

For weeks, my mother tried to guess the identity of my girlfriend. "It's Bitsy, right?— the one we met on the Vineyard? Or no, wait, it's not Sheila's daughter, the redhead, is it?" I told her over and over it was no one she knew, when what I really meant was that Julia was no one she would recognize.

"I know what's right for Anna," Julia tells me, "but I'm not sure she's mature enough to make her own decisions."

I pick up another piece of antipasto. "If you think she's justified in filing the petition, then what's the conflict?"

"Commitment," Julia says dryly. "Would you like me to define that for you?"

"You know, it's impolite to unsheathe your claws at the dinner table."

"Right now, every time Anna's mom confronts her, she backs off. Every time something happens with Kate, she backs off. And in spite of what she thinks she's capable of, she hasn't made a decision of this magnitude before—considering what the consequences are going to be to her sister."

"What if I told you that by the time we have our hearing, she'll be able to make that decision?"

Julia glances up. "Why are you so sure that'll happen?"

"I'm always sure of myself."

She plucks an olive out of the tray between us. "Yeah," she says quietly. "I remember that."

Although Julia must have had her suspicions, I didn't tell her about my parents, my house. As we drove into Newport in my Jeep, I pulled into the driveway of a huge brick mansion. "Campbell," Julia said. "You're kidding."

I circled the loop of the driveway and turned out the other side. "Yeah, I am."

That way, when I pulled into the house two driveways down, the sprawling Georgian with its rows of beech trees and its slope to the Bay, it wasn't quite as imposing. At the very least, it was smaller than the first place.

Julia shook her head. "Your parents are going to take one look at me and pull us apart with a crowbar."

"They're gonna love you," I told her, the first time I lied to Julia, but not the last.

Julia ducks beneath the table with a plateful of pasta. "Here you go, Judge," she says. "So what's with the dog?"

"He translates for my Spanish-speaking clients."

"Really."

I grin at her. "Really."

She leans forward, narrowing her eyes. "You

know, I have six brothers. I know how you guys work."

"Do tell."

"And give away my trade secrets? I don't think so." She shakes her head. "Maybe Anna hired you because you're just as evasive as she is."

"She hired me because she saw my name in the paper," I say. "Nothing more to it than that."

"But why'd you take **her** on? This isn't your usual case."

"How would you know what my usual case is?"

It is said lightly, a joke, but Julia goes mute, and there's my answer: all these years, she's been following my career.

Sort of like I've been following hers.

I clear my throat, uncomfortable, and point to her face. "You've got sauce . . . over there."

She lifts her napkin and wipes the side of her mouth, but misses completely. "Did I get it off?" she asks.

Leaning forward with my own napkin, I clean the small spot—but then I don't move away. My hand rests on her cheek. Our eyes lock, and in that instance, we are young again and learning the shape of each other.

"Campbell," Julia says, "don't do this to me."

"Do what?"

"Push me off the same cliff twice."

When the cell phone in my coat pocket rings, we both jump. Julia inadvertently knocks over her glass of Chianti while I answer. "No, calm down. Calm down. Where are you? Okay, I'm on my way." Julia stops mopping the table as I hang up. "I have to go."

"Is everything all right?"

"That was Anna," I say. "She's at the Upper Darby Police Station."

On the way back to Providence, I tried to come up with at least one awful death per mile for my parents. Bludgeoning, scalping. Skinning alive and sprinkling with salt. Pickling in gin, although I don't know whether that would be considered torture or simply Nirvana.

It was possible they saw me sneaking into the guest room, bringing Julia down the servants' stairs to the rear door of the house. It is possible they could make out our silhouettes as we stripped off our clothes and waded into the Bay. Maybe they watched her legs wrap around me, watched me lay her down on a bed made of sweatshirts and flannel.

Their excuse, given the next morning over eggs Benedict, was an invitation to a party at the Club that night—black-tie, family only. An invitation that, of course, didn't include Julia.

It was so hot out by the time we pulled up to her house that some enterprising boy had pried open the fire hydrant, and kids bounced like popcorn through the stream. "Julia, I never should have dragged you home to meet my parents."

"There's a lot of stuff you shouldn't do," she admitted. "And most of it involves me."

"I'll call you before graduation," I said, as she kissed me and got out of the Jeep.

But I didn't call. And I didn't meet up with her at graduation. And she thinks she knows why, but she doesn't.

• • •

The curious thing about Rhode Island is that it has absolutely no feng shui. By this I mean that there's a Little Compton, but no Big Compton. There's an Upper Darby but no Lower Darby. There are all sorts of places defined in terms of something else that doesn't actually exist.

Julia follows me in her own car. Judge and I must break a land-speed record, because it seems less than five minutes have passed since the phone call and the moment we walk into the station to find Anna hysterical beside the desk sergeant. She flies toward me, frantic. "You've got to help," she cries. "Jesse got arrested."

"What?" I stare at Anna, who tore me away from a very good meal, not to mention a conversation I really would rather have followed to its conclusion. "Why is this my problem?"

"Because I need you to get him out," Anna explains slowly, as if I am a moron. "You're a lawyer."

"I'm not **his** lawyer."

"But can't you be?"

"Why don't you call your mother," I suggest. "I hear she's taking new clients."

Julia whacks me on the arm. "Shut up." She turns to Anna. "What happened?"

"Jesse stole a car and he got nailed."

"Give me more details," I say, already regretting this.

"It was a Humvee, I think. A big, yellow one."

There's one big yellow Humvee in this entire state, and it belongs to Judge Newbell. A headache begins between my eyes. "Your brother stole a judge's car, and you want me to get him out?"

Anna blinks at me. "Well, **yeah**."

Jesus. "Let me go talk to the officer." Leaving Anna in Julia's care, I walk to the desk sergeant, who—I swear it—is already laughing at me. "I'm representing Jesse Fitzgerald," I sigh.

"Sorry to hear that."

"It was Judge Newbell's, wasn't it?"

The officer smiles. "Yup."

I take a deep breath. "The kid doesn't have a record."

"That's because he just turned eighteen. He's got a juvy record a mile long."

"Look," I say. "His family's going through a lot right now. One sister's dying; the other one is suing her parents. Can you cut me a break here?"

The officer looks over at Anna. "I'll talk to the AG for you, but you'd better plead the kid, because I'm quite sure Judge Newbell doesn't want to come testify."

After a little more negotiation I walk back toward Anna, who leaps up the minute she sees me. "Did you fix it?"

"Yeah. But I'm never doing this again, and I'm not done with you." I stalk toward the rear of the station, where the holding cells are.

Jesse Fitzgerald lies on his back on the metal bunk, one arm thrown over his eyes. For a moment I stand outside his cell. "You know, you are the best argument I've ever seen for natural selection."

He sits up. "Who the hell are you?"

"Your fairy godmother. You dumb little shit—do you realize you stole a judge's Humvee?"

"Well, how was I supposed to know whose car it was?"

"Maybe because of the judicial vanity plate that says ALLRISE?" I say. "I'm a lawyer. Your sister asked me to represent you. Against my better judgment, I've agreed."

"No kidding? So can you get me out?"

"They're going to let you go on PR bail. You need to give them your license and agree to live at home, which you already do, so that shouldn't be a problem."

Jesse considers this. "Do I have to give them my car?"

"No."

You can actually see the gears churning. A kid like Jesse couldn't care less about a piece of paper that permits him to drive, just so long as he has wheels. "That's cool, then," he says.

I motion to an officer waiting nearby, who unlocks the cell so that Jesse can leave. We walk side by side to the waiting area. He is as tall as I am, but unfinished around the edges. His face lights up as we turn the corner, and for a moment I think he is capable of redemption, that maybe he feels enough for Anna to be an ally for her.

But he ignores his sister, and instead approaches Julia. "Hey," he says. "Were you worried about me?"

I want, in that moment, to lock him back up. **After** I kill him.

"Get away," Julia sighs. "Come on, Anna. Let's go find something to eat."

Jesse looks up. "Excellent. I'm starving."

"Not you," I say. "We're going to court."

On the day I graduated from Wheeler, the locusts came. They arrived like a thick summer storm, tangling in the branches of trees and thudding hard on the ground. The meteorologists had a field day, trying to explain the phenomenon. They mentioned biblical plagues and El Niño and our prolonged drought. They recommended umbrellas, broad-brimmed hats, staying indoors.

The graduation ceremony, however, was held outside under a large white canvas tent. As the salutatorian spoke, his message was punctuated by the suicide leap of bugs. Locusts rolled off the sloped roof, falling into the laps of spectators.

I hadn't wanted to come, but my parents forced me to go. Julia found me while I was putting on my cap. She wrapped her arms around my waist. She tried to kiss me.

"Hey," she said. "Which side of the earth did you drop off?"

I remember thinking that in our white gowns, we looked like ghosts. I pushed her away from me. "Don't. Okay? Just don't."

In every graduation photo my parents took, I was smiling as if this new world were a place I actually wanted to live in, while all around me insects fell, big as fists.

What is ethical to a lawyer differs from what's ethical to the rest of the world. In fact, we have a written code—the Rules of Professional Responsibility—which we have to read, be tested on, and follow in order to maintain a practice. But these very standards require us to do things that most people consider immoral. For example, if you walk into my office and say, "I killed the Lindbergh baby," I might ask you where the body is. "Under my bedroom floor," you tell me, "three feet down below the foundation of the house." If I am to do my job correctly, I can't tell a soul where that baby is. I could be disbarred, in fact, if I do.

All this means is that I'm actually educated to think that morals and ethics do not necessarily go hand in hand.

"Bruce," I say to the prosecutor, "my client will waive information. And if you get rid of some of these traffic misdemeanors, I swear he'll never come within fifty feet of the judge or his car again."

I wonder how much the general population of this country knows that the legal system has far more to do with playing a good hand of poker than it does with justice.

Bruce is an all right guy. Plus, I happen to know he's just been assigned to a double murder; he doesn't want to waste his time with Jesse Fitzgerald's conviction.

"You know, we're talking about Judge Newbell's Humvee, Campbell," he says.

"Yes. I am aware of that," I answer gravely, when what I'm thinking is that anyone vain enough to drive a Humvee is practically asking to have it ripped off.

"Let me talk to the judge," Bruce sighs. "I'm probably going to get eviscerated for suggesting it, but I'll tell him that the cops don't mind if we give the kid a break."

Twenty minutes later, we have signed all the forms, and Jesse stands beside me in the front of the court. Twenty-five minutes later he is on probation, officially, and we walk out onto the courthouse steps.

It is one of those summer days that feel like a memory welling up in your throat. On days like this, I would have been sailing with my father.

Jesse tips his head back. "We used to fish for tadpoles," he says out of nowhere. "Catch them up in a bucket, and then watch their tails turn into legs. Not a single one, I swear it, ever made it to frog." He turns to me and pulls a pack of cigarettes out of his shirt pocket. "Want one?"

I haven't smoked since I was in law school. But I find myself taking a cigarette and lighting up. Judge watches life happen, lolling his tongue. Beside me, Jesse strikes a match. "Thanks," he says. "For what you're doing for Anna."

A car passes by, its radio playing one of those songs that stations never play in winter. A blue stream of smoke flares out from Jesse's mouth. I wonder if he's ever been sailing. If there's a memory he's held on to all these years—sitting on the front lawn and feeling the grass cool down after sunset, holding a sparkler on the Fourth of July until it burned his fingers. We all have something.

She left the note underneath the windshield wiper of my Jeep seventeen days after graduation. Before I even opened it I wondered how she got to Newport, how she made her way back. I carried it out to the Bay to read on the rocks; and after I was done I held it up and sniffed at it, in case it smelled like her.

I was not technically allowed to drive, but that hardly mattered. We met, as per that note, at the cemetery.

Julia sat in front of the headstone, her arms clasped around her knees. She looked up when she saw me. "I wanted you to be different."

"Julia, it's not you."

"No?" She got to her feet. "I don't have a trust fund, Campbell. My father doesn't own a yacht. If you were crossing your fingers, expecting me to turn into Cinderella one of these days, you got it all wrong."

"I don't care about any of that."

"Bullshit you don't." Her eyes narrowed. "What did you think, that it would be fun to go slumming? Did you do it to piss off your parents? And now you can scrape me off your shoe like I'm something you stepped in by accident?" She struck out at me, clipping me across the chest. "I don't need you. I never needed you."

"Well, I fucking needed you!" I shouted back at her. When she turned I grabbed her shoulders and I kissed her. I took the things I couldn't bring myself to say, and poured them into her.

There are some things we do because we convince ourselves it would be better for everyone involved. We tell ourselves that it's the right thing to do, the altruistic thing to do. It's far easier than telling ourselves the truth.

I pushed Julia away from me. Walked down that cemetery hill. Didn't look back.

Anna sits in the passenger seat, which doesn't go over well with Judge. He hangs his sorry face into the front, right between us, panting up a storm. "Today wasn't a very good harbinger of what's to come," I tell her.

"What are you talking about?"

"If you want the right to make major decisions, Anna, then you need to start making them now. Not relying on the rest of the world to clean up the messes."

She scowls at me. "This is all because I called you to help my brother? I thought you were my **friend.**"

"I already told you once I'm not your friend; I'm your attorney. There's a seminal difference."

"Fine." She fumbles with the lock. "I'll go back to the police and tell them to rearrest Jesse." She nearly succeeds in pushing the passenger door open, although we are traveling on a highway.

I grab the handle and slam it shut. "Are you crazy?"

"I don't know," she answers. "I'd ask you what you think, but it's probably not in the job description."

With a yank of the wheel, I pull the car to the shoulder of the road. "You know what I think? The reason no one ever asks you for your opinion about anything important is because you change your mind so often they don't know **what** to believe. Take me, for example. I don't even know if we're still petitioning a judge for medical emancipation."

"Why wouldn't we be?"

"Ask your mother. Ask Julia. Every time I turn around someone informs me that you don't want to go through with this." I look down at the armrest, where her hand sits—purple sparkle polish, nails bitten to the quick. "If you want to be treated like an adult by the court, you need to start acting like one. The only way I can fight for you, Anna, is if you can prove to everyone that you can fight for yourself when I walk away."

I pull the car back onto the road, and glance at her sidelong, but Anna sits with her hands wedged between her thighs, her face set mutinously ahead. "We're almost at your house," I say dryly. "Then you can get out and give the door a good slam in my face."

"We're not going to my house. I need to go to the fire station. My dad and I are staying there for a while."

"Is it my imagination, or did I not spend a couple of hours at the family court yesterday arguing this very point? And I thought you told Julia that you **didn't** want to be separated from your mother? This is exactly what I'm talking about, Anna," I say, banging my hand on the steering wheel. "What the hell do you really want?"

When she blows, it is remarkable. "You want to know what I want? I'm sick of being a guinea pig. I'm sick of nobody asking me how I feel about all this. I'm sick, but I'm never fucking sick enough for this family." She opens the car door while it is still moving, and takes off at a dead run to the firehouse, a few hundred feet in the distance.

Well. Deep in the recesses of my little client is the potential to make other people listen. It means that on the stand, she'll hold up better than I imagined.

And on the heels of that thought: Anna might be able to testify, but what she's said makes her seem unsympathetic. Immature, even. Or in other words, highly unlikely to convince the judge to rule in her favor.

BRIAN

FIRE AND HOPE ARE CONNECTED, just so you know. The way the Greeks told it, Zeus put Prometheus and Epimetheus in charge of creating life on earth. Epimetheus made the animals, giving out bonuses like swiftness and strength and fur and wings. By the time Prometheus made man, all the best qualities had been given out. He settled for making them walk upright, and he gave them fire.

Zeus, pissed off, took it away. But Prometheus saw his pride and joy shivering and unable to cook. He lit a torch from the sun and brought it to man again. To punish Prometheus, Zeus had him chained to a rock, where an eagle fed on his liver. To punish man, Zeus created the first woman—Pandora—and gave her a gift, a box she was forbidden to open.

Pandora's curiosity got the best of her, and one day she opened that box. Out came plagues and misery and mischief. She managed to shut the lid tight before hope escaped. It's the only weapon we have left to fight the others.

Ask any fireman; he'll tell you it's true. Hell. Ask any father.

"Come on up," I say to Campbell Alexander, when he arrives with Anna. "There's fresh coffee." He follows me up the stairs, his German shepherd trailing. I pour two cups. "What's the dog for?"

"He's a chick magnet," the lawyer says. "Got any milk?"

I pass him the carton from the fridge, then sit down with my own mug. It's quiet up here; the boys are downstairs washing the engines and doing their daily maintenance.

"So." Alexander takes a sip of his coffee. "Anna tells me that you've both moved out."

"Yeah. I sort of figured you might want to ask me about that."

"You do realize that your wife is opposing counsel," he says carefully.

I meet his eye. "I suppose by that you mean do I realize that I shouldn't be sitting here talking to you."

"That only becomes an issue if your wife is still representing you."

"I never asked Sara to represent me."

Alexander frowns. "I'm not sure she's aware of that."

"Look, with all due respect, this may seem like an incredibly big deal, and it is, but we have another incredibly big deal going on at the same time. Our older daughter's been hospitalized and . . . well, Sara's fighting on two fronts."

"I know. And I'm sorry about Kate, Mr. Fitzgerald," he says.

"Call me Brian." I cup my hands around my mug. "And I would like to speak to you . . . without Sara around."

He leans back in the folding chair. "How about right now?"

It's not a good time, but it will never be a good time for this. "Okay." I take a deep breath. "I think Anna's right."

At first I'm not sure Campbell Alexander's

even heard me. Then he asks, "Are you willing to tell that to the judge at a hearing?"

I look down at my coffee. "I think I have to."

By the time Paulie and I responded to this morning's ambulance call, the boyfriend already had the girl in a shower. She sat on the bottom, her legs splayed around the drain, fully dressed. Her hair was matted to the front of her face, but even if it wasn't, I'd have known that she was unconscious.

Paulie got right inside and started to drag her out. "Her name's Magda," the boyfriend said. "She's gonna be okay, right?"

"Is she diabetic?"

"What does that matter?"

For Christ's sake. "Tell me what you were using," I demanded.

"We were just getting drunk," the boyfriend said. "Tequila."

He was no more than seventeen. Old enough to have heard the myth that a shower will bring someone out of a heroin overdose. "Let me explain this to you. My buddy and I want to help Magda, to save her life. But if you tell me that she's got alcohol in her system and it turns out that it's a drug instead, whatever we give her could backfire and make her even worse. You get that?"

By then, just outside the shower stall, Paulie had wrestled Magda out of her shirt. There were tracks up and down her arms. "If it's tequila, then they've been shooting it up. Coma cocktail?"

I took the Narcan out of the paramedic bag and handed Paulie the equipment for a micro-drip. "So, um," the boy said, "you're not going to tell the cops, are you?"

In one quick move, I grabbed him by the neck of his shirt and pushed him up against the wall. "Are you that fucking stupid?"

"It's just that my parents will kill me."

"You didn't seem to care much if you killed yourself. Or her." I jerked his head toward the girl, who by then was vomiting all over the floor. "You think life is something you can throw out like a piece of trash? You think you OD, and get a sec-ond chance?"

I was yelling hard into his face. I felt a hand on my shoulder—Paulie. "Step down, Cap," he said under his breath.

Slowly I realized that the kid was trembling in front of me, that he really had nothing to do with the reason I was yelling. I walked away to clear my head. Paulie finished up with the patient and then came back to me. "You know, if it's too much, we can cover for you," he offered. "The chief'll give you as much time off as you want."

"I need to work." Over his shoulder I could see the girl pinking up; the boy sobbing into his hands beside her. I looked Paulie in the eye. "When I'm not here," I explained, "I have to be there."

The lawyer and I finish up our coffee. "Second cup?" I offer.

"I'd better not. I have to get back to the office."

We nod at each other, but there is really nothing left to say. "Don't worry about Anna," I add. "I'll make sure she gets whatever she needs."

"You might want to check in at home, too," Alexander says. "I just got your son released on PR bail for stealing a judge's Humvee."

He puts his coffee cup in the sink and leaves me holding this information, knowing sooner or later, it will force me to my knees.

SARA

1997

NO MATTER HOW MANY TIMES you drive to the emergency room, it never becomes routine. Brian carries our daughter in his arms, blood running down her face. The triage nurse waves us inside, shepherds the other kids to the bank of plastic chairs where they can wait. A resident comes into the cubicle, all business. "What happened?"

"She went over the handlebars of her bike," I said. "She landed on concrete. There doesn't seem to be any evidence of concussion, but there's a scalp lac at the hairline of about an inch and a half."

The doctor lays her down gently on the table, snaps on gloves, and peers at her forehead. "Are you a doctor or a nurse?"

I try to smile. "Just used to this."

It takes eighty-two stitches to sew up the gash. Afterward, with a bright white patch of gauze taped to her head, and a hefty dose of pediatric Tylenol swimming through her veins, we walk out to the waiting area, hand in hand.

Jesse asks her how many stitches she needed. Brian tells her she was just as brave as a firefighter. Kate glances at Anna's fresh bandage. "I like it better when I get to sit out here," she says.

It starts when Kate screams in the bathroom. I race upstairs and jimmy the lock to find my nine-year-old standing in front of a toilet spattered with blood. Blood runs down her legs, too, and has soaked through her underpants. This is the calling card for APL—hemorrhage in all sorts of masks and disguises. Kate's had rectal bleeding before, but she was a toddler; she would not remember. "It's all right," I say calmly.

I get a warm washcloth to clean her up,

and find a sanitary napkin for her under-wear. I watch her try to position the bulk of the pad between her legs. This is the moment I would have had with her when she got her period; will she live long enough for that?

"Mom," Kate says. "It's back."

"Clinical relapse." Dr. Chance takes off his glasses and presses his thumbs to the cor-ners of his eyes. "I think a bone marrow transplant's the way to go."

My mind jumps to a memory of an inflat-able Bozo punching bag I had when I was Anna's age; filled with sand at the bottom, I'd whack it only to have it pop back up.

"But a few months ago," Brian says, "you told us they were dangerous."

"They are. Fifty percent of patients who receive BMTs are cured. The other half don't survive the chemo and the radiation leading up to the transplant. Some are killed by the complications they develop after the trans-plant's done."

Brian looks at me, and then speaks the fear that ripples between us. "Then why would we even put Kate at risk?"

"Because if you don't," Dr. Chance explains, "she will die."

The first time I call the insurance company, they hang up on me by mistake. The second time, I wait through Muzak for twenty-two minutes before reaching a customer service representative. "Can I have your policy number?"

I give her the one all municipal employees get, and Brian's Social Security number. "How can I help you?"

"I spoke to someone there a week ago," I explain. "My daughter has leukemia, and needs a bone marrow transplant. The hospital explained that our insurance company needs to sign off on coverage."

A bone marrow transplant costs from $100,000 upward. Needless to say, we don't have that kind of cash lying around. But just because a doctor has recommended the transplant doesn't mean that our insurance company will agree.

"That sort of procedure needs a special review—"

"Yes, I know. That's where we were a week ago. I'm calling because I haven't heard back from you yet."

She puts me on hold, so that she can look up my file. I hear a subtle click, and then the tinny voice of a recorded operator. **If you'd like to make a call . . .**

"Shit!" I slam down the phone.

Anna, vigilant, pokes her head around the doorway. "You said a bad word."

"I know." I pick up the receiver and hit the redial button. I wind my way through the touch-tone menu. Finally, I reach a living person. "I was just disconnected. Again."

It takes this rep five more minutes to take down all the same numbers and names and history I have already given her predecessors. "We actually **have** reviewed your daughter's case," the woman says. "Unfortunately, at this time, we don't think that procedure is in her best interests."

I feel heat rush to my face. "Is dying?"

In preparation for the bone marrow harvest, I have to give Anna ongoing growth factor shots, just like I once gave Kate after her initial cord blood transplant. The intent is to hyper-pack Anna's marrow, so that when it is time to withdraw the cells, there will be plenty for Kate.

Anna has been told this, too, but all she knows is that twice a day, her mother has to give her a shot.

We use EMLA cream, a topical anesthetic. The cream is supposed to keep her from feeling the prick of the needle, but she still yells. I wonder if it hurts as much as having your six-year-old stare you in the eye and say she hates you.

"Mrs. Fitzgerald," the insurance company's customer service supervisor says, "we appreciate where you're coming from. Truly."

"Somehow, I find that very hard to believe,"

I say. "Somehow I doubt that you have a daughter in a life-or-death situation, and that your advisory board isn't looking solely at the bottom line cost of a transplant." I have told myself that I will not lose my temper, and already thirty seconds into this phone call with the insurance company, I have ceded the battle.

"AmeriLife will pay ninety percent of what's considered reasonable and customary for a donor lymphocyte infusion. However, should you still choose to do a bone marrow transplant, we are willing to cover ten percent of the costs."

I take a deep breath. "The doctors on your board who recommended this—what's their specialty?"

"I don't—"

"It's not acute promyelocytic leukemia, though, is it? Because even an oncologist who graduated last in his class from some hack medical school in Guam could probably tell you that a DLI isn't going to work as a cure. That three months from now, we'll be having this same discussion again. Plus, if you'd asked a doctor who had any familiarity with my daughter's particular disease burden, he'd tell you that repeating a treatment that's already been tried is highly unlikely to produce results in an APL patient, because they develop a resistance. Which means that AmeriLife is basically agreeing to throw money down a toilet, but not to spend it on the one thing that might actually have a chance of saving my child's life."

There is a pregnant bubble of silence on the other end of the phone. "Mrs. Fitzgerald," the supervisor suggests, "it is my understanding that if you follow this protocol, the insurance company would have no problems then paying for the transplant."

"Except that my daughter might not be alive by then to get it. We aren't talking about a car, where we can try a used part first and if it doesn't work, get a new one shipped in. We're talking about a human being. A human being. Do you automatons there even know what the hell that is?"

This time, I'm expecting the click when I am disconnected.

• • •

Zanne shows up the night before we are due to go to the hospital to begin Kate's preparatory transplant regimen. She lets Jesse help her set up her portable office, takes a phone call from Australia, and then comes into the kitchen so that Brian and I can catch her up on daily routines. "Anna's got gymnastics on Tuesday," I tell her. "Three o'clock. And I expect the oil truck to come sometime this week."

"The trash goes out on Wednesday," Brian adds.

"**Don't** walk Jesse into school. Apparently, that's anathema for sixth-graders."

She nods and listens and even takes notes, and then says she has a couple of questions. "The fish . . ."

"Gets fed twice a day. Jesse can do it, if you remind him."

"Is there an official bedtime?" Zanne asks.

"Yeah," I reply. "Do you want me to give you the real one, or the one you can use if you're going to tack on an extra hour as a special treat?"

"Anna's eight o'clock," Brian says. "Jesse's ten. Anything else?"

"Yes." Zanne reaches into her pocket and takes out a check made out to us, for $100,000.

"Suzanne," I say, stunned. "We can't take that."

"I know how much it costs. You can't cover it. I can. Let me."

Brian picks up the check and hands it back to her. "Thank you," he says. "But actually, we've got the transplant covered."

This is news to me. "We do?"

"The guys at the station sent out a call to arms, nationwide, and got a bunch of donations from other firefighters." Brian looks at me. "I just found out today."

"Really?" Inside me a weight lifts.

He shrugs. "They're my brothers," he explains.

I turn to Zanne and hug her. "Thank you. For even offering."

"It's here if you need it," she answers.

But we don't. We are able to do this, at least.

• • •

"Kate!" I call the next morning. "It's time to go!"

Anna is curled on Zanne's lap on the couch. She pulls her thumb out of her mouth but she doesn't say good-bye.

"Kate!" I yell again. "We're leaving!"

Jesse smirks over his Nintendo controls. "Like you'd really take off without her."

"**She** doesn't know that. Kate!" Sighing, I swing up the stairs toward her bedroom.

The door is closed. With a soft knock, I push it open, and find Kate in the final throes of making her bed. The quilt is pulled tight enough to bounce a dime off its middle; the pillows have been fluffed and centered. Her stuffed animals, relics at this point, sit on the window seat in gradated succession, tallest to smallest. Even her shoes have been neatly arranged in her closet, and the mess on her desk has vanished.

"Okay." I haven't even **asked** her to clean up. "Clearly, I'm in the wrong bedroom."

She turns. "It's in case I don't come back," she says.

• • •

When I first became a parent I used to lie in bed at night and imagine the most horrible succession of maladies: the bite of a jellyfish, the taste of a poisonous berry, the smile of a dangerous stranger, the dive into a shallow pool. There are so many ways a child can be harmed that it seems nearly impossible one person alone could succeed at keeping him safe. As my children got older, the hazards only changed: inhaling glue, playing with matches, small pink pills sold behind the bleachers of the middle school. You can stay up all night and still not count all the ways to lose the people you love.

It seems to me, now that this is more than just a hypothetical, that a parent falls one of two ways when told a child has a fatal disease. Either you dissolve into a puddle, or you take the blow on the cheek and force yourself to lift your face again for more. In this, we probably look a lot like the patients.

Kate is semi-conscious on her bed, her central line tubes blooming like a fountain from her chest. The chemo has made her throw up thirty-two times, and has given her mouth sores and such bad mucositis that she sounds like a cystic fibrosis patient.

She turns to me and tries to speak, but coughs up phlegm instead. "Drown," she chokes out.

Raising the suction tube she's clutching in her hands, I clear out her mouth and throat. "I'll do it while you rest," I promise, and that is how I come to breathe for her.

An oncology ward is a battlefield, and there are definite hierarchies of command. The patients, they're the ones doing the tour of duty. The doctors breeze in and out like conquering heroes, but they need to read your child's chart to remember where they've left off from the previous visit. It is the nurses who are the seasoned sergeants—the ones who are there when your baby is shaking with such a high fever she needs to be bathed in ice, the ones who can teach you how to flush a central venous catheter, or suggest which patient floor kitchens might still have Popsicles left to be stolen, or tell you which dry cleaners know how to remove the stains of blood and chemotherapies from clothing. The nurses know the name of your daughter's stuffed walrus and show her how to make tissue paper flowers to twine around her IV stand. The doctors may be mapping out the war games, but it is the nurses who make the conflict bearable.

You get to know them as they know you, because they take the place of friends you once had in a previous life, the one before diagnosis. Donna's daughter, for example, is studying to be a vet. Ludmilla, on the graveyard shift, wears laminated pictures of Sanibel Island clipped like charms to her stethoscope, because it's where she wants to retire. Willie, the male nurse, has a weakness for chocolate and a wife expecting triplets.

One night during Kate's induction, when I have been awake for so long that my body has forgotten how to segue into sleep, I turn on the TV while she sleeps. I mute it, so that the volume won't disturb her. Robin Leach is walking through the palatial home of some-one Rich and Famous. There are gold-plated bidets and hand-carved teak beds, a pool in the shape of a butterfly. There are ten-car garages and red clay tennis courts and eleven roaming peacocks. It's a world I can't even wrap my head around—a life I would never imagine for myself.

Sort of like this one used to be.

I can't even really remember what it was like to hear a story about a mother with breast cancer or a baby born with congenital heart problems or any other medical burden, and to feel myself crack down the middle: half sympathetic, half grateful that my own family was safe. We have **become** that story, for everyone else.

I don't realize I'm crying until Donna kneels down in front of me and takes the TV remote out of my hand. "Sara," the nurse says, "can I get you something?"

I shake my head, embarrasseed to have broken down, even more ashamed to be caught. "I'm fine," I insist.

"Yeah, and I'm Hillary Clinton," she says.

She reaches for my hand and tugs me upright, drags me toward the door.

"Kate—"

"—will not even miss you," Donna finishes.

In the small kitchenette where there is coffee brewing twenty-four hours a day, she fixes a cup for each of us. "I'm sorry," I say.

"For what? Not being made of granite?"

I shake my head. "It just doesn't end." Donna nods, and because she completely understands, I find myself talking. And talking. And when I have spilled all my secrets, I take a deep breath and realize that I have been talking for an hour straight. "Oh my God," I say. "I can't believe I've wasted so much of your time."

"It wasn't a waste," Donna replies. "And besides, my shift ended a half hour ago."

My cheeks flame. "You ought to go. I'm sure you have somewhere else you'd much rather be."

But instead of leaving, Donna folds me into her ample arms. "Honey," she says, "don't we all?"

• • •

The door to the ambulatory operating suite yawns open into a small room packed with gleaming silver instruments—a mouth gilded with braces. The doctors and nurses she has met are masked and gowned, only recognizable by their eyes. Anna tugs at me until I kneel down beside her. "What if I changed my mind?" she says.

I put my hands on her shoulders. "You don't have to do this if you don't want to, but I know that Kate is counting on you. And Daddy and me."

She nods once, then slips her hand into mine. "Don't let go," she tells me.

A nurse shepherds her in the right direction, onto the table. "Wait'll you see what we've got for you, Anna." She draws a heated blanket over her.

The anesthesiologist wipes a red-tinged gauze pad around an oxygen mask. "Have you ever gone to sleep in a strawberry field?"

They work their way down Anna's body, applying gelled pads that will be hooked to monitors to track her heart and her breathing. They administer to her while she's lying on her back, although I know they will flip her over to draw marrow from her hipbones.

The anesthesiologist shows Anna the accordion mechanism on his equipment. "Can you blow up that balloon?" he asks, and places the mask over Anna's face.

All this time, she doesn't let go of my hand. Finally, her grip slackens. She fights at the last minute, her body already asleep but straining forward at the shoulders. One nurse holds Anna down; the other restrains me. "It's just the way the medicine affects the body," she explains. "You can give her a kiss now."

So I do, through my mask. I whisper a thank-you, too. I walk out of the swinging door and peel off my paper hat and booties. I watch through the postage-stamp window as Anna is rolled to her side and an impossibly long needle is lifted from a sterile tray.

Then I go upstairs to wait with Kate.

Brian sticks his head into Kate's room. "Sara," he says, exhausted, "Anna's asking for you."

But I cannot be in two places at one time. I

hold the pink emesis basin up to Kate's mouth as she vomits again. Beside me, Donna helps lower Kate back onto her pillow. "I'm a little busy right now," I say.

"Anna's asking for you," Brian repeats, that's all.

Donna looks from him to me. "We'll be fine till you get back," she promises, and after a moment, I nod.

Anna is on the pediatric floor, one that doesn't have the hermetically sealed rooms necessary for protective isolation. I hear her crying before I even enter the room. "Mommy," she sobs. "It hurts."

I sit down on the side of the bed and fold her into my arms. "I know, sweetie."

"Can you stay here?"

I shake my head. "Kate's sick. I'm going to have to go back."

Anna pulls away. "But **I'm** in the hospital," she says. "I'm in the hospital!"

Over her head, I glance at Brian. "What are they giving her for pain?"

"Very little. The nurse said they don't like to overmedicate kids."

"That's ridiculous." When I stand, Anna whimpers and grabs for me. "Be right back, honey."

I accost the first nurse I can find. Unlike the staff in oncology, these RNs are unfamiliar. "She was given Tylenol an hour ago," the woman explains. "I know she's a little uncomfortable—"

"Roxicet. Tylenol with codeine. Naproxen. And if it's not on the doctor's orders call and ask whether it can be put on there."

The nurse bristles. "With all due respect, Mrs. Fitzgerald, I do this every day, and—"

"So do I."

When I go back to Anna's room, I am carrying a pediatric dose of Roxicet, which will either relieve her aches or knock her out so that she no longer feels them. I walk in to find Brian's big hands fumbling a Lilliputian clasp on the back of a necklace, as he hangs a locket around Anna's neck. "I thought you deserved your own gift, since you were giving one to your sister," he says.

Of course Anna should be honored for donating her bone marrow. Of course she deserves recognition. But the thought of rewarding someone for their suffering, frankly, never entered my mind. We've all been doing it for so long.

They both glance up when I come through the doorway. "Look at what Daddy got me!" Anna says.

I hold out the plastic dosage cup, a poor second-best.

Shortly after ten o'clock, Brian brings Anna to Kate's room. She moves slowly, like an old woman, leaning on Brian for support. The nurses help her into a mask and gown and gloves and booties so that she can be allowed in—a compassionate breach of protocol, as children are not usually allowed to visit protective isolation.

Dr. Chance stands beside the IV pole, holding up the bag of marrow. I turn Anna so that she can see it. "That," I tell her, "is what you gave us."

Anna makes a face. "It's gross. You can have it."

"Sounds like a plan," Dr. Chance says, and the rich ruby marrow begins to feed into Kate's central line.

I place Anna on the bed. There is room for both of them, shoulder to shoulder. "Did it hurt?" Kate asks.

"Kind of." Anna points to the blood running through the plastic tubes into the slit in Kate's chest. "Does that?"

"Not really." She sits up a little. "Hey, Anna?"

"Yeah?"

"I'm glad it came from you." Kate reaches for Anna's hand and places it just below the central line's catheter, a spot that falls precariously near her heart.

Twenty-one days after the bone marrow transplant, Kate's white cell counts begin to rise, proof of engraftment. To celebrate, Brian insists that he is taking me out to dinner. He arranges for a private-duty nurse for Kate, makes reservations at XO Café, and even brings me a black dress from my closet. He forgets pumps, so I wind up wearing my scruffy hiking clogs with it.

The restaurant is nearly full. Almost immediately after we are seated, the sommelier comes to ask if we want wine. Brian orders a Cabernet Sauvignon.

"Do you even know whether that's red or white?" I do not think, in all these years, I have seen Brian drink anything but beer.

"I know it's got alcohol in it, and I know we're celebrating." He lifts his glass after the sommelier pours it. "To our family," he toasts.

We click glasses and take sips. "What are you getting?" I ask.

"What do you want me to get?"

"The filet. That way I can taste it if I get the sole." I fold my menu. "Did you hear the results of the last CBC?"

Brian looks down at the table. "I was sort of hoping that we could come here to get away from all that. You know. Just talk."

"I'd like to talk," I admit. But when I look at Brian, the information that leaps to my lips is about Kate, not us. I have no call to ask him about his day—he has taken three weeks off from the station. We are connected by and through sickness.

We fall back into silence. I look around XO Café and notice that chatter happens mostly at tables where the diners are young and hip. The older couples, the ones sporting wedding bands that wink with their silverware, eat without the pepper of conversation. Is it because they are so comfortable, they already know what the other is thinking? Or is it because after a certain point, there is simply nothing left to say?

When the waiter arrives to take our order, we both turn eagerly, grateful for someone who keeps us from having to recognize the strangers we have become.

We leave the hospital with a child who is different from the one we brought in. Kate moves cautiously, checking the drawers of the nightstand for anything she might have left behind. She has lost so much weight that the jeans I brought do not fit; we have to use two bandannas knotted together as a makeshift belt.

Brian has gone down ahead of us to bring the car around. I zip the last Tiger Beat and CD into Kate's duffel bag. She pulls a fleece cap on over her smooth, bare scalp and winds a scarf tight around her neck. She puts on a mask and gloves; now that we are venturing out of the hospital, **she** is the one who will need protection.

We walk out the door to the applause of the nurses we have come to know so well. "Whatever you do, **don't** come back and see us, all right?" Willie jokes.

One by one, they walk up to say their good-byes. When they have all dispersed, I smile at Kate. "Ready?"

Kate nods, but she doesn't step forward. She stands rigid, fully aware that once she sets foot outside this doorway, everything changes. "Mom?"

I fold her hand into mine. "We'll do it together," I promise, and side by side, we take the first step.

• • •

The mail is full of hospital bills. We have learned that the insurance company will not talk to the hospital billing department, and vice versa, but neither one thinks that the charges are accurate—which leads them to charge us for procedures we shouldn't have to cover, in the hopes that we are stupid enough to pay them. Managing the monetary aspect of Kate's care is a full-time job that neither Brian nor I can do.

I leaf through a grocery store flyer, an AAA magazine, and a long-distance rate announcement before I open the letter from the mutual fund. It's not something I really pay attention to; Brian usually manages finances that require more than basic checkbook balancing. Besides, the three funds we have are all earmarked for the kids' education. We are not the sort of family that has enough spare change to play the stock market.

Dear Mr. Fitzgerald:

This is to confirm your recent redemption from fund #323456, Brian D. Fitzgerald Custodian for Katherine S.

Fitzgerald, in the amount of $8,369.56. This disbursement effectively closes the account.

As banking errors go, this is a pretty major one. We've been off by pennies in our checking account, but at least I've never lost eight thousand dollars. I walk out of the kitchen and into the yard, where Brian is rolling an extra garden hose. "Well, either someone at the mutual fund screwed up," I say, handing the letter to him, "or the second wife you're supporting is no longer a secret."

It takes him one moment too long to read it, the same moment that I realize that this is not a mistake after all. Brian wipes his forehead with the back of one wrist. "I took that money out," he says.

"Without telling me?" I cannot imagine Brian doing such a thing. There have been times, in the past, where we dipped into the children's accounts, but only because we were having a month too tight to swing the cost of groceries and the mortgage, or because we needed the down payment for a new car when our old one had finally been put to rest. We'd lie awake in bed feeling guilt press down like an extra quilt, promising each other that we would put that money right back where it belonged as soon as humanly possible.

"The guys at the station, they tried to raise some money, like I told you. They got ten thousand dollars. With this added to it, the hospital's willing to work out some kind of payment plan for us."

"But you said—"

"I know what I said, Sara."

I shake my head, stunned. "You **lied** to me?"

"I didn't—"

"Zanne offered—"

"I won't let your sister take care of Kate," Brian says. "**I'm** supposed to take care of Kate." The hose falls to the ground, dribbles and spits at our feet. "Sara, she's not going to live long enough to use that money for college."

The sun is bright; the sprinkler twitches on the grass, spraying rainbows. It is far too beautiful a day for words like these. I turn and run into the house. I lock myself in the bathroom.

A moment later, Brian bangs on the door. "Sara? Sara, I'm sorry."

I pretend I can't hear him. I pretend I haven't heard anything he's said.

At home, we all wear masks so that Kate doesn't have to. I find myself checking her fingernails while she brushes her teeth or pours cereal, to see if the dark ridges made by the chemo have disappeared—a sure sign of the bone marrow transplant's success. Twice a day I give Kate growth factor shots in the thigh, a necessity until her neutrophil count tops one thousand. At that point, the marrow will be reseeding itself.

She can't go back to school yet, so we get her lessons sent home. Once or twice she has come with me to pick Anna up from kindergarten, but refuses to get out of the car. She will troop to the hospital for her routine CBC, but if I suggest a side trip to the video store or Dunkin' Donuts afterward, she begs off.

One Saturday morning, the door to the girls' bedroom is ajar; I knock gently. "Want to go to the mall?"

Kate shrugs. "Not now."

I lean against the doorframe. "It'll be good to get out of the house."

"I don't want to." Although I am sure she does not even realize she is doing it, she skims her palm over her head before tucking her hand into her back pocket.

"Kate," I begin.

"Don't say it. Don't tell me that nobody's going to stare at me, because they will. Don't tell me it doesn't matter, because it does. And don't tell me I look fine because that's a lie." Her eyes, lash-bare, fill with tears. "I'm a freak, Mom. **Look** at me."

I do, and I see the spots where her brows have gone missing, and the slope of her endless brow, and the small divots and bumps that are usually hidden under a cover of hair. "Well," I say evenly. "We can fix this."

Without another word, I walk out of her room, knowing Kate will follow. I pass Anna, who abandons her coloring book to trail behind her sister. In the basement, I pull out a pair of ancient electric grooming clippers we found when we bought the house, and plug them in. Then I cut a swath right down the middle of my scalp.

"Mom!" Kate gasps.

"What?" A tumble of brown waves falls onto Anna's shoulder; she picks them up delicately. "It's only hair."

With another swipe of the razor, Kate starts to smile. She points out a spot that I've missed, where a small thatch stands like a forest. I sit down on an overturned milk crate and let her shave the other side of my head herself. Anna crawls onto my lap. "Me next," she begs.

An hour later, we walk through the mall holding hands, a trio of bald girls. We stay for hours. Everywhere we go, heads turn and voices whisper. We are beautiful, times three.

THE WEEKEND

There is no fire without some smoke.

—JOHN HEYWOOD, **Proverbes**

JESSE

DON'T DENY IT—you've driven by a bulldozer or front-end loader on the side of a
highway, after hours, and wondered why the
road crews leave the equipment out there
where anyone, meaning me, could steal it. My
first truckjacking was years ago; I put a
cement mixer out of gear on a slope and
watched it roll into a construction company's
base trailer. Right now there's a dump truck a
mile away from my house; I've seen it sleeping
like a baby elephant next to a pile of Jersey
barriers on I-195. Not my first choice of
wheels, but beggars can't be choosers; in the
wake of my little run-in with the law, my
father's taken my car into custody, and is
keeping it at the fire station.

Driving a dump truck turns out to be a hell

of a lot different than driving my car. First, you fill up the whole freaking road. Second, it handles like a tank, or at least like what I suppose a tank would handle like if you didn't have to join an army full of uptight, power-crazy assholes to drive one. Third—and least palatable—people see you coming. When I roll up to the underpass where Duracell Dan makes his cardboard home, he cowers behind his line of thirty-three-gallon drums. "Hey," I say, swinging out of the cab of the truck. "It's just me."

It still takes Dan a minute to peek between his hands, make sure I'm telling him the truth. "Like my rig?" I ask.

He gets up gingerly and touches the streaked side of the truck. Then he laughs. "Your Jeep been taking steroids, boy."

I load up the rear of the cab with the materials I need. How cool would it be if I just backed the truck up to a window, dumped in several bottles of my Arsonist's Special, and drove away with the place bursting into flames? Dan stands by the driver's-side door. **Wash Me,** he writes across the grit.

"Hey," I say, and for no reason except the fact that I've never done it before, I ask him if he wants to come.

"For real?"

"Yeah. But there's a rule. Whatever you see and whatever we do, you can't tell anyone about it."

He pretends to lock up his lips and toss the key. Five minutes later, we're on our way to an old shed that used to be a boathouse for one of the colleges. Dan fiddles with the controls, raising and lowering the truck bed while we're tooling along. I tell myself that I've invited him along to add to the thrill—one more person who knows only makes it more exciting. But it's really because there are some nights when you just want to know there's someone else besides you in this wide world.

When I was eleven years old I got a skateboard. I never asked for one; it was a guilt gift. Over the years I got quite a few of these big ticket items, usually in conjunction with one of Kate's episodes. My parents would shower her with all kinds of cool shit whenever she had to have something done to her; and since Anna was usually involved, she got some amazing presents, too, and then a week later my parents would feel bad about the inequality and would buy me some toy to make sure I didn't feel left out.

Anyway, I cannot even begin to tell you how amazing that skateboard was. It had a skull on the bottom that glowed in the dark, and from the teeth dripped green blood. The wheels were neon yellow and the gritty surface, when you stepped on it in your sneakers, made the sound of a rock star clearing his throat. I skimmed it up and down the driveway, around the sidewalks, learning how to pop wheelies and kickflips and ollies. There was only one rule: I wasn't supposed to take it into the street, because cars could come around at any minute; kids could get hit in an instant.

Well, I don't need to tell you that eleven-year-old budding derelicts and house rules are like oil and water. By the end of my first week with this board I thought I'd rather slide down a razor blade into alcohol than tool up and down the sidewalk yet one more time with all the toddlers on their Big Wheels.

I begged my father to take me to the Kmart parking lot, or the school basketball court, or anywhere, really, where I could play around a little. He promised me that on Friday, after Kate had a routine bone marrow aspiration, we could all go out to the school. I could bring my skateboard, Anna could bring her bike, and if Kate felt up to it, she could Rollerblade.

God, was I looking forward to that. I greased the wheels and polished up the bottom of the skateboard and practiced a double helix on the driveway ramp I'd made of old scrap plywood and a fat log. The minute I saw the car—my mom and Kate returning from the hematologist—I ran out to the porch so we wouldn't waste any time.

My mother, it turned out, was in a huge hurry, too. Because the door to the van slid open and there was Kate, covered with blood. "Get your father," my mother ordered, holding a wad of tissues up to Kate's face.

It wasn't like she hadn't had nosebleeds

before. And my mom was always telling me, when it freaked me out, that the bleeding looked way worse than it actually was. But I got my father, and the two of them hustled Kate into the bathroom and tried to keep her from crying, because it only made everything harder.

"Dad," I said. "When are we going?"

But he was busy wadding up toilet paper, bunching it up under Kate's nose.

"Dad?" I repeated.

My father looked right at me, but he didn't answer. And his eyes were dazed and staring through me, like I was made out of smoke.

That was the first time I thought that maybe I was.

The thing about flame is that it's insidious—it sneaks, it licks, it looks over its shoulder and laughs. And fuck, it's beautiful. Like a sunset eating everything in its path. For the first time, I have someone to admire my handiwork. Beside me, Dan makes a small sound at the back of his throat—respect, no doubt. But when I look at him, proud, I see that he's got his head ducked into the greasy collar of his army-surplus coat. He's got tears running down his face.

"Dan, man, what's going on?" Granted, the guy is nuts, but still. I put my hand on his shoulder and you'd think, from his reaction, that a scorpion just landed there. "You scared of the fire, Danny? You don't have to be. We're far enough away. We're safe." I give him what I hope is an encouraging smile. What if he freaks out and starts screaming, calls down some wandering cop?

"That shed," Dan says.

"Yeah. No one's gonna miss it."

"That's where the rat lives."

"Not anymore," I answer.

"But the rat . . ."

"Animals make their own way out of a fire. I'm telling you. The rat will be totally cool. Chill."

"But what about the newspapers? He has one with President Kennedy's assassination . . ."

It occurs to me that the rat is most likely not a rodent, but another homeless guy. One using this shed as a shelter. "Dan, are you saying someone lives in there?"

He looks at the crowning flames and his eyes fill. Then he repeats my own words. "Not anymore," he says.

Like I said, I was eleven, so even to this day I can't tell you how I made my way from our house in Upper Darby to the middle of downtown Providence. I suppose it took me a few hours; I suppose I believed that with my new superhero's cloak of invisibility, maybe I could just disappear and reappear somewhere else entirely.

I tested myself. I walked through the business district, and sure enough, people passed right by me, their eyes on the cracks of the pavement or staring straight ahead like corporate zombies. I walked by a long wall of mirrored glass on the side of a building, where I could see myself. But no matter how many faces I made, no matter how long I stood there, none of the people funneling around me had anything to say.

I wound up that day at the middle of an intersection, smack under the traffic light, with taxis honking and a car swerving off to the left and a pair of cops running to keep me from getting killed. At the police station, when my dad came to get me, he asked what the hell I'd been thinking.

I hadn't been thinking, actually. I was just trying to get to a place where I'd be noticed.

First I take off my shirt and dunk it into a puddle on the side of the road; then wrap it around my head and face. The smoke is already billowing, angry black clouds. In the hollow of my ear is the sound of sirens. But I have made a promise to Dan.

What hits me first is the heat, a wall that's way more solid than it looks. The frame of the shed stands out, an orange X ray. Inside, I can't see a foot in front of me.

"Rat," I yell out, already regretting the smoke that leaves me raw-throated and hoarse. "Rat!"

No answer. But the shed isn't all that big. I get down on my hands and knees and begin to feel my way around.

I only have one really bad moment, when I

put my hand down by accident on something that was made of metal before it became a searing brand. My skin sticks to it, blisters immediately. By the time I fall over a booted foot I'm sobbing, sure I will never get out. I feel my way up Rat, haul his limp body over my shoulder, stagger back the way I came.

Through some little joke of God, we make it outside. By now, the engines are pulling up, charging their lines. Maybe my father is even here. I stay under the screen of smoke; I dump Rat on the ground. With my heart racing, I run in the other direction; leaving the rest of this res-cue to people who actually want to be heroes.

ANNA

DID YOU EVER WONDER how we all got here? On Earth, I mean. Forget the song and dance about Adam and Eve, which I know is a load of crap. My father likes the myth of the Pawnee Indians, who say that the star deities populated the world: Evening Star and Morning Star hooked up and gave birth to the first female. The first boy came from the Sun and the Moon. Humans rode in on the back of a tornado.

Mr. Hume, my science teacher, taught us about this primordial soup full of natural gases and muddy slop and carbon matter that somehow solidified into one-celled organisms called choanoflagellates . . . which sound a lot more like a sexually transmitted disease than the start of the evolutionary chain, in my opinion. But even once you get there, it's a huge leap from an amoeba to a monkey to a whole thinking person.

The really amazing thing about all this is no matter what you believe, it took some doing to get from a point where there was nothing, to a point where all the right neurons fire and pop so that we can make decisions.

More amazing is how even though that's become second nature, we all still manage to screw it up.

On Saturday morning, I am at the hospital with Kate and my mother, all of us doing our best to pretend that two days from now, my trial won't begin. You'd think this is hard, but actually, it's much easier than the alternative. My family is famous for lying to ourselves by omission: if we don't talk about it, then—**presto!**—there's no more lawsuit, no more kidney failure, no worries at all.

I'm watching **Happy Days** on the TVLand channel. Those Cunninghams, they're not so different from us. All they ever seem to worry about is whether Richie's band will be hired at

Al's place, or if Fonzie will win the kissing con-test, when even I know that in the '50s Joanie should have been having air raid drills at school and Marion was probably popping Valium and Howard would have been freaking out about commie attacks. Maybe if you spend your life pretending you're on a movie set, you don't ever have to admit that the walls are made out of paper and the food is plastic and the words in your mouth aren't really yours.

Kate is trying to do a crossword puzzle. "What's a four-letter word for vessel?" she asks.

Today is a good day. By this I mean she feels up to yelling at me for borrowing two of her CDs without asking (for God's sake, she was practically comatose; it isn't like she would have been able to give her permission); she feels up to trying this crossword.

"Vat," I suggest. "Urn."

"Four letters."

"Ship," my mother offers. "Maybe they're thinking of that kind."

"Blood," Dr. Chance says, coming into the room.

"That's five letters," Kate replies, in a tone

that's much more pleasant than the one she used with me, I might add.

We all like Dr. Chance; by now, he might as well be the sixth member of our family.

"Give me a number." He means on the pain scale. "Five?"

"Three."

Dr. Chance sits down on the edge of her bed. "It may be a five in an hour," he cautions. "It may be a nine."

My mother's face has gone the color of an eggplant. "But Kate's feeling great right now!" she cheerleads.

"I know. But the lucid moments, they're going to get briefer and further apart," Dr. Chance explains. "This isn't the APL. This is renal failure."

"But after a transplant—" my mother says.

All the air in the room, I swear, turns into a sponge. You'd be able to hear a hummingbird's wings, that's how quiet it gets. I want to slink out of the room like mist; I don't want this to be my fault.

Dr. Chance is the only one brave enough to look at me. "As I understand it, Sara, the availability of an organ is under debate."

"But—"

"Mom," Kate interrupts. She turns to Dr. Chance. "How long are we talking about?"

"A week, maybe."

"Wow," she says softly. "Wow." She touches the edge of the newspaper, rubs her thumb over the point at its edge. "Will it hurt?"

"No," Dr. Chance promises. "I will make sure of that."

Kate lays the paper in her lap and touches his arm. "Thanks. For the truth, I mean."

When Dr. Chance looks up, his eyes are red-rimmed. "Don't thank me." He gets up so heavily that I think he must be made of stone, and leaves the room without speaking another word.

My mother, she folds into herself, that's the only way to explain it. Like paper, when you put it deep into the fireplace, and instead of burning, it simply seems to vanish.

Kate looks at me, and then down at all the tubes that anchor her to the bed. So I get up and walk toward my mother. I put a hand on her shoulder. "Mom," I say. "Stop."

She lifts her head and looks at me with haunted eyes. "No, Anna. **You** stop."

It takes me a little while, but I break away. **"Anna,"** I murmur.

My mother turns. "What?"

"A four-letter word for vessel," I say, and I walk out of Kate's room.

Later that afternoon, I'm turning in circles on the swivel chair in my dad's office at the fire station, with Julia sitting across from me. On the desk are a half-dozen pictures of my family. There's one with Kate as a baby, wearing a knit hat that looks like a strawberry. Another with Jesse and me, grinning just as wide as the bluefish balanced between our hands. I used to wonder about the fake pictures that came in frames you buy at the store—ladies with smooth brown hair and show-me smiles, grapefruit-headed babies on their sibling's knees—people who in real life probably were strangers brought together by a talent scout to be a phony family.

Maybe it's not so different from real photos, after all.

I pick up one picture that shows my mother and father looking tanned and younger than I can ever remember them being. "Do you have a boyfriend?" I ask Julia.

"No!" she says, way too fast. When I glance up, she just sort of shrugs. "Do you?"

"There's this one guy, Kyle McFee, that I thought I liked but now I'm not sure." I pick up a pen and start to unscrew the whole thing, pull out the skinny little tube of blue ink. It would be so cool to have one of these built inside you, like a squid; you could point your finger and leave your mark on anything you wanted.

"What happened?"

"I went to a movie with him, like on a date, and when it was over and we stood up he was—" I turn bright red. "Well, you know." I wave in the general vicinity of my lap.

"Ah," Julia says.

"He asked me whether I'd ever taken wood shop at school—I mean, God, **wood** shop?— and I go to tell him no and bam, I'm staring **right there."** I put the decapitated pen down on my dad's blotter. "When I see him now around town it's all I can think about." I stare up at her, a thought coming at me. "Am I a pervert?"

"No, you're thirteen. And for the record, so

is Kyle. He couldn't help it happening any more than you can help thinking about it when you see him. My brother Anthony used to say there were only two times a guy could get excited: during the day, and during the night."

"Your brother used to talk to you about stuff like that?"

She laughs. "I guess so. Why, wouldn't Jesse?"

I snort. "If I asked Jesse a question about sex, he'd laugh so hard he'd bust a rib, and then he'd give me a stash of Playboys and tell me to do research."

"How about your parents?"

I shake my head. My dad is out of the question—because he's my dad. My mom's too distracted. And Kate is in the same clueless boat I'm in. "Did you and your sister ever fight over the same guy?"

"Actually, we don't go for the same type."

"What's your type?"

She thinks about it. "I don't know. Tall. Dark-haired. Breathing."

"Do you think Campbell's cute?"

Julia nearly falls out of her chair. "What?"

"Well, I mean, for an **older** guy."

"I could see where some women . . . might find him attractive," she says.

"He looks like a character on one of the soaps that Kate likes." I run my thumbnail into the groove of wood on the desk. "It's weird. That I get to grow up and kiss someone and get married."

And Kate doesn't.

Julia leans forward. "What's going to happen if your sister dies, Anna?"

One of the pictures on the desk is of me and Kate. We are little—maybe five and two. It is before her first relapse, but after her hair grew back. We're standing on the edge of a beach, wearing matching bathing suits, playing patty-cake. You could fold this picture in half and think it was a mirror image—Kate small for her age and me tall; Kate's hair a different color but with the same natural part and flip at the bottom; Kate's hands pressed up against mine. Until now, I don't think I've really realized how much alike we are.

The phone rings just before ten o'clock that night, and to my surprise it's my name that's paged throughout the firehouse. I pick up the extension in the kitchen area, which has been cleaned and mopped for the night. "Hello?"

"Anna," my mother says.

Immediately, I assume she's calling about Kate. There isn't much else for her to say to me, given the way we left things earlier at the hospital. "Is everything okay?"

"Kate's asleep."

"That's good," I reply, and then wonder if it really is.

"I called for two reasons. The first is to say that I'm sorry about this morning."

I feel very small. "Me too," I admit. In that minute, I remember how she used to tuck me in at night. She'd go to Kate's bed first, and lean down, and announce that she was kissing Anna. And then she'd come to my bed and say she'd come to hug Kate. Every time, it cracked us up. She'd turn off the light, and for long moments after she left, the room still smelled of the lotion she used on her skin to keep it as soft as the inside of a flannel pillowcase.

"The second reason I called," my mother says, "was just to say good night."

"That's all?"

In her voice, I can hear a smile. "Isn't that enough?"

"Sure," I tell her, although it isn't.

Because I can't fall asleep, I slip out of my bed at the fire station, past my father, who's snoring. I steal the **Guinness Book of World Records** from the men's room and lie down on the roof of the station to read by moonlight. An eighteen-month-old baby named Alejandro fell 65 feet 7 inches from the window of his parents' apartment in Murcia, Spain, and became the infant to survive the longest fall. Roy Sullivan, of Virginia, survived seven lightning strikes, only to commit suicide after being spurned by a lover. A cat was found in rubble eighty days after a Taiwanese earthquake that killed 2,000, and made a full recovery. I find myself reading and rereading the section called "Survivors and Lifesavers," adding listings in my head. **Longest surviving APL patient,** it would read. **Most ecstatic sister.**

My father finds me when I have put the book aside and started searching for Vega. "Can't see much tonight, huh?" he asks, taking a seat beside me. It is a night wrapped in clouds; even the moon seems covered with cotton.

"Nope," I say. "Everything's fuzzy."

"You try the telescope?"

I watch him fiddle with the scope for a while, and then decide that it's just not worth it tonight. I suddenly remember being about seven, riding beside him in the car, and asking him how grown-ups found their way to places. After all, I had never seen him pull out a map.

"I guess we just get used to taking the same turns," he said, but I wasn't satisfied.

"Then what about the first time you go somewhere?"

"Well," he said, "we get directions."

But what I want to know is who got them the **very** first time? What if no one's ever been where you're going? "Dad?" I ask, "is it true that you can use stars like a map?"

"Yeah, if you understand celestial navigation."

"Is it hard?" I'm thinking maybe I should learn. A backup plan, for all those times I feel like I'm just wandering in circles.

"It's pretty jazzy math—you have to measure the altitude of a star, figure out its position using a nautical almanac, figure out what you **think** the altitude should be and what direction the star should be in based on where you think you are, and compare the altitude you measured with the one you calculated. Then you plot this on a chart, as a line of position. You get several lines of position to cross, and that's where you go." My father takes one look at my face and smiles. "Exactly," he laughs. "Never leave home without your GPS."

But I bet I could figure it out; it isn't really all that confusing. You head toward the place where all those different positions cross, and you hope for the best.

If there was a religion of Annaism, and I had to tell you how humans made their way to Earth, it would go like this: in the beginning, there was nothing at all but the moon and the sun. And the moon wanted to come out during the day, but there was something so much brighter that seemed to fill up all those hours. The moon grew hungry, thinner and thinner, until she was just a slice of herself, and her tips were as sharp as a knife. By accident, because that is the way most things happen, she poked a hole in the night and out spilled a million stars, like a fountain of tears.

Horrified, the moon tried to swallow them up. And sometimes this worked, because she got fatter and rounder. But mostly it didn't, because there were just so many. The stars kept coming, until they made the sky so bright that the sun got jealous. He invited the stars to his side of the world, where it was always bright. What he didn't tell them, though, was that in the daytime, they'd never be seen. So the stupid ones leaped from the sky to the ground, and they froze under the weight of their own foolishness.

The moon did her best. She carved each of these blocks of sorrow into a man or a woman. She spent the rest of her time watching out so that her other stars wouldn't fall. She spent the rest of her time holding on to whatever scraps she had left.

BRIAN

JUST BEFORE SEVEN A.M. on Sunday, an octopus walks into the station. Well, it is actually a woman dressed like an octopus, but when you see something like that, distinctions hardly matter. She has tears running down her face and holds a Pekingese dog in her multiple arms. "You have to help me," she says, and that's when I remember: this is Mrs. Zegna, whose house was gutted by a kitchen fire a few days ago.

She plucks at her tentacles. "This is the only clothing I have left. A Halloween costume. Ursula. It's been rotting in a U-Store-It locker in Taunton with my Peter Paul and Mary album collection."

I gently sit her down in the chair across from my desk. "Mrs. Zegna, I know your house is uninhabitable—"

"Uninhabitable? It's **wrecked!**"

"I can put you in touch with a shelter. And if

you like, I can speak to your insurance company to expedite things."

She lifts one arm to wipe her eyes, and eight others, drawn by strings, rise in unison. "I don't have home insurance. I don't believe in living my life expecting the worst."

I stare at her for a moment. I try to remember what it is like to be taken aback by the very possibility of disaster.

When I get to the hospital, Kate is lying on her back, holding tight to a stuffed bear she's had since she was seven. She's hooked up to one of those patient-managed morphine drips, and her thumb pushes down on the button every now and then, although she is fast asleep.

One of the chairs in the room folds out into a cot with a mattress thin as a wafer; this is where Sara is curled. "Hey," she says, pushing her hair out of her eyes. "Where's Anna?"

"Still sleeping like only a kid can. How was Kate's night?"

"Not bad. She was in a little pain between two and four."

I sit down on the edge of her cot. "It meant a lot to Anna, you calling last night."

When I look into Sara's eyes, I see Jesse—they have the same coloring, the same features. I wonder if Sara looks at me and thinks of Kate. I wonder if that hurts.

It is hard to believe that once, this woman and I sat in a car and drove the entire length of Route 66, and never ran out of things to say. Our conversations now are an economy of facts, full of blue chip details and insider information.

"Do you remember that fortune-teller?" I ask. When she looks at me blankly, I keep talking. "We were out in the middle of Nevada, and the Chevy ran out of gas . . . and you wouldn't let me leave you in the car while I looked for a service station?"

Ten days from now, when you're still walking in circles, they're going to find me with vultures eating out my insides, Sara had said, and she'd fallen into step beside me. We hiked back four miles to the shanty we'd passed, a gas station. It was run by an old guy and his sister, who advertised herself as a psychic. **Let's do it,** Sara begged, but a reading cost five bucks and I only had ten. **Then we'll get**

half the gas, and ask the psychic when we can expect to run out the next time, Sara said, and like always, she convinced me.

Madame Agnes was the kind of blind that scares children, with cataract eyes that looked like an empty blue sky. She put her knobby hands on Sara's face to read her bones, and said that she saw three babies and a long life, but that it wouldn't be good enough. **What's that supposed to mean?** Sara asked, incensed, and Madame Agnes explained that fortunes were like clay, and could be reshaped at any time. But you could only remake your own future, not anyone else's, and for some people that just wasn't good enough.

She put her hands on my face and said only one thing: **Save yourself.**

She told us we would run out of gas again just over the Colorado border, and we did.

Now, in the hospital room, Sara looks at me blankly. "When did we go to Nevada?" she asks. Then she shakes her head. "We need to talk. If Anna is really going through with this hearing on Monday, then I need to review your testimony."

"Actually." I look down at my hands. "I'm going to speak on Anna's behalf."

"What?"

With a quick glance over my shoulder to make sure Kate is still sleeping, I do my best to explain. "Sara, believe me, I've thought long and hard about this one. And if Anna's through being a donor for Kate, we've got to respect that."

"If you testify for Anna, the judge is going to say that at least one of her parents is capable of supporting this petition, and he's going to rule in her favor."

"I know that," I say. "Why else would I do it?"

We stare at each other, speechless, unwilling to admit what lies at the end of each of these roads.

"Sara," I ask finally, "what do you want from me?"

"I want to look at you and remember what it used to be like," she says thickly. "I want to go back, Brian. I want you to take me back."

But she is not the woman I used to know, the woman who traveled a countryside counting prairie dog holes, who read aloud the classifieds of lonely cowboys seeking women and told me, in the darkest crease of the night, that she would love me until the moon lost its footing in the sky.

To be fair, I am not the same man. The one who listened. The one who believed her.

SARA

2001

BRIAN AND I ARE SITTING on the couch, sharing sections of the newspaper, when Anna walks into the living room. "If I mow the lawn, like, until I get married," she asks, "can I have $614.96 right now?"

"Why?" we say simultaneously.

She rubs her sneaker into the carpet. "I need a little cash."

Brian folds the national news section. "I didn't think Gap jeans had gotten quite that expensive."

"I **knew** you'd be like this," she says, ready to huff away.

"Hang on." I sit up, rest my elbows on my knees. "What is it you want to buy?"

"What difference does it make?"

"Anna," Brian responds, "we're not forking

over six hundred bucks without knowing what it's for."

She weighs this for a minute. "It's something on eBay."

My ten-year-old surfs eBay?

"Okay," she sighs. "It's goaltender leg pads."

I look at Brian, but he doesn't seem to understand, either. "For hockey?" he says.

"Well, **duh**."

"Anna, you don't play hockey," I point out, and when she blushes, I realize this may not be the case at all.

Brian presses her into an explanation. "A couple of months ago, the chain fell off my bike right in front of the hockey rink. A bunch of guys were practicing, but their goalie had mono, and the coach said he'd pay me five bucks to stand in net and block shots. I borrowed the sick kid's equipment, and the thing is . . . I wasn't that bad at it. I **liked** it. So I kept coming back." Anna smiles shyly. "The coach asked me to join the team for real, before the tournament. I'm the first girl on it, ever. But I have to have my own equipment."

"Which costs $614?"

"And ninety-six cents. That's just the leg pads, though. I still need a chest protector and catcher and a glove and a mask." She stares at us expectantly.

"We have to talk about it," I tell her.

Anna mutters something that sounds like **Figures**, and walks out of the room.

"Did you know she was playing hockey?" Brian asks me, and I shake my head. I wonder what else my daughter has been hiding from us.

We are about to leave the house to watch Anna playing hockey for the first time when Kate announces she isn't going. "Please Mom," she begs. "Not when I look like this."

She has an angry red rash all over her cheeks, palms, soles, and chest, and a moon face, courtesy of the steroids she takes to treat it. Her skin is rough and thickened.

These are the calling cards of graft-versus-host disease, which Kate developed after her bone marrow transplant. For the past four years, it's come and gone, flaring up when we least expect it. Bone marrow is an organ, and like a heart or a liver, a body can reject it. But sometimes, instead, the transplanted marrow begins to reject the body it's been put in.

The good news is that if that happens, all the cancer cells are under siege, too—something Dr. Chance calls graft-versus-leukemia disease. The bad news is the symptomology: the chronic diarrhea, the jaundice, the loss of range of motion in her joints. The scarring and sclerosis wherever there's connective tissue. I am so accustomed to this that it doesn't phase me, but when the graft-versus-host disease flares up this badly, I let Kate stay home from school. She is thirteen, and appearance is paramount. I respect her vanity, because there is so little of it.

But I cannot leave her alone in the house, and we have promised Anna we'll come watch her play. "This is really important to your sister."

In response, Kate flops onto the couch and pulls a throw pillow over her face.

Without saying another word I walk to the hall closet and pull a variety of items from drawers. I hand the gloves to Kate, then jam the hat on her head and wind the scarf around her nose and mouth so that only her eyes are visible. "It'll be cold in the rink," I say, in a voice that leaves no room for anything but acceptance.

I barely recognize Anna, stuffed and trussed and tied into equipment that, eventually, we wound up borrowing from the coach's nephew. You cannot tell, for example, that she is the only girl on the ice. You cannot tell that she is two years younger than every other player out there.

I wonder if Anna can hear the cheering through her helmet, or if she's so focused on what's coming toward her that she blocks it all out, concentrating instead on the scrape of the puck and the smack of the sticks.

Jesse and Brian sit on the edge of their seats; even Kate—so reluctant to come—is getting into the game. The opposing goalie, compared to Anna, moves in slow motion. The action switches like a current, the play moving from the far goal toward Anna's. The center passes to the right wing, who skates for broke, his blades slicing through the roar of the cheering crowd. Anna steps forward, sure of where the puck is going a moment before it arrives, her knees bent in, her elbows pointed out.

"Unbelievable," Brian says to me after the second period. "She's got natural talent as a goalie."

That much, I could have told him. Anna saves, every time.

That night Kate wakes up with blood streaming out of her nose, her rectum, and the sockets of her eyes. I have never seen so much blood, and even as I try to stanch the flow I wonder how much of it she can stand to lose. By the time we reach the hospital, she is disoriented and agitated, finally slipping into unconsciousness. The staff pump her full of plasma, blood, and platelets to replace the lost blood, which seems to leak out of her just as quickly. They give her IV fluids to prevent hypovolemic shock, and intubate her. They take CT scans of her brain and her lungs to see how far the bleeding has spread.

In spite of all the times we have run to the

ER in the middle of the night, all the times Kate's relapsed with sudden symptoms, Brian and I know it has never been quite this bad. A nosebleed is one thing; system failure is another. Twice now, she's had cardiac arrhythmias. The hemorrhaging keeps her brain, heart, liver, lungs, and kidneys from receiving the flow they need to work.

Dr. Chance takes us into the little lounge at the end of the pediatric ICU floor. It is painted with smiley-face daisies. On one wall is a growth chart, a four-foot-tall inchworm: **How Big Can I Grow?**

Brian and I sit very still, as if we will be rewarded for good behavior. "Arsenic?" Brian repeats. "Poison?"

"It's a very new therapy," Dr. Chance explains. "You get it intravenously, for twenty-five to sixty days. To date, we haven't effected a cure with it. That's not to say it might not happen in the future, but at the moment, we don't even have five-year survival curves—that's how new the drug is. As it is, Kate's exhausted cord blood, allogeneic transplant, radiation, chemo, and ATRA. She's lived ten years past what any of us would have expected."

I find myself nodding already. "Do it," I say, and Brian looks down at his boots.

"We can try it. But in all likelihood, the hemorrhaging will still beat out the arsenic," Dr. Chance tells us.

I stare at the growth chart on the wall. Did I tell Kate I loved her before I put her to bed last night? I cannot remember. I cannot remember at all.

Shortly after two A.M., I lose Brian. He slips out when I am falling asleep beside Kate's bed and doesn't come back for over an hour. I ask for him at the nurse's desk; I search the cafeteria and the men's room, all empty. Finally I locate him at the end of the hallway, in a tiny atrium that was named in some poor dead child's honor, a room of light and air and plastic plants that a neutropenic patient could enjoy. He sits on an ugly brown corduroy couch, writing furiously with a blue crayon on a piece of scrap paper.

"Hey," I say quietly, remembering how the

kids would color together on the floor of the kitchen, crayons spilled like wildflowers between them. "Trade you a yellow for your blue."

Brian glances up, startled. "Is—"

"Kate's fine. Well, she's the same." Steph, the nurse, has already given her the first induction of arsenic. She has also given her two blood transfusions, to make up for what she's losing.

"Maybe we should bring Kate home," Brian says.

"Well, of course we—"

"I mean now." He steeples his hands. "I think she'd want to die in her own bed."

That word, between us, explodes like a grenade. "She isn't going to—"

"Yes, she is." He looks at me, his face carved by pain. "She is **dying**, Sara. She will die, either tonight or tomorrow or maybe a year from now if we're really lucky. You heard what Dr. Chance said. Arsenic's not a cure. It just postpones what's coming."

My eyes fill up with tears. "But I love her," I say, because that is reason enough.

"So do I. Too much to keep doing this." The paper he has been scribbling on falls out of his hands and lands at my feet; before he can reach it I pick it up. It is full of tearstains, of cross-outs. **She loved the way it smelled in Spring,** I read. **She could beat anyone at gin rummy. She could dance even if there wasn't music playing.** There are notes on the side, too: **Favorite color: pink. Favorite time of day: twilight. Used to read** Where the Wild Things Are, **over and over, and still knows it by heart.**

All the hair stands up on the back of my neck. "Is this . . . a **eulogy?**"

By now, Brian is crying, too. "If I don't do it now, I won't be able to when it's really time."

I shake my head. "It's not time."

I call my sister at three-thirty in the morning. "I woke you," I say, realizing the minute Zanne gets on the phone that for her, for everyone normal, it is the middle of the night.

"Is it Kate?"

I nod, even though she cannot hear that. "Zanne?"

"Yeah?"

I close my eyes, feel the tears squeeze out.

"Sara, what's the matter? Do you want me to come down there?"

It is hard to speak around the enormous pressure in my throat; truth expands until it can choke you. As kids, Zanne's bedroom and mine shared a hallway, and we used to fight about leaving the light on through the night. I wanted it burning; she didn't. **Put a pillow over your head,** I used to tell her. **You can make it dark, but I can't make it light.**

"Yes," I say, sobbing freely now. "Please."

Against all odds, Kate survives for ten days on intense transfusions and arsenic therapy. On the eleventh day of her hospitalization, she slips into a coma. I decide I will keep a bedside vigil until she wakes up. And I do this for exactly forty-five minutes, until I receive a phone call from the principal of Jesse's school.

Apparently, the metal sodium is stored in the high school science laboratory in small containers of oil, because of its volatile reaction with air. Apparently, it is water-reactive, too, creating hydrogen and heat. Apparently, my ninth-grader was bright enough to real-ize this, which is why he stole the sample, flushed it down the toilet, and exploded the school's septic tank.

After he is expelled for three weeks by the principal, a man who has the decency to ask after Kate while basically telling me that my eldest is destined for the State Penitentiary, Jesse and I drive back to the hospital. "Needless to say, you're grounded."

"Whatever."

"Until you're forty."

Jesse slouches, and if it is possible, his brows knit even more closely together. I wonder when, exactly, I gave up on him. I wonder why, when Jesse's history is not by any stretch as disappointing as his sister's.

"The principal's a dick."

"You know what, Jess? The world's full of them. You will always be up against someone. Something."

He glares at me. "You could take a conver-sation about the frigging Red Sox and some-how turn it back to Kate."

We pull into the hospital parking lot, but I

make no move to shut off the car. Rain pelts the windshield. "We're all pretty gifted at that. Or were you blowing up the septic tank for some other reason?"

"You don't know what it's like being the kid whose sister is dying of cancer."

"I have a fairly good idea. Since I'm the **mother** of the kid who is dying of cancer. You're absolutely right, it does suck. And sometimes I feel like blowing something up, too, just to get rid of that feeling that I'm going to explode any minute." I glance down and notice a bruise the size of a half-dollar, right in the crook of his arm. There's a matching one on the other side. It is telling, I suppose, that my mind immediately races to heroin, instead of leukemia, as it would with his sisters. "What's that?"

He folds his arms. "Nothing."

"What is it?"

"None of your business."

"It **is** my business." I pull down his forearm. "Is that from a needle?"

He lifts his head, eyes blazing. "Yeah, Ma. I shoot up every three days. Except I'm not doing smack, I'm getting blood taken out of me on the third floor here." He stares at me. "Didn't you wonder who else was keeping Kate in platelets?"

He gets out the car before I can stop him, leaving me staring out a windshield where nothing is clear anymore.

Two weeks after Kate is admitted to the hospital, the nurses convince me to take a day off. I come home and shower in my own bathroom, instead of the one used by the medical stafff. I pay overdue bills. Zanne, who is still with us, makes me a cup of coffee; it is fresh and ready when I come down with my hair wet and combed."Anyone call?"

"If by **anyone** you mean the hospital, then no." She flips the page of the cookbook she's reading. "This is such bullshit," Zanne says. "There **is** no joy in cooking."

The front door opens and slams shut. Anna comes racing into the kitchen and stops abruptly at the sight of me. "What are **you** doing here?"

"I live here," I say.

Zanne clears her throat. "Contrary to appearances."

But Anna doesn't hear her, or doesn't want to. She has a smile as wide as a canyon on her face, and brandishes a note in front of me. "It was sent to Coach Urlicht. Read it read it read it!"

Dear Anna Fitzgerald,

Congratulations on being accepted into the Girls in Goal Summer Hockey Camp. This year camp will be held in Minneapolis, from July 3–17. Please fill out the attached paperwork and medical history and return by 4/30/01. See you on the ice!

Coach Sarah Teuting

I finish scanning the letter. "You let Kate go to that sleep-away camp when she was my age, the one for kids with leukemia," Anna says. "Do you have any idea who Sarah Teuting is? The goalie on Team USA, and I don't just get to **meet** her, I get to have her tell me what

I'm doing wrong. Coach got a full scholarship for me, so you don't even have to pay a dime. They'll fly me out on a plane and give me a dorm room to stay in and everything and nobody gets a chance like this, ever—"

"Honey," I say carefully, "you can't do this."

She shakes her head, as if she's trying to make my words fit. "But it's not now, or anything. It's not till next summer."

And Kate might be dead by then.

It is the first time I can remember Anna ever indicating that she sees an end to this time line, a moment when she might finally be free of obligation to her sister. Until that point, going to Minnesota is not an option. Not because I am afraid of what might happen to Anna there, but because I am afraid of what might happen to Kate while her sister is gone. If Kate survives this latest relapse, who knows how long it will be before another crisis happens? And when it does, we will need Anna—her blood, her stem cells, her tissue—right here.

The facts hang between us like a filmy curtain. Zanne gets up and puts her arm around Anna. "You know what, bud? Maybe we should talk about this with your mom some other time—"

"No." Anna refuses to budge. "I want to know why I can't go."

I run a hand down my face. "Anna, don't make me do this."

"Do **what**, Mom," she says hotly. "I don't make **you** do anything."

She crumples the letter and runs out of the kitchen. Zanne smiles weakly at me. "Welcome back," she says.

Outside, Anna picks up a hockey stick and starts to shoot against the wall of the garage. She keeps this up for nearly an hour, a rhythmic beat, until I forget she is out there and begin to think a home might have its own pulse.

Seventeen days after Kate is admitted to the hospital, she develops an infection. Her body spikes a fever. She is pancultured—blood, urine, stool, and sputum sent out to isolate the organism—but is put on a broad-spectrum antibiotic right away in the hopes that whatever is making her sick might respond.

Steph, our favorite nurse, stays late some nights just so that I don't have to face this by myself. She brings me **People** magazines filched from the day surgery waiting rooms, and holds sunny one-sided conversations with my unconscious daughter. She is a model of resolve and optimism on the surface, but I have seen her eyes cloud with tears as she is sponge-bathing Kate, in the moments when she doesn't think I can see her.

One morning, Dr. Chance comes in to check on Kate. He wraps his stethoscope around his neck and sits down in a chair across from me. "I wanted to be invited to her wedding."

"You will," I insist, but he shakes his head.

My heart beats a little faster. "A punch bowl, that's what you can buy. A picture frame. You can make a toast."

"Sara," Dr. Chance says, "you need to say good-bye."

Jesse spends fifteen minutes in Kate's closed room, and comes out looking for all the world like a bomb about to explode. He runs through the halls of the pediatric ICU ward. "I'll go," Brian says. He heads down the corridor in Jesse's direction.

Anna sits with her back to the wall. She is angry, too. "I'm not doing this."

I crouch down next to her. "There is nothing, believe me, I'd rather make you do less. But if you don't, Anna, then one day, you're going to wish you had."

Belligerent, Anna walks into Kate's room, climbs onto a chair. Kate's chest rises and falls, the work of the respirator. All the fight goes out of Anna as she reaches out to touch her sister's cheek. "Can she hear me?"

"Absolutely," I answer, more for myself than for her.

"I won't go to Minnesota," Anna whispers. "I won't ever go anywhere." She leans close. "Wake up, Kate."

We both hold our breath, but nothing happens.

• • •

I have never understood why it is called losing a child. No parent is that careless. We all know exactly where our sons and daughters are; we just don't necessarily want them to be there.

Brian and Kate and I are a circuit. We sit on each side of the bed and hold each other's hands, and one of hers. "You were right," I tell him. "We should have taken her home."

Brian shakes his head. "If we hadn't tried the arsenic, we'd spend the rest of our lives asking why not." He brushes back the pale hair that surrounds Kate's face. "She's such a good girl. She's always done what you ask her to do." I nod, unable to speak. "That's why she's hanging on, you know. She wants your permission to leave."

He bends down to Kate, crying so hard he cannot catch his breath. I put my hand on his head. We are not the first parents to lose a child. But we are the first parents to lose **our** child. And that makes all the difference.

• • •

When Brian falls asleep, draped over the foot of the bed, I take Kate's scarred hand between both of mine. I trace the ovals of her nails and remember the first time I painted them, when Brian couldn't believe I'd do that to a one-year-old. Now, twelve years later, I turn over her palm and wish I knew how to read it, or better yet, how to edit that lifeline.

I pull my chair closer to the hospital bed. "Do you remember the summer we signed you up for camp? And the night before you left, you said you'd changed your mind and wanted to stay home? I told you to get a seat on the left side of the bus, so that when it pulled away, you'd be able to look back and see me there, waiting for you." I press her hand against my cheek, hard enough to leave a mark. "You get that same seat in Heaven. One where you can watch me, watching you."

I bury my face in the blankets and tell this daughter of mine how much I love her. I squeeze her hand one last time.

Only to feel the slightest pulse, the tiniest grasp, the smallest clutch of Kate's fingers, as she claws her way back to this world.

ANNA

HERE'S MY QUESTION: What age
are you when you're in Heaven? I mean, if it's
Heaven, you should be at your beauty-queen
best, and I doubt that all the people who die of
old age are wandering around toothless and
bald. It opens up a whole additional realm of
questions, too. If you hang yourself, do you
walk around all gross and blue, with your
tongue spitting out of your mouth? If you are
killed in a war, do you spend eternity minus
the leg that got blown up by a mine?

I figure that maybe you get a choice. You fill
out the application form that asks you if you
want a star view or a cloud view, if you like
chicken or fish or manna for dinner, what age
you'd like to be seen as by everyone else. Like
me, for example, I might pick seventeen, in the
hopes I grow boobs by then, and even if I'm a

pruny centegenarian by the time I die, in Heaven I'd be young and pretty.

Once at a dinner party I heard my father say that even though he was old old old, in his heart he was twenty-one. So maybe there is a place in your life you wear out like a rut, or even better, like the soft spot on the couch. And no matter what else happens to you, you come back to that.

The problem, I suppose, is that everyone's different. What happens in Heaven when all these people are trying to find each other after so many years spent apart? Say that you die and start looking around for your husband, who died five years ago. What if you're picturing him at seventy, but he hit his groove at sixteen and is wandering around suave as can be?

Or what if you're Kate, and you die at sixteen, but in Heaven you choose to look thirty-five, an age you never got to be here on Earth. How would **anyone** ever be able to find you?

Campbell calls my father at the station when we're having lunch, and says that opposing counsel wants to talk about the case. Which is a really stupid way to put it, since we all know he's talking about my mother. He says we have to meet at three o'clock in his office, no matter that it's Sunday.

I sit on the floor with Judge's head in my lap. Campbell is so busy he doesn't even tell me not to do it. My mother arrives right on the dot and (since Kerri the secretary is off today) walks in by herself. She has made a special effort to pull her hair back into a neat bun. She's put on some makeup. But unlike Campbell, who wears this room like an overcoat he can shrug on and off, my mom looks completely out of place in a law firm. It is hard to believe that my mother used to do this for a living. I guess she used to be someone else, once. I suppose we all were.

"Hello," she says quietly.

"Ms. Fitzgerald," Campbell replies. Ice.

My mother's eyes move from my father, at the conference table, to me, on the floor. "Hi," she says again. She steps forward, like she is going to hug me, but she stops.

"You called this meeting, Counselor," Campbell prompts.

My mother sits down. "I know. I was . . .

well, I'm hoping that we can clear this up. I want us to make a decision, together."

Campbell raps his fingers on the table. "Are you offering us a deal?"

He makes it sound so businesslike. My mother blinks at him. "Yes, I guess I am." She turns her chair toward me, as if only the two of us are in the room. "Anna, I know how much you've done for Kate. I also know she doesn't have many chances left . . . but she might have this one."

"My client doesn't need coercing—"

"It's okay, Campbell," I say. "Let her talk."

"If the cancer comes back, if this kidney transplant doesn't work, if things don't wind up the way we all wish they would for Kate—well, I will never ask you to help your sister again . . . but Anna, will you do this one last thing?"

By now, she looks very tiny, smaller even than me, as if I am the parent and she is the child. I wonder how this optical illusion took place, when neither of us has moved.

I glance at my father, but he's gone boulder-still, and he seems to be doing everything he can to follow the grain of wood in the conference table instead of getting involved.

"Are you indicating that if my client willingly donates a kidney, then she will be absolved of all other medical procedures that may be necessary in the future to prolong Kate's life?" Campbell clarifies.

My mother takes a deep breath. "Yes."

"We need, of course, to discuss it."

When I was seven, Jesse went out of his way to make sure I wasn't stupid enough to believe in Santa. **It's Mom and Dad,** he explained, and I fought him every step of the way. I decided to test the theory. So that Christmas I wrote to Santa, and asked for a hamster, which is what I wanted most in the world. I mailed the letter myself in the school secretary's mailbox. And I steadfastly did not tell my parents, although I dropped other hints about toys I hoped for that year.

On Christmas morning, I got the sled and the computer game and the tie-dyed comforter I had mentioned to my mother, but I did not get that hamster because she didn't know about it. I learned two things that year: that neither Santa, nor my parents, were what I wanted them to be.

Maybe Campbell thinks this is about the law, but really, it's about my mother. I get up from the floor and fly into her arms, which are a little like that spot in life I was talking about before, so familiar that you slide right back to the place where you fit. It makes my throat hurt, and all those tears I've been saving come out of their hiding place. "Oh, Anna," she cries into my hair. "Thank God. Thank God."

I hug her twice as tight as I would normally, trying to hold on to this moment the same way I like to paint the slanted light of summer on the back wall of my brain, a mural to stare at during the winter. I put my lips right up to her ear, and even as I speak I wish I wasn't. "I can't."

My mother's body goes stiff. She pulls away from me, stares at my face. Then she pushes a smile onto her lips that is broken in several spots. She touches the crown of my head. That's it. She stands up, straightens her jacket, and walks out of the office.

Campbell gets out of his seat, too. He crouches down in front of me, in the place where my mother was. Eye to eye, he looks more serious than I have ever seen him look. "Anna," he says. "Is this really what you want?"

I open my mouth. And find an answer.

JULIA

"Do you think I like Campbell **because** he's an asshole," I ask my sister, "or in **spite** of it?"

Izzy shushes me from the couch. She is watching **The Way We Were,** a movie she's seen twenty-thousand times. It is on her list of Movies You Cannot Click Past, which also includes **Pretty Woman, Ghost,** and **Dirty Dancing.** "If you make me miss the end, Julia, I'll kill you."

" 'See ya, Katie,' " I quote for her. " 'See ya, Hubbell.' "

She throws a couch pillow at me and wipes her eyes as the theme music swells. "Barbra Streisand," Izzy says, "is the bomb."

"I thought that was a gay **men's** stereo-type." I look up over the table of papers I have been studying in preparation for tomorrow's hearing. This is the decision I will render to the judge, based on what is in Anna Fitzgerald's best interests. The problem is, it doesn't matter whether I side in her favor or against her. Either way I will be ruining her life.

"I thought we were talking about Campbell," Izzy says.

"No, **I** was talking about Campbell. **You** were swooning." I rub my temples. "I thought you might be sympathetic."

"About Campbell Alexander? I'm not sympathetic. I'm apathetic."

"You're right. That **is** what kind of pathetic you are."

"Look, Julia. Maybe it's hereditary," Izzy says. She gets up and starts rubbing the muscles of my neck. "Maybe you have a gene that attracts you to absolute jerks."

"Then you have it, too."

"Well." She laughs. "Case in point."

"I **want** to hate him, you know. Just for the record."

Reaching over my shoulder, Izzy takes the

Coke I'm drinking and finishes it off. "What happened to this being strictly professional?"

"It is. There's just a very vocal minority opposition group in my mind wishing otherwise."

Izzy sits back down on the couch. "The problem, you know, is that you never forget your first one. And even if your brain's smart about it, your body's got the IQ of a fruit fly."

"It's just so easy with him, Iz. It's like we're picking up where we left off. I already know everything I need to about him and he already knows everything he needs to about me." I look at her. "Can you fall for someone because you're lazy?"

"Why don't you just screw him and get it out of your system?"

"Because," I say, "as soon as it's over, that's one more piece of the past I won't be able to get rid of."

"I can fix you up with one of my friends," Izzy suggests.

"They all have vaginas."

"See, you're looking at the wrong stuff,

Julia. You ought to be attracted to someone for what they've got inside them, not for the package it's presented in. Campbell Alexander may be gorgeous, but he's like marzipan frosting on a sardine."

"You think he's gorgeous?"

Izzy rolls her eyes. "You," she says, "are doomed."

When the doorbell rings, Izzy goes to look through the peephole. "Speak of the devil."

"It's Campbell?" I whisper. "Tell him I'm not here."

Izzy opens the door just a few inches. "Julia says she's not here."

"I'm going to kill you," I mutter, and walk up behind her. Pushing her out of the way, I undo the chain and let Campbell and his dog inside.

"The reception here just keeps getting warmer and fuzzier," he says.

I cross my arms. "What do you want? I'm working."

"Good. Sara Fitzgerald just offered us a plea bargain. Come out to dinner with me and I'll tell you all about it."

"I am **not** going out to dinner with you," I tell him.

"Actually, you are." He shrugs. "I know you, and eventually you're going to give in because even more than you don't want to be with me, you want to know what Anna's mother said. Can't we just cut to the chase?"

Izzy starts laughing. "He **does** know you, Julia."

"If you don't go willingly," Campbell adds, "I have no problem using brute force. Although it's going to be considerably more difficult for you to cut your filet mignon if your hands are tied together."

I turn to my sister. "Do something. Please."

She waves at me. "See ya, Katie."

"See ya, Hubbell," Campbell replies. "**Great** movie."

Izzy looks at him, considering. "Maybe there's hope," she says.

"Rule number one," I tell him. "We talk about the trial, and nothing but the trial."

"So help me God," Campbell adds. "And may I just say you look beautiful?"

"See, you've already broken the rule."

He pulls into a parking lot near the water and cuts the engine. Then he gets out of the car and comes around to my side to help me out. I look around, but I don't see anything resembling a restaurant. We are at a marina filled with sailboats and yachts, their honey-colored decks tanning in the late sun. "Take off your sneakers," Campbell says.

"No."

"For God's sake, Julia. This isn't the Victorian age; I'm not going to attack you because I see your ankle. Just do it, will you?"

"Why?"

"Because right now you've got an enormous pole up your ass and this is the only G-rated way I can think of to make you relax." He pulls off his own deck shoes and sinks his feet into the grass growing along the edge of the parking lot. "Ahhh," he says, and he spreads his arms wide. "Come on, Jewel. Carpe diem. Summer's almost over; better enjoy it while you can."

"What about the plea bargain—"

"What Sara said is going to remain the same whether or not you go barefoot."

I still do not know if he's taken on this case because he's a glory hound, because he wants the PR, or if he simply wanted to help Anna. I want to believe the latter, idiot that I am. Campbell waits patiently, the dog at his side. Finally I untie my sneakers and peel off my socks. I step out onto the strip of lawn.

Summertime, I think, is a collective unconscious. We all remember the notes that made up the song of the ice cream man; we all know what it feels like to brand our thighs on a playground slide that's heated up like a knife in a fire; we all have lain on our backs with our eyes closed and our hearts beating across the surface of our lids, hoping that this day will stretch just a little longer than the last one, when in fact it's all going in the other direction. Campbell sits down on the grass. "What's rule number two?"

"That I get to make up all the rules," I say. When he smiles at me, I'm lost.

• • •

Last night, Seven the Bartender slipped a martini into my waiting hand and asked me what I was hiding from.

I took a sip before I answered, and reminded myself why I hate martinis—they're straight bitter alcohol, which of course is the point, but they also taste that way, which is always somehow disappointing. "I'm not hiding," I told him. "I'm here, aren't I?"

It was early at the bar, just dinnertime. I stopped in on my way back from the fire station, where I'd been with Anna. Two guys were making out in a booth in the corner, one lone man was sitting at the other end of the bar. "Can we change the channel?" He gestured toward the TV, which was broadcasting the evening news. "Jennings is so much hotter than Brokaw."

Seven flicked the remote, then turned back to me. "You're not hiding, but you're sitting in a gay bar at dinnertime. You're not hiding, but you're wearing that suit like it's armor."

"Well, I'd definitely take fashion advice from a guy with a pierced tongue."

Seven lifted a brow. "One more martini, and I could convince you to go see my man Johnston and get your own done. You can take the pink hair dye out of the girl, but you never lose those roots."

I took another sip of the martini. "You don't know me."

At the end of the bar, the other customer lifted his face to Peter Jennings and smiled.

"Maybe," Seven said, "but neither do you."

Dinner turns out to be bread and cheese— well, a baguette and Gruyère—on board a thirty-foot sailboat. Campbell rolls up his pants like a castaway and sets the rigging and hauls line and catches the wind until we are so far away from the shore of Providence that it is only a line of color, a distant, jeweled necklace.

After a while, when it becomes clear to me that any information Campbell feels like providing me with won't be doled out until after dessert, I give in. I lie on my back with my arm draped over the sleeping dog. I watch the sail, loose now, flap like the great white wing of a pelican. Campbell comes up from belowdecks, where he's been hunting down a corkscrew, and holds out two glasses of red wine. He sits down on the other side of Judge and scratches behind the German shepherd's ears. "You ever think about being an animal?"

"Figuratively? Or literally?"

"Rhetorically," he says. "If you hadn't drawn that human card."

I think about this for a while. "Is this a trick question? Like, if I say killer whale you're going to tell me that means I'm a ruthless, cold-blooded, bottom-feeder fish?"

"They're mammals," Campbell says. "And no. It's just a simple, making-polite-conversation inquiry."

I turn my head. "What would you be?"

"I asked you first."

Well, a bird is out of the question; I'm too scared of heights. I don't think I have the right attitude to be a cat. And I am too much of a loner to function in a pack, like a wolf or a dog. I think of saying something like **tarsier** just to show off, but then he'll ask what the hell that is and I can't remember if it is a rodent or a lizard. "A goose," I decide.

Campbell bursts out laughing. "As in Mother? Or Silly?"

It is because they mate for life, but I would rather fall overboard than tell him this. "What about you?"

But he doesn't answer me directly. "When I asked Anna the same question, she told me she'd be a phoenix."

The image of the mythical creature rising from the ashes glitters in my mind. "They don't really exist."

Campbell strokes the dog's head. "She said that depends on whether or not there's someone who can see them." Then he looks up at me. "How do you see her, Julia?"

The wine I have been drinking suddenly tastes bitter. Was all this—the charm, the picnic, the sunset sail—engineered to tip my hand in his favor at tomorrow's trial? Whatever I recommend as guardian ad litem will weigh heavily in Judge DeSalvo's decision, and Campbell knows it.

Until this moment, I had not realized that someone could break your heart twice, along the very same fault lines.

"I'm not going to tell you what my decision is," I say stiffly. "You can wait to hear it when you call me as a witness." I grab for the anchor and try to reel it in. "I'd like to go back now, please."

Campbell yanks the line out of my hand. "You already told me that you don't think it's in Anna's best interests to be a kidney donor for her sister."

"I also told you she's incapable of making that decision by herself."

"Her father moved her out of the house. He can be her moral compass."

"And how long is that going to last? What about the next time?" I am furious at myself for falling for this. For agreeing to go out to dinner, for letting myself believe that Campbell might want to **be** with me, rather than **use** me. Everything—from his compliments on my looks to the wine sitting on the deck between us—has been coldly calculated to help him win his case.

"Sara Fitzgerald offered us a deal," Campbell says. "She said if Anna donates the kidney, she will never ask her to do anything for her sister again. Anna turned it down."

"You know, I could have the judge throw you in jail for this. It's completely unethical to try to seduce me into changing my mind."

"**Seduce** you? All I did was lay the cards on the table for you. I made **your** job easier."

"Oh, right. Forgive me," I say sarcastically. "This isn't about **you.** This isn't about me writing my report with a definite slant toward your client's petition. If you were an animal, Campbell, you know what you'd be? A toad. No, actually, you'd be a parasite on the belly of a toad. Something that takes what it needs without giving a single thing back."

A vein throbs blue in his temple. "Are you finished?"

"Actually, I'm not. Is anything that comes out of your mouth ever honest?"

"I did not lie to you."

"No? What's the dog for, Campbell?"

"Jesus Christ, will you shut up already?" Campbell says, and he pulls me into his arms and kisses me.

His mouth moves like a silent story; he tastes like salt and wine. There is no moment of relearning, of adjusting the patterns of the past fifteen years; our bodies remember where to go. He licks my name along the course of my throat. He presses himself so close to me that any hurt left on the surface between us spreads thin, becomes a binding instead of a boundary.

When we break away to breathe again, Campbell stares at me. "I'm still right," I whisper.

It is the most natural thing in the world when Campbell pulls my old sweatshirt up over my head, works at the clasp of my bra. When he kneels before me with his head over my heart, when I feel the water rocking the hull of the boat, I think that maybe this is the place for us. Maybe there are entire worlds where there are no fences, where feeling bears you like a tide.

MONDAY

How great a matter a little fire kindleth!

—THE NEW TESTAMENT,
James 3:5

CAMPBELL

WE SLEEP IN THE TINY CABIN, moored to its slip. Tight quarters, but that hardly seems to matter: all night long, she fits herself around me. She snores, just a little. Her front tooth is crooked. Her eyelashes are as long as the nail of my thumb.

These are the minutiae that prove, more than anything else, the difference between us now that fifteen years have passed. When you're seventeen, you don't think about whose apartment you want to sleep in. When you're seventeen, you don't even see the pearl-pink of her bra, the lace that arrows between her legs. When you're seventeen it's all about the now, not the after.

What I had loved about Julia—there, I've said it now—was that she didn't need anyone. At Wheeler, even when she stood out with her pink hair and quilted army-surplus jacket and combat boots, she did this without apology. It was a great irony that the very fact of a relationship with her would diminish her appeal, that the moment she came to love me back and depend on me as much as I depended on her, she would no longer be a truly independent spirit.

No way in hell was I going to be the one to take that quality away from her.

After Julia, there weren't all that many women. None whose names I took the time to remember, anyway. It was far too complicated to maintain the façade; instead, I chose the coward's rocky route of one-night stands. Out of necessity—medical and emotional—I have gotten rather skilled at being an escape artist.

But there are a half-dozen times this past night when I had the opportunity to leave. While Julia was sleeping, I even considered how to do it: a note pinned to the pillow, a message scrawled on the deck with her cherry lipstick. And yet the urge to do this was nowhere near as strong as the need to wait just one more minute, one more hour.

From the spot where he's curled up on the galley table tight as a cinnamon bun, Judge raises his head. He whines a little, and I completely understand. Detangling myself from Julia's rich forest of hair, I slip out of the bed. She inches into the warm spot I've left behind.

I swear, it makes me hard again.

But instead of doing what comes naturally—that is, calling in sick with some latent strain of smallpox and making the clerk of the court reschedule the hearing so that I can spend the day getting laid—I pull on my pants and go above-deck. I want to make sure I'm at the courthouse before Anna, and need to shower and change. I leave Julia the keys to my car—it's a short walk to my place. It's only when Judge and I are on our way home that I realize unlike every other bloodshot morning that I have left a woman, I haven't fashioned some charming symbol of my exit for Julia, something to lessen the blow of abandonment upon waking.

I wonder if this was an oversight. Or if I have been waiting all this time for her to come back, so that I can grow up.

● ● ●

When Judge and I arrive at the Garrahy building for the hearing, we have to fight our way through the reporters who have lined up for the Main Event. They thrust microphones in my face, and inadvertently step on Judge's paws. Anna will take one look at walking this gauntlet, and bolt.

Inside the front door, I flag down Vern. "Get us some security out here, will you?" I tell him. "They're going to eat the witnesses alive."

Then I see Sara Fitzgerald, already waiting. She is wearing a suit that most likely hasn't seen the outside of the plastic dry cleaner's bag for a decade, and her hair is pulled back severely into a barrette. She doesn't carry a briefcase, but a knapsack instead. "Good morning," I say evenly.

The door blows open and Brian enters, looking from Sara to me. "Where's Anna?"

Sara takes a step forward. "Didn't she come here with you?"

"She was already gone when I got back from a call at five A.M. She left a note and said she'd meet me here." He glances at the door, at the jackals on the other side. "I bet she took off."

Again, there is the sound of a seal being breached, and then Julia surfs into the courthouse on a crest of shouts and questions. She smooths back her hair, gets her bearings, then looks at me and loses them again.

"I'll find her," I say.

Sara bristles. "No, I will."

Julia looks at each of us. "Find who?"

"Anna is temporarily absent," I explain.

"Absent?" Julia says. "As in disappeared?"

"Not at all." This isn't a lie, either. For Anna to have disappeared, she would have had to appear in the first place.

I realize that I even know where I am headed— at the same moment that Sara understands it, too. In that moment she lets me take the lead. Julia grabs my arm as I am walking toward the door. She shoves my car keys into my hand. "Now you do understand why this isn't going to work?"

I turn to her. "Julia, listen. I want to talk about what's going on between us, too. But this isn't the right time."

"I was talking about **Anna**. Campbell, she's waffling. She couldn't even show up for her own court date. What does that say to you?"

"That everyone gets scared," I answer finally, fair warning for all of us.

•   •   •

The shades to the hospital room are drawn, but that doesn't keep me from seeing the angel pallor of Kate Fitzgerald's face, the web of blue veins mapping out the last-chance path of medication running under her skin. Curled up on the foot of the bed is Anna.

At my command, Judge waits by the door. I crouch down. "Anna, it's time to go."

When the door to the hospital room opens, I'm expecting either Sara Fitzgerald or a doctor with a crash cart. Instead, to my shock, Jesse stands on the threshold. "Hey," he says, as if we are old friends.

How did you get here? I almost ask, but realize I don't want to hear the answer. "We're on our way to the courthouse. Need a lift?" I ask dryly.

"No thanks. I thought since everyone was going to be there, I'd stay here." His eyes do not waver from Kate. "She looks like shit."

"What do you expect," Anna answers, awake now. "She's dying."

Again, I find myself staring at my client. I should know better than most that motivations are never what they seem to be, but I still cannot figure her out. "We need to go."

In the car, Anna rides shotgun while Judge takes a seat in the back. She starts telling me about some crazy precedent she found on the internet, where a guy in Montana in 1876 was legally prohibited from using the water from a river that originated on his brother's land, even though it meant all his crops would dry up. "What are you doing?" she asks, when I deliberately miss the turn to the courthouse.

Instead I pull over next to a park. A girl with a great ass jogs by, holding on to the leash of one of those froufrou dogs that looks more like a cat. "We're gonna be late," Anna says after a moment.

"We already are. Look, Anna. What's going on here?"

She gives me one of those patented teenage looks, as if to say that there's no way she and I descended from the same evolutionary chain. "We're going to court."

"That's not what I'm asking. I want to know why we're going to court."

"Well, Campbell, I guess you cut the first day of law school, but that's pretty much what happens when someone files a lawsuit."

I level my gaze on her, refusing to be bested. "Anna, why are we going to court?"

She doesn't blink. "Why do you have a service dog?"

I rap my fingers on the steering wheel and look out over the park. A mother pushes a stroller now, across the same spot where the jogger was, oblivious to the kid who's trying his best to crawl out. A titter of birds explodes from a tree. "I don't talk about this with anyone," I say.

"I'm not just anyone."

I take a deep breath. "A long time ago I got sick and wound up with an ear infection. But for whatever reason, the medicine didn't work and I got nerve damage. I'm totally deaf in my left ear. Which isn't such a big deal, in the long run, but there are certain lifestyle issues I couldn't handle. Like hearing a car approach, you know, but not being able to tell what direction it's coming from. Or having someone behind me at the grocery store who wants to pass by me in the aisle, but I don't hear her ask. I got trained with Judge so that in those circumstances, he could be my ears." I hesitate. "I don't like people feeling sorry for me. Hence, the big secret."

Anna stares at me carefully. "I came to your office because just for once, I wanted it to be about me instead of Kate."

But this selfish confession saws out of her sideways; it just doesn't fit. This lawsuit has never been about Anna wanting her sister to die, but simply that **she** wants a chance to **live**. "You're lying."

Anna crosses her arms. "Well, you lied first. You hear perfectly fine."

"And you're a brat." I start to laugh. "You remind me of me."

"Is that supposed to be a good thing?" Anna says, but she's smiling.

The park is starting to get more crowded. An entire school group walks the path, toddlers tethered together like sled-dog huskies, pulling two teachers in their wake. Someone zooms past on a racing bike, wearing the colors of the U.S. Postal Service. "C'mon. I'll treat you to breakfast."

"But we're late."

I shrug. "Who's counting?"

•　•　•

Judge DeSalvo is not a happy man; Anna's little field trip this morning has cost us an hour and a half. He glares at me when Judge and I hurry into his chambers for the pretrial conference. "Your Honor, I apologize. We had a veterinary emergency."

I feel, rather than see, Sara's mouth drop open. "That's not what opposing counsel indicated," the judge says.

I look DeSalvo right in the eye. "Well, it's what happened. Anna was kind enough to help me by keeping the dog calm while the sliver of glass was removed from his paw."

The judge is dubious. But there are laws against handicapped discrimination, and I'm playing them to the hilt; the last thing I want is for him to blame Anna for this delay. "Is there any way of resolving this petition without a hearing?" he asks.

"I'm afraid not." Anna may not be willing to share her secrets, which I can only respect, but she knows that she wants to go through with this.

The judge accepts my answer. "Mrs. Fitzgerald, I take it you're still representing yourself?"

"Yes, Your Honor," she says.

"All right then." Judge DeSalvo glances at each of us. "This is family court, Counselors. In family court, and especially in hearings like these, I tend to personally relax the rules of evidence because I don't want a contentious hearing. I'm able to filter out what is admissible and what is not, and if there's something truly objectionable, I'll listen to the objection, but I would prefer that we get through this hearing quickly, without worrying about form." He looks directly at me. "I want this to be as painless as possible for everyone involved."

We move into the courtroom—one that's smaller than the criminal courts, but intimidating all the same. I swing into the lobby to pick Anna up along the way. As we cross through the doorway, she stops dead. She glances at the vast paneled walls, the rows of chairs, the imposing bench. "Campbell," she whispers, "I won't have to stand up there and talk, right?"

The fact is, the judge will most likely want to hear what she has to say. Even if Julia comes out in support of her petition, even if Brian says he will help Anna, Judge DeSalvo may want her to take the stand. But telling her this right now is only going to get her all worked up—and that's not any way to start a hearing.

I think about the conversation in the car, when Anna called me a liar. There are two reasons to not tell the truth—because lying will get you what you want, and because lying will keep someone from getting hurt. It's for both of these reasons that I give Anna this answer. "Well," I say, "I doubt it."

"Judge," I begin, "I know it's not traditional practice, but there's something I'd like to say before we start calling witnesses."

Judge DeSalvo sighs. "Isn't this sort of standing on ceremony exactly what I asked you **not** to do?"

"Your Honor, I wouldn't ask if I didn't think it was important."

"Make it quick," the judge says.

I stand up and approach the bench. "Your Honor, all of Anna Fitzgerald's life she has been medically treated for her sister's good, not her own. No one doubts Sara Fitzgerald's love for all her children, or the decisions she's made that have prolonged Kate's life. But today we have to doubt the decisions she's made for **this** child."

I turn, and see Julia watching me carefully. And suddenly I remember that old ethics assignment, and know what I have to say. "You might remember the recent case of the firefighters in Worcester, Massachusetts, who were killed in a blaze started by a homeless woman. She knew the fire had started and she left the building, but she never called 911 because she thought she might get into trouble. Six men died that night, and yet the State couldn't hold this woman responsible, because in America—even if the consequences are tragic—you are not responsible for someone else's safety. You aren't obligated to help anyone in distress. Not if you're the one who started the fire, not if you're a passerby to a car wreck, not if you're a perfectly matched donor."

I look at Julia again. "We're here today because there's a difference in our system of justice between what's legal and what's moral. Sometimes it's easy to tell them apart. But every now and then, especially when they rub up against each other, right sometimes looks wrong, and wrong sometimes looks right." I walk back to my seat, and stand in front of it. "We're here today," I finish, "so that this Court can help us all see a little more clearly."

My first witness is opposing counsel. I watch Sara walk to the stand unsteadily, a sailor getting her sea legs again. She manages to get herself into the seat and be sworn in without ever breaking her gaze away from Anna.

"Judge, I'd like permission to treat Mrs. Fitzgerald as a hostile witness."

The judge frowns. "Mr. Alexander, I truly would hope that both you and Mrs. Fitzgerald can stand to be civilized, here."

"Understood, Your Honor." I walk toward Sara. "Can you state your name?"

She lifts her chin a fraction. "Sara Crofton Fitzgerald."

"You are the mother of the minor child Anna Fitzgerald?"

"Yes. And also of Kate and Jesse."

"Isn't it true that your daughter Kate was diagnosed with acute promyelocytic leukemia at age two?"

"That's right."

"At that time did you and your husband decide to conceive a child who would be genetically programmed to be an organ donor for Kate, so that she could be cured?"

Sara's face hardens. "Not the words I would choose, but that was the story behind Anna's conception, yes. We were planning to use Anna's umbilical cord blood for a transplant."

"Why didn't you try to find an unrelated donor?"

"It's much more dangerous. The risk of mortality would have been far higher with someone who wasn't related to Kate."

"So how old was Anna when she first donated an organ or tissue to her sister?"

"Kate had the transplant a month after Anna was born."

I shake my head. "I didn't ask when Kate received it; I asked when Anna donated it. The cord blood was taken from Anna moments after birth, isn't that right?"

"Yes," Sara says, "but Anna wasn't even aware of it."

"How old was Anna the next time she donated some body part to Kate?"

Sara winces, just as I have expected. "She was five when she gave donor lymphocytes."

"What does that involve?"

"Drawing blood from the crooks of her arms."

"Did Anna agree to let you put a needle in her arm?"

"She was five years old," Sara answers.

"Did you ask her if you could put a needle in her arm?"

"I asked her to help her sister."

"Isn't it true that someone had to physically hold Anna down to get the needle in her arm?"

Sara looks at Anna, closes her eyes. "Yes."

"Do you call that voluntary participation, Mrs. Fitzgerald?" From the corner of my eye I can see Judge DeSalvo's brows draw together. "The first time you took lymphocytes from Anna, were there any side effects?"

"She had some bruising. Some tenderness."

"How long was it before you took blood again?"

"A month."

"Did she have to be held down that time, too?"

"Yes, but—"

"What were her side effects then?"

"The same." Sara shakes her head. "You don't understand. It wasn't like I didn't see what was happening to Anna, every time she underwent a procedure. It doesn't matter which of your children you see in that situation—every single time, it breaks you apart."

"And yet, Mrs. Fitzgerald, you managed to get past that sentiment," I say, "because you took blood from Anna a third time."

"It took that long to get all the lymphocytes," Sara says. "It's not an exact procedure."

"How old was Anna the next time she had to undergo medical treatment for her sister's well-being?"

"When Kate was nine she got a raging infection and—"

"Again, that's not what I asked. I want to know what happened to **Anna** when she was six."

"She donated granulocytes to fight Kate's infection. It's a process a lot like a lymphocyte donation."

"Another needle stick?"

"That's right."

"Did you ask her if she was willing to donate the granulocytes?"

Sara doesn't answer. "Mrs. Fitzgerald," the judge prompts.

She turns toward her daughter, pleading. "Anna, you know we never did any of these things to hurt you. It hurt **all** of us. If you got the bruises on the outside, then we got them on the inside."

"Mrs. Fitzgerald," I step between her and Anna. "**Did you ask her?**"

"Please don't do this," Sara says. "We all know the history. I'll stipulate to whatever it is you're trying to do in the process of crucifying me. I'd rather just get this part over with."

"Because it's hard to hear it hashed out again, isn't it?" I know I'm walking a fine line, but behind me there is Anna, and I want her to know that someone here is willing to go the distance for her. "Added up like this, it doesn't seem quite so innocuous, does it?"

"Mr. Alexander, what **is** the point of this?" Judge DeSalvo says. "I am well aware of the number of procedures Anna's undergone."

"Because we have Kate's medical history, Your Honor, not Anna's."

Judge DeSalvo looks between us. "Be brief, Counselor."

I turn to Sara. "Bone marrow," she says wood-enly, before I can ask the question. "She was put under general anesthesia because she was so young, and needles were put into the crests of her hips to draw out the marrow."

"Was it one needle stick, like the other proce-dures?"

"No," Sara says quietly. "It was about fifteen."

"Into the bone?"

"Yes."

"What were the side effects for Anna this time around?"

"She had some pain, and was given some analgesics."

"So this time, Anna had to be hospitalized over-night . . . and she needed medication herself?"

Sara takes a minute to compose herself. "I was told that donating marrow isn't consid-ered a particularly invasive procedure for a donor. Maybe I was just waiting to hear those words; maybe I needed to hear them at that time. And maybe I was not thinking as much of Anna as I should have been, because I was so focused on Kate. But I know beyond a doubt that—like everyone else in our family—Anna wanted nothing more than for her sister to be cured."

"Well, sure," I reply, "so that you'd stop sticking needles in her."

"Enough, Mr. Alexander," Judge DeSalvo interjects.

"Wait," Sara interrupts. "I have something to say." She turns to me. "You think you can lay it all out in words, black-and-white, as if it's that easy. But you only represent one of my daughters, Mr. Alexander, and only in this courtroom. I represent both of them equally, everywhere, every place. I **love** both of them equally, everywhere, every place."

"But you admitted that you've always considered Kate's health, not Anna's, in making these choices," I point out. "So how can you claim to love both of them equally? How can you say that you haven't been favoring one child in your decisions?"

"Aren't you asking me to do that very thing?" Sara asks. "Only this time, to favor the other child?"

Anna

WHEN YOU ARE A KID you have your own language, and unlike French or Spanish or whatever you start learning in fourth grade, this one you're born with, and eventually lose. Everyone under the age of seven is fluent in **Ifspeak;** go hang around with someone under three feet tall and you'll see. What if a giant funnelweb spider crawled out of that hole over your head and bit you on the neck? What if the only antidote for venom was locked up in a vault on the top of a mountain? What if you lived through the bite, but could only move your eyelids and blink out an alphabet? It doesn't really matter how far you go; the point is that it's a world of possibility. Kids think with their brains cracked wide open; becoming an adult, I've decided, is only a slow sewing shut.

• • •

During the first recess, Campbell takes me to a conference room for privacy and buys me a Coke that isn't cold. "So," he says. "What do you think so far?"

Being in the courtroom is weird. It's like I've turned into a ghost—I can watch what's going on, but even if I felt like speaking no one would be able to hear me. Add to that the very bizarre way I have to listen to everyone talk about my life as if they can't see me sitting right there, and you've landed in my surreal little corner of earth.

Campbell pops open his 7 UP and sits down across from me. He pours a little into a paper cup for Judge, and then takes a good long drink. "Comments?" he says. "Questions? Unadulterated praise for my skillful litigation?"

I shrug. "It's not like I expected."

"What do you mean?"

"I guess I figured when it started, I'd know for sure that I was doing the right thing. But when my mom was up there, and you were asking her all those questions . . . " I glance up at him.

"That part about it not being simple. She's right."

What if I was the one who was sick? What if Kate had been asked to do what I've done? What if one of these days, some marrow or blood or whatever actually worked, and that was the end? What if I could look back on all this one day and feel good about what I did, instead of feeling guilty? What if the judge doesn't think I'm right?

What if he does?

I can't answer a single one of these, which is how I know that whether I'm ready or not, I'm growing up.

"Anna." Campbell gets up and comes around to my side of the table. "Now is not the time to start changing your mind."

"I'm not changing my mind." I roll the can between my palms. "I think I'm just saying that even if we win, we don't."

When I was twelve I started baby-sitting for twins who live down the street. They're only six, and they don't like the dark, so I usually wind up sitting between them on a stool that's shaped like the stubby foot of an elephant, toenails and all. It never fails to amaze me how quickly a kid can shut off an energy switch—they'll be climbing the curtains and bam, five minutes later, they're conked out. Was I ever like that? I can't remember, and it makes me feel ancient.

Every now and then one of the twins will fall asleep before the other one. "Anna," his brother will say, "how many years till I can drive?"

"Ten," I tell him.

"How many years till you can drive?"

"Three."

Then the talk will split off like the spokes of a spiderweb—what kind of car will I buy; what will I be when I grow up; does it suck to get homework every night in middle school. It's totally a ploy to stay up a little bit later. Sometimes I fall for it, mostly I just make him go to sleep. See, I get a round hollow spot in my belly knowing I could tell him what's coming, but also knowing it would come out sounding like a warning.

The second witness Campbell calls is Dr. Bergen, the head of the medical ethics committee at Providence Hospital. He has salt-and-pepper hair and a face dented in like a potato. He is smaller than you'd expect, too, given the fact that it takes him just short of a millennium to recite his credentials.

"Dr. Bergen," Campbell starts, "what's an ethics committee?"

"A diverse group of doctors, RNs, clergy, ethicists, and scientists, who are assigned to review individual cases to protect patients' rights. In Western Bioethics, there are six principles we try to follow." He ticks them off on his fingers. "Autonomy, or the idea that any patient over age eighteen has the right to refuse treatment; veracity, which is basically informed consent; fidelity—that is, a health-care provider fulfilling his duties; beneficence, or doing what's in the best interests of the patient; nonmaleficence—when you can no longer do good, you shouldn't do harm . . . like performing major surgery on a terminal patient who's 102 years old; and finally, justice—that no patient should be discriminated against in receiving treatment."

"What does an ethics committee do?"

"Generally, we're called to convene when there's a discrepancy about patient care. For example, if a physician feels it's in the patient's best interests to go on with extraordinary measures, and the family doesn't—or vice versa."

"So you don't see every case that passes through a hospital?"

"No. Only when there are complaints, or if the attending physician asks for a consultation. We review the situation and make recommendations."

"Not decisions?"

"No," Dr. Bergen says.

"What if the patient complaining is a minor?" Campbell asks.

"Consent isn't necessary until age thirteen. We rely on parents to make informed choices for their children until that point."

"What if they can't?"

He blinks. "You mean if they're not physically present?"

"No. I mean if there's another agenda they're adhering to, that in some way keeps them from making choices in the best interests of that child?"

My mother stands up. "Objection," she says. "He's speculating."

"Sustained," Judge DeSalvo replies.

Without missing a beat, Campbell turns back to his witness. "Do parents control their children's health-care decisions until age eighteen?"

Well, I could answer that. Parents control everything, unless you're like Jesse and you do enough to upset them that they'd rather ignore you than pretend you actually exist.

"Legally," Dr. Bergen says. "However, once a child reaches adolescence, although they can't give formal consent, they have to agree to any hospital procedure—even if their parents have already signed off on it."

This rule, if you ask me, is like the law against jaywalking. Everyone knows you're not supposed to do it, but that doesn't actually stop you.

Dr. Bergen is still talking. "In the rare instance where a parent and an adolescent patient disagree, the ethics committee weighs several factors: whether the procedure is in the adolescent's best interests, the risk/benefit scenario, the age and maturity of the adolescent, and the argument he or she presents."

"Has the ethics committee at Providence Hospital ever met regarding the care of Kate Fitzgerald?" Campbell asks.

"On two occasions," Dr. Bergen says. "The first involved allowing her to enter a trial for peripheral blood stem cell transplant in 2002, when her bone marrow transplant and several other options had failed. The second, more recently, involved whether or not it would be in her best interests to receive a donor kidney."

"What was the outcome, Dr. Bergen?"

"We recommended that Kate Fitzgerald receive a peripheral blood stem cell transplant. As for the kidney, our group was split on that decision."

"Can you explain?"

"Several of us felt that, at this point, the patient's health care had deteriorated to a point where major invasive transplant surgery was going to do more harm than good. Others believed that without a transplant, she would still die, and therefore the benefits outweighed the risk."

"If your team was split, then who gets to decide what will ultimately happen?"

"In Kate's case, because she is still a minor, her parents."

"During either of the times that your committee met regarding Kate's medical treatment, did you discuss the risks and benefits to the donor?"

"That wasn't the issue at stake—"

"What about the consent of the donor, Anna Fitzgerald?"

Dr. Bergen looks right at me, sympathetic, which it turns out is worse even than him thinking I'm a horrible person for filing this petition in the first place. He shakes his head. "It goes without saying that no hospital in the country is going to take a kidney out of a child who doesn't want to donate it."

"So, theoretically, if Anna was fighting this decision, the case would most likely land on your desk?"

"Well—"

"Has Anna's case landed on your desk, Doctor?"

"No."

Campbell advances toward him. "Can you tell us why?"

"Because she isn't a patient."

"Really?" He pulls a stack of papers out from his briefcase, and hands them to the judge, and then to Dr. Bergen. "These are Anna Fitzgerald's hospital records at Providence Hospital for the past thirteen years. Why would there be records for her, if she wasn't a patient?"

Dr. Bergen flips through them. "She's had several invasive procedures," he admits.

Go, Campbell, I think. I am not one to believe in knights who ride in to rescue damsels in distress, but I bet it feels a little like this. "Doesn't it strike you as odd that in thirteen years, given the thickness of this file and the fact it exists in the first place, the medical ethics committee never once convened to discuss what was being done to Anna?"

"We were under the impression that donation was her wish."

"Are you telling me that if Anna had previously said she didn't want to give up lymphocytes or granulocytes or cord blood or even a bee sting kit in her backpack—the ethics committee would have acted differently?"

"I know where you're going with this, Mr. Alexander," the psychiatrist says coldly. "The problem is that this kind of medical situation hasn't existed before. There **is** no precedent. We're trying to feel our way as best we can."

"Isn't your job as an ethics committee to look at situations that haven't existed before?"

"Well. Yes."

"Dr. Bergen, in your expert opinion, is it ethically right for Anna Fitzgerald to have been asked to donate parts of her own body repeatedly for thirteen years?"

"Objection!" my mother calls out.

The judge strokes his chin. "I want to hear this."

Dr. Bergen glances at me again. "Quite frankly, even before I knew that Anna didn't want to be a participant, I voted **against** her donating a kidney to her sister. I don't believe Kate would live through the transplant, and therefore Anna would undergo a serious operation for no reason at all. Up until this point, however, I think that the risk of the procedures was small, compared to the benefit the family as a whole received, and I support the choices the Fitzgeralds made for Anna."

Campbell pretends to consider this. "Dr.

Bergen, what kind of car do you drive?"

"A Porsche."

"Bet you like it."

"I do," he says guardedly.

"What if I told you that you have to give up your Porsche before you leave this courtroom, because that action will save Judge DeSalvo's life?"

"That's ridiculous. You—"

Campbell leans in. "What if you had no choice? What if, today, psychiatrists simply have to do whatever lawyers decide is in the best interests of others?"

He rolls his eyes. "In spite of the high drama you're alluding to, Mr. Alexander, there are basic donor rights, safeguards put into place in medicine, so that the greater good doesn't steamroll the pioneers who help create it. The United States has a long and nasty history of the abuse of informed consent, which is what led to laws relating to Human Subjects Research. It keeps people from being used as experimental lab rats."

"Then tell us," Campbell says, "how the hell did Anna Fitzgerald slip through the cracks?"

• • •

When I was only seven months old, there was a block party in our neighborhood. It's just as bad as you're thinking: Jell-O molds and towers of cheese cubes and dancing in the street to music piped out of someone's living room stereo. I, of course, have no personal recollection of any of this—I was plopped down in one of those walkers they made for babies before babies started overturning them and cracking their heads open.

At any rate, I was in my walker, tooling around between the tables and watching the other kids, so the story goes, when I sort of lost my footing. Our block is canted at an angle, and suddenly the wheels were moving faster than I could make them stop. I whizzed past adults, under the barricade the cops had put up at the end of the road to shut it off to traffic, and I was heading right for a main drag full of cars.

But Kate came out of nowhere and ran after me. She somehow managed to grab me by the back of my shirt moments before I got hit by a passing Toyota.

Every now and then, someone on the block

brings this up. Me, I remember it as the time she saved me, instead of the other way around.

My mother gets her first chance to play lawyer. "Dr. Bergen," she says, "how long have you known of my family?"

"I've been at Providence Hospital for ten years now."

"In those ten years, when some aspect of Kate's treatment was presented to you, what did you do?"

"Come up with a plan of action that was recommended," he says. "Or an alternate, if possible."

"When you did, at any point in your report did you mention that Anna shouldn't be a part of it?"

"No."

"Did you ever say this would hurt Anna considerably?"

"No."

"Or put her in grave medical danger herself?"

"No."

Maybe it's not Campbell, after all, who will

turn out to be my white knight. Maybe it's my mother.

"Dr. Bergen," she asks, "do you have kids?"

The doctor looks up. "I have a son. He's thirteen."

"Have you ever looked at these cases that come to the medical ethics committee and put yourself in a patient's shoes? Or better yet, a parent's shoes?"

"I have," he admits.

"If you were me," my mother says, "and the medical ethics committee handed you back a piece of paper with a suggested course of action that would save your son's life, would you question them further . . . or would you just jump at the chance?"

He doesn't answer. He doesn't have to.

Judge DeSalvo calls a second recess after that. Campbell says something about getting up and stretching my legs. So I start to follow him out, walking right past my mother. As I pass by, I feel her hand on my waist, tugging down my T-shirt, which is riding up in the back. She hates the spaghetti-strap girls, the ones who come to school in halters and low-riders, like they're trying out as dancers in a Britney Spears video instead of going to math class. I can almost hear her voice: Please **tell me that shrank in the wash.**

She seems to realize mid-tug that maybe she shouldn't have done this. I stop, and Campbell stops, too, and her face goes bright red. "Sorry," she says.

I put my hand over hers and tuck my shirt into the back of my jeans where it should be. I look at Campbell. "Meet you outside?"

He's giving me a look that has **Bad Idea** written all over it, but he nods and heads down the aisle. Then my mother and I are nearly alone in the courtroom. I lean forward and kiss her on the cheek. "You did really great up there," I tell her, because I don't know how to say what I really want to: that the people you love can surprise you every day. That maybe who we are isn't so much about what we do, but rather what we're capable of when we least expect it.

SARA

2002

KATE MEETS TAYLOR AMBROSE when they are sitting side by side, hooked up to IVs. "What are you here for?" she asks, and I immediately look up from my book, because in all the years that Kate has been receiving outpatient treatment I cannot remember her initiating a conversation.

The boy she is talking to is not much older than she is, maybe sixteen to her fourteen. He has brown eyes that dance, and is wearing a Bruins cap over his bald head. "The free cocktails," he answers, and the dimples in his cheeks deepen.

Kate grins. "Happy hour," she says, and she looks up at the bag of platelets being infused into her.

"I'm Taylor." He holds out his hand. "AML."

"Kate. APL."

He whistles, and raises his brows. "Ooh," he says. "A rarity."

Kate tosses her cropped hair. "Aren't we all?"

I watch this, amazed. Who is this flirt, and what has she done with my little girl?

"Platelets," he says, scrutinizing the label on her IV bag. "You're in remission?"

"Today, anyway." Kate glances at his pole, the telltale black bag that covers the Cytoxan. "Chemo?"

"Yeah. Today, anyway. So, Kate," Taylor says. He has that rangy puppy look of a sixteen-year-old, one with knobby knees and thick fingers and cheekbones he hasn't yet grown into. When he crosses his arms, the muscles swell. I realize he's doing this on purpose, and I duck my head to hide a smile. "What do you do when you're not at Providence Hospital?"

She thinks, and then a slow smile lights her up from the inside out. "Wait for something that makes me come back."

This makes Taylor laugh out loud. "Maybe sometime we can wait together," he says, and he passes her a wrapper from a gauze pad. "Can I have your phone number?"

Kate scribbles it down as Taylor's IV begins to beep. The nurse comes in and unhooks his line. "You're outta here, Taylor," she says. "Where's your ride?"

"Waiting downstairs. I'm all set." He gets out of the padded chair slowly, almost weakly, the first reminder that this is not some casual conversation. He slips the piece of paper with our phone number into his pocket. "Well, I'll call you, Kate."

When he leaves Kate lets all her breath out in a dramatic finish. She rolls her head after him. "Oh my God," she gasps. "He is gorgeous."

The nurse, checking her flow, grins. "Tell me about it, honey. If only I were thirty years younger."

Kate turns to me, blooming. "You think he'll call?"

"Maybe," I say.

"Where do you think we'll go out?"

I think of Brian, who has always said that Kate can date . . . when she's forty. "Let's take one step at a time," I suggest. But inside, I am singing.

The arsenic, which ultimately put Kate into remission, worked its magic by wearing her down. Taylor Ambrose, a drug of an entirely different sort, works his magic by building her up. It becomes a habit: when the phone rings at seven P.M., Kate flies from the dinner table and hides in a closet with the portable receiver. The rest of us clear the dinner plates and spend time in the living room and get ready for bed, hearing little more than giggles and whispers, and then Kate emerges from her cocoon, flushed and glowing, first love beating like a hummingbird at the pulse in her throat. Every time it happens, I can't stop staring. It is not that Kate is so beautiful, although she is; it's that I never really let myself believe that I would see her all grown up.

I follow her into the bathroom one night, after one of her marathon phone sessions. Kate stares at herself in the mirror, pursing her lips and raising her brows in a come-hither pose. Her hand comes up to her cropped hair—after the chemo, it never grew back in waves, just thick straight tufts that she usually cultivates with mousse to look like bedhead. She holds her palm out, as if she still expects to see hair shedding.

"What do you think he sees when he looks at me?" Kate asks.

I come to stand behind her. She is not the child that mirrors me—that would be Jesse—and yet when you put us side by side, there are definite similarities. It's not in the shape of the mouth but the set of it, the sheer determination that silvers our eyes.

"I think he sees a girl who knows what he's been through," I tell her honestly.

"I got on the internet and read up on AML," she says. "His leukemia's got a pretty high cure rate." She turns to me. "When you care more if someone else lives than you do about yourself . . . is that what love's like?"

It is hard, all of a sudden, to pull an answer through the tunnel of my throat. "Exactly."

Kate runs the tap and washes her face with a foam of soap. I hand her a towel, and as she rises from the cloud of it, she says, "Something bad's going to happen."

On alert, I search her out for clues. "What's the matter?"

"Nothing. But that's the way it works. If there's something as good as Taylor in my life, I'm going to pay for it."

"That's the stupidest thing I've ever heard," I say out of habit, yet there is a truth to this. Anyone who believes that people have ultimate control of what life hands to them needs only to spend a day in the shoes of a child with leukemia. Or her mother. "Maybe you're finally getting a break," I say.

Three days later, during a routine CBC, the hematologist tells us that Kate is once again throwing promyelocytes, the first slide down a steep slope of relapse.

I have never eavesdropped, at least not intentionally, until the night that Kate comes back from her first date with Taylor, to see a movie. She tiptoes into her room and sits down on Anna's bed. "You awake?" she asks.

Anna rolls over, groans. "I am now." Sleep slips away from her, like a shawl falling to the floor. "How was it?"

"Wow," Kate says, and she laughs. "Wow."

"How wow? Like, tonsil hockey wow?"

"You are so disgusting," Kate whispers, although there's a smile behind it. "But he is a really good kisser." She dangles this like a fisherman.

"Get out!" Anna's voice shines. "So what was it like?"

"Flying," Kate answers. "I bet it feels just the same way."

"I don't get what that has in common with someone slobbering all over you."

"God, Anna, it's not like he spits on you."

"What does Taylor taste like?"

"Popcorn." She laughs. "And guy."

"How did you know what to do?"

"I didn't. It just kind of happened. Like the way you play hockey."

This, finally, makes sense to Anna. "Well," she says, "I do feel pretty good when I'm doing that."

"You have no idea," Kate sighs. There is some movement; I imagine her stripping off her clothes. I wonder if Taylor is imagining the same, somewhere.

Pillow is punched, cover yanked back, sheets rustle as Kate gets into bed and rolls onto her side. "Anna?"

"Hmm?"

"He has scars on his palms, from graft-versus-host," Kate murmurs. "I could feel them when we were holding hands."

"Was it gross?"

"No," she says. "It was like we matched."

At first, I can't get Kate to agree to undergo the peripheral blood stem cell transplant. She refuses because she doesn't want to be hospitalized for chemo, doesn't want to have to sit in reverse isolation for the next six weeks when she could be going out with Taylor Ambrose. "It's your life," I point out to her, and she looks at me as if I'm crazy.

"Exactly," she says.

In the end, we compromise. The oncology

team agrees to let Kate begin her chemo as an outpatient, in preparation for a transplant from Anna. At home, she agrees to wear a mask. At the first indication of her counts dropping, she'll be hospitalized. They aren't happy; they worry it will affect the procedure, but like me they also understand that Kate has reached the age where she can bargain with her will.

As it turns out, this separation anxiety is all for naught, since Taylor shows up for Kate's first outpatient chemo appointment. "What are you doing here?"

"I can't seem to stay away," he jokes. "Hey, Mrs. Fitzgerald." He sits down beside Kate in the empty adjoining chair. "God, it feels good to be in one of these without an IV hookup."

"Rub it in," Kate mutters.

Taylor puts his hand on her arm. "How far into it are you?"

"Just started."

He gets up and sits on the wide arm of Kate's chair, picks the emesis basin up from Kate's lap. "A hundred bucks says you can't make it till three without tossing your cookies."

Kate glances at the clock. It is 2:50. "You're on."

"What did you have for lunch?" He grins, wicked. "Or should I guess based on the colors?"

"You're disgusting," Kate says, but her smile is as wide as the sea. Taylor puts his hand on her shoulder. She leans into the contact.

The first time Brian touched me, he saved my life. There had been cataclysmic downpours in Providence, a nor'easter that swelled the tides and put the parking lot at the courthouse entirely underwater. I was clerking then, when we were evacuated. Brian's department was in charge; I walked onto the stone steps of the building to see cars floating by, and abandoned purses, and even a terrified paddling dog. While I had been filing briefs, the world I knew had been submerged. "Need a hand?" Brian asked, dressed in his full turnout gear, and he held out his arms. As he swam me to higher ground, rain struck my face and pelted my back. I wondered how—in a deluge—I could feel like I was being burned alive.

"What's the longest you've ever gone before throwing up?" Kate asks Taylor.

"Two days."

"Get out."

The nurse glances up from her paperwork. "True," she confirms. "I saw it with my own eyes."

Taylor grins at her. "I told you, I'm a master at this." He looks at the clock: 2:57.

"Don't you have anywhere else you'd rather be?" Kate says.

"Trying to weasel out of the bet?"

"Trying to spare you. Although—" Before she can finish, she goes green. Both the nurse and I rise from ours seats, but Taylor reaches Kate first. He holds the vomit basin beneath her chin and when she starts retching, he rubs his hand in slow circles on her upper back.

"It's okay," he soothes, close to her temple.

The nurse and I exchange glances. "Looks like she's in good hands," the nurse says, and she leaves to take care of another patient.

When Kate is finished, Taylor puts the basin aside and wipes her mouth with a tissue. She looks up at him, glow-eyed and flushed, her nose still running. "Sorry," she mutters.

"For what?" Taylor says. "Tomorrow, it could be me."

I wonder if all mothers feel like this the moment they realize their daughters are growing up—as if it is impossible to believe that the laundry I once folded for her was doll-sized; as if I can still see her dancing in lazy pirouettes along the lip of the sandbox. Wasn't it yesterday that her hand was only as big as the sand dollar she found on the beach? That same hand, the one that's holding a boy's; wasn't it just holding mine, tugging so that I might stop and see the spiderweb, the milkweed pod, any of a thousand moments she wanted me to freeze? Time is an optical illusion—never quite as solid or strong as we think it is. You would assume that, given everything, I saw this coming. But watching Kate watch this boy, I see I have a thousand things to learn.

"I'm some fun date," Kate murmurs.

Taylor smiles at her. "Fries," he says. "For lunch."

Kate smacks his shoulder. "You are disgusting."

He raises one brow. "You lost the bet, you know."

"I seem to have left my trust fund at home."

Taylor pretends to study her. "OK, I know what you can give me instead."

"Sexual favors?" Kate says, forgetting I am here.

"Gee, I don't know." Taylor laughs. "Should we ask your mom?"

She goes plum-red. "Oops."

"Keep this up," I warn, "and your next date will be during a bone marrow aspiration."

"You know the hospital has this dance, right?" Suddenly, Taylor is jittery; his knee bobs up and down. "It's for kids who are sick. There are doctors and nurses there, in case, and it's held in one of the conference rooms at the hospital, but for the most part it's just like a regular prom. You know, lame band, ugly tuxes, punch spiked with platelets." He swallows. "I'm just kidding about that last part. Well, I went last year, stag, and it was pretty dumb, but I figure since you're a patient and I'm a patient maybe this year we could, like, go together."

Kate, with an aplomb I never would have guessed she possesses, considers the offer. "When is it?"

"Saturday."

"As it turns out, I don't have plans to kick the bucket that day." She beams at him. "I'd love to."

"Cool," Taylor says, smiling. "Very cool." He reaches for a fresh basin, careful of Kate's IV line, which snakes down between them. I wonder if her heart is pumping faster, if it will affect the medication. If she'll be sicker, sooner rather than later.

Taylor settles Kate into the crook of his arm. Together, they wait for what comes next.

"It's too low," I say, as Kate holds a pale yellow dress up below her neck. From the spot on the boutique floor where she is sitting, Anna offers up her opinion, too: "You'd look like a banana."

We have been shopping for a prom dress for hours. Kate has only two days to prepare for this dance, and it has become an obsession: what she will wear, how she will do her makeup, if the band is going to play anything remotely decent. Her hair, of course, is not an issue; after chemo she lost it all. She hates wigs—they feel like bugs on her scalp, she says—but she's too self-conscious to go commando. Today, she has wrapped a batik scarf around her head, like a proud, pale African queen.

The reality of this outing hasn't matched Kate's dreams. Dresses that normal girls wear to proms bare the midriff or shoulders, where Kate's skin is riddled and thickened with scarring. They cling in all the wrong places. They are cut to showcase a healthy, hale body, not to hide the lack of it.

The saleswoman who hovers like a hummingbird takes the dress from Kate. "It's actually quite modest," she pushes. "It really does cover up a fair amount of cleavage."

"Will it cover this?" Kate snaps, popping open the buttons of her peasant blouse to reveal her recently replaced Hickman catheter, which sprouts from the center of her chest.

The saleswoman gasps before she can remember to stop herself. "Oh," she says faintly.

"Kate!" I scold.

She shakes her head. "Let's just get out of here."

As soon as we are on the street in front of the boutique I lace into her. "Just because you're angry, you don't have to take it out on the rest of the world."

"Well, she's a bitch," Kate retorts. "Did you see her looking at my scarf?"

"Maybe she just liked the pattern," I say dryly.

"Yeah, and maybe I'm going to wake up tomorrow and not be sick." Her words fall like boulders between us, cracking the sidewalk. "I'm not going to find a stupid dress. I don't know why I even told Taylor I'd go in the first place."

"Don't you think every other girl who's going to that dance is in the same boat? Trying to find gowns that cover up tubes and bruises and wires and colostomy bags and God knows what?"

"I don't care about anyone else," Kate says.

"I wanted to look good. Really good, you know, for one night."

"Taylor already thinks you're beautiful."

"Well I don't!" Kate cries. "I don't, Mom, and maybe I want to just **once**."

It is a warm day, one where the ground beneath our feet seems to be breathing. The sun beats down on my head, on the back of my neck. What do I say to that? I have never been Kate. I have prayed and begged and wanted to be the one who's sick in lieu of her, some devil's Faustian bargain, but that is not the way it's happened.

"We'll sew something," I suggest. "You can design it."

"You don't know how to sew," Kate sighs.

"I'll learn."

"In a day?" She shakes her head. "You can't fix it every time, Mom. How come I know that, and you don't?"

She leaves me on the sidewalk and storms off. Anna runs after her, loops her arm through Kate's elbow, and drags her into a storefront a few feet away from the boutique, while I hurry to catch up.

It is a salon, filled with gum-cracking hair-stylists. Kate is struggling to get away from Anna, but Anna, she can be strong when she wants to be. "Hey," Anna says, getting the attention of the receptionist. "Do you work here?"

"When I'm forced to."

"You guys do prom hairstyles?"

"Sure," the stylist says. "Like an updo?"

"Yeah. For my sister." Anna looks at Kate, who has stopped fighting. A smile glows slowly across her face, like a firefly caught in a jelly jar.

"That's right. For me," Kate says mischievously, and she unwinds the scarf from her bald head.

Everyone in the salon stops speaking. Kate stands regally straight. "We were thinking of French braids," Anna continues.

"A perm," Kate adds.

Anna giggles. "Maybe a nice chignon."

The stylist swallows, caught between shock and sympathy and political correctness. "Well, um, we might be able to do something for you." She clears her throat. "There's always, you know, extensions."

"Extensions," Anna repeats, and Kate bursts out laughing.

The stylist begins to look behind the girls, toward the ceiling. "Is this like a **Candid Camera** thing?"

At that, my daughters collapse into each other's arms, hysterical. They laugh until they cannot catch their breath. They laugh until they cry.

As a chaperone at the Providence Hospital Prom, I am in charge of the punch. Like every other food item provided for the celebrants, it's neutropenic. The nurses—fairy godmothers for the night—have converted a conference room into a fantasy dance hall, complete with streamers and a disco ball and mood lighting.

Kate is a vine twined around Taylor. They sway to completely different music than the song that is playing. Kate wears her obligatory blue mask. Taylor has given her a corsage made of silk flowers, because real ones can carry diseases that immunocompromised patients can't fight off. In the end, I did not wind up sewing a dress; I found one online at Bluefly.com: a gold sheath, cut in a V for Kate's catheter. But over this is a long-sleeved, sheer shirt, one that wraps at the waist and glimmers when she turns this way and that so when you notice the strange triple tubing coming out by her breastbone, you wonder if it was only a trick of the light.

We took a thousand photos before leaving the house. When Kate and Taylor had escaped and were waiting for me in the car, I went to put the camera away and found Brian in the kitchen with his back to me. "Hey," I said. "You going to wave us off? Throw rice?"

It was only when he turned around that I realized he'd come in here to cry. "I didn't expect to see this," he said. "I didn't think I'd get to have this memory."

I fitted myself against him, working our bodies so tight it felt as if we'd been carved from the same smooth stone. "Wait up for us," I whispered, and then I left.

Now, I hand a cup of punch to a boy whose hair is just starting to fall out in small tufts. It sheds on the black lapel of his tuxedo. "Thanks," he says, and I see he has the most beautiful eyes, dark and still as a panther's. I glance away and realize that Kate and Taylor are gone.

What if she's sick? What if he's sick? I have promised myself I wouldn't be overprotective, but there are too many children here for the staff to really keep track of. I ask another parent to take over my punch station and then I search out the ladies' room. I check the supply closet. I walk through empty hallways and dark corridors and even the chapel.

Finally I hear Kate's voice through a cracked doorway. She and Taylor stand under a spotlight moon, holding hands. The court-yard they've found is a favorite for the residents during the daytime; many doctors who wouldn't otherwise see the light of the sun take their lunches out here.

I am about to ask if they're all right when Kate speaks. "Are you afraid of dying?"

Taylor shakes his head. "Not really. Sometimes, though, I think about my funeral. If people will say good things, you know, about

me. If anyone will cry." He hesitates. "If anyone will even come."

"I will," Kate promises.

Taylor dips his head toward Kate's, and
she sways closer, and I realize that this is why
I followed them. I knew this was what I
would find, and like Brian, I wanted one
more picture of my daughter, one that I
might worry between my fingers like a piece
of sea glass. Taylor lifts up the edges of her
blue hygienic mask and I know I should stop
him, I know I have to, but I don't. This much I
want her to have.

When they kiss, it is beautiful: those
alabaster heads bent together, smooth as
statues—an optical illusion, a mirror image
that's folding into itself.

When Kate goes into the hospital for her
stem cell transplant, she's an emotional
wreck. She is far less concerned with the
runny fluid being infused into her catheter
than she is with the fact that Taylor hasn't
called her in three days, and has in fact not

returned her calls either. "Did you have a fight?" I ask, and she shakes her head. "Did he say he was going somewhere? Maybe it was an emergency," I say. "Maybe this has nothing to do with you at all."

"Maybe it does," Kate argues.

"Then the best revenge is getting healthy enough to give him a piece of your mind," I point out. "I'll be right back."

In the hallway, I approach Steph, a nurse who has just come on duty and who's known Kate for years. The truth is, I am just as surprised about Taylor's lack of communication as Kate is. He knew she was coming in here.

"Taylor Ambrose," I ask Steph. "Has he been in today?"

She looks at me and blinks.

"Big kid, sweet. Hung up on my daughter," I joke.

"Oh, Sara . . . I thought for sure someone would have told you," Steph says. "He died this morning."

•   •   •

I don't tell Kate, not for a month. Not until the day Dr. Chance says Kate is well enough to leave the hospital, until Kate has already convinced herself she was better off without him. I cannot begin to tell you the words I use; none of them are big enough to bear the weight behind them. I mention how I went to Taylor's house and spoke to his mother; how she broke down in my arms and said she'd wanted to call me, but there was a part of her that was so jealous it swallowed all her speech. She told me that Taylor, who'd come home from the prom walking on air, had walked into her bedroom in the middle of the night, with a 105 degree fever. How maybe it was viral and maybe it was fungal but he'd gone into respiratory distress and then cardiac arrest and after thirty minutes of trying the doctors had to let him go.

I don't tell Kate something else Jenna Ambrose said—that afterward, she went inside and stared at her son, who wasn't her son anymore. That she sat for five whole hours, sure he was going to wake up. That even now she hears noise overhead and thinks Taylor is moving around his room, and that the half-second she is gifted before she remembers the truth is the only reason she gets up each morning.

"Kate," I say, "I'm so sorry."

Kate's face crumples. "But I loved him," she replies, as if this should be enough.

"I know."

"And you didn't tell me."

"I couldn't. Not when I thought it might make you stop fighting back, yourself."

She closes her eyes and turns onto her side on the pillow, crying so hard that the monitors she's still hooked to begin to beep and bring in the nursing staff.

I reach for her. "Kate, honey, I did what was best for you."

She refuses to look in my direction. "Don't talk to me," she murmurs. "You're good at that."

Kate stops speaking to me for seven days and eleven hours. We come home from the hospital; we go about our business of reverse isolation; we pick through the motions because we have done it before. At night I lie in bed next to Brian and wonder why he can sleep. I stare at the ceiling and think that I have lost my daughter before she's even gone.

Then one day I walk by her bedroom and find her sitting on the floor with photographs all around. There are, as I expect, the ones of her and Taylor that we took before the prom—Kate dressed to the nines with that telltale surgical mask covering her mouth. Taylor has drawn a lipstick smile on it, for the sake of the photos, or so he said.

It had made Kate laugh. It seems impossible that this boy, who was so solid a presence when the flash went off mere weeks ago, simply is not here anymore; a pang goes through me, and immediately on its heels a single word: practice.

But there are other photos, too, from when Kate was younger. One of Kate and Anna on the beach, crouched over a hermit crab. One of Kate dressed up like Mr. Peanut for Halloween. One of Kate with cream cheese all over her face, holding up two halves of a bagel like eyeglasses.

In another pile are her baby pictures—all taken when she was three, or younger. Gap-toothed and grinning, backlit by a sloe-eyed sun, unaware of what was to come. "I don't remember being her," Kate says quietly, and these first words make a bridge of glass, one that shifts beneath my feet as I step into the room.

I put my hand beside hers, at the edge of one photo. Bent at a corner, it shows Kate as a toddler being tossed into the air by Brian, her hair flying behind her, her arms and legs starfish-splayed, certain beyond a doubt that when she fell to earth again, there would be a safe landing, sure that she deserved nothing less.

"She was beautiful," Kate adds, and with her pinky she strokes the glossy vivid cheek of the girl none of us ever got to know.

JESSE

THE SUMMER I WAS FOURTEEN my parents sent me to boot camp on a farm. It was one of those action-adventures for troubled kids, you know, get up at four A.M. to do the milking and how much trouble can you really get into? (The answer, if you're interested: score pot off the ranch hands. Get stoned. Tip cows.) Anyway, one day I was assigned to Moses Patrol, or that's what we called the poor son of a bitch who pulled herding duty with the lambs. I had to follow about a hundred sheep around a pasture that didn't have one goddamned tree to provide even a sliver of shade.

To say a sheep is the dumbest fucking animal on earth is probably an understatement. They get caught in fences. They get lost in four-foot-square pens. They forget where to find their food, although it's been in the same place for a thousand days straight. And they're not the little puffy darlings you picture when you go to sleep, either. They stink. They bleat. They're annoying as hell.

Anyway, the day I was stuck with the sheep, I had filched a copy of **Tropic of Cancer** and I was folding down the pages that came closest to good porn, when I heard someone scream. I was perfectly sure, mind you, that it wasn't an animal, because I'd never heard anything like this in my life. I ran toward the sound, sure I was going to find someone thrown from a horse with their leg twisted like a pretzel or some yoho who'd emptied his revolver by accident into his own guts. But lying on the side of the creek, with a bevy of ewes in attendance, was a sheep giving birth.

I wasn't a vet or anything, but I knew enough to realize that when any living creature makes a racket like that, things aren't going according to plan. Sure enough, this poor sheep had two little hooves dangling out of her privates. She lay on her side, panting. She rolled one flat black eye toward me, then just gave up.

Well, nothing was dying on my patrol, if only because I knew that the Nazis who ran the camp would make me bury the damn animal. So I shoved the other sheep out of the way. I got down on my knees and grabbed the knotty slick hooves and yanked while the ewe screamed like any mother whose child is ripped away from her.

The lamb came out, its limbs folded like the parts of a Swiss Army knife. Over its head was a silver sac that felt like the inside of your cheek when you run your tongue around it. It wasn't breathing.

I sure as shit wasn't going to put my mouth over a sheep and do artificial respiration, but I used my fingernails to rip apart the skin sac, to yank it down from the neck of the lamb. And it turned out, that was all it needed. A minute later it unbent its clothespin legs and started whickering for its mother.

There were, I think, twenty lambs born during that summer session. Every time I passed the pen I could pick mine out from a crowd. He looked like all the others, except that he moved with a little more spring; he always seemed to have the sun shining off the oil in its wool. And if you happened to get him calm enough to look you in the eye, the pupils had gone milky white, a sure sign that he'd walked on the other side long enough to remember what he was missing.

I tell you this now because when Kate finally stirs in that hospital bed, and opens her eyes, I know she's got one foot on the other side already, too.

"Oh my God," Kate says weakly, when she sees me. "I wound up in Hell after all."

I lean forward in my chair and cross my arms. "Now, sis, you know I'm not that easy to kill." Getting up, I kiss her on the forehead, letting my lips stay an extra second. How is it that mothers can read fever that way? I can only read imminent loss. "How you doing?"

She smiles at me, but it's like a cartoon drawing when I've seen the real thing hanging in the Louvre. "Peachy," she says. "To what do I owe the honor of your presence?"

Because you won't be here much longer, I think, but I do not tell her this. "I was in the neighborhood. Plus there's a really hot nurse who works this shift."

This makes Kate laugh out loud. "God, Jess. I'm gonna miss you."

She says it so easily that I think it surprises both of us. I sit down on the edge of the bed and trace the little puckers in the thermal blanket. "You know—" I begin a pep talk, but she puts her hand on my arm.

"Don't." Then her eyes come alive, for just a moment. "Maybe I'll get reincarnated."

"Like as Marie Antoinette?"

"No, it's got to be something in the future. You think that's crazy?"

"No," I admit. "I think we probably all just keep running in circles."

"So what will you come back as, then?"

"Carrion." She winces, and something beeps, and I panic. "You want me to get someone?"

"No, you're fine," Kate answers, and I'm sure she doesn't mean it this way, but it pretty much makes me feel like I've swallowed lightning.

I suddenly remember an old game I used to play when I was nine or ten, and was allowed to ride my bike until it got dark. I used to make little bets with myself as I watched the sun getting lower and lower on the horizon: if I hold my breath to twenty seconds, the night won't come. If I don't blink. If I stand so still a fly lands on my cheek. Now, I find myself doing the same thing, bargaining to keep Kate, even though that isn't the way it works.

"Are you afraid?" I blurt out. "Of dying?"

Kate turns to me, a smile sliding over her mouth. "I'll let you know." Then she closes her eyes. "I'm just gonna rest a second," she manages, and she is asleep again.

It's not fair, but Kate knows that. It doesn't take a whole long life to realize that what we deserve to have, we rarely get. I stand up, with that lightning bolt branding the lining of my throat, which makes it impossible to swallow, so everything gets backed up like a dammed river. I hurry out of Kate's room and far enough down the hall where I won't disturb her, and then I lift my fist and punch a hole in the thick white wall and still this isn't enough.

BRIAN

HERE IS THE RECIPE to blow something up:
a Pyrex bowl; potassium chloride—found at
health food stores, as a salt substitute. A
hydrometer. Bleach. Take the bleach and pour it
into the Pyrex, put it onto a stove burner.
Meanwhile, weigh out your potassium chloride
and add to the bleach. Check it with the
hydrometer and boil until you get a reading of
1.3. Cool to room temperature, and filter out the
crystals that form. This is what you will save.

It's hard to be the one always waiting. I mean,
there's something to be said for the hero who
charges off to battle, but when you get right down
to it there's a whole story in who's left behind.

I'm in what has to be the ugliest courtroom

on the East Coast, sitting in chairs until it's my turn, when suddenly my beeper goes off. I look at the number, groan, and try to figure out what to do. I'm a witness later, but the department needs me right now.

It takes a few talking heads but I get permission from the judge to remove myself from the premises. I leave through the front door, and immediately I'm assailed with questions and cameras and lights. It is everything I can do not to punch these vultures, who want to rip apart the bleached bones of my family.

When I couldn't find Anna the morning of the hearing, I headed home. I looked in all her usual haunts—the kitchen, the bedroom, the hammock out back—but she wasn't there. As a last resort I climbed the garage stairs to the apartment Jesse uses.

He wasn't home either, although by now this is hardly a surprise. There was a time when Jesse disappointed me regularly; eventually, I told myself not to expect anything from him, and as a result, it has gotten easier for me to take what comes. I knocked on the door and yelled for Anna, for Jesse, but no one answered. Although there was a key to this apartment on my own set, I stopped short of letting myself inside. Turning on the stairs, I knocked over the red recycling bin I personally empty every Tuesday, since God forbid Jesse can remember to drag it out to the curb himself. A tenpin of beer bottles, lucent green, tumbled out. An empty jug of laundry detergent, an olive jar, a gallon container from orange juice.

I put everything back in, except for the orange juice container, which I've told Jesse isn't recyclable and which he puts in the bin nonetheless every damn week.

The difference between these fires and the other ones was that now the stakes have been ratcheted up a notch. Instead of an abandoned warehouse or a shack at the side of the water, it is an elementary school. This being summer, no one was on the premises when the fire was started. But there's no question in my mind it was due to unnatural causes.

When I get there, the engines are just loading up after salvage and overhaul. Paulie comes over to me right away. "How's Kate?"

"She's okay," I tell him, and I nod toward the mess. "What'd you find?"

"He pretty much managed to gut the whole north side of the facility," Paulie says. "You doing a walk through?"

"Yeah."

The fire began in the teacher's lounge; the char patterns point like an arrow to the origin. A collection of synthetic stuffing that hasn't burned clean through is still visible; whoever set this was smart enough to light his fire in the middle of a pile of couch cushions and stacks of paper. I can still smell the accelerant; this time it was as simple as gasoline. Bits of glass from the exploded Molotov cocktail litter the ashes.

I wander to the far side of the building, peer through a broken window. The guys must have vented the fire here. "You think we'll catch this little fuck, Cap?" asks Caesar, coming into the room. Still in his turnout gear, with a smudge across his left cheek, he looks down at the debris in the fire line. Then he bends down, and with his heavy glove, picks up a cigarette butt. "Unbelievable. The secretary's desk melted down to a puddle, but a goddamn tobacco stick survives."

I take it out of his hands and turn it over in my palm. "That's because it wasn't here when the fire started. Someone had a nice smoke while he watched this, and then he walked away." I tip it onto the side, to where the yellow meets the filter, and read the brand.

Paulie sticks his head in the shattered window, looking for Caesar. "We're heading back. Get on the truck." Then he turns to me. "Hey, just so you know, we didn't break this one."

"I wasn't gonna make you pay for it, Paulie."

"No, I mean, we vented the roof. This was already broken when we got here." He and Caesar leave, and a few moments later I hear the heavy drag of the engine pulling away.

It could have been a stray baseball, or a Frisbee. But even in the summertime, janitors monitor public property. A broken window is too much of a hazard to be left alone; it would have been taped up or boarded.

Unless the same guy who started the fire knew where to bring in oxygen, so that the flames would race through the wind tunnel created by that vacuum.

I look down at the cigarette in my hand, and crush it.

You need 56 grams of these reserved crystals. Mix with distilled water. Heat to a boil and cool again, saving the crystals, pure potassium chlorate. Grind these to the consistency of face powder, and heat gently to dry. Melt five parts Vaseline with five parts wax. Dissolve in gasoline and pour this liquid onto 90 parts potassium chlorate crystals in a plastic bowl. Knead. Allow the gasoline to evaporate.

Mold into a cube and dip in wax to make it waterproof. This explosive requires a blasting cap of at least a grade A3.

When Jesse opens the door to his apartment, I am waiting on the couch. "What are you doing here?" he asks.

"What are **you** doing here?"

"I live here," Jesse says. "Remember?"

"Do you? Or are you using this as a place to hide?"

He takes out a cigarette from a pack in his front pocket and lights up. Merits. "I don't know what the fuck you're talking about. Why aren't you in court?"

"How come there's muriatic acid under your sink?" I ask. "Considering that we don't have a pool?"

"Hello? Is this, like, the Inquisition?" He scowls. "I used it when I was working with those tile layers last summer; you can clean up grout with it. To tell you the truth I didn't even know I still had it."

"Then you probably wouldn't know, Jess, that when you put it into a bottle with a piece of aluminum foil with a rag stuffed into the top, it blows up pretty damn well."

He goes very still. "Are you accusing me of something? Because if you are, just say it, you bastard."

I get up from the couch. "Okay. I want to know if you scored the bottles before you made the cocktails, so that they'd break easier. I want to know if you realized how close that homeless guy was to dying when you set the warehouse on fire for kicks." Reaching behind me, I lift the empty

Clorox container from his recycle bin. "I want to know why the hell this is in your trash, when you don't do your own laundry and God knows you don't clean, yet there's an elementary school six miles from here that's been gutted with an explosive made of bleach and brake fluid?" I have him by the shoulders now, and although Jesse could break away if he really tried, he lets me shake him until his head snaps back. "Jesus Christ, Jesse!"

He stares at me, his face blank. "Are you about done?"

I let him go and he backs away, teeth bared. "Then tell me I'm wrong," I challenge.

"I'll tell you more than that," he yells. "I mean, I totally understand that you've spent your life believing that everything that's wrong in the universe all traces back to me, but news flash, Dad, this time you're totally off base."

Slowly, I take something out of my pocket and press it into Jesse's hand. The Merit cigarette butt settles in the hollow of his palm. "Then you shouldn't have left your calling card."

There is a point when a structure fire is raging out of control that you simply have to give it the distance to burn itself out. So you move back to safety, to a hill out of the wind, and you watch the building eat itself alive.

Jesse's hand comes up, trembling, and the cigarette rolls to the floor at our feet. He covers his face, presses his thumbs to the corners of his eyes. "I couldn't save her." The words are ripped from his center. He hunches his shoulders, sliding backward into the body of a boy. "Who . . . who did you tell?"

He is asking, I realize, whether the police will be coming after him. Whether I have spoken to Sara about this.

He is asking to be punished.

So I do what I know will destroy him: I pull Jesse into my arms as he sobs. His back is broader than mine. He stands a half-head taller than me. I don't remember seeing him go from that five-year-old, who wasn't a genetic match, to the man he is now, and I guess this is the problem. How does someone go from thinking that if he cannot rescue, he must destroy? And do you blame him, or do you blame the folks who should have told him otherwise?

I will make sure that my son's pyromania ends here and now, but I won't tell the cops or the fire chief about this. Maybe that's nepotism, maybe it's stupidity. Maybe it's because Jesse isn't all that different from me, choosing fire as his medium, needing to know that he could command at least one uncontrollable thing.

Jesse's breathing evens against me, like it used to when he was so small, when I used to carry him upstairs after he'd fallen asleep in my lap. He used to hit me over and over with questions: **What's a two-inch hose for, a one-inch? How come you wash the engines? Does the can man ever get to drive?** I realize that I cannot remember exactly when he stopped asking. But I do remember feeling as if something had gone missing, as if the loss of a kid's hero worship can ache like a phantom limb.

CAMPBELL

DOCTORS HAVE THIS THING about being subpoenaed: they let you know, with every syllable of every word, that no moment of this testimony will make up for the fact that while they were sitting on the witness stand under duress, patients were waiting, people were dying. Frankly, it pisses me off. And before I know it, I can't help myself, I am asking for a bathroom break, leaning down to retie my shoe, gathering my thoughts and stuffing sentences with pregnant pauses—whatever it takes to keep them cooling their heels just a few seconds more.

Dr. Chance is no exception to the rule. From the onset he's anxious to leave. He checks his watch so often you'd think he was about to miss a train. The difference this time around is that Sara Fitzgerald is just as anxious to get him out of the courtroom. Because the patient who is waiting, the person who is dying, is Kate.

But beside me, Anna's body throws heat. I get up, continue my questioning. Slowly. "Dr. Chance, were any of the treatments that involved donations from Anna's body 'sure things'?"

"Nothing in cancer is a sure thing, Mr. Alexander."

"Was that explained to the Fitzgeralds?"

"We carefully explain the risks of every procedure, because once you begin treatments, you compromise other bodily systems. What we wind up doing for one treatment successfully may come back to haunt you the next time around." He smiles at Sara. "That said, Kate's an incredible young woman. She wasn't expected to live past age five, and here she is at sixteen."

"Thanks to her sister," I point out.

Dr. Chance nods. "Not many patients have both the strength of body and the good fortune to have a perfectly matched donor available to them."

I stand up, my hands in my pockets. "Can you tell the Court how the Fitzgeralds came to consult Providence Hospital's preimplantation genetic diagnosis team to conceive Anna?"

"After their son was tested and found to be an unsuitable donor for Kate, I told the Fitzgeralds about another family I'd worked with. They'd tested all the patient's siblings, and none qualified, but then the mother got pregnant during the course of treatment and that child happened to be a perfect match."

"Did you tell the Fitzgeralds to conceive a genetically programmed child to serve as a donor for Kate?"

"Absolutely not," Chance says, affronted. "I just explained that even if none of the existing children was a match, that didn't mean that a future child might not be."

"Did you explain to the Fitzgeralds that this child, as a perfectly genetically programmed match, would have to be available for all these treatments for Kate throughout her life?"

"We were talking about a single cord blood treatment at the time," Dr. Chance says. "Subsequent donations came about because Kate didn't respond to the first one. And because they offered more promising results."

"So if tomorrow scientists were to come up

with a procedure that would cure Kate's cancer if Anna only cut off her head and gave it to her sister, would you recommend that?"

"Obviously not. I would never recommend a treatment that risked another child's life."

"Isn't that what you've done for the past thirteen years?"

His face tightens. "None of the treatments have caused significant long-term harm to Anna."

I take a piece of paper out of my briefcase and hand it to the judge, and then to Dr. Chance. "Can you read the part that's marked?"

He puts on a pair of glasses and clears his throat. "I understand that anesthesia involves potential risks. These risks may include, but are not limited to: adverse drug reactions, sore throat, injury to teeth and dental work, damage to vocal cords, respiratory problems, minor pain and discomfort, loss of sensation, headaches, infection, allergic reaction, awareness during general anesthesia, jaundice, bleeding, nerve injury, blood clot, heart attack, brain damage, and even loss of bodily function or of life."

"Are you familiar with this form, Doctor?"

"Yes. It's a standard consent form for a surgical procedure."

"Can you tell us who the patient receiving it was?"

"Anna Fitzgerald."

"And who signed the consent form?"

"Sara Fitzgerald."

I rock back on my heels. "Dr. Chance, anesthesia carries a risk of life impairment or death. Those are pretty strong long-term effects."

"That's exactly why we have a consent form. It's to protect us from people like you," he says. "But realistically, the risk is extremely small. And the procedure of donating marrow is fairly simple."

"Why was Anna being anesthetized for such a simple procedure?"

"It's less traumatic for a child, and they're less likely to squirm around."

"And after the procedure, did Anna experience any pain?"

"Maybe a little," Dr. Chance says.

"You don't remember?"

"It's been a long time. I'm sure even Anna's forgotten about it by now."

"You think?" I turn to Anna. "Should we ask her?"

Judge DeSalvo crosses his arms.

"Speaking of risk," I continue smoothly. "Can you tell us about the research that's been done on the long-term effects of the growth factor shots she's taken twice now, prior to harvest for transplant?"

"Theoretically, there shouldn't be any long-term sequelae."

"Theoretically," I repeat. "Why theoretically?"

"Because the research has been done on lab animals," Dr. Chance admits. "Effects on humans are still being tracked."

"How comforting."

He shrugs. "Physicians don't tend to prescribe drugs that have the potential to wreak havoc."

"Have you ever heard of thalidomide, Doctor?" I ask.

"Of course. In fact, recently, it's been resurrected for cancer research."

"And it was a milestone drug once before," I point out. "With catastrophic effects. Speaking of which . . . this kidney donation—are there risks associated with the procedure?"

"No more than for most surgeries," Dr. Chance says.

"Could Anna die from complications of this surgery?"

"It's highly unlikely, Mr. Alexander."

"Well, then, let's assume Anna comes through the procedure with flying colors. How will having a single kidney affect her for the rest of her life?"

"It won't, really," the doctor says. "That's the beauty of it."

I hand him a flyer that has come from the nephrology department of his own hospital. "Can you read the highlighted section?"

He slips on his glasses again. "Increased chance of hypertension. Possible complications during pregnancy." Dr. Chance glances up. "Donors are advised to refrain from contact sports to eliminate the risk of harming their remaining kidney."

I clasp my hands behind my back. "Did you know that Anna plays hockey in her free time?"

He turns toward her. "No. I didn't."

"She's a goalie. Has been for years now." I let this sink in. "But since this donation is hypothetical, let's concentrate on the ones that have already happened. The growth factor shots, the

DLI, the stem cells, the lymphocyte donations, the bone marrow—all of these myriad treatments Anna endured—in your expert opinion, Doctor, are you saying that Anna has not undergone any significant medical harm from these procedures?"

"Significant?" He hesitates. "No, she has not."

"Has she received any significant benefit from them?"

Dr. Chance looks at me for a long moment. "Sure," he says. "She's saving her sister."

Anna and I are eating lunch upstairs at the courthouse when Julia walks in. "Is this a private party?"

Anna waves her inside, and Julia sits down without so much as a glance toward me. "How are you doing?" she asks.

"Okay," Anna replies. "I just want it to be over."

Julia opens up a packet of salad dressing and pours it over the lunch she's brought. "It will be, before you know it."

She looks at me when she says this, briefly.

That's all it takes for me to remember the

smell of her skin, and the spot below her breast where she has a beauty mark in the shape of a crescent moon.

Suddenly Anna gets up. "I'm going to take Judge for a walk," she announces.

"Like hell you are. There are reporters out there, still."

"I'll walk him in the hallway, then."

"You can't. He has to be walked by me; it's part of his training."

"Then I'm going to pee," Anna says. "That's something I'm still allowed to do by myself, right?"

She walks out of the conference room, leaving Julia and me and everything that shouldn't have happened but did.

"She left us alone on purpose," I realize.

Julia nods. "She's a smart kid. She can read people very well." Then she sets down her plastic fork. "Your car is full of dog hair."

"I know. I keep asking Judge to pull it back in a ponytail but he never listens."

"Why didn't you just get me up?"

I grin. "Because we were anchored in a no-wake zone."

Julia, however, doesn't even crack a smile. "Was last night a joke to you, Campbell?"

That old adage pops into my head: **If you want to see God laugh, make a plan.** And because I am a coward, I grab the dog by his collar. "I need to walk him before we're called back into court."

Julia's voice follows me to the door. "You didn't answer me."

"You don't want me to," I say. I don't turn around. That way I don't have to see her face.

When Judge DeSalvo adjourns us for the day at three because of a weekly chiropractic appointment, I walk Anna out to the lobby to find her father—but Brian's gone. Sara looks around, surprised. "Maybe he got a fire call," she says. "Anna, I'll—"

But I put my hand on Anna's shoulder. "I'll take you to the fire station."

In the car, she is quiet. I pull into the station parking lot and leave the engine running. "Listen," I tell her, "you may not have realized it, but we had a great first day."

"Whatever."

She gets out of my car without another word and Judge hops up into the vacated front seat. Anna walks toward the station, but then veers left. I start to pull back out, and then against my better judgment turn off the engine. Leaving Judge in the car, I follow her around the back of the building.

She stands like a statue, her face turned up to the sky. What am I supposed to do, say? I have never been a parent; I can barely take care of myself.

As it turns out, Anna starts speaking first. "Did you ever do something you knew was wrong, even though it felt right?"

I think of Julia. "Yeah."

"Sometimes I hate myself," Anna murmurs.

"Sometimes," I tell her, "I hate myself, too."

This surprises her. She looks at me, and then at the sky again. "They're up there. The stars. Even when you can't see them."

I put my hands into my pockets. "I used to wish on a star every night."

"For what?"

"Rare baseball cards for my collection. A

golden retriever. Young, hot female teachers."

"My dad told me that a bunch of astronomers found a new place where stars are being born. Only it's taken us 2,500 years to see them." She turns to me. "Do you get along with your parents?"

I think about lying to her, but then I shake my head. "I used to think I'd be just like them when I grew up, but I'm not. And the thing is, somewhere along the way, I stopped wanting to be like them, anyway."

The sun washes over her milky skin, lights the line of her throat. "I get it," Anna says. "You were invisible, too."

TUESDAY

A little fire is quickly trodden out;

Which, being suffered, rivers can not
quench.

—WILLIAM SHAKESPEARE,
King Henry VI

CAMPBELL

BRIAN FITZGERALD IS MY LOCK. Once
the judge realizes that at least one of Anna's parents agrees with her decision to stop being a
donor for her sister, granting her emancipation
won't be quite as great a leap. If Brian does what
I need him to—namely, tell Judge DeSalvo that
he knows Anna has rights, too, and that he's prepared to support her—then whatever Julia says in
her report will be a moot point. And better still,
Anna's testimony would only be a formality.

Brian shows up with Anna early the next
morning, wearing his captain's uniform. I paste
a smile on my face and get up, walking toward
them with Judge. "Morning," I say. "Everyone
ready?"

Brian looks at Anna. Then he looks at me.
There is a question right there on the verge of

his lips, but he seems to be doing everything he can not to ask it.

"Hey," I say to Anna, brainstorming. "Want to do me a favor? Judge could use a couple of quick runs up and down the stairs, or he's going to get restless in court."

"Yesterday you told me I couldn't walk him."

"Well, today you can."

Anna shakes her head. "I'm not going anywhere. The minute I leave you're just going to talk about me."

So I turn to Brian again. "Is everything all right?"

At that moment, Sara Fitzgerald comes into the building. She hurries toward the courtroom, and seeing Brian with me, pauses. Then she turns slowly away from her husband and continues inside.

Brian Fitzgerald's eyes follow his wife, even after the doors close behind her. "We're fine," he says, an answer not meant for me.

"Mr. Fitzgerald, were there times that you disagreed with your wife about having Anna participate in medical treatments for Kate's benefit?"

"Yes. The doctors said that it was only cord blood we needed for Kate. They'd be taking part of the umbilicus that usually gets thrown out after giving birth—it wasn't anything that the baby was ever going to miss, and it certainly wasn't going to hurt her." He meets Anna's eye, gives her a smile. "And it worked for a little while, too. Kate went into remission. But in 1996, she relapsed again. The doctors wanted Anna to donate some lymphocytes. It wasn't going to be a cure, but it would hold Kate over for a while."

I try to draw him along. "You and your wife didn't see eye to eye over this treatment?"

"I didn't know if it was such a great idea. This time Anna was going to know what was happening, and she wasn't going to like it."

"What did your wife say to make you change your mind?"

"That if we didn't draw blood from Anna this time, we'd need marrow soon anyway."

"How did you feel about that?"

Brian shakes his head, clearly uncomfortable. "You don't know what it's like," he says quietly, "until your child is dying. You find yourself saying things and doing things you don't want to do or say. And you think it's something you have a choice about, but then you get up a little closer to it, and you see you had it all wrong." He looks up at Anna, who is so still beside me I think she has forgotten to breathe. "I didn't want to do that to Anna. But I couldn't lose Kate."

"Did you have to use Anna's bone marrow, eventually?"

"Yes."

"Mr. Fitzgerald, as a certified EMT, would you ever perform a procedure on a patient who didn't present with any physical problems?"

"Of course not."

"Then why did you, as Anna's father, think this invasive procedure, which carried risk to Anna herself and no personal physical benefit, was in her best interests?"

"Because," Brian says, "I couldn't let Kate die."

"Were there other points, Mr. Fitzgerald, when you and your wife disagreed over the use of Anna's body for your other daughter's treatment?"

"A few years ago, Kate was hospitalized

and . . . losing so much blood nobody thought she'd make it through. I thought maybe it was time to let her go. Sara didn't."

"What happened?"

"The doctors gave her arsenic, and it kicked in, putting Kate into remission for a year."

"Are you saying that there was a treatment which saved Kate, that didn't involve the use of Anna's body?"

Brian shakes his head. "I'm saying . . . I'm saying I was so sure Kate was going to die. But Sara, she didn't give up on Kate and she came back fighting." He looks over at his wife. "And now, Kate's kidneys are giving out. I don't want to see her suffering. But at the same time, I don't want to make the same mistake twice. I don't want to tell myself it's over, when it doesn't have to be."

Brian has become an emotional avalanche, headed right for the glass house I have been meticulously crafting. I need to reel him in. "Mr. Fitzgerald, did you know your daughter was going to file a lawsuit against you and your wife?"

"No."

"When she did, did you speak to Anna about it?"

"Yes."

"Based on that conversation, Mr. Fitzgerald, what did you do?"

"I moved out of the house with Anna."

"Why?"

"At the time I believed Anna had the right to think this decision out, which wasn't something she'd be able to do living in our house."

"After having moved out with Anna, after having spoken to her at great lengths about why she's initiated this lawsuit—do you agree with your wife's request to have Anna continue to be a donor for Kate?"

The answer we have rehearsed is **no**; this is the crux of my case. Brian leans forward to reply. "Yes, I do," he says.

"Mr. Fitzgerald, in your opinion . . ." I begin, and then I realize what he's just done. "Excuse me?"

"I still wish Anna would donate a kidney," Brian admits.

Staring at this witness who has just completely fucked me over, I scramble for footing. If Brian won't support Anna's decision to stop being a donor, then the judge will find it far harder to rule in favor of emancipation.

At the same time, I'm patently aware of the smallest sound that has escaped from Anna, the quiet break of soul that comes when you realize that what looked like a rainbow was actually only a trick of the light. "Mr. Fitzgerald, you're willing to have Anna undergo major surgery and the loss of an organ to benefit Kate?"

It is a curious thing, watching a strong man fall to pieces. "Can you tell me what the right answer is here?" Brian asks, his voice raw. "Because I don't know where to look for it. I know what's right. I know what's fair. But neither of those apply here. I can sit, and I can think about it, and I can tell you what should be and what ought to be. I can even tell you there's got to be a better solution. But it's been thirteen years, Mr. Alexander, and I still haven't found it."

He slowly sinks forward, too big in that tiny space, until his forehead rests on the cool bar of wood that borders the witness stand.

Judge DeSalvo calls for a ten-minute recess before Sara Fitzgerald will begin her cross-examination, so that the witness can have a few moments to himself. Anna and I go downstairs to the vending machines, where you can spend a dollar on weak tea and weaker soup. She sits with her heels caught on the rungs of a stool, and when I hand her her cup of hot chocolate she sets it down on the table without drinking.

"I've never seen my dad cry," she says. "My mom, she would lose it all the time over Kate. But Dad—well, if he fell apart, he made sure to do it where we weren't watching."

"Anna—"

"Do you think I did that to him?" she asks, turning to me. "Do you think I shouldn't have asked him to come here today?"

"The judge would have asked him to testify even if you didn't." I shake my head. "Anna, you're going to have to do it yourself."

She looks up at me, wary. "Do what?"

"Testify."

Anna blinks at me. "Are you **kidding?**"

"I thought that the judge would clearly rule in your favor if he saw that your father was willing to support your choices. But unfortunately, that's not what just happened. And I have no idea what Julia's going to say—but even if she comes down on your side, Judge DeSalvo will still need to be convinced that you're mature enough to make these choices on your own, independent of your parents."

"You mean I have to get up there? Like a witness?"

I have always known that at some point, Anna would have to take the stand. In a case about emancipation of a minor, it stands to reason that a judge would want to hear from the minor herself. Anna might be acting skittish about testifying, but I believe that subconsciously, it's what she really wants to do. Why else go to the trouble of instigating a lawsuit, if not to make sure that you finally get to speak your mind?

"You told me yesterday I wouldn't have to testify," Anna says, getting agitated.

"I was wrong."

"I hired you so that **you** could tell everyone what I want."

"It doesn't work that way," I say. "You started this lawsuit. You wanted to be someone other than the person your family's made you for the past thirteen years. And that means you have to pull back the curtain and show us who she is."

"Half the grown-ups on this planet have no idea who they are, but they get to make decisions for themselves every day," Anna argues.

"They aren't thirteen. Listen," I say, getting to what I imagine is the crux of the matter. "I know, in the past, standing up and speaking your mind hasn't gotten you anywhere. But I promise you, this time, when you talk, every-one will listen."

If anything, this has the reverse effect of what I've intended. Anna crosses her arms. "There is no way I'm getting up there," she says.

"Anna, being a witness isn't really that big a deal—"

"It **is** a big deal, Campbell. It's the **hugest** deal. And I'm **not** doing it."

"If you don't testify, we lose," I explain.

"Then find another way to win. **You're** the lawyer."

I'm not going to rise to that bait. I drum my fingers on the table for patience. "Do you want to tell me why you're so dead set against this?"

She glances up. "No."

"No, you're not doing it? Or no, you won't tell me?"

"There are just some things I don't like talking about." Her face hardens. "I thought you, of all people, would be able to understand that."

She knows exactly what buttons to push. "Sleep on it," I suggest tightly.

"I'm not going to change my mind."

I stand up and dump my full cup of coffee into the trash. "Well then," I tell her. "Don't expect me to be able to change your life."

SARA

Present Day

THERE IS A CURIOUS THING that happens with the passage of time: a calcification of character. See, if the light hits Brian's face the right way, I can still see the pale blue hue of his eyes that has always made me think of an island ocean I had yet to swim in. Beneath the fine lines of his smile, there is the cleft of his chin—the first feature I looked for in the faces of my newborn children. There is his resolve, his quiet will, and a steady peace with himself that I have always wished would rub off on me. These are the base elements that made me fall in love with my husband; if there are times I do not recognize him now, maybe this isn't a drawback. Change isn't always for the worst; the shell that forms around a piece of sand looks to some people like an irritation, and to others, like a pearl.

Brian's eyes dart from Anna, who is picking at a scab on her thumb, to me. He watches me like a mouse watches a hawk. There is something about this that makes me ache; is this really what he thinks of me?

Does everyone?

I wish there was not a courtroom between us. I wish I could walk up to him. **Listen,** I would say, **this is not how I thought our lives would go; and maybe we cannnot find our way out of this alley. But there is no one I'd rather be lost with.**

Listen, I'd say, **maybe I was wrong.**

"Mrs. Fitzgerald," Judge DeSalvo asks, "do you have any questions for the witness?"

It is, I realize, a good term for a spouse. What else does a husband or a wife do, but attest to each other's errors in judgment?

I get up slowly from my seat. "Hello, Brian," I say, and my voice is not nearly as steady as I would have hoped.

"Sara," he answers.

Following that exchange, I have no idea what to say.

A memory washes over me. We had

wanted to get away, but couldn't decide where to go. So we got into the car and drove, and every half hour we'd let one of the kids pick an exit, or tell us to turn right or left. We wound up in Seal Cove, Maine, and then stopped, because Jesse's next direction would have landed us in the Atlantic. We rented a cabin with no heat, no electricity—and our three kids afraid of the dark.

I do not realize I have been speaking out loud until Brian answers. "I know," he says. "We put so many candles on that floor I thought for sure we'd burn the place down. It rained for five days."

"And on the sixth day, when the weather cleared, the greenheads were so bad we couldn't even stand to be outside."

"And then Jesse got poison ivy and his eyes swelled shut . . ."

"Excuse me," Campbell Alexander interrupts.

"Sustained," Judge DeSalvo says. "Where is this going, Counselor?"

We hadn't been going anywhere, and the place we wound up was awful, and still I wouldn't have traded that week for the world. When you don't know where you're headed, you find places no one else would ever think to explore. "When Kate wasn't sick," Brian says slowly, carefully, "we've had some great times."

"Don't you think Anna would miss those, if Kate were gone?"

Campbell is out of his seat, just as I'd expect. "Objection!"

The judge holds up his hand, and nods to Brian for his answer.

"We all will," he says.

And in that moment, the strangest thing happens. Brian and I, facing each other and poles apart, flip like magnets sometimes can; and instead of pushing each other away we suddenly seem to be on the same side. We are young and pulse-to-pulse for the first time; we are old and wondering how we have walked this enormous distance in so short a period of time. We are watching fireworks on television on a dozen New Year's Eves, three sleeping children wedged between us in our bed, pressed so tight that I can feel Brian's pride even though we two are not touching.

Suddenly it does not matter that he has moved out with Anna, that he has questioned some of the decisions about Kate. He did what he thought was right, just the same as me, and I can't fault him for it. Life sometimes gets so bogged down in the details, you forget you are living it. There is always another appointment to be met, another bill to pay, another symptom presenting, another uneventful day to be notched onto the wooden wall. We have synchronized our watches, studied our calendars, existed in minutes, and completely forgotten to step back and see what we've accomplished.

If we lose Kate today, we will have had her for sixteen years, and no one can take that away. And ages from now, when it is hard to bring back the picture of her face when she laughed or the feel of her hand inside mine or the perfect pitch of her voice, I will have Brian to say, **Don't you remember? It was like this.**

The judge's voice breaks into my reverie. "Mrs. Fitzgerald, are you finished?"

There has never been a need for me to

cross-examine Brian; I have always known his answers. What I've forgotten are the questions.

"Almost." I turn to my husband. "Brian?" I ask. "When are you coming home?"

In the bowels of the court building are a sturdy row of vending machines, none of which have anything you'd want to eat. After Judge DeSalvo calls a recess, I wander down there, and stare at the Starbursts and the Pringles and the Cheetos trapped in their corkscrew cells.

"The Oreos are your best shot," Brian says from behind me. I turn around in time to see him feed the machine seventy-five cents. "Simple. Classic." He pushes two buttons and the cookies begin their suicide plunge to the bottom of the machine.

He leads me to the table, scarred and stained by people who have carved their eternal initials and graffitied their inner thoughts across the top. "I didn't know what to say to you on the stand," I admit, and then hesitate. "Brian? Do you think we've been good parents?" I am thinking of Jesse, who I gave up on so long ago. Of Kate, who I could not fix. Of Anna.

"I don't know," Brian says. "Does anyone?"

He hands me the package of Oreos. When I open my mouth to tell him I'm not hungry, Brian pushes a cookie inside. It is rich and rough against my tongue; suddenly I am famished. Brian brushes the crumbs from my lips as if I am made of fine china. I let him. I think maybe I have never tasted anything this sweet.

Brian and Anna move back home that night. We both tuck her in; we both kiss her. Brian goes to take a shower. In a little while, I will go to the hospital, but right now I sit down across from Anna, on Kate's bed. "Are you going to lecture me?" she asks.

"Not the way you think." I finger the edge of one of Kate's pillows. "You're not a bad person because you want to be yourself."

"I never—"

I hold up a hand. "What I mean is that

those thoughts, they're human. And just because you turn out differently than everyone's imagined you would doesn't mean that you've failed in some way. A kid who gets teased in one school might move to a different one, and be the most popular girl there, just because no one has any other expectations of her. Or a person who goes to med school because his entire family is full of doctors might find out that what he really wants to be is an artist instead." I take a deep breath, and shake my head. "Am I making any sense?"

"Not really."

That makes me smile. "I guess I'm saying that you remind me of someone."

Anna comes up on an elbow. "Who?"

"Me," I say.

When you have been with your partner for so many years, they become the glove compartment map that you've worn dog-eared and white-creased, the trail you recognize so well you could draw it by heart and for this very reason keep it with you on journeys at all times. And yet, when you least expect it, one day you open your eyes and there is an unfamiliar turnoff, a vantage point that wasn't there before, and you have to stop and wonder if maybe this landmark isn't new at all, but rather something you have missed all along.

Brian lies beside me on the bed. He doesn't say anything, just puts his hand on the valley made by the curve of my neck. Then he kisses me, long and bittersweet. This I expect, but not the next—he bites down on my lip so hard that I taste blood. "Ow," I say, trying to laugh a little, make light of this. But he doesn't laugh, or apologize. He leans forward, licks it off.

It makes me jump inside. This is Brian, and this is not Brian, and both of these things are remarkable. I run my own tongue over the blood, copper and slick. I open like an orchid, make my body a cradle, and feel his breath travel down my throat, over my breasts. He rests his head for a moment on my belly, and just as much as that bite was unexpected, there is now a pang of the familiar—this is what he would do each night, a ritual, when I was pregnant.

Then he moves again. He rises over me, a second sun, and fills me with light and heat. We are a study of contrasts—hard to soft, fair to dark, frantic to smooth—and yet there is something about the fit of us that makes me realize neither of us would be quite right without the other. We are a Möbius strip, two continuous bodies, an impossible tangle.

"We're going to lose her," I whisper, and even I don't know if I'm talking about Kate or about Anna.

Brian kisses me. "Stop," he says.

After that we don't talk anymore. That's safest.

WEDNESDAY

Yet from those flames,

No Light, but rather darkness visible.

—JOHN MILTON, **Paradise Lost**

JULIA

IZZY IS SITTING IN THE LIVING ROOM when I come back from my morning run. "You okay?" she asks.

"Yeah." I unlace my sneakers, wipe the sweat off my forehead. "Why?"

"Because normal people don't go jogging at 4:30 A.M."

"Well, I had some energy to burn off." I go into the kitchen, but the Braun coffeemaker I've programmed to have my hazelnut ready at this very moment hasn't done its job. I check Eva's plug, and press some of her buttons, but the whole LED display is shot. "Dammit," I say, yanking the cord out of the wall. "This isn't old enough to be broken."

Izzy comes up beside me and fiddles with the system. "Is she under warranty?"

"I don't know. I don't care. All I know is when you pay for something that's supposed to give you a cup of coffee, you deserve to get your fucking cup of coffee." I slam down the empty glass carafe so hard it breaks in the sink. Then I slide down against the cabinets and start to cry.

Izzy kneels down next to me. "What did he do?"

"The same exact thing, Iz," I sob. "I am so damn stupid."

She puts her arms around me. "Boiling oil?" she suggests. "Botulism? Castration? You pick."

That makes me smile a little. "You'd do it, too."

"Only because you'd do it right back for me."

I lean against my sister's shoulder. "I thought lightning wasn't supposed to strike in the same place twice."

"Sure it does," Izzy tells me. "But only if you're too dumb to move."

•   •   •

The first person to greet me at court the next morning isn't a person at all, but Judge the dog. He comes slinking around a corner with his ears flattened, no doubt running away from the sound of his owner's raised voice. "Hey," I say, soothing, but Judge wants none of it. He latches on to the bottom of my suit jacket—Campbell's paying the dry cleaning bill, I swear it—and starts to drag me toward the fray.

I can hear Campbell before I turn the corner. "I wasted time, and manpower, and you know what, that's not the worst of it. I wasted my own good judgment about a client."

"Yeah, well, you aren't the only one who judged wrong," Anna argues back. "I hired *you* because I thought you had a spine." She pushes past me. "Asshole," she mutters under her breath.

In that moment, I remember the way I felt when I woke up alone on that boat: Disappointed. Drifting. Angry at myself, for getting into this situation.

Why the hell wasn't I angry at Campbell?

Judge leaps up on Campbell, scraping at his chest with his paws. "Get down!" he orders, and then he turns around and sees me. "You weren't supposed to hear all that."

"I'll bet."

He sits heavily on a bridge chair in the conference room and passes his hand over his face. "She refuses to take the stand."

"Well, for God's sake, Campbell. She can't confront her mother in her own living room, much less in a cross-exam. What did you expect?"

He looks up at me, piercing. "What are you going to tell DeSalvo?"

"Are you asking because of Anna, or because you're afraid of losing this trial?"

"Thanks, but I gave my conscience up for Lent."

"Aren't you going to ask yourself why a thirteen-year-old girl's gotten under your skin?"

He grimaces. "Why don't you just butt out, Julia, and ruin my case like you were planning to do in the first place?"

"This isn't your case, it's Anna's. Although

I can certainly see why you'd think other-wise."

"What's that supposed to mean?"

"You're cowards. You're both hell-bent on running away from yourself," I say. "I know what consequences Anna's afraid of. What about you?"

"I don't know what you're talking about."

"No? Where's the one-liner? Or is it too hard to joke about something that hits so close to the bone? You back away every time someone gets close to you. It's okay if Anna's just a client, but the minute she becomes someone you care about, you're in trouble. Me, well, a quick fuck's just fine, but making an emotional attachment, that's out of the question. The only relationship you have is with your dog, and even that's some enormous State secret."

"You are way out of line, Julia—"

"No, actually, I'm probably the only per-son who's qualified to let you know exactly what a jerk you are. But that's okay, right? Because if everyone thinks you're a jerk, no one will bother getting too close." I stare at him a beat longer. "It's disappointing to know that someone can see right through you, isn't it, Campbell."

He gets up, stone-faced. "I have a case to try."

"You do that," I say. "Just make sure you separate justice from the client who needs it. Otherwise, God forbid, you may actually find out that you have a working heart."

I walk off before I can embarrass myself any further, and hear Campbell's voice reach out to me. "Julia. It's not true."

I close my eyes, and against my better judgment, turn around.

He hesitates. "The dog. I—"

But whatever he is about to admit is interrupted by Vern's appearance in the doorway. "Judge DeSalvo's on the warpath," he interrupts. "You're late, and the mini-mart was sold out of coffee milk."

I meet Campbell's gaze. I wait for him to finish his sentence. "You're my next witness," he says evenly, and the moment is gone before I can even remember it existed.

CAMPBELL

IT'S GETTING HARDER and harder to be a bastard.

By the time I get into the courtroom, my hands are trembling. Part of it, of course, is the same old same old. But part of it involves the fact that my client is about as responsive as a boulder beside me; and the woman I'm crazy about is the one I am about to put on the witness stand. I glance once at Julia as the judge enters; she makes a point of looking away.

My pen rolls off the table. "Anna, can you get that for me?"

"I don't know. I'd be wasting time and manpower, wouldn't I?" she says, and the goddamn pen stays on the floor.

"Are you ready to call your next witness, Mr. Alexander?" Judge DeSalvo asks, but before I can even say Julia's name Sara Fitzgerald asks to approach the bench.

I gear up for yet another complication, and sure enough, opposing counsel doesn't disappoint. "The psychiatrist that I've asked to call as a witness has an appointment at the hospital this afternoon. Would it be all right with the Court if we took her testimony out of order?"

"Mr. Alexander?"

I shrug. It's just a stay of execution for me, when you get right down to it. So I sit down beside Anna and watch a small, dark woman with a bun twisted ten degrees too tight for her face take the stand. "Please state your name and address for the record," Sara begins.

"Dr. Beata Neaux," the psychiatrist says. "1250 Orrick Way, Woonsocket."

Dr. No. I look around the courtroom, but apparently I'm the only James Bond fan. I take out a legal pad and write a note to Anna: **If she married Dr. Chance, she'd be Dr. Neaux-Chance.**

A smile twitches at the corner of Anna's mouth. She picks up the pen that dropped and writes back: **If she got a divorce and then married Mr. Buster, she'd be Dr. Neaux-Chance-Buster.**

We both start to laugh, and Judge DeSalvo clears his throat and looks at us. "Sorry, Your Honor," I say.

Anna passes me another note: **I'm still mad at you.**

Sara walks toward her witness. "Can you tell us, Doctor, the nature of your practice?"

"I'm a child psychiatrist."

"How did you first meet my children?"

Dr. Neaux glances at Anna. "About seven years ago, you brought in your son, Jesse, because of some behavioral problems. Since then I've met with all the children, over various occasions, to talk about different issues that have come up."

"Doctor, I called you last week and asked you to prepare a report giving your expert opinion about psychological harm Anna might suffer if her sister dies."

"Yes. In fact, I did a little research. There was a similar case in Maryland in which a girl was asked to be a donor for her twin. The psychiatrist who examined the twins found they had such a strong identification with each other that if the expected successful results were achieved, it would be of immense benefit to the donor." She looks at Anna. "In my opinion, you're looking at a very similar set of circumstances here. Anna and Kate are very close, and not just genetically. They live together. They hang out together. They have literally spent their entire lives together. If Anna donates a kidney that saves her sister's life, it's a tremendous gift—and not just to Kate. Because Anna herself will continue to be part of the intact family by which she defines herself, rather than a family that's lost one of its members."

This is such a load of psychobabble bullshit I can barely see to swim through it, but to my shock, the judge seems to be taking this with great sincerity. Julia, too, has her head tilted and a tiny frown line between her brows. Am I the only person in the room with a functioning brain?

"Moreover," Dr. Neaux continues, "there are several studies that indicate children who serve as donors have higher self-esteem, and feel more important within the family structure. They consider themselves superheroes, because they can do the one thing no one else can."

That's the most off-the-mark description of Anna Fitzgerald I have ever heard.

"Do you think that Anna is capable of

making her own medical decisions?" Sara asks.

"Absolutely not."

Big surprise.

"Whatever decision she makes is going to have overtones for this entire family," Dr. Neaux says. "She's going to be thinking of that while making her decision, and therefore, it will never truly be independent. Plus, she's only thirteen years old. Developmentally her brain isn't wired yet to look that far ahead, so any decision will be made based on her immediate future, rather than the long term."

"Dr. Neaux," the judge interrupts, "what would you recommend, in this case?"

"Anna needs the guidance of someone with more life experience . . . someone who has her best interests in mind. I'm happy to work with the family, but the parents need to be the parents, here—because the children can't be."

When Sara turns the witness over to me, I go in for the kill. "You're asking us to believe that donating a kidney will net Anna all these fabulous psychological perks."

"That's correct," Dr. Neaux says.

"Doesn't it stand to reason, then, that if she

donates that same kidney—and her sister dies as a result of the operation—then Anna will suffer significant psychological trauma?"

"I believe her parents will help her reason through that."

"What about the fact that Anna's saying she **doesn't** want to be a donor anymore," I point out. "Isn't that important?"

"Absolutely. But like I said, Anna's current state of mind is driven by the short-term consequences. She doesn't understand how this decision is really going to play out."

"Who does?" I ask. "Mrs. Fitzgerald may not be thirteen, but she lives each day waiting for the other shoe to drop in terms of Kate's health, don't you think?"

Grudgingly, the psychiatrist nods.

"You might say she defines her own ability to be a good mother by keeping Kate healthy. In fact, if her actions keep Kate alive, she herself benefits psychologically."

"Of course."

"Mrs. Fitzgerald would be much better off in a family that included Kate. Why, I'd even go as far as to say that the choices she makes in her life are not at all independent, but rather colored by issues concerning Kate's health care."

"Probably."

"Then by your own reasoning," I finish, "isn't it true that Sara Fitzgerald looks, feels, and acts like a donor for Kate?"

"Well—"

"Except she's not offering her own bone marrow and blood. Just Anna's."

"Mr. Alexander," the judge warns.

"And if Sara fits the psychological profile of a closely related donor personality who can't make independent decisions, then why is she any more capable of making this choice than Anna?"

From the corner of my eye, I can see Sara's stunned face. I can hear the judge banging his gavel. "You're right, Dr. Neaux—parents need to be parents," I say. "But sometimes that isn't good enough."

JULIA

JUDGE DESALVO CALLS for a ten-minute break. I put down my knapsack, a Guatemalan weave, and start washing my hands when the door to one of the bathroom stalls opens. Anna comes out, hesitating for just a moment. Then she turns on the tap beside me.

"Hey," I say.

Anna goes to dry her hands under the blower. The air doesn't feed out, not reading the sensor of her palm for some reason. She waves her fingers beneath the machine again, then stares at them, as if trying to make sure that she's not invisible. She bangs on the metal.

When I lean over and wave a hand beneath it, hot air breathes into my palm.

We share this small warmth, hobos around a kettle-bellied fire. "Campbell tells me you don't want to testify."

"I don't really want to talk about it," Anna says.

"Well, sometimes to get what you want the most, you have to do what you want the least."

She leans against the bathroom wall and crosses her arms. "Who died and made you Confucius?" Anna turns away, then reaches down to pick up my knapsack for me. "I like this. All the colors."

I take it and slip it over my shoulder. "I saw old women weaving them, when I was in South America. It takes twenty spools of thread to make this pattern."

"Truth's like that," Anna says, or it's what I think she says, but by then she has left the room.

I am watching Campbell's hands. They move around a lot while he is talking; he almost seems to use them to punctuate whatever he's saying. But they're trembling a little, too, and I attribute this to the fact that he doesn't know what I'm going to say. "As the guardian ad litem," he asks, "what are your recommendations in this case?"

I take a deep breath and look at Anna. "What I see here is a young woman who has spent her life feeling an enormous responsibility for her sister's well-being. In fact, she knows she was brought into this world to carry that responsibility." I glance at Sara, sitting at her table. "I think that this family, when they conceived Anna, had the best of intentions. They wanted to save their older daughter; they believed Anna would be a welcome addition to the family—not just because of what she would provide genetically, but also because they wanted to love her and watch her grow up well."

Then I turn to Campbell. "I also understand completely how, in this family, it became critical to do anything that was humanly possible to save Kate. When you love someone, you'll do anything you can to keep them with you."

As a little girl, I used to wake up in the middle of the night remembering my wildest dreams—I was flying; I was locked in a chocolate factory; I was queen of a Caribbean isle. I would wake with the smell of frangipani in my hair or clouds caught in the hem of my nightgown until I realized that I was somewhere different. And no matter how hard I tried, I might fall asleep again but I could not will myself back into the fabric of that dream I'd been having.

Once, during the night Campbell and I spent together, I woke up in his arms to find him still sleeping. I traced the geography of his face: from the cliff of his cheekbone to the whirlpool of his ear to the laugh lines ravined beside his mouth. Then I closed my eyes and for the first time in my life fell right back into the dream, in the very spot where I'd left it.

"Unfortunately," I say to the Court, "there is also a point when you have to step back and say that it's time to let go."

•   •   •

For a month after Campbell dumped me, I did not get out of bed except when forced to go to Mass or to sit at the dinner table. I stopped washing my hair. Under my eyes were dark circles. Izzy and I, at very first glance, looked completely different.

On the day that I mustered the courage to get out of bed of my own volition, I went to Wheeler and trolled around the boat-house, carefully staying hidden until I found a boy on the sailing team—a summer session student—who was taking out one of the school's skiffs. He had blond hair, instead of Campbell's black. He was stocky, not tall and lean. I pretended I needed a ride home.

Within an hour I had fucked him in the backseat of his Honda.

I did it because if there was someone else, then I wouldn't smell Campbell on my skin and taste him on the inside of my lips. I did it because I had been feeling so hollow inside that I feared floating away, like a helium balloon that rose so high you couldn't even see the faintest splash of color.

I felt this boy whose name I couldn't be bothered to remember grunting and heaving inside me; I was that empty and that far away. And suddenly I knew what became of all those lost balloons: they were the loves that slipped out of our fists; the blank eyes that rose in every night sky.

"When I first was given this assignment two weeks ago," I tell the judge, "and I started to look at the dynamics of this family, it seemed to me that medical emancipation was in Anna's best interests. But then I realized I was guilty of making judgments the way everyone else in this family does—based solely on physiological effects, instead of psychological ones. The easy part of this decision is to figure out what's medically right for Anna. Bottom line: it is not in her best interests to donate organs and blood that has no medical benefit for Anna herself but prolongs her sister's life."

I see Campbell's eyes spark; this endorsement has surprised him. "It's harder to come up with a solution, though—because although it may not be in Anna's best interests to be a donor for her sister, her own family is incapable of making informed decisions about that. If Kate's illness is a runaway train, then everyone reacts from crisis to crisis without figuring out the best way to bring this into the station. And using the same analogy, her parents' pressure is a switch on the track—Anna isn't mentally or physically strong enough to guide her own decisions, knowing what their wishes are."

Campbell's dog gets up and begins to whine. Distracted, I turn to the noise. Campbell pushes away Judge's snout, never taking his eyes off me.

"I see no one in the Fitzgerald family who can make unbiased decisions about Anna's health care," I admit. "Not her parents, and not Anna herself."

Judge DeSalvo frowns down at me. "Then Ms. Romano," he asks, "what's your recommendation to the court?"

CAMPBELL

SHE'S NOT GOING to veto the petition.

That's my first incredible thought—that my case isn't going down in flames yet, even after Julia's testimony. My second thought is that Julia is as ripped up about this case and what it's done to Anna as I am, except she's put it out there on display for everyone to see.

Judge has chosen this moment to become a colossal pain in the ass. He sinks his teeth into my coat and starts tugging, but I'll be damned if I'm going to break before I hear Julia finish.

"Ms. Romano," DeSalvo asks, "what's your recommendation to the court?"

"I don't know," she says softly. "I'm sorry. This is the first time I've ever served as a guardian ad litem and been unable to reach a

recommendation, and I know that's not acceptable. But on one hand I have Brian and Sara
Fitzgerald, who have done nothing but make
choices throughout the course of both their
daughters' lives out of love. Put that way, they
certainly don't seem like the wrong decisions—
even if they aren't the right decisions for both of
those daughters anymore."

She turns to Anna, and beside me I can feel
her sit a little straighter, prouder. "On the other
hand, I have Anna, who after thirteen years is
standing up for herself—even though it may
mean losing the sister she loves." Julia shakes
her head. "It's a Solomon's choice, Your Honor.
But you're not asking me to split a baby in half.
You're asking me to split a family."

When I feel a tug on my other arm I start to
slap the dog away again, but then realize that this
time, it's Anna. "Okay," she whispers.

Judge DeSalvo excuses Julia from the stand.
"Okay what?" I whisper back.

"Okay I'll talk," Anna says.

I stare at her in disbelief. Judge is whining
now, and batting his nose against my thigh,
but I can't risk a recess. All it will take for

Anna to change her mind is a split second. "You sure?"

But she doesn't answer me. She stands up, drawing all attention in the courtroom to herself. "Judge DeSalvo?" Anna takes a deep breath. "I have something to say."

ANNA

LET ME TELL YOU about the first time I had to give an oral report in class: it was third grade, and I was in charge of talking about the kangaroo. They're pretty interesting, you know. I mean, not only are they found on Australia alone, like some kind of mutant evolutionary strain—they have the eyes of deer and the useless paws of a *T. Rex*. But the most fascinating thing about them is the pouch, of course. This baby, when it gets born, is like the size of a germ and manages to crawl under the flap and tuck itself inside, all while its clueless mother is bouncing around the Outback. And that pouch isn't like they make it out on Saturday morning cartoons—it's pink and wrinkled like inside your lip, and full of important motherish plumbing. I'll bet you didn't know kangaroos don't just carry one joey at a time. Every now and then there will be a miniature sibling, tiny and jellied and stuck in the bottom while her older sister scrapes around with enormous feet and makes herself comfortable.

As you can see, I clearly knew my stuff. But when it was nearly my turn, just as Stephen Scarpinio was holding up a papier-mâché model of a lemur, I knew that I was going to be sick. I went up to Mrs. Cuthbert, and told her if I stayed to do this assignment, no one was going to be happy.

"Anna," she said, "if you tell yourself you feel fine, you will."

So when Stephen finished, I got up. I took a deep breath. "Kangaroos," I said, "are marsupials that live only in Australia."

Then I projectile vomited over four kids who had the bad luck to be sitting in the front row.

For the whole rest of the year, I was called KangaRalph. Every now and then some kid would go on a plane on vacation, and I'd go to my cubby to find a barf bag pinned to the front of my fleece pullover, a makeshift marsupial pouch. I was the school's greatest embarrassment until Darren Hong went to capture the flag in gym and accidentally pulled down Oriana Bertheim's skirt.

I'm telling you this to explain my general aversion to public speaking.

But now, on the witness stand, there's even more to be worried about. It's not that I'm nervous, like Campbell thinks. I am not afraid of clamming up, either. I'm afraid of saying too much.

I look out at the courtroom and see my mother, sitting at her lawyer table, and at my father, who smiles at me just the tiniest bit. And suddenly I can't believe I ever thought I might be able to go through with this. I get to the edge of my seat, ready to apologize for wasting everyone's time and bolt—only to realize that Campbell looks positively awful. He's sweating, and his pupils are so big they look like quarters set deep in his face. "Anna," Campbell asks, "do you want a glass of water?"

I look at him and think, Do **you?**

What I want is to go home. I want to run away to a place where no one knows my name and pretend to be a millionaire's adopted daughter, the heir to a toothpaste manufacturing kingdom, a Japanese pop star.

Campbell turns to the judge. "May I confer for a moment with my client?"

"Be my guest," Judge DeSalvo says.

So Campbell walks up to the witness stand and leans so close that only I can hear him. "When I was a kid I had a friend named Joseph Balz," he whispers. "Imagine if Dr. Neaux had married **him.**"

He backs away while I am still smiling, and thinking that maybe, just maybe, I can last for another two or three minutes up here.

Campbell's dog is going crazy—he's the one who needs water or something, from the looks of it. And I'm not the only one to notice. "Mr. Alexander," Judge DeSalvo says, "please control your animal."

"No, Judge."

"Excuse me?!"

Campbell goes tomato red. "I was speaking to the dog, Your Honor, like you asked." Then he turns to me. "Anna, why did you want to file this petition?"

A lie, as you probably know, has a taste all its own. Blocky and bitter and never quite right, like when you pop a piece of fancy chocolate into your mouth expecting toffee filling and you get lemon zest instead. "She asked," I say, the first two words that will become an avalanche.

"Who asked what?"

"My mom," I say, staring at Campbell's shoes. "For a kidney." I look down at my skirt, pick at a thread. Just maybe I will unravel the whole thing.

About two months ago, Kate was diagnosed with kidney failure. She got tired easily, and lost weight, and retained water, and threw up a lot. The blame was pinned to a bunch of different things: genetic abnormalities, granulocyte-macrophage colony-stimulating factor—growth hormone shots Kate had once taken to boost marrow production, stress from other treatments. She was put on dialysis to get rid of the toxins zipping around her bloodstream. And then, the dialysis stopped working.

One night, my mother came into our room when Kate and I were just hanging out. She had my father with her, which meant we were in for a more heavy discussion than who-left-the-sink-running-by-accident. "I've been doing some reading on the internet," my mother said. "Transplants of typical organs aren't nearly as difficult to recover from as bone marrow transplants."

Kate looked at me and popped in a new CD. We both knew where this was headed. "You can't exactly pick up a kidney at Kmart."

"I know. It turns out that you only need to match a couple of HLA proteins to be a kidney donor—not all six. I called Dr. Chance to ask if I might be a match for you, and he said in normal cases, I probably would."

Kate hears the right word. "Normal cases?"

"Which you're not. Dr. Chance thinks you'd reject an organ from the general donor pool, just because your body has already been through so much." My mother looked down at the carpet. "He won't recommend the procedure unless the kidney comes from Anna."

My father shook his head. "That's invasive surgery," he said quietly. "For both of them."

I started thinking about this. Would I have to be in the hospital? Would it hurt? Could people live with just one kidney?

What if I wound up with kidney failure when I was, like, seventy? Where would I get **my** spare?

Before I could ask any of this, Kate spoke. "I'm not doing it again, all right? I'm sick of it. The hospitals and the chemo and the radiation and the whole freaking thing. Just leave me alone, will you?"

My mother's face went white. "Fine, Kate. Go ahead and commit suicide!"

She put her headphones on again, turned the music up so loud that I could hear it. "It's not suicide," she said, "if you're already dying."

"Did you ever tell anyone that you didn't want to be a donor?" Campbell asks me, as his dog starts doing helicopters in the front of the courtroom.

"Mr. Alexander," Judge DeSalvo says, "I'm

going to call a bailiff to remove your . . . pet."

It's true, the dog is totally out of control. He's barking and leaping up with his front paws on Campbell and running in those tight circles. Campbell ignores both Judges. "Anna, did you decide to file this lawsuit all by yourself?"

I know why he's asking; he wants everyone to know I'm capable of making choices that are hard. And I even have my lie, quivering like the snake it is, caught between my teeth. But what I mean to say isn't quite what slips out. "I was kind of convinced by someone."

This is, of course, news to my parents, whose eyes hammer onto me. It's news to Julia, who actually makes a small sound. And it's news to Campbell, who runs a hand down his face in defeat. This is exactly why it's better to stay silent; there is less of a chance of screwing up your life and everyone else's.

"Anna," Campbell says, "who convinced you?"

I am small in this seat, in this state, on this lonely planet. I fold my hands together, holding between them the only emotion I've managed to keep from slipping away: regret. "Kate."

The entire courtroom goes silent. Before I can say anything else, the lightning bolt I have been expecting strikes. I cringe, but it turns out that the crash I've heard isn't the earth opening up to swallow me whole. It is Campbell, who's fallen to the floor, while his dog stands nearby with a very human look on his face that says **I told you so.**

BRIAN

IF YOU TRAVEL IN SPACE for three years and come back, four hundred years will have passed on Earth. I am only an armchair astronomer, but I have the odd sense that I have returned from a journey to a world where nothing quite makes sense. I thought I had been listening to Jesse, but it turns out I haven't been listening to him at all. I **have** listened carefully to Anna, and yet it seems there is a piece missing. I try to work through the few things she has said, tracing them and trying to make sense of them the way the Greeks somehow found five points in the sky and decided it looked like a woman's body.

Then it hits me—I am looking in the wrong place. The Aboriginal people of Australia, for example, look between the constellations of the Greeks and the Romans into the black wash of sky, and find an emu hiding under the Southern Cross where there are no stars. There are just as many stories to be told in the dark spots as there are in the bright ones.

Or this is what I'm thinking, anyway, when my daughter's lawyer falls to the floor in the throes of an epileptic seizure.

Airway, breathing, circulation. Airway, for someone having a grand mal seizure, is the biggie. I jump over the gate of the gallery and have to fight the dog out of the way; he's come to stand over Campbell Alexander's twitching body like a sentry. The attorney enters the tonic phase with a cry, as air is forced out by the contraction of his breathing muscles. He lays rigid on the ground. Then the clonic phase starts, and his muscles fire randomly, repeatedly. I turn him on his side, in case he vomits, and start looking for something to stick between his jaws so that he won't bite off his own tongue, when the most amazing thing happens—that dog knocks over Alexander's briefcase and pulls out something that looks like a rubber bone but is actually a bite block, and drops it into my hand. Distantly I am aware of the judge sealing off the court-room. I yell to Vern to call for an ambulance.

Julia is at my side immediately. "Is he all right?"

"He's gonna be fine. It's a seizure."

She looks like she's on the verge of tears. "Can't you do something?"

"Wait," I say.

She reaches for Campbell, but I draw her hand away. "I don't understand why it happened."

I don't know if Campbell does, himself. I do know that there are some things, though, that occur without a direct line of antecedents.

Two thousand years ago the night sky looked com-pletely different, and so when you get right down to it, the Greek conceptions of star signs as related to birth dates are grossly inaccurate for today's day and age. It's called the Line of Procession: back then the sun didn't set in Taurus, but in Gemini. A September 24 birthday didn't mean you were a Libra, but a Virgo. And there was a thirteenth zodiac constella-tion, Ophiuchus the Serpent Bearer, which rose between Sagittarius and Scorpio for only four days.

The reason it's all off kilter? The earth's axis wobbles. Life isn't nearly as stable as we want it to be.

Campbell Alexander vomits on the courtroom rug, then coughs his way to consciousness in the judge's chambers. "Take it easy," I say, helping him sit. "You had a bad one."

He holds his head. "What happened?"

Amnesia, on both sides of the event, is pretty common. "Blacked out. Looked like a grand mal to me."

He glances down at the IV line Caesar and I have placed. "I don't need that."

"Like hell you don't," I say. "If you don't take antiseizure meds, you'll be back on that floor in no time."

Relenting, he leans back against the couch and stares at the ceiling. "How bad was it?"

"Pretty bad," I admit.

He pats Judge on the head—the dog's been inseparable. "Good boy. Sorry I didn't listen." Then he looks down at his pants—wet and reeking, another common effect of a grand mal. "Shit."

"Close enough." I hand him a spare pair from

one of my uniforms, something I had the department bring along. "You need help?"

He shakes me off and tries, one-handedly, to take off his trousers. Without a word I reach over and undo the fly, help him change. I do this without thinking, the way I'd lift up the shirt of a woman who needed CPR; but all the same, I know it's killing him.

"Thanks," he says, taking great care to zip his own fly. We sit for a second. "Does the judge know?" When I don't answer, Campbell buries his face in his hands. "Christ. Right in front of **everyone?"**

"How long have you hidden it?"

"Since it started. I was eighteen. I got into a car crash, and they started up after that."

"Head trauma?"

He nods. "That's what they said."

I clasp my hands together between my knees. "Anna was pretty freaked out."

Campbell rubs his forehead. "She was . . . testifying."

"Yeah," I say. "Yeah."

He looks up at me. "I have to get back in there."

"Not yet." At the sound of Julia's voice, we both

turn. She stands in the doorway, staring at Campbell as if she has never seen him before, and I suppose in all fairness she hasn't, not like this.

"I'll, uh, go see if the boys have filed their report yet," I murmur, and I leave them.

Things don't always look as they seem. Some stars, for example, look like bright pinholes, but when you get them pegged under a microscope you find you're looking at a globular cluster—a million stars that, to us, presents as a single entity. On a less dramatic note there are triples, like Alpha Centauri, which up close turns out to be a double star and a red dwarf in close proximity.

There's an indigenous tribe in Africa that tells of life coming from the second star in Alpha Centauri, the one no one can see without a high-powered observatory telescope. Come to think of it, the Greeks, the Aboriginals, and the Plains Indians all lived continents apart and all, independently, looked at the same septuplet knot of the Pleiades and believed them to be seven young girls running away from something that threatened to hurt them.

Make of it what you will.

CAMPBELL

THE ONLY THING comparable to the aftermath of a grand mal seizure is waking up on the pavement with a hangover from the mother of all frat parties and immediately being run over by a truck. On second thought, maybe a grand mal is worse. I am covered in my own filth, hooked up to medicine and falling apart at the seams, when Julia walks toward me. "It's a seizure dog," I say.

"No kidding." Julia holds out her hand for Judge to sniff. She points to the couch beside me. "Can I sit down?"

"It's not catching, if that's what you mean."

"It wasn't." Julia comes close enough that I can feel the heat from her shoulder, inches away from mine. "Why didn't you tell me, Campbell?"

"Christ, Julia, I didn't even tell my parents." I try to look over her shoulder into the hallway. "Where's Anna?"

"How long has this been going on?"

I try to get up, and manage to lift myself a half inch before my strength gives out. " I have to get back in there."

"Campbell."

I sigh. "A while."

"A while, as in a week?"

Shaking my head, I say, "A while, as in two days before we graduated from Wheeler." I look up at her. "The day I took you home, all I wanted was to be with you. When my parents told me I had to go to that stupid dinner at the country club, I followed them in my own car, so I could make a quick escape—I was planning on driving back to your house, that night. But on the way to dinner, I got into a car accident. I came through with a few bruises, and that night, I had the first seizure. Thirty CT scans later, the doctors still couldn't really tell me why, but they made it pretty clear I'd have to live with it forever." I take a deep breath. "Which is what made me realize that no one else should have to."

"What?"

"What do you want me to say, Julia? I wasn't good enough for you. You deserved better than some freak who might fall down frothing at the mouth any old minute."

Julia goes perfectly still. "You might have let me make up my own mind."

"What difference would it have made? Like you really would have gotten great satisfaction guarding me like Judge does when it happens; wiping up after me, living at the end of my life." I shake my head. "You were so incredibly independent. A free spirit. I didn't want to be the one who took that away from you."

"Well, if I'd had the choice, maybe I wouldn't have spent the past fifteen years thinking there was something the matter with me."

"You?" I start to laugh. "Look at you. You're a knockout. You're smarter than I am. You're on a career track and you're family-centered and you probably even can balance your checkbook."

"And I'm lonely, Campbell," Julia adds. "Why do you think I had to learn to act so independent? I also get mad too quickly, and I hog the covers, and my second toe is longer than my big one. My hair has its own zip code. Plus, I get certifiably crazy when I've got PMS. You don't love someone because they're perfect," she says. "You love them in spite of the fact that they're not."

I don't know how to respond to that; it's like being told after thirty-five years that the sky, which I've seen as a brilliant blue, is in fact rather green.

"And another thing—this time, you don't get to leave **me**. I'm going to leave **you**."

If possible, that only makes me feel worse. I try to pretend it doesn't hurt, but I don't have the energy. "So go."

Julia settles next to me. "I will," she says. "In another fifty or sixty years."

ANNA

I KNOCK ON THE DOOR of the men's room, and then walk inside. On one wall is a really long, gross urinal. On the other, washing his hands in a sink, is Campbell. He's wearing a pair of my dad's uniform pants. He looks different now, as if all the straight lines that had been used to draw his face have been smudged. "Julia said you wanted me to come in here," I say.

"Yeah, I wanted to talk to you alone, and all the conference rooms are upstairs. Your dad doesn't think I ought to tackle that just yet." He wipes his hands on a towel. "I'm sorry about what happened."

Well, I don't even know if there's a decent answer to that. I chew on my lower lip. "Is that why I couldn't pat the dog?"

"Yeah."

"How does Judge know what to do?"

Campbell shrugs. "It's supposed to have something to do with scent or electrical impulses that an animal can sense before a human can. But I think it's because we know each other so well." He pats Judge on the neck. "He gets me somewhere safe before it happens. I usually have about twenty minutes' lead time."

"Huh." I am suddenly shy. I've been with Kate when she's really, really sick, but this is different. I hadn't been expecting this from Campbell. "Is this why you took my case?"

"So that I could have a seizure in public? Believe me, no."

"Not that." I look away from him. "Because you know what it's like to not have any control over your body."

"Maybe," Campbell says thoughtfully. "But my doorknobs did sorely need polishing."

If he's trying to make me feel better, he's failing miserably. "I told you having me testify wasn't the greatest idea."

He puts his hands on my shoulders. "Anna,

come on. If I can go back in there after that performance, you sure as hell can climb into the hot seat for a few more questions."

How am I supposed to fight that logic? So I follow Campbell back into the courtroom, where nothing is the way it was just an hour ago. With everyone watching him like he's a ticking bomb, Campbell walks up to the bench and turns to the court in general. "I'm very sorry about that, Judge," he says. "Anything for a ten-minute break, right?"

How can he make jokes about something like this? And then I realize: it's what Kate does, too. Maybe if God gives you a handicap, he makes sure you've got a few extra doses of humor to take the edge off.

"Why don't you take the rest of the day, Counselor," Judge DeSalvo offers.

"No, I'm all right now. And I think it's important that we get to the bottom of this." He turns to the court reporter. "Could you, uh, refresh my memory?"

She reads back the transcript, and Campbell nods, but he acts like he's hearing my words, regurgitated, for the very first time. "All right,

Anna, you were saying Kate asked you to file this lawsuit for medical emancipation?"

Again, I squirm. "Not quite."

"Can you explain?"

"She didn't ask me to file the lawsuit."

"Then what did she ask you?"

I steal a glance at my mother. She knows; she has to know. Don't make me say it out loud.

"Anna," Campbell presses, "what did she ask you?"

I shake my head, tight-lipped, and Judge DeSalvo leans over. "Anna, you're going to have to give us an answer to this question."

"Fine." The truth bursts out of me; a raging river, now that the dam's washed away. "She asked me to kill her."

The first thing that was wrong was that Kate had locked the door to our bedroom, when there wasn't really a lock, which meant she'd either pushed up furniture or pennied it shut. "Kate," I yelled, banging, because I was sweaty and gross from hockey practice and I wanted to take a shower and change. "Kate, this isn't fair."

I guess I made enough noise, because she opened up. And that was the second thing: there was something just wrong about the room. I glanced around, but everything seemed to be in place—most importantly, none of my stuff had been messed with—and yet Kate still looked like she'd swilled a mystery.

"What's your problem?" I asked, and then I went into the bathroom, turned on the shower, and smelled it—sweet and almost angry, the same boozy scent I associated with Jesse's apartment. I started opening up cabinets and rummaging through towels and trying to find the proof, no pun intended, and sure enough there was a half-empty bottle of whiskey hidden behind the boxes of tampons.

"Looky here . . ." I said, brandishing it and walking back into the bedroom, thinking I had a great little wedge of blackmail to use to my advantage for a while, and then I saw Kate holding the pills.

"What are you doing?"

Kate rolled over. "Leave me alone, Anna."

"Are you crazy?"

"No," Kate said. "I'm just sick of waiting for something that's going to happen anyway. I think I've fucked up everyone's life long enough, don't you?"

"But everyone's worked so hard just to keep you alive. You can't kill yourself."

All of a sudden Kate started to cry. "I know. I can't."

It took me a few moments to realize this meant she'd already tried before.

My mother gets up slowly. "It's not true," she says, her voice stretched thin as glass. "Anna, I don't know why you'd say that."

My eyes fill up. "Why would I make it up?"

She walks closer. "Maybe you misunderstood. Maybe she was just having a bad day, or being dramatic." She smiles in the pained way of people who really want to cry. "Because if she was that upset, she would have told me."

"She couldn't tell you," I reply. "She was too afraid if she killed herself she'd be killing you, too." I cannot catch my breath. I am sinking in a tar pit; I am running and the ground's gone beneath my feet. Campbell asks the judge for a few minutes so that I can pull myself together, but even if Judge DeSalvo answers, I am crying so hard I don't hear it. "I don't want her to die, but I know she doesn't want to live like this, and I'm the one who can give her what she wants." I keep my eyes on my mother, even as she swims away from me. "I've always been the one who can give her what she wants."

The next time it came up was after my mother came into our room to talk about donating a kidney. "Don't do it," Kate said, when they were gone.

I glanced at her. "What are you talking about? Of course I'm going to do it."

We were getting undressed, and I noticed that we had picked the same pajamas—shiny satin ones printed with cherries. As we slid into bed I thought we looked like we did as little kids, when our parents would dress us similarly because they thought it was cute.

"Do you think it would work?" I asked. "A kidney transplant?"

Kate looked at me. "It might." She leaned over, her hand on the light switch. "Don't do it," she repeated, and it wasn't until I heard her a second time that I understood what she was really saying.

My mother is a breath away from me, and in her eyes are all the mistakes she's ever made. My father comes up and puts his arm around her shoulders. "Come sit down," he whispers into her hair.

"Your Honor," Campbell says, getting to his feet. "May I?"

He walks toward me, Judge right beside him. I am just as shaky as he is. I think about that dog an hour ago. How did he know for sure what Campbell really needed, and when?

"Anna, do you love your sister?"

"Of course."

"But you were willing to take an action that might kill her?"

Something flashes inside me. "It was so she

wouldn't have to go through this anymore. I thought it was what she wanted."

He goes silent; and I realize at that moment: he knows.

Inside me, something breaks. "It was . . . it was what I wanted, too."

We were in the kitchen, washing and drying the dishes. "You hate going to the hospital," Kate said.

"Well, duh." I put the forks and spoons, clean, back into their drawer.

"I know you'd do anything to not have to go there anymore."

I glanced at her. "Sure. Because you'd be healthy."

"Or dead." Kate plunged her hands into the soapy water, careful not to look at me. "Think about it, Anna. You could go to your hockey camps. You could choose a college in a whole different country. You could do anything you want and never have to worry about me."

She pulled these examples right out of my head, and I could feel myself blushing, ashamed that they were even up there to be drawn out into the open. If Kate was feeling guilty about being a burden, then I was feeling twice as guilty for knowing she felt that way. For knowing I felt that way.

We didn't talk after that. I dried whatever she handed me, and we both tried to pretend we didn't know the truth: that in addition to the piece of me that's always wanted Kate to live, there's another, horrible piece of me that sometimes wishes I were free.

There, they understand: I am a monster. I started this lawsuit for some reasons I'm proud of and many I'm not. And now Campbell will see why I couldn't be a witness—not because I was scared to talk in front of everyone—but because of all these terrible feelings, some of which are too awful to speak out loud. That I want Kate alive, but also want to be myself, not part of her. That I want the chance to grow up, even if Kate can't. That Kate's death would be the worst thing that's ever happened to me . . . and also the best.

That sometimes, when I think about all this, I hate myself and just want to crawl back to where I was, to the person they want me to be.

Now the whole courtroom is looking at me, and I'm sure that the witness stand or my skin or maybe both is about to implode. Under this magnifying glass, you can see right down to the rotten core at the heart of me. Maybe if they keep staring at me, I will go up in blue, bitter smoke. Maybe I will disappear without a trace.

"Anna," Campbell says quietly, "what made you think that Kate wanted to die?"

"She said she was ready."

He walks up until he is standing right in front of me. "Isn't it possible that's the same reason she asked you to help her?"

I look up slowly, and unwrap this gift Campbell's just handed me. What if Kate wanted to die, so that I could live? What if after all these years of saving Kate, she was only trying to do the same for me?

"Did you tell Kate you were going to stop being a donor?"

"Yes," I whisper.

"When?"

"The night before I hired you."

"Anna, what did Kate say?"

Until now, I hadn't really thought about it, but Campbell has triggered the memory. My sister had gotten very quiet, so quiet that I wondered if she'd fallen asleep. And then she turned to me with all the world in her eyes, and a smile that crumbled like a fault line.

I glance up at Campbell. "She said thanks."

SARA

IT IS JUDGE DESALVO'S IDEA to take a field trip of sorts, so that he can talk to Kate. When we all reach the hospital, she is sitting up in bed, absently staring at the TV set that Jesse flicks through with the remote. She is thin, her skin cast yellow, but she's conscious. "The tin man," Jesse says, "or the scarecrow?"

"Scarecrow would get the stuffing knocked out of him," Kate says. "Chynna from the WWF, or the Crocodile Hunter?"

Jesse snorts. "The Croc dude. Everyone knows the WWF is fake." He glances at her. "Gandhi or Martin Luther King, Jr.?"

"They wouldn't sign the waiver."

"We're talking **Celebrity Boxing** on Fox, babe," Jesse says. "What makes you think they bother with a waiver?"

Kate grins. "One of them would sit down in the ring, and the other wouldn't put his mouthguard in." This is the moment I walk inside. "Hey, Mom," she asks, "who'd win on Hypothetical Celebrity Boxing—Marcia or Jan Brady?"

She notices then that I am not alone. As the whole crowd dribbles into the room, her eyes widen, and she pulls the covers up higher. She looks right at Anna, but her sister refuses to meet her eye. "What's going on?"

The judge steps forward, takes my arm. "I know you want to talk to her, Sara, but I need to talk to her." He walks forward, extending his hand. "Hi, Kate. I'm Judge DeSalvo. I was wondering if I could maybe speak to you for a few minutes? Alone," he adds, and one by one, everyone else leaves the room.

I am the last to go. I watch Kate lean back against the pillows, suddenly exhausted again. "I had a feeling you'd come," she tells the judge.

"Why?"

"Because," Kate says, "it always comes back to me."

About five years ago a new family bought the house across the street and knocked it down, wanting to rebuild something different. A single bulldozer and a half-dozen waste bins were all it took; in less than a morning this structure, which we'd seen every time we walked outside, was reduced to a pile of rubble. You'd think a house would last forever, but the truth is a strong wind or a wrecking ball can devastate it. The family inside is not so different.

Nowadays I can hardly remember what that old house looked like. I walk out the front door and never recall the stretch of months that the gaping lot stood out, conspicuous in its absence, like a lost tooth. It took some time, you know, but the new owners? They did rebuild.

When Judge DeSalvo comes outside, grim and troubled, Campbell, Brian, and I get to our feet. "Tomorrow," he says. "Closing's at nine A.M." With a nod to Vern to follow, he walks down the hallway.

"Come on," Julia tells Campbell. "You're at the mercy of my chaperonage."

"That's not a real word." But instead of following her, he walks toward me. "Sara," he says simply, "I'm sorry." He gives me one more gift: "You'll take Anna home?"

The minute they leave, Anna turns to me. "I really need to see Kate."

I slide an arm around her. "Of course you can."

We go inside, just our family, and Anna sits down on the edge of Kate's bed. "Hey," Kate murmurs, her eyes opening.

Anna shakes her head; it takes a moment for her to find the right words. "I tried," she says finally, her voice catching like cotton on thorns, as Kate squeezes her hand.

Jesse sits down on the other side. The three of them in one spot; it makes me think of the Christmas card photo we would take each October, balancing them in height order in the wings of a maple tree or on a stone wall, one frozen moment for everyone to remember them by.

"Alf or Mr. Ed," Jesse says.

The corners of Kate's mouth turn up. "Horse. Eighth round."

"You're on."

Finally Brian leans down, kisses Kate's forehead. "Baby, you get a good night's sleep." As Anna and Jesse slip into the hall, he kisses me good-bye, too. "Call me," he whispers.

And then, when they are all gone, I sit down beside my daughter. Her arms are so thin I can see the bones shifting as she moves; her eyes seem older than mine.

"I guess you have questions," Kate says.

"Maybe later," I answer, surprising myself. I climb up onto the bed and fold her into my embrace.

I realize then that we never have children, we receive them. And sometimes it's not for quite as long as we would have expected or hoped. But it is still far better than never having had those children at all. "Kate," I confess, "I'm so sorry."

She pushes back from me, until she can look me in the eye. "Don't be," she says fiercely. "Because I'm not." She tries to smile, tries so damn hard. "It was a good one, Mom, wasn't it?"

I bite my lip, feel the heaviness of tears. "It was the best," I answer.

THURSDAY

One fire burns out another's burning,

One pain is lessen'd by another's
anguish.

—WILLIAM SHAKESPEARE,
Romeo and Juliet

CAMPBELL

IT'S RAINING.

When I come out to the living room, Judge has his nose pressed against the plate glass wall that makes up one whole side of the apartment. He whines at the drops that zigzag past him. "You can't get them," I say, patting him on the head. "You can't get to the other side."

I sit down on the rug beside him, knowing I need to get up and get dressed and go to court; knowing that I ought to be reviewing my closing argument again and not sitting here idle. But there is something mesmerizing about this weather. I used to sit in the front seat of my father's Jag, watching the raindrops run their kamikaze suicide missions from one edge of the windshield to the wiper blade. He liked to leave the wipers on intermittent, so that the world went runny on my side of the glass for whole blocks of time. It made me crazy. **When you drive,** my father used to say when I complained, **you can do what you want.**

"You want the shower first?"

Julia stands in the open doorway of the bedroom, wearing one of my T-shirts. It hits her at mid-thigh. She curls her toes into the carpet.

"You go ahead," I tell her. "I could always just step out on the balcony instead."

She notices the weather. "Awful out, isn't it?"

"Good day to be stuck in court," I answer, but without any great conviction. I don't want to face Judge DeSalvo's decision today, and for once it has nothing to do with fear of losing this case. I've done the best I could, given what Anna admitted on the stand. And I hope like hell that I've made her feel a little better about what she's done, too. She doesn't look like an indecisive kid anymore, that much is true. She doesn't look selfish. She just looks like the rest of us—trying to figure out exactly who she is, and what to make of it.

The truth is, as Anna once told me, nobody's going to win. We are going to give our closing arguments and hear the judge's opinion and even then, it won't be over.

Instead of heading back to the bathroom, Julia approaches. She sits down cross-legged beside me and touches her fingers to the plate of glass. "Campbell," she says, "I don't know how to tell you this."

Everything inside me goes still. "Fast," I suggest.

"I hate your apartment."

I follow her eyes from the gray carpet to the black couch, to the mirrored wall and the lacquered bookshelves. It is full of sharp edges and expensive art. It has the most advanced electronic gadgets and bells and whistles. It is a dream residence, but it is nobody's home.

"You know," I say. "I hate it, too."

JESSE

IT'S RAINING.

I go outside, and start walking. I head down the street and past the elementary school and through two intersections. I am soaked to the bone in about five minutes flat. That's when I start to run. I run so fast that my lungs start to ache and my legs burn, and finally when I cannot move another step I fling myself down on my back in the middle of the high school soccer field.

Once, I took acid here during a thunderstorm like this one. I lay down and watched the sky fall. I imagined the raindrops melting away my skin. I waited for the one stroke of lightning that would arrow through my heart, and make me feel one hundred percent alive for the first time in my whole sorry existence.

The lightning, it had its chance, and it didn't come that day. It doesn't come this morning, either.

So I get up, wipe my hair out of my eyes, and try to come up with a better plan.

ANNA

IT'S RAINING.

The kind of rain that comes down so heavy it sounds like the shower's running, even when you've turned it off. The kind of rain that makes you think of dams and flash floods, arks. The kind of rain that tells you to crawl back into bed, where the sheets haven't lost your body heat, to pretend that the clock is five minutes earlier than it really is.

Ask any kid who's made it past fourth grade and they can tell you: water never stops moving. Rain falls, and runs down a mountain into a river. The river finds it way to the ocean. It evaporates, like a soul, into the clouds. And then, like everything else, it starts all over again.

BRIAN

IT'S RAINING.

Like the day Anna was born—New Year's Eve, and way too warm for that time of year. What should have been snow become a torrential downpour. Ski slopes had to close for Christmas, because all their runs got washed out. Driving to the hospital, with Sara in labor beside me, I could barely see through the windshield.

There were no stars that night, what with all the rain clouds. And maybe because of that, when Anna arrived I said to Sara, "Let's name her Andromeda. Anna, for short."

"Andromeda?" she said. "Like the sci-fi book?"

"Like the princess," I corrected. I caught her eye over the tiny horizon of our daughter's head. "In the sky," I explained, "she's between her mother and her father."

SARA

IT'S RAINING.

Not an auspicious beginning, I think. I shuffle my index cards on the table, trying to look more skilled than I actually am. Who was I kidding? I am no lawyer, no professional. I have been nothing more than a mother, and I have not even done a very square job of that.

"Mrs. Fitzgerald?" the judge prompts.

I take a deep breath, stare down at the gibberish in front of me, and grab the whole sheaf of index cards. Standing up, I clear my throat, and start to read aloud. "In this country we have a long legal history of allowing parents to make decisions for their children. It's part of what the courts have always found to be the constitutional right to privacy. And given all the evidence this court has heard—"

Suddenly, there is a crash of lightning, and I drop all my notes onto the floor. Kneeling, I scramble to pick them up, but of course now they are out of order. I try to rearrange what I have in front of me, but nothing makes sense.

Oh, hell. It's not what I need to say, anyway.

"Your Honor," I ask, "can I start over?" When he nods, I turn my back on him, and walk toward my daughter, who is sitting beside Campbell.

"Anna," I tell her, "I love you. I loved you before I ever saw you, and I will love you long after I'm not here to say it. And I know that because I'm a parent, I'm supposed to have all the answers, but I don't. I wonder every single day if I'm doing the right thing. I wonder if I know my children the way I think I do. I wonder if I lose my perspective in being your mother, because I'm so busy being Kate's."

I take a few steps forward. "I know I jump at every sliver of possibility that might cure Kate, but it's all I know how to do. And even if you don't agree with me, even if Kate doesn't agree with me, I want to be the one who says I told you so. Ten years from now, I want to see your children on your lap and in your arms, because that's when you'll understand. I have a sister, so I know—that relationship, it's all about fairness: you want your sibling to have exactly what you have—the same amount of toys, the same number of meatballs on your spaghetti, the same share of love. But being a mother is completely different. You want your child to have more than you ever did. You want to build a fire underneath her and watch her soar. It's bigger than words." I touch my chest. "And it still all manages to fit very neatly inside here."

I turn to Judge DeSalvo. "I didn't want to come to court, but I had to. The way the law works, if a petitioner takes action—even if that's your own child—you must have a reaction. And so I was forced to explain, eloquently, why I believe that I know better than Anna what is best for her. When you get down to it, though, explaining what you believe isn't all that easy. If you say that you believe something to be true, you might mean one of two things— that you're still weighing the alternatives, or that you accept it as a fact. I don't logically see how one single word can have contradictory definitions, but emotionally, I completely understand. Because there are times I think what I am doing is right, and there are other times I second-guess myself every step of the way.

"Even if the court found in my favor today, I couldn't force Anna to donate a kidney. No one could. But would I beg her? Would I want to, even if I restrained myself? I don't know, not even after speaking to Kate, and after hearing from Anna. I am not sure what to believe; I never was. I know, indisputably, only two things: that this lawsuit was never really about donating a kidney . . . but about having choices. And that nobody ever really makes decisions entirely by themselves, not even if a judge gives them the right to do so."

Finally, I face Campbell. "A long time ago I used to be a lawyer. But I'm not one anymore. I am a mother, and what I've done for the past eighteen years in that capacity is harder than anything I ever had to do in a courtroom. At the beginning of this hearing, Mr. Alexander, you said that none of us is obligated to go into a fire and save someone else from a burning building. But that all changes if you're a parent and the person in that burning building is your child. If that's the case, not only would everyone understand if you ran in to get your child—they'd practically expect it of you."

I take a deep breath. "In my life, though, that building was on fire, one of my children was in it—and the only opportunity to save her was to send in my other child, because she was the only one who knew the way. Did I know I was taking a risk? Of course. Did I realize it meant maybe losing both of them? Yes. Did I understand that maybe it wasn't fair to ask her to do it? Absolutely. But I also knew that it was the only chance I had to keep both of them. Was it legal? Was it moral? Was it crazy or foolish or cruel? I don't know. But I do know it was right."

Finished, I sit down at my table. The rain beats against the windows to my right. I wonder if it will ever let up.

CAMPBELL

I GET TO MY FEET, look at my notecards, and—like Sara—toss them into the trash. "Like Mrs. Fitzgerald just said, this case isn't about Anna donating a kidney. It isn't about her donating a skin cell, a single blood cell, a rope of DNA. It's about a girl who is on the cusp of becoming **someone**. A girl who is thirteen—which is hard, and painful, and beautiful, and difficult, and exhilarating. A girl who may not know what she **wants** right now, and she may not know who she **is** right now, but who deserves the chance to find out. And ten years from now, in my opinion, I think she's going to be pretty amazing."

I walk toward the bench. "We know that the Fitzgeralds were asked to do the impossible—make informed health-care decisions for two of their children, who had opposing medical interests. And if we—like the Fitzgeralds—don't know what the right decision is, then the person who has to have the final say is the person whose body it is . . . even if that's a thirteen-year-old. And ultimately, that too is what this case is about: the moment when perhaps a child knows better than her parents.

"I know that when Anna made the choice to file this lawsuit, she did not do it for all the self-centered reasons you might expect of a thirteen-year-old. She didn't make this decision because she wanted to be like other kids her age. She didn't make this decision because she was tired of being poked and prodded. She didn't make this decision because she was afraid of the pain."

I turn around, and smile at her. "You know what? I wouldn't be surprised if Anna gives her sister that kidney after all. But what I think doesn't matter. Judge DeSalvo, with all due respect, what **you** think doesn't matter. What Sara and Brian and Kate Fitzgerald think doesn't matter. What Anna thinks **does**." I walk back toward my chair. "And that's the only voice we ought to be listening to."

•   •   •

Judge DeSalvo calls for a fifteen-minute recess to render his decision, and I use it to walk the dog. We circle the little square of green behind to the Garrahy building, with Vern keeping an eye on the reporters who are waiting for a verdict. "Come on already," I say, as Judge makes his fourth loop around, in search of the ultimate spot. "No one's watching."

But this turns out to not be entirely true. A kid, no older than three or four, breaks away from his mother and comes crashing toward us. "Puppy!" he yells. He stretches out his hands in hot pursuit, and Judge steps closer to me.

His mother catches up a moment later. "Sorry. My son's going through a canine stage. Can we pet him?"

"No," I say automatically. "He's a service dog."

"Oh." The woman straightens, pulls her son away. "But you aren't blind."

I'm epileptic, and this is my seizure dog. I think about coming clean, for once, for the first time. But then again, you have to be able to laugh at yourself, don't you? "I'm a lawyer," I say, and I grin at her. "He chases ambulances for me."

As Judge and I walk off, I'm whistling.

• • •

When Judge DeSalvo comes back to the bench he brings a framed picture of his dead daughter, which is how I know that I've lost this case. "One thing that has struck me through the presentation of the evidence," he begins, "is that all of us in this courtroom have entered into a debate about the quality of life versus the sanctity of life. Certainly the Fitzgeralds have always believed that having Kate alive and part of the family was crucial—but at this point the sanctity of Kate's existence has become completely intertwined with the quality of Anna's life, and it's my job to see whether those two can be separated."

He shakes his head. "I'm not sure that any of us is qualified to decide which of those two is the most important—least of all myself. I'm a father. My daughter Dena was killed when she was twelve years old by a drunk driver, and when I rushed to the hospital that night, I would have given anything for another day with her. The Fitzgeralds have had fourteen years of being in that position—of being asked to give anything to keep their daughter alive a little bit longer. I respect their decisions. I admire their courage. I envy the fact that they even had these opportunities. But as both attorneys have pointed out, this case is no longer about Anna and a kidney, it's about how these decisions get made and how we decide who should make them."

He clears his throat. "The answer is that there is no good answer. So as parents, as doctors, as judges, and as a society, we fumble through and make decisions that allow us to sleep at night— because morals are more important than ethics, and love is more important than law."

Judge DeSalvo turns his attention to Anna, who shifts uncomfortably. "Kate doesn't want to die," he says gently, "but she doesn't want to live like this, either. And knowing that, and knowing the law, there's really only one decision I can make. The sole person who should be allowed to make that choice is the very one who lies at the heart of the issue."

I exhale heavily.

"And by that, I don't mean Kate, but Anna."

Beside me, she sucks in her breath. "One of the issues brought up during these past few days has involved whether or not a thirteen-year-old is capable of making choices as weighty as these. I'd argue, though, that age is the least likely variable here for basic understanding. In fact, some of the adults here seem to have forgotten the simplest childhood rule: You don't take something away from someone without asking permission. Anna," he asks, "will you please stand up?"

She looks at me, and I nod, standing up with her. "At this time," Judge DeSalvo says, "I'm going to declare you medically emancipated from your parents. What that means is that even though you will continue to live with them, and even though they can tell you when to go to bed and what TV shows you can't watch and whether you have to finish your broccoli, with regards to any medical treatment, you have the last word." He turns toward Sara. "Mrs. Fitzgerald, Mr. Fitzgerald—I'm going to order you to meet with Anna and her pediatrician and discuss the terms of this verdict so that the doctor understands he needs to deal directly with Anna. And just so that she has additional guidance, should she need it, I'm going to ask Mr. Alexander to assume medical power of attorney for her until age eighteen, so that he may assist her in making some of the more difficult decisions. I'm not in any way suggesting that these decisions should not be made in conjunction with her parents—but I am finding that the final decision will rest with Anna alone." The judge pins his gaze on me. "Mr. Alexander, will you accept this responsibility?"

With the exception of Judge, I have never had to take care of anyone or anything before. And now I will have Julia, and I will have Anna. "I'd be honored," I say, and I smile at her.

"I want those forms signed before you leave the courthouse today," the judge orders. "Good luck, Anna. Stop by every now and then, and let me know how you are."

He bangs his gavel, and we rise as he leaves the courtroom. "Anna," I say, when she remains still and shocked beside me. "You did it."

Julia reaches us first and leans over the gallery railing to hug Anna. "You were very brave." Over Anna's shoulder she grins at me. "And so were you."

But then Anna steps away, and finds herself facing her parents. There is a foot between them, and a universe of time and comfort. It isn't until that moment that I realize I have begun already to think of Anna as older than her biological age, yet here she is unsure and unable to make eye contact. "Hey," Brian says, bridging the gap, pulling his daughter into a rough embrace. "It's okay." And then Sara slips into this huddle, her arms coming around both of them, all their shoulders forming the wide wall of a team that has to reinvent the very game they play.

ANNA

VISIBILITY SUCKS. The rain, if possible, is coming down even harder. I have this brief vision of it pummeling the car so hard it crunches like an empty Coke can, and just like that it's harder for me to breathe. It takes a second for me to realize that this has nothing to do with the shitty weather or latent claustrophobia, but with the fact that my throat is only half as wide as usual, tears hardening it like an artery, so that everything I do and say involves twice as much work.

I have been medically emancipated for a whole half hour now. Campbell says the rain is a blessing, it's kept the reporters away. Maybe they will find me at the hospital and maybe they won't, but by then I will be with my family and it won't really matter. My parents left

before us; we had to fill out the stupid paperwork. Campbell offered to drop me off when
we were through, which is nice considering I
know he wants nothing more than to hook up
with Julia, which they seem to think is some
tremendous mystery, but **so** isn't. I wonder
what Judge does, when it's the two of them. I
wonder if he feels left out.

"Campbell?" I ask, out of nowhere. "What do
you think I should do?"

He doesn't pretend to not know what I'm
talking about. "I just fought very hard at a trial
for **your** right to choose, so I'm not going to tell
you what I think."

"Great," I say, settling deep into my seat. "I
don't even know who I really am."

"I know who you are. You're the premier
doorknob caddy in all of Providence
Plantations. You've got a wise mouth, and you
pick the crackers out of the Chex Mix, and you
hate math and . . ."

It's kind of cool, watching Campbell try to
fill in all the blanks.

". . . you like boys?" he finishes, but that
one's a question.

"Some of them are okay," I admit, "but they probably all grow up to be like you."

He smiles. "God forbid."

"What are you going to do next?"

Campbell shrugs. "I may actually have to take on a paying case."

"So you can continue to support Julia in the style to which she's accustomed?"

"Yeah," he laughs. "Something like that."

It gets quiet for a moment, so all I can hear is the squelch of the windshield wipers. I slip my hands under my thighs, sit on them. "What you said at the trial . . . do you really think I'll be amazing in ten years?"

"Why, Anna Fitzgerald, are you fishing for compliments?"

"Forget I said anything."

He glances at me. "Yes, I do. I imagine you'll be breaking guy's hearts, or painting in Montmartre, or flying fighter jets, or hiking through undiscovered countries." He pauses. "Maybe all of the above."

There was a time when, like Kate, I'd wanted to be a ballerina. But since then I've gone through a thousand different stages: I wanted to be an astronaut. I wanted to be a paleontologist. I wanted to be a backup singer for Aretha Franklin, a member of the Cabinet, a Yellowstone National Park ranger. Now, based on the day, I sometimes want to be a microsurgeon, a poet, a ghost hunter.

Only one thing's a constant. "Ten years from now," I say, "I'd like to be Kate's sister."

BRIAN

MY BEEPER GOES OFF just as Kate starts another course of dialysis. An MVA, two cars, with PI—a motor vehicle accident with injuries. "They need me," I tell Sara. "You'll be okay?"

The ambulance is headed to the corner of Eddy and Fountain, a bad intersection to begin with, rendered worse by this weather. By the time I arrive, the cops have blocked off the area. It's a T-bone: the two vehicles rammed together by sheer force into a conglomerate of twisted steel. The truck made out better; the smaller BMW is literally bent like a smile around its front end. I get out of the car and into the pouring rain, find the first policeman I can. "Three injured," he says. "One's already en route."

I find Red working the Jaws of Life, trying to cut through the driver's side of the second car to get to the victims. "What have you got?" I shout over the sirens.

"First driver went through the windshield," he yells back. "Caesar took her in the ambulance. The second ambulance is on its way. There are two people in here, from what I can see, but both doors are accordions."

"Let me see if I can crawl over the top of the truck." I start to work my way up the slick metal and shattered glass. My foot goes through a hole I couldn't see in the flatbed, and I curse and try to get myself untangled. With careful movements I pull myself into the pleated cab of the truck, maneuver myself forward. The driver must have flown out the windshield over the height of the little BMW; the entire front end of the Ford-150 has plowed through the sports car's passenger side, as if it were made of paper.

I have to crawl out what was the window of the truck, because the engine is between me and whoever's inside the BMW. But if I twist myself a certain way, there is a tiny space where I can nearly fit myself, one that puts me up against the tempered glass, spiderweb-shattered, stained red with blood. And just as Red forces the driver's side door free with the Jaws and a dog comes whimpering out, I realize that the face pressed up against the other side of the broken window is Anna's.

"Get them out," I yell, "get them out now!" I do not know how I force myself back out of this snarled skeleton to knock Red out of the way; how I unhook Campbell Alexander from his seat belt and drag him to lay in the street with the rain pelting around him; how I reach inside to where my daughter is still and wide-eyed, strapped into her belt the way she is supposed to be and Jesus God no.

Paulie comes out of nowhere and lays his hands on her and before I know what I'm doing I deck him, sending him sprawling. "Fuck, Brian," he says, holding his jaw.

"It's Anna. Paulie, it's Anna."

When they understand, they try to hold me back and do this work for me, but it is my baby, my baby, and I am having none of it. I get her onto a backboard and strap her down, let them load her onto the ambulance. I tip back the bottom of her chin, ready to intubate, but see the little scar she got from falling on Jesse's ice skate, and fall apart. Red moves me aside and does it instead, then takes her pulse. "It's weak, Cap," he says, "but it's there."

He puts in an IV line while I pick up the radio and call in our ETA. "Thirteen-year-old female, MVA, severe closed head injury . . ." When the cardiac monitor blanks out, I drop the receiver and start CPR. "Get the paddles," I order, and I pull open Anna's shirt, cut through the lace of the bra she wanted so badly but doesn't need. Red shocks her, and gets the pulse back, bradycardia with ventricular escape beats.

We bag her and put in an IV. Paulie screams into the loading zone for ambulances and throws open the back doors. On the trailer, Anna is immobile. Red grabs my arm, hard. "Don't think about it," he says, and he takes the head of Anna's stretcher and rushes her into the ER.

They will not let me into the trauma room. A flock of firefighters dribble in for support. One of them goes up to get Sara, who arrives frantic. "Where is she? What happened?"

"A car accident," I manage. "I didn't know who it was until I got there." My eyes fill up. Do I tell her that she is not breathing independently? Do I tell her that the EKG flatlined? Do I tell her that I have spent the past few minutes questioning every single thing I did on that call, from the way

I crawled over the truck to the moment I pulled her from the wreckage, certain that my emotion compromised what should have been done, what could have been done?

At that moment I hear Campbell Alexander, and the sound of something being thrown against a wall. "Goddammit," he says. "Just tell me whether or not she was brought here!"

He bursts out of the doorway of another trauma room, his arm in a cast, his clothes bloodied. The dog, limping, is at his side. Immediately, Campbell's eyes home in on mine. "Where's Anna?" he asks.

I don't answer, because what the hell can I say. And that's all it takes for him to understand. "Oh, Jesus," he whispers. "Oh God, no."

The doctor comes out of Anna's room. He knows me; I am here four nights a week. "Brian," he says soberly, "she's not responding to noxious stimuli."

The sound that comes out of me is primal, inhuman, all-knowing. "What does that mean?" Sara's words peck at me. "What is he saying, Brian?"

"Anna's head hit the window with great force, Mrs. Fitzgerald. It caused a fatal head injury. A respirator is keeping her breathing right now, but she's not showing any indications of neurological activity . . . she's brain dead. I'm sorry," the doctor says. "I really am." He hesitates, looks from me to Sara. "I know it's not something you even want to think about right now, but there's a very small window . . . is organ donation something you'd like to consider?"

There are stars in the night sky that look brighter than the others, and when you look at them through a telescope you realize you are looking at twins. The two stars rotate around each other, sometimes taking nearly a hundred years to do it. They create so much gravitational pull there's no room around for anything else. You might see a blue star, for example, and realize only later that it has a white dwarf as a companion— that first one shines so bright, by the time you notice the second one, it's really too late.

Campbell is the one who actually answers the doctor. "I have power of attorney for Anna," he explains, "not her parents." He looks from me, to Sara. "And there is a girl upstairs who needs that kidney."

SARA

IN THE ENGLISH LANGUAGE there are orphans and widows, but there is no word for the parent who loses a child.

They bring her back down to us after the donated organs are removed. I am the last to go in. In the hallway, already, are Jesse and Zanne and Campbell and some of the nurses we've grown close to, and even Julia Romano—the people who needed to say goodbye.

Brian and I walk inside, where Anna lies tiny and still on the hospital bed. A tube feeds down her throat, a machine breathes for her. It is up to us to turn it off. I sit down on the edge of the bed and pick up Anna's hand, still warm to the touch, still soft inside mine. It turns out that after all these years I have spent anticipating a moment like this, I am completely at a loss. Like coloring the sky in with a crayon; there is no language for grief this big. "I can't do this," I whisper.

Brian comes up behind me. "Sweetheart, she's not here. It's the machine keeping her body alive. What makes Anna Anna is already gone."

I turn, bury my face against his chest. "But she wasn't supposed to," I sob.

We hold each other, then, and when I feel brave enough I look back down at the husk that once held my youngest. He is right, after all. This is nothing but a shell. There is no energy to the lines of her face; there is a slack absence to her muscles. Under this skin they have stripped her of organs that will go to Kate and to other, nameless, second-chance people.

"Okay." I take a deep breath. I put my hand on Anna's chest as Brian, trembling, flips off the respirator. I rub her skin in small circles, as if this might make it easier. When the monitors flatline, I wait to see some change in her. And then I feel it, as her heart stops beating beneath my palm—that tiny loss of rhythm, that hollow calm, that utter loss.

EPILOGUE

When along the pavement,

Palpitating flames of life,

People flicker round me,

I forget my bereavement,

The gap in the great constellation,

The place where a star used to be.

> —D. H. LAWRENCE,
> "Submergence"

KATE

2010

THERE SHOULD BE A STATUTE of limitation on grief. A rule book that says it is all right to wake up crying, but only for a month. That after forty-two days you will no longer turn with your heart racing, certain you have heard her call out your name. That there will be no fine imposed if you feel the need to clean out her desk; take down her artwork from the refrigerator; turn over a school portrait as you pass—if only because it cuts you fresh again to see it. That it is okay to measure the time she has been gone, the way we once measured her birthdays.

For a long time, afterward, my father claimed to see Anna in the night sky. Sometimes it was the wink of her eye, sometimes the shape of her profile. He insisted that stars were people who were so well loved they were traced in constellations, to live forever. My mother believed, for a long time, that Anna would come back to her. She began to look for signs—plants that bloomed too early, eggs with double yolks, salt spilled in the shape of letters.

And me, well, I began to hate myself. It was, of course, all my fault. If Anna had never filed that lawsuit, if she hadn't been at the courthouse signing papers with her attorney, she never would have been at that particular intersection at that particular moment. She would be here, and I would be the one coming back to haunt her.

For a long time, I was sick. The transplant nearly failed, and then, inexplicably, I began the long steep climb upward. It has been eight years since my last relapse, something not even Dr. Chance can understand. He thinks it is a combination of the ATRA and the arsenic therapy—some contributing delayed effect—but I know better. It is that someone had to go, and Anna took my place.

Grief is a curious thing, when it happens unexpectedly. It is a Band-Aid being ripped away, taking the top layer off a family. And the underbelly of a household is never pretty, ours no exception. There were times I stayed in my room for days on end with headphones on, if only so that I would not have to listen to my mother cry. There were the weeks that my father worked round-the-clock shifts, so that he wouldn't have to come home to a house that felt too big for us.

Then one morning, my mother realized that we had eaten everything in the house, down to the last shrunken raisin and graham cracker crumb, and she went to the grocery store. My father paid a bill or two. I sat down to watch TV and watched an old I Love Lucy and started to laugh.

Immediately, I felt like I had defiled a shrine. I clapped my hand over my mouth, embarrassed. It was Jesse, sitting beside me on the couch, who said, "She would have thought it was funny, too."

See, as much as you want to hold on to the bitter sore memory that someone has left this world, you are still in it. And the very act of living is a tide: at first it seems to make no difference at all, and then one day you look down and see how much pain has eroded.

I wonder how much she keeps tabs on us. If she knows that for a long time, we were close to Campbell and Julia, even went to their wedding. If she understands that the reason we don't see them anymore is because it just plain hurt too much, because even when we didn't talk about Anna, she lingered in the spaces between the words, like the smell of something burning.

I wonder if she was at Jesse's graduation from the police academy, if she knows that he won a citation from the mayor last year for his role in a drug bust. I wonder if she knew that Daddy fell deep into a bottle after she left, and had to claw his way out. I wonder if she knows that, now, I teach children how to dance. That every time I see two little girls at the barre, sinking into pliés, I think of us.

She still takes me by surprise. Like nearly a year after her death, when my mother came home with a roll of film she'd just developed of my high school graduation. We sat down at the kitchen table together, shoulder to shoulder, trying not to mention as we looked at all our double-wide grins that there was someone missing from the photo.

And then, as if we'd conjured her, the last picture was of Anna. It had been that long since we'd used the camera, plain and simple. She was on a beach towel, holding out one hand toward the photographer, trying to get whoever it was to stop taking her picture.

My mother and I sat at the kitchen table staring at Anna until the sun set, until we had memorized everything from the color of her ponytail holder to the pattern of fringe on her bikini. Until we couldn't be sure we were seeing her clearly anymore.

• • •

My mother let me have that picture of Anna. But I didn't frame it; I put it into an envelope and sealed it and stuffed it far back into a corner drawer of a filing cabinet. It's there, just in case one of these days I start to lose her.

There might be a morning when I wake up and her face isn't the first thing I see. Or a lazy August afternoon when I can't quite recall anymore where the freckles were on her right shoulder. Maybe one of these days, I will not be able to listen to the sound of snow falling and hear her footsteps.

When I start to feel this way I go into the bathroom and I lift up my shirt and touch the white lines of my scar. I remember how, at first, I thought the stitches seemed to spell out her name. I think about her kidney working inside me and her blood running through my veins. I take her with me, wherever I go.

OUT O

Also by Shirley MacLaine

SHIRLEY MacLAINE

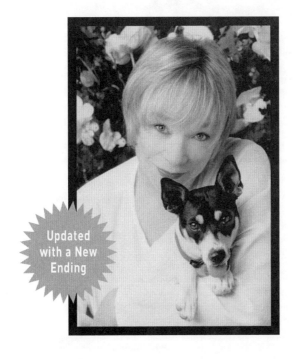

Updated with a New Ending

OUT ON A LEASH

How Terry's Death Gave Me New Life

ATRIA BOOKS

New York   London   Toronto   Sydney   New Delhi

ATRIA
BOOKS

An Imprint of Simon & Schuster, Inc.
1230 Avenue of the Americas
New York, NY 10020

Photographs on insert pages 1, 3, 4, 5, 6, 8 (bottom), 10 (bottom), 11 (top), 14–15,
and 16 are courtesy of David Weininger; photographs in the insert on pages 2
(bottom), 7, 8 (top), 9, 10 (top), 11 (bottom), 12–13 are courtesy of the author;
photograph in the insert on page 2 (top), is courtesy of Roger Wood/Corbis.

This Atria Books hardcover edition November 2017

ATRIA BOOKS and colophon are trademarks of Simon & Schuster, Inc.

For information about special discounts for bulk purchases,
please contact Simon & Schuster Special Sales at 1-866-506-1949 or
business@simonandschuster.com.

The Simon & Schuster Speakers Bureau can bring authors to your
live event. For more information, or to book an event, contact the
Simon & Schuster Speakers Bureau at 1-866-248-3049 or visit our
website at www.simonspeakers.com.

Interior design by Joel Avirom, Jason Snyder, and Meghan Day Healey

Manufactured in the United States of America

10   9   8   7   6   5   4   3   2

ISBN 978-1-5011-8245-7
ISBN 978-1-5011-8431-4 (ebook)

For Allene, who put wind under Terry's wings,
For Mort, who always understood me,
And for Terry, who helps me live in the light
of expressing what we both feel.

"All knowledge, the totality of all questions and answers, is contained in the dog."

—*Franz Kafka*

"I explained to St. Peter I'd rather stay here,

Outside the Pearly Gate.

I won't be a nuisance, I won't even bark,

I'll be very patient and wait.

I'll be here, chewing on a celestial bone,

No matter how long you may be.

I'd miss you so much if I went in alone,

It wouldn't be Heaven for me."

—*Author unknown*

Introduction

I f we are lucky, there comes a point in our lives when the past becomes a memory of things we are no more and we are faced with inventing a new future. This is the moment when we are finally free to make choices outside the powerful tug of expectation, ambition, and struggle. We have reached what I call the age of reason. Now we can choose to live not for others, but for ourselves, and we can take time to explore a life of inner knowledge for which we were always too busy.

For me the chaos of city life, heightened by the fear of terrorism and the culture of technology that forced me to remember codes and numbers to access even my own personal information, further pushed me to reevaluate what life should be about. I realized I was inundated by information and misinformation from our

1

leadership and the media—and that it was slowly erod-
ing my spirit. I was falling out of touch with my own
inner truth. These realizations were slow in coming, but
the important thing is that they finally did arrive.

So, many years ago, I decided to make my year-
round home on an 8,000-acre Spanish land grant that
used to be an old cattle ranch just outside of Santa Fe,
New Mexico. It's a peaceful place, and sometimes deaf-
eningly silent, with ancient energies that communicate
to me in nameless ways. I live there with people who
take care of me, and friends who come and stay, as well
as nine dogs, three horses, ducks, platoons of birds, a
pond, streams, deer, elk, bears, mountain lions, coyotes,
and a host of spectacular plant life. But the most important being on the ranch was my little dog, Terry.

I "acquired" Terry in Malibu, California, where I
lived for fifty years and still keep a place for meetings.
She and I grew closer and closer during the few years it
took me to distance myself from Malibu, with its easy
access to the movie business, and to shift my life to the
high desert wilderness. But as with all events that are

life-changing, I woke up one morning and knew in my soul that the city part of my life was over. I was moving on to a new adventure that would lead me to realize that perhaps Terry had acquired *me*.

This book is about hearing a deeper song of being that has made me more optimistic about what the future of life on this planet could be. It is based on the truth as I see it, and as it has been shown to me through the eyes of a dog. More to the point, I'm having a new experience with love. I have deeply enjoyed the love of my intimate relationships with friends, lovers, a husband, work, creativity, fame, travel, success, money, politics, controversy, and even struggle. But the love that has come to me through Terry is an exultant confirmation that love exists in many realities and forms, all of them longing to be acknowledged through wisdom, humor, simplicity, silence, and the wordless language of the heart.

Here is an account of what Terry has taught me, now that I am taking time to listen. Her thoughts as they come to me are not articulated in English, but in a purer, more direct form, in a language I call "humanimal." I know that I am touching deeper truths because of the knowledge Terry shared with me, so I've set down those insights into words here, in hopes that you may benefit from them as well.

I published an earlier edition of this book in 2003, which was necessarily an incomplete story because there were many years still to come in my relationship with Terry. When my beloved Terry passed away in 2016, the most surprising part of our story occurred. And that is why I felt compelled to revise and update this book—to share with you all that Terry has helped me to discover.

This book, then, is a rumination, an ongoing conversation between Terry and me. Those of you who have an animal and live in close proximity to nature will understand immediately. If you haven't allowed an animal or nature to "acquire" you, the journey through yourself will take a little longer. Either way, this journey is the only one worth taking.

The answers we seek are ours to create.

Part I:
MIND

Shirley

Have I discovered that I am capable of unconditional love? Sometimes I lie in bed, holding Terry, overcome with the wonder of it all. She has slowed me down, letting me understand that time is just an invention of man as she takes me to a world where everything is known concurrently. Her tolerance gives me peace. Her free spirit gives me courage. Her playfulness entertains me beyond all comedy I've ever known. Terry negotiates my life as though she has traveled it before, and she knows my thoughts as though she were part of me. We communicate in a game that is sometimes playful and at other times profoundly serious, because we both realize it is the basis for my newfound ability to feel and accept love without reservation.

I have had many female friends whom I enjoyed because they understood the power of allowing others just to be, the power of patience, and even the power of subservience at certain times. But I've never had a girlfriend like this. She is my confidante, my sense of home, and my deepest venture into the intimacy of myself. She has taken me on a road away from this world into a new world of happiness and inner peace. The happiness comes from what I've found; the inner peace comes from what I did not even know was there before.

I cuddle with Terry and understand for the first time what it means to weep for the sheer joy of it. Her purity humbles me. Her warmth brings me comfort, and her breathing is a reminder that God has created involuntary acts so that we need not always control and manipulate our surroundings to survive; simply by being we can also evolve.

When Terry stirs in her sleep, it always makes me smile. When I hear her moving through her dreams I long to join her there, and I wonder if she can remember her dreams in the morning. I wish I could understand the dimensions of her life that she seems so fully able to appreciate in mine. She always seems to be telling me something, something that I haven't yet touched, or something that I am unwilling to embrace in the world I understand.

When I'm away from Terry I'm back to square one. I want to return home, where I know she waits to give me the secrets of the night, to share her knowledge of the moon. She waits for me to understand what it is to be female. She wants me home from the yang world, and I know the wait is sometimes too long. I wonder where she is. Is she sitting by the front door? Lying on the bed with her feet up in the air? Is she feeling alone? Why *did* I leave her to come out into a world that is so confused, so upset, and so off balance when I can be with Terry in a state of bliss, where another living being accepts me totally and I accept her the same way?

Terry weaves her bouncing spirit through the threads of my life. I hug her with my heart. She *is* my heart and part of my soul, playing through the shadows of all my concerns and lighting them up with her bubbly prancing. Why have I never felt this way before? I am at once exalted and ashamed because I have known so many, have given myself to and taken from so many, and yet this is the first time that I feel peace. My old world sometimes wonders where I've gone. What am I doing? Who am I with? Why have I disappeared? Why do I not seem to mind that I have disappeared?

I feel removed from all but my closest friends. As for the rest, I find I have nothing to contribute to their competitive conversations. I am not particularly interested in their moneymaking prowess, in their over-achieving, and their living by the rules. I am even beginning to be bored by their favorite topic: aging. I am not much interested in gyms and workouts, or even vanity, anymore; my face is becoming prettier to me as I learn to love myself. What I *am* interested in is taking a walk for the sheer pleasure of every step. I'm interested in eating much smaller amounts of food and exercising moderately, because I feel better when I do. I'm interested in caring for my skin and my face because it loves attention. And yes, I am interested in loving the space in which I live and the person that I am in this space. Here Terry loves me and accepts me, sometimes with hints of sadness for what I don't understand, and with steady joy for what I might someday come to know.

Terry

*My Mistress Mother can be **so** serious sometimes. She thinks too much. She asks too many questions. My canine mother let me join my MM so I could teach her that she already knows much more than she thinks she does.*

*On the bright side, my Mistress Mother does call me Twinklebutt, Sparklefeet, and Honeyhunk. And she **can** just let herself have a good time with me, even if she wants to know **why**. I try to tell her that when she's happy, that's all that matters.*

I have a wonderful time with my MM. She hardly ever scolds me. When she does it's usually because I have decided to provoke her. I like to stir her up, and besides, she can be really cute when she's upset. She does feel guilty about it afterward, which I love to put to good purpose—

along with all the other emotions that a child can bring out in a mother.

My MM truly does care for me. She feeds me whatever I want, which is why my Twinklebutt sometimes won't fit under an airplane seat. She also takes me almost everywhere. She drives me in the car, which I love. I chase my shadows in the car. I chase shadows anywhere, which really intrigues MM because she doesn't really understand what a shadow is. I will have to teach her.

When I'm in the car, I love to hurl myself against the windows, barking and snarling. None of this has anything to do with my real feelings, but it entertains my MM and it tests her ability to focus when she's on the road. I notice that she's very careful to take my leash off when I'm in the car, so I don't accidentally hang myself. I know we never die, so that wouldn't be a problem for me, but she carefully avoids anything that could be dangerous to me.

I have known my Mistress Mother before, in an Egyptian lifetime, when I was the animal god Anubis, and she was a minor, mortal princess. As a deity who had knowl-

edge of the afterlife in ancient Egypt, I presided on a throne decorated with animals and hieroglyphs, and my MM sat at my feet inquiring incessantly about the nature of life and what happened after we died. I tried to teach her then, but she never really understood, so I'm going to try to teach her again in this lifetime. (In those days all Egyptians were grappling with the same questions, although I must say they were further along in their understanding than people are today; now people are too cynical and suspicious.)

I have told MM that I'm going to live eighteen years in human time. That's a good number because eight and one is nine. I don't know if she knows that's the number of completion, but I do. She's going to live much longer than that, and one of the reasons she will is because I am going to bring her the gift of simplicity. That is why I am in her life: to cut down on everything but the simple joy of being happy.

I watched my MM for a long time before I decided to be born, then I began this part of my journey with MM in a pet shop in Malibu. I don't really remember how I got into the pet shop, but she was walking by on her way to do some shopping. I could see that one of the big questions in her little human mind was: what is love? I felt that it was time for her to buy me, so I called her in. "Come into the pet shop. Come into the pet shop." When she walked in I began my little sparkle-footed, twinkle-butted dance around the cage. I knew that she had been a dancer, so I put on my best prancing steps and they definitely got her attention.

My Mistress Mother likes to think she is practical. When she learned that I was a rat terrier she thought I could help with mice on the ranch where she lives. Concerned that the other dogs on the ranch might kill a cat, my MM had been looking for another ranch dog, which was good. She was ready to hear me want her, call her, and demand to be owned and brought up by her.

My Mistress Mother doesn't do much of anything that doesn't have practical use. Some think she is a good actor. Others think she is a good dancer, or singer. For my MM, none of these measure up to her sense of being a practical person. I have watched her choose to play theaters that are closer to the freeway turnoff instead of theaters that have good acoustics or even a great stage. No, she would rather be practical.

My MM did, after all, have a Canadian mother, and Canadian people tend to be practical. Her father, on the other hand, was a dreamer, although sometimes the dream was no fun. He grew up in a small town in Virginia, and looking down on him I saw that he used to tie dogs' and cats' tails together and watch them fight (which may be why my MM has this fascination with inner peace). Also, she was born at the end of April, which makes her a Taurus, an earth sign, so she likes having her feet planted solidly on the ground. Some would say her head is now too much in the stars, but she even looks at the starry aspect of things in a very practical way. Although she seems to be one of the free spirits of the planet, she never really has thrown caution to the winds. She has always had a way of making sure her survival was ensured. She thinks that is her job in life. I know that mine is to help her get over that. Not that I don't want her to survive, but I understand that she should have more sparkle-footed, twinkle-butted moments.

Shirley

Terry is part of my destiny. She drew me into her life because it was time. In fact she imposed herself on what I thought was my well-regulated time. She insisted on giving love to me, on being so adorable that I had to welcome her into my life. Terry has given me a new vista, full of flowers, bees, birds, and worms. She has brought new kinds of play to me. She has given the chase new meaning. She makes frolicking with insects an alert game. She even gives begging dignity. She begs for play, food, touch; she begs for my arms, my lap, my warmth, at times my love itself. And all the while she is teaching me by example.

Terry lives in profound honesty. She lunges and grabs at life with barks and snorts and kisses and jumps. She asks for love unashamedly and returns it without reservation. She is my teacher, my friend, my sister, my daughter, and my mother. She is now part of me. I cannot leave her alone for more than a few hours. I know that she is self-sufficient in her own soul, but I also know how much she enjoys being with me. When I'm away, does she wonder whatever happened to me? I think so, because I feel the same way.

Time doesn't matter anymore, except to remind me to come home to her. How is it possible that Terry now rules my schedule? How is it possible that through the merging of our souls she now dictates where I live? How is it possible that I am no longer free, yet I know that I have found true freedom? I no longer travel unless Terry will be happy with it. I won't stay out all night with friends because I know that the other half of me is waiting. I'm much more meticulous with my habits because I have to be careful about hers: I have water with me at all times because I know Terry needs water at all times; I brush my hair more frequently because I like to brush *her* hair more frequently.

How is it possible that another little soul could have so imposed herself on my life that I have changed the very fundamentals by which I live? She has made me read differently, think differently, and act differently. I feel that I am loved without judgment, without boundaries, and without blame. In response to Terry I am loving unconditionally for the first time.

I think I may have known Terry throughout the ages. She may even be here to teach me that I can satisfy my incessant search for truth and meaning before I die. Perhaps she is a messenger from God. Perhaps in her warm little body and soul lies all I need to know of life and death and spirit. Perhaps it is all a joke that the universe is playing on me. The truth is hiding in plain sight. Perhaps the TRUTH is my dog Terry, and the joke is that dog spelled backward is God.

Terry

My MM keeps asking herself, What is love? From what I can see, most humans don't know the answer to that question. They don't know how to love, or do it for the wrong reasons, and what starts out being about what they think is love and romance usually ends up being about money. My MM's questions about love are the reason I'm in her life. Interestingly, male canines and male humans don't have much to say on this subject that's helpful. It's the female of the species that seems to be most profoundly interested.

I deeply love my MM and she deeply loves me too, but she doesn't know how to deal with it. Every now and then, to snap her out of confusion, I will spring myself up into her arms, drag her shoes around and use them for chewy toys, or stare at the Milk-Bone box, all to distract her. My favorite trick, though, is to refuse to get out of the car in the middle of a snowy winter. I will sit in the car, shivering in the cold, just so she will worry about me instead of her own problems. Sometimes, if she wants to go for a beach walk in the warm sun, I will wait until the sun goes down before I'll say, "Okay, now I'm ready." Because I'm royalty.

Sometimes I like to play princess. (I wouldn't dare play a god in this lifetime.) My MM has arranged with a half-dozen restaurants in various cities to allow me to sit beside her in a booth when she's having a delicious seven-course meal. Whether I'm in a restaurant in Santa Fe or a hotel in New York, people might say, "Oh, here comes Princess Terry again." I sit there exactly like royalty and refuse any meat bones that the cook might whip up for me in the kitchen so they'll know that's beneath my dignity. They all think it's charming; I know it's absurd, because I prefer people food.

It is often said that dogs have masters and cats have staff. I am a dog that has a staff. Of course, even a princess like me has to be careful not to be too aloof, so I insist on greeting every human I see, regardless of who he or she may be; an upright statesman or a beggar lying on the street both get the same greeting. I jump on them and kiss their faces. Most of the time I lightly nip their noses too, and whenever I do that they always say, "Animals love me, especially dogs."

Whenever I want people to pay more attention to me, I assume a dignified seated position and then I shiver. Then they all come over to me, sometimes as many as a dozen people at once, and say, "Oh, the poor little thing, why is she shivering?" They give me a treat or they pet me, or they chastise my MM. "Why is she so afraid?" Of course I am neither cold nor afraid. I'm ready to start teaching my next lesson.

I also love to twirl for people. I twirl around two or three times and they think I'm so talented. Then they give me treats and fuss over me. I don't remember how I learned to twirl. It might have been from watching MM dance. Whenever we have company I twirl.

My Mistress Mother once took me to a very fancy party where several elderly women, covered with expen-

sive glittering stones, thought it was shocking that a dog should be in attendance, roaming between legs and feet under the table. I heard my mistress say, "Well, just wait, soon you'll be feeding her off your plate." And, sure enough, before long I was being fed from a half-dozen laps. I twirled many times that night.

I enjoy being adorable, but it's difficult with the harem of dogs at my mistress's ranch, because the females are on to me. However, I control every new environment I'm in, within about, I would say, three minutes; one for mind, one for body, and one for spirit.

My favorite environment is my MM's bed, where I love to sleep curled up in her arms. I also enjoy pushing her out of bed with my legs, which are very strong because she takes me on long walks. In Malibu we walk on the beach, and on the ranch we walk in the mountains. I also like to put my head up above the covers so that I can snuggle against my MM's cheek. She loves cuddling me. She buries her face in my fur and squiggles around with her nose. She loves the way I smell because she puts parsley in my water to prevent the doggie smell that most humans don't like. I smell very sweet. I've heard a lot of MM's friends say that.

I like to protect my MM, and sometimes I even protect her in her sleep. I can enter my Mistress Mother's dreams, so if she is dreaming about something scary, I sit on her stomach and bark to wake her up.

Without a wake-up bark, my Mistress Mother is a late riser. She likes to go to bed around two in the morning and get up about ten, so now I've made that natural for me. When the clock squeals for no good reason, an appointment or something, I ignore it. I crawl farther under the covers, exactly where my MM would like to be if she wasn't so anxious to do what is expected of her.

When MM begins her morning exercises that's when I like to sneak out, jump on her back and nip at her hair, or lick the nape of her neck—anything to turn her away from the boring drone of that CNN. Then I will go grab a toy. I know where I've hidden everything in every single room; I have toys under every single pillow or table. I rotate my *toys, finding the ones most difficult for my MM to locate. I will then jump in the air and throw the toys, knowing MM will turn away from the news to catch them.*

I never understood why it's so important to know what's going on in the world every single day, especially when most of it isn't exactly true anyway. But then I suppose my MM has no idea why I stop dozens of times every fifty yards when we walk. No matter how many mornings we walk the same path, God gives me more to see, and smell, and understand. I love it when my MM notices some small thing in my world, freeing her from hers, even if only for a breath. I take enormous pleasure in making her stop many times, knowing this keeps her from being so goal-oriented.

When my Mistress Mother wants to take me out in the snow or the cold, I'm perfectly happy to go, but sometimes I don't want to wear the coats she buys for me, which include a beautiful yellow wool coat, a plaid coat, and even a raincoat. But if I just want to go out in my own natural coat instead, I simply crawl under the middle of our big bed where she can't get me dressed. She always waits for me and usually when I come out she doesn't force me to wear anything.

I hope you don't think that I'm poking fun at my Mistress Mother's love for me. That's not it at all. What I am really doing is trying to teach her to be simpler in the ways of joy, simpler in the ways of love, simpler in the ways of life. One of the best ways to do that is through humor.

Did you hear about the dyslexic agnostic who lies awake at night wondering if there really is a Dog?

Shirley

I love to walk. I've done so much rigorous exercise in order to stay in shape for dancing that I'm happy to take it slower in my advancing years. LSD walking, I call it: Long, Slow, Distance walking. I'm learning to allow the path to become the journey. In this way I'm not only savoring the exquisite beauty of nature but also the pleasures of ruminating, of sifting and sorting through my own thoughts and feelings.

With Terry accompanying me I'm learning there are many dimensions to being alive that I never considered before, simply because I always felt it necessary to have a purpose. When I walked across northern Spain (the Santiago de Compostela Camino) I realized how much of an overachiever I was. I'm learning how to let that go, and walking, especially with Terry, has helped me do so. Walking has become a form of meditation. I can't say I've attained the ability to walk without having a single thought, but I am enjoying the new experience of just *being*. I'm learning that from Terry.

I would like to be able to happily walk without knowing where I'm going. I would like to be able to walk farther than is safe. I would like to walk away, to let myself off my own leash to be in a place where my thoughts and feelings can exist solely for their own sakes. Terry can do that already. She has a sense of peace that I aspire to. There's nothing like a dog to help you know who you are—and what you're capable of being.

When Terry and I are in Malibu one of our favorite pleasures is taking a long walk on the beach. I'm no longer surprised when Terry begins to jump with excitement as soon as I just *think* about going to the beach. Often she seems to know my thoughts before I do. By the time I've put on my sun hat Terry is down the stairs and out on the sand. For the next few minutes she leaps and barks until I throw something she can chase. When my sense of balance is challenged I negotiate a little moonwalk to avoid stepping on Terry dancing underfoot, which excites her even more.

Terry's favorite beach activity is chasing wet sand, so I pick up a long-handled scoop that I'll use to fling the sand as far out in front of me as I can. Terry will then run like a streak of furry lightning, her paws barely touching the ground, to launch herself twisting and twirling on the ocean breeze to catch every possible grain of sand. I don't need to stock up on Frisbees, or rubber balls, or anything else a pet store has to offer. Wet sand is all she wants. When we pass other beach walkers, they stare in disbelief at what Terry does in the air, and at the rudimentary nature of her chasing toy. She likes the sand because all the other dogs like balls and sticks. I don't mind; not only do I get a good upper-body workout this way, I also never have to bend over to retrieve anything. Terry would never lower herself to bring an object back to lie at my feet anyway. Such an act would be demeaning.

Terry stops unexpectedly, still as a perched statue on the beach in front of me, and waits for me to catch up. This gives me the opportunity to step into a fast-paced stride. I reach Terry and keep right on going. She, meantime, maintains her frozen stance, which finally forces me to turn back to get her. She loves interrupting my stride.

When another dog approaches, Terry simply sets her ears in antenna position and waits. If the new dog seems friendly, Terry's tail wags like a runaway metronome and she romps to meet her new friend. If the dog looks hostile, Terry waits for the dog to reach her, then rolls over on her back and flattens her ears in supplication, allowing the dog to have his way with her. This is actually a form of seduction. Today she allowed a big German shepherd to believe he was in control, and then she bounded to her feet and began to play. The huge male was astonished and thrown off balance. Sometimes she keeps playing until the game becomes a romp, but today she simply trotted off, leaving the huge shepherd abandoned and confused, a helpless giant.

Terry

I love to play on the beach with my MM. Sometimes when I'm chasing sand I will see huge dogs come bounding toward me. I always roll over on my back and let them think they are in charge. But I have this act down. MM knows it too. She's never concerned for me because she knows that in the end TERRY RULES.

It's people in uniforms who sometimes bother me. Once the Dog Police came out on the beach to arrest me and take me to dog jail because I didn't have my leash on. I knew what they were thinking so I jumped into my MM's arms and started my shivering act. MM was furious; she held me close and screamed at them. She called them Fascists and threatened to sue them if they hurt me. They were very upset by her behavior and turned away, leaving me safe. I licked my MM's face and understood more than ever how much she loves me. She knows that as we walk through this lifetime together I am her spiritual teacher. She is out on my leash . . . my spiritual leash.

I love to walk on the beach when the sun goes into the water. Sometimes this means the moon will go up soon. If it goes up tonight maybe I can use it to teach MM more about the light of reflection. After all, everything is a reflection. Although I'm happy here in Malibu I can't wait to go to our ranch in New Mexico because there are other kinds of reflections there: reflections of trees and birds and insects and shadows from the rocky mountains and hills, and of course reflections from my family of dog friends. And there are no humans in uniforms.

Shirley

As we romp and play at the water's edge, I am in turmoil.
I'm being offered a role in a movie being shot partly on
location in Northern Ireland. It's a wonderful script with
Lord Richard Attenborough directing, but I haven't been
able to find a way to bring Terry with me, and the location
shoot will take six weeks. The U.K. has a quarantine re-
quirement for dogs. The old 180-day quarantine has been
lifted, but I don't understand what the new procedures are.
Even if Terry would have to remain in quarantine for only
a few weeks, I don't think I could bear it. The thought of
her in a cage for just one night breaks my heart.

I've contacted the British embassy, the airlines,
and veterinarians, but nobody will give me a straight
answer when I ask if there's a way to get around the

quarantine. It's far-fetched, but I've been thinking of hiring someone to fly with Terry to Germany or France and then drive her into the U.K. I would want to be with her, though, for the drive, which would mean adding a week of extra time to my schedule.

When Elizabeth Taylor shot a movie in the U.K., she rented a yacht where she could work and live with her dog. I can't afford a yacht. Believe me, I know all this is completely impractical, if not delusional. Will I really allow my dog to be the determining factor in my career? I have good friends who would give Terry the best of care, but I'd still worry so much about her being alone—not to mention how *I'd* feel being without her.

Terry senses my thoughts as she runs toward me and leaps into my arms. I look down at her as she gazes into my face unflinchingly, the rolling waves reflected in her eyes. She kisses my hand and nips my fingers. If I were away from her, would I feel her giving me lick-kisses on my cheek or pushing against my legs, only to look down and find that she wasn't really there?

Terry

Poor MM. She is plagued with worries, like a ringing in her ears that won't go away. I am everything to her, but she doesn't trust that I am also everywhere. I could put my spirit on a wave and send it across the ocean to her, but I don't want her to know that yet. It's time for her to decide what love means. I know she'll be so unhappy without me, there's no way she could focus on her work: She'll wonder, maybe Terry's not getting her vitamins, maybe Terry's not eating, or maybe Terry's sulking under the bed.

I don't like it when my MM has to be away from me, and I know it's not particularly sensitive, but sometimes when she comes home I find ways to communicate my displeasure so she'll think twice before leaving me next time. I'll turn away if she strokes me. I'll sleep with my

*back to her if she takes a nap. Basically, I'll have nothing
to do with her until I decide she has gotten my point. I
know this hurts her but I **really** don't like her to be away.
Once, to show my displeasure, I pooped on her white rug
even though she left the outside door open for me. That
really made her upset, which upset me, and neither of us
should be upset.*

*Once my MM left me for two whole days. She had
some important business and couldn't take me with her. Her
housekeeper, Nellie, was cleaning on the other side of the
house, and I was under our big bed pouting and feeling mis-
erable, so I decided to tell Nellie how I felt. Using my soul
language, I shouted very loud, "Tell her NO. I mean it! NO!"*

*Nellie was really scared because she thought some-
one else was in the house. She came running to our bedroom and looked around. I yelled again, "Tell her not to
go away for so long again!"*

Nellie ran away, terrified.

*When my MM came back, Nellie told her what had
happened. She said she had heard a ghost. But MM knew*

it was me—and she has never left me for that long since. That's the truth!

And that's what I'll do if she can't take me to Northern Ireland. I'll make the "NO" so loud she'll hear me across the ocean. The producer of the movie is still having trouble raising all the money anyway, so I don't have to worry for a while.

However, when my Mistress Mother does go out for a few hours without me, I do appreciate it when she tells me what she wants me to do when she's gone, like to take care of the house, or to make sure everything is peaceful. This way I know I have a job to do. I usually try to stay in communication with her when she's driving on the road because, as I've said before, I love to go in the car with her. I always know when she's coming home and I always go right by the door when she's about a mile away so she'll think I've been sitting there the whole time.

Shirley

I think I understand Terry's inner life—her sorrows and her joys—but she is still a dog and something about her will always remain a little elusive. Terry may not be able to study physics, or paint a picture, but I bet she could find her way across the country to come back to me. What is intelligence? Terry is capable of remarkable tranquillity, and according to Hindu philosophers tranquillity is the highest emotion because it lies underneath all the others, waiting to be discovered. Terry is teaching me to feel more purely and more intensely, and not to be so wracked by intellectual and emotional ambivalence. I've always thought of myself as direct and honest, but I am nothing along those lines compared to Terry.

Our human language is full of indications of how

much dogs mean to us. Someone who is a champion is "top dog." Somebody who is not favored to win is an "underdog." People compete in a "dog-eat-dog" world, and suffer through the "dog days" of August. When our priorities are misplaced, the "tail wags the dog." A book that's well worn is "dog-eared." People who look victimized have "hangdog" expressions. Why do we sometimes call people a "dirty dog"? And why is a "bitch" the most humiliating thing you can call a woman? Dogs have not only stepped into our hearts but into our lexicons.

If dogs are important to us, there is ample evidence that the depth of feeling runs both ways. I know many examples of dogs who, after their masters passed, experienced such loneliness that they never recovered. There's the famous account of the Japanese dog that used to meet his owner at the train station in Shibuya, Tokyo, every night after work and walk home with him. When the man died at his place of work and never came home again, the dog continued to meet the train for fifteen years until he finally rejoined his master in heaven. A friend of mine who had AIDS couldn't take care of his dog anymore so he gave the dog to a good family. The dog ran away and walked thirty miles back to my friend's house. My friend returned him to the new owner, and soon after that, my friend died. His dog died within two hours.

When we get back from a walk on the beach Terry will sometimes sit on the balcony for hours, gazing at the horizon. What does she see? Can she see into the underlying cycles of time—or beyond them? Does she see spirit guides? Dog playmates? Relatives who have passed on? Is she seeing God? Is this why she likes to be perched atop something high, giving her a grander vista? When the wind blows Terry goes into a kind of reverie, as though she is receiving messages from other dimensions.

What does Terry think when she chases the shadow of a seagull flying overhead? Does she think that the shadow is solid, or is she pouncing on a moment that once was but is no more? She's interested beyond measure in shadows, particularly moving shadows, and I'd love to know why.

When Terry plays outside on the beach with other friends, she checks in every twenty minutes or so to see that I am still there, to remind me that she's fine, to stretch, to yawn, and to look up at me. Is she trying to say, I will be patient until you join me in the interplay of darkness and light, when I can show you what you're missing? She bounds into the sunlit ocean waves and buries her face in the salty water, only to leap into the air at the shadow of a dive-bombing pelican. Who is this little sprite of a fur person? When I walk with her and she scampers under the pilings of people's seaside homes I revel in her unbounded freedom, and I am filled with the wonder of knowing that I was holding and cuddling her the night before.

Some friends say I'm losing my mind over the intimacy I feel with this dog. Sometimes I think they are right. I have lived with dogs all my life—golden retrievers, German shepherds, mutts, malamutes, Australian shepherds, huskies, always good-sized dogs—but this is the first time I've had a terrier in my adult life.

I did have a little terrier when I was small. Her name was Trixie. Perhaps that's why I have inherited Terry now. Maybe Terry is Trixie, come around again. She certainly has the same traits, but then again, as a terrier, she would. Somehow I find comfort in the knowledge that we are all like terriers, or snowflakes—with a beauty in common that is only enhanced by our uniqueness. Yet that same image adds to my anxiety, for most humans fight and fear our differences. We are all one under God, yet we will always be part of the puzzle of suffering until we find a remedy for separation, not only from each other but, more profoundly, from what Native Americans call the "Great Spirit All There Is."

Terry

My Mistress Mother knows I can see things that she cannot. All animals can. We can **hear** *colors and* **see** *sounds. Red, orange, yellow, green, blue, indigo, and violet: Each color has a frequency, and we canines can hear those vibrations. We also* **see** *how sounds vibrate and what voices* **look** *like. Our ears and eyes are fine-tuned instruments, just like our other senses. I know when the ocean is disturbed or even angry. I hear and see nature because I am nature. But MM is not in that state of mind, poor thing. She is not a princess of simplicity like I am.*

That peaceful way of living is there for all of us, but my MM and her friends are too busy taking care of things they think they have to do in a day. This is why they can't sleep well at night. It's also why my friends and I sleep so much. We don't feel stressed. We're peaceful. We see things in our sleep-state but we don't really care if we remember them or not. We know we are perfect just as we are, which is why we have such dignity. Humans marvel at our talent for forgiveness, yet we feel we have nothing to forgive. We know everything is exactly as it should be. Sometimes humans try our patience and upset nature in general. They should be especially careful of what they're dumping into the ocean because someday the ocean is going to get very mad and hit back. That could really happen, of course; it already did, a long time ago.

As far as shadows are concerned, we know all about them. We canines play with shadows because we know they are just part of the game. All of life is a game, so we live to be happy. The shadowy fears that humans see as causes for their anxiety are really only parts of themselves.

Humans don't understand pecking order, either. They don't realize that they have lived before and will live again; a being who was once leader of the pack may soon be a puppy, clinging to life. We understand that. It makes us humble.

We see many dimensions, including past, present, and future, and we know they are all happening simultaneously. We know that people have invented time. We know that living in every single moment is all there is. It's so simple, yet my MM and the rest of the humans don't get it. How can they have time to do those things that upset them when there's no such thing as time? I sometimes think they invented time so they'd always have something to worry about. I don't like to watch my MM and her friends fret about silly things, like what to wear. That's why I sometimes give my MM a hard time about putting on my store-bought coat before going out into the snow and rain. I have my own coat. I am completely naked, but I am also fully clothed and protected.

People are often surprised when they feel our little cold noses, but do they know why our noses are so cold? We are regulated by nature to be warm inside but our noses are never really hot unless we're taking on a sickness.

When my MM is brushing her teeth with her jammies on and she's leaning over the sink, I like to go and stick my cold nose against her butt so she'll shriek with surprise.

Speaking of butts, I remember a time when my MM was giving a dinner party and she served spare ribs. I begged and begged for those leftover ribs, and finally she gave them to me. I ate all the meat off of them and then I ate the bones and I was very sick the next day. Nobody should ever feed us bones that splinter, no matter how much we beg. Our bones have to be big and thick, like they were when we were wolves and hunted in packs. My Mistress Mom was very worried about me. I wasn't just shivering, I really didn't feel good, and when she saw something was wrong she took me to the doctor. I remember the doctor spent the entire day up my butt getting the splintered bones out of my insides. If they hadn't come out, I could have been punctured, which is not a good thing for anybody.

I've heard my MM and her friends wonder why dogs smell each other's butts. We learn a lot from sniffing butts. We can tell what our friends have eaten, where they've been, and even whether or not they've been well. We can also tell whether or not they are nice or threatening. I've noticed a lot of people now call each other "assholes" on TV, so perhaps humans are beginning to see that we're right about the importance of butts.

*Even though we dogs are perfect, we do have some problems. For example, when males of our species go around lifting their legs and peeing to mark their territory, this is not a good thing. Maybe marking territory is something we learned from the humans, since we've been bonded to them for so long. Perhaps by setting a good example, and not peeing on each other, people could stop our males from doing that too. Nothing belongs to anybody, it all belongs to everybody, and all of us and all of it belong to the Great Spirit God anyway. We all just **use** territory. Nobody **owns** it.*

If any of my friends come along to eat out of my dish, I let them do it and I will always let them do it, although I suppose if I was starving, that might be another story. But instead of people spending all that stuff they call money on weapons to protect themselves, I think they should spend that money to feed everybody; then nobody would be angry or frightened in the first place.

I heard on MM's TV that a human dies every ten seconds from not having enough food, and that there are eight hundred million starving people in the world. I'm glad I am my MM's dog when I hear that, but shouldn't people's children be treated as well as their dogs? No wonder so many people are angry. When I feel angry it's because I'm afraid. Humans will do terrible things to keep from being afraid. And why are they afraid? They're afraid that they don't have enough. And why are they afraid they don't have enough? They're afraid that if they don't have enough they will die. But the truth of the matter is, nothing and nobody ever dies, and **that** *is one of the biggest secrets of all. Nothing ever dies; it just changes form. And that's the Big Truth.*

Shirley

The producers tell me that the movie in Ireland may very well start shooting this summer. I've checked everywhere for ways to get past the quarantine laws but I'm not making any headway. The most plausible advice I've been given is to go to Paris and find a veterinarian who will keep Terry for a few weeks and say she's been there longer, certifying that she is rabies-free. Then we could travel through the Chunnel to England.

Terry is used to me; I don't want her to have to adjust to being away from me for a long time, assuming she even could. And to be honest, I suffer from canine separation anxiety myself. I never thought this would happen to me.

During my various travels around the world, I never liked to go with anyone else. I liked to be able to pick up at a moment's notice or stay in one place until I had had enough of it. Life was a spontaneous, unpredictable adventure. I traveled light and unencumbered. As my father often said, "He travels fastest who travels alone."

When I have had to leave people I loved, I knew that they and I would grieve, but that eventually we would get on with our lives. I knew, despite what we might think, we were not dependent on each other. Not so with Terry. I'm now dependent on the love she brings out in me. I don't want to be away from the reminder of that love.

The producer of the movie now says we'll begin shooting in May, just after Easter. Maybe I can put "dependent on Terry being with me" into my contract, and let the producer sort out the details.

Terry

Perhaps I should play the Hollywood game too. Here are my demands: Put me in MM's contract, overseas first-class tickets all the way.

Shirley

There is nothing sadder for a dog than being left alone, and many dog experts believe that there is nothing comparable in human experience to the degree of loneliness experienced by an isolated dog. Terry needs to speak and be spoken to. She needs to touch and be touched. She needs to love and be loved. I know this is true for humans too, so why won't we acknowledge it the way dogs do?

Terry can live happily and at ease in two worlds: hers and mine. That makes her much more clever than I am, but I am making some progress. Terry may have levels of perception that I can't comprehend, but as far as the five senses go, in some ways she is better equipped than I am, and in others, she's not. A dog, for example, has one taste bud for every six of ours, which is why dogs can eat the same food every day and seem content.

I know dogs have favorite foods and I would gladly become a cook for Terry, but she is happy with whatever I give her, except for fruit. She doesn't like fruit.

A dog's vision is comparable to that of a human being, although it's not quite as good. Dogs' eyes are very much more sensitive to movement than ours. And yet dogs can be easily spooked by something they see. One day, Terry barked at a statue of Buddha in my house for hours. I wonder why. Was she frightened, or did she feel something familiar, and want to communicate?

Dogs have much better hearing than we humans do; they can hear sounds four times farther away. Terry is constantly freezing in her tracks, one paw up, indicating that she's heard something outside of my range. Terry's ears also move independently, so she can get a better directional fix than I can. A dog can locate the source of a sound in six hundredths of a second. That's why I so often see Terry stop to listen and then immediately go racing off in a specific direction.

And of course it's well known that dogs are able to detect higher-pitched sounds than we are. That's why

Terry always seems to find chipmunks and squirrels and other ground rodents that are emitting high-frequency signals beyond the reach of the human ear. Terry can hear a storm coming long before I can, or maybe she just smells the electricity in the air. I wonder if she can hear fish swimming.

A dog's sense of touch is also extremely sensitive. Terry's entire body is covered with nerve endings. Dogs sense air flowing through extremely sensitive hairs located above their eyes, on their faces, or below the jaw. That might be why Terry raises her head when she stops and focuses far out on the ocean. When she raises her head, this also enhances her ability to smell. Maybe she smells the dolphins and the whales. It's well known that dogs have as many as 300 million olfactory receptors in their noses, compared to humans' paltry six million.

The relationship between emotions and sensory experiences allows dogs to be in constant touch with their emotional core, which is why we see dogs live through such a wide range of emotions in any one day.

Because a dog's sensory world is so rich, it's in constant interplay with its own emotional world.

I think as humans our best test of morality may be our attitude toward those who are at our mercy, namely animals. I'm more and more convinced that the love I have for a dog is as important or greater than any love I could have for a man or woman because it's a completely voluntary and selfless love. And Terry returns my love so openly, so fiercely, that I begin to see what is possible between human beings. It's funny to think that I've been so interested in life on other planets when I haven't even begun to understand the alien life on my own world.

Terry

We are taking one last quick beach romp before we go to the ranch for Easter. I dash once more into the waves and chase the shadows of a squadron of seagulls. I decide not to dig out picnics abandoned on the sand, and I don't lap up any salt water even though I'm thirsty; MM says it's bad for me. Soon we have to leave for the airport, so MM is turning around to go back to our beach house. Now when she tosses wet sand into the air it hits her in the face, because the wind is blowing the wrong way. She'll get tired of that very quickly, and will walk faster so we can get ready to go on the plane. I'll be good and tired and ready to go to sleep under the seat, dreaming of dolphins because I know they bring good luck.

Airports are my favorite places to observe how humans react to me. My MM has a little rolling case for me so she can pull me like a piece of luggage. Whenever we get to a waiting lounge or the Red Carpet place, she opens the case and people are surprised to see my little head pop out. I'm careful not to scamper around where food is being served, because that's against health code rules. But everybody always wants to play with me. You would think I had landed from a friendly planet and no one had ever seen my kind before when I come out of my case and twinkle up to people.

We are leaving for New Mexico. There has been a terror alert, and even though I am sometimes called "Terry the Terror," I can't understand why I have to keep going in and out of my case. I go through the beeping screening arch, and then they make me get out of my case, and then people in uniforms feel my stomach and rummage around in my empty case. I see my MM is also being felt by a female in uniform; she is taking off MM's shoes, and asking her if there is metal in her bra.

I am immediately attracted to one of the big, strong female security agents because she seems so stern, so I scamper over to her and jump up to be petted. She is so mad, she steps back and shouts, "Get down! Get down!" My MM replies, "Oh, she's just a dog, she's just a little playmate." The security agent leads MM into a little cubicle and I hear her say "I want to see everything that's underneath your clothes." I don't know what's going on because I'm left outside while other people try to pet me. What did I do wrong? I look under the cubicle as MM lifts her skirt and shirt. The lady does not touch her, but she is not being nice. I can see why I chose to make her happier.

Now we are on the plane to New Mexico. We are all settled in our spaces. I am under the seat in front of my Mistress Mother but my little doggie bag case sticks out just a little bit. The male flight attendant is bending over us looking very closely at my case. My MM says, "Well, it's got a tag that says 'Approved by America West.'" The attendant says, "It doesn't fit." I realize we might have a problem. He bends over and tries to push me farther under the seat. He is hurting my back so I growl. A few other people in first class hear me. Up to now they must have *thought I was a piece of luggage. I see them looking over. The attendant keeps saying, "It doesn't fit," and every time he tries to push me in farther I growl. My MM is getting embarrassed because she doesn't want to feel she is getting special treatment, but she hates what he's doing to me.*

Another flight attendant comes over. Because she's a female I think everything will be all right. But when my MM shows her the America West approval tag, the male attendant says, "That doesn't matter if the case doesn't fit." The female attendant doesn't seem to know what to do.

The other passengers begin to speak up. "C'mon, let's go, it doesn't matter." But the male flight attendant just stands there looking at me. There is a lot of commotion because now everyone knows what is going on and my MM won't give up and he won't give up. Half an hour goes by while other people in uniforms come on and off the plane. There is more confusion. Now the pilot is coming out. I hear him ask, "What's the dog's name?" My MM says to him, "Terry. She and I have always flown America

West because this case is approved." He asks, "You don't fly Southwest?" She says, "No, they don't allow dogs." He says, "Do you take Terry everywhere?" My MM answers, "Yes."

The pilot is reaching down and rolling my case into the aisle. "Okay, Terry," he says, "we'll take you into the cockpit." His voice sounds so sweet.

The pilot has taken me into the cockpit and now he's even giving me a treat. I wish I could twirl for him, but of course I can't get out of my case. I know my MM is probably fuming in her seat, but I know she's also grateful to the nice pilot.

Everybody who was trying to help leaves the plane and now I feel the familiar push of the plane taking off. I know it's time for me to be quiet and sleep. I can feel my MM decide to call America West by a new name—from now on she will call it America Worst!

Shirley

Once, when I was on a Christmas vacation in Palm Beach, Florida, I lost Terry. We were staying with some friends in a beautiful home, but Terry did not have dogs to play with. There were too many sophisticated grown-ups around, so Terry decided to go down to the beach by herself. She was missing for two hours. I was frantic, but I have a council of angels, and I asked them where Terry had gone. They directed me south. I walked along the beach until I came to a country club, where one of the attendants told me that a little white-and-black terrier had followed a group of kids to the country club, and then an elderly gentleman, who was worried about the dog, took her home with him. He pointed me in the direction of the man's house.

I walked over to it, and there was Terry, having the time of her life playing with a bunch of other dogs. She had her dog tag on, but of course the two telephone numbers listed were in California and in New Mexico, so the man couldn't contact me. Terry, being of a mind of timelessness, had no idea that her being gone would worry me. I have relied on my council of angels ever since. In fact I believe we always play and walk with our angels, and they always try to get our attention when we're too busy thinking and worrying.

Terry

Humans should play more for no reason, like the angels do. Angels play in all kinds of ways. For example, since I am an earth angel I love to charge at nothing in the middle of the night, and sometimes it wakes my MM up, but perhaps she should be more aware of the night sounds. Perhaps she should be more aware of the glory of the moon. I bay at the moon and gaze at the stars, hoping that she will take the cue and do it more herself. I want my MM's angel child to come out and play more. I love to charge at thunder when a rainstorm comes up. To me, the weather is entertainment, but it is also a reflection of turmoil in human emotions. We natural beings know that nature follows consciousness. It's nothing to be afraid of, except when people don't understand that nature will be strange and chaotic when they are. I love to return from my charging at the night to nuzzle into my MM's neck and tell her to be careful how she treats nature. She giggles when my nose is too cold, but I'm not sure she understands my point about nature. I nuzzle up against her shoulder and cuddle myself into her arms to keep her warm and hope she gets what I'm trying to teach her. Sometimes we watch movies, especially Stuart Little *and* Stuart Little II. *I love those two. Perhaps my being a rat terrier has something to do with it.*

Once my MM took me to a ball in celebration of a ballet company, and she said the theme of the ball was Cinderella. I remembered having seen the minds of children when they read Cinderella. *It was really nice. I liked the ball that Cinderella went to and found her prince, so I loved the idea of attending with MM. But when we arrived at the ball, three big people dressed in rat suits greeted us. Even their faces looked exactly like rats, whiskers and all, because they were wearing some kind of rat hoods. They were so big there was no way I could charge at them. MM* said not to worry but I ran away and hid in the Cinderella carriage. Everybody laughed and said I was cute, but I didn't feel cute. I was afraid the human rats would charge at **me**. I tried to shiver like I do when I want attention but I was too scared.

After that terrifying experience, I had to ask myself why I attack anything. I think it might be because it runs away, and I love to catch things that run away. But as far as hurting anything, I would rather roll over on my back and be adorable with my feet up in the air, inviting whoever or whatever to do what they want with me. Maybe even rats, especially if they are as big as they were that day!

I know my MM loves to watch me sitting contentedly in my world of other-dimensional communication. Being in many worlds simultaneously takes silence and concentration. I practice this every day. I wish MM would take more time for silence and concentration. Still, I don't mind being distracted when my MM comes over to me after an upsetting phone call and just hugs me. That helps her. She has also learned to make little sniffing sounds in *my ear and all over my face, like other dogs do with me. It makes me think that she is finally, on some level, entering my world of wisdom.*

When it comes to just being, I know that my MM is more capable of this than most people because her practical needs are being met. Other people have their work, their pressures, children to feed, chores, and other things that go along with busy human lives. MM is past all that so she can afford to "just be," although she still needs to **be** *better. I know that many of my furry friends wish their owners would take time to just be too. If they would just take an hour, even if it meant getting up earlier, my furry friends would get up with them and help them "just be," silently connecting with all there is.*

This business of just being is really what they call "profound." It's especially important now for humans because what they have made of their lives is really not natural. Once they sit with a twinkling leaf that shimmers in the sun, or watch a sparrow bounce around in the seeds, or get involved with water flowing over a rock, once they see the importance of that, they will begin to absorb that "being" information into their lives. That's what I do for my Mistress Mother; that's what all pets do for their masters and mistresses. When they're with us their blood pressure drops and their hearts become healthier. We serve a great purpose to humans just by being ourselves. This is why we are magical to them.

I love to be mischievous and bawdy with MM. She wouldn't like a dull and placid dog anyway. I love to make her laugh, even with my bathroom humor. I love to have her watch me when I go out for my morning poop. In the middle of my search for a good place I love to suddenly squat down and pretend to notice a cactus needle in my hind leg. I lift my leg in the middle of a poop just so she'll know I'm capable of multitasking. This always makes her laugh.

I'm very respectful of my Mistress Mom when she's on an important phone call, or when she is reading a script, or when she is writing something. She doesn't realize it but I am helping her write these very words. But when I sense a break in her focus, I run from the other side of the room and jump into her lap so she'll think I'm just a dog. This surprises her, and sometimes shocks her, but then she always laughs and cuddles me. When she cuddles me, I don't know who gets more pleasure, she or I. So it's not that I'm an even-keeled, entertaining soul-being. I can also be a very unpredictable one. Whatever works. But I also want her to get back to her writing because she has reached an age when she is really looking at the meaning of life in a deep way, which is why she loves me so much.

Shirley

In the *Mahabharata,* the celebrated Indian epic poem written more than 2,000 years ago, a great emperor is making a trek to the Himalayas, accompanied by his four brothers and his wife, when a small dog attaches himself to the retinue. As the trip progresses, one by one the members of the royal party fall victim to the hardships of the road, and die, until the emperor's only remaining companion is his adopted dog. When they reach the end of their journey at the gates of heaven, the King of the Heavenly Gates comes to greet the emperor in regal and godly splendor. He then says, "But the dog cannot come with you. You will achieve immortality equal to mine, but you must leave the dog." The emperor replies, "No, I can't, he is devoted to me; he has been with me all along this arduous journey." And the King of the Heavenly Gates says, "There is no place in heaven for persons with dogs. Abandon the dog." Calmly but firmly the emperor responds, "I will under no circumstances abandon this dog just to achieve happiness for myself." So the King of the Heavenly Gates tries to convince him one last time, "If you give up the dog you will acquire the world of heaven. You've already given up your brothers and wife. You have obtained heaven through your very own deeds. You have already abandoned everything else. How can you be so confused as to not give up a dog?" The emperor still refuses, saying he abandoned his wife and brothers because they were already dead, but he will not abandon the living dog. At that point the dog reveals himself to be none other than the great god Dharma, god of cosmic order and moral principle, who tells the emperor he has passed this final test of his virtue.

Of course dog spelled backward is God.

Terry

Because of what happened on America Worst, my MM has been talking about finding someone who owns an airplane. I don't know if she means marrying someone who has an airplane, or finding a very close companion-friend who has an airplane. What would happen if that friend with the airplane wanted to share the bed with my Mistress Mom and me? I think that could be very difficult, so I hope airport security relaxes enough so that we can have our life together without a man involved. She doesn't know that I can read the pillow she has on her bed that says, "The more I know about MEN the more I love my Dog." When I read this it makes me feel secure in our future.

When strangers come to my MM's home or to her movie trailer, I always jump up in their laps and kiss them as though I have known them all their lives, which I have. That makes them feel very loved. When I play princess I want all the attention I can get any way, and of course I want everyone to love me too. So everybody wins as long as it's not women with black dresses and pearls, who are afraid that dog hair is something that no outfit needs. However, most strangers are so happy with the attention and love I lavish on them that they don't really look down to see what their clothes look like. Anyway, no outfit is complete without dog hair. Basically, dog hairs are threads of love from heaven.

When we arrive at a hotel, I know what the concierge's uniforms look like now, so while my MM is checking in I go right over to the concierge and jump up, lick his face, and gently nip his nose. When he takes all my Mistress Mom's bags up to the room, I run around in circles and help him unpack the bags. Sometimes I even drag out my MM's undies so that he gets a big laugh. After I have connected with the concierge, I know he'll want to come and take me for walks when my mom is busy. He'll also talk to me about other people in the hotel, but I would never divulge those secrets. He gives me treats too.

Since I go everywhere with my Mistress Mom, I'm at her side when she works on a movie. The word gets around when I am on a movie set. I find myself loving the lights. I gravitate to them because then people can see me do my tricks, they can see me be adorable. I also like the Teamsters, who are a union. I like the Teamsters because they let me into their trailer, let me watch football, let me chase the players on the TV screen, and give me lots of treats. In fact, they even get extra popcorn and lots of food for me from the catering table. So I am a Teamsters dog when I'm on the set.

Once while working on a movie MM had really bad shoulder pain. She wrenched her shoulder during one of her workouts, and she was writhing in agony down on the floor of her trailer. I jumped up on her shoulder and hugged it. I hugged it very tight. Then I ran and got my favorite Teamster and he gave my MM some medicine and she was all better. And now every morning when I see her *down on the floor doing her exercises, I run up to her and I hug her shoulder and her arm, because I don't want her to hurt herself. I hope she understands that's what I'm doing.*

The Teamsters take turns taking me on walks, and bringing me food from the catering tables. They are really tired by the end of the day, but they still come in early the next morning when my MM is in the makeup trailer to play with me all over again. I know I'm a girl, but I feel like one of them. Sometimes I wait in my Mistress Mom's trailer for her to come back from a scene; when she does she wears these funny things on her head that she calls wigs, but they look like strange hats to me. Sometimes she has blond-wig hats, sometimes she has long brown-wig hats, and sometimes she has gray-wig hats. Sometimes when she hasn't had time to visit the hairdresser, her own hair is the color of the gray-wig hat. But now I'm telling secrets that my Mistress Mom doesn't want anybody else to know.

I also like to watch her in the makeup chair because she doesn't wear makeup in real life. She puts on makeup to become "the character." When she becomes the charac-

ter, she plays with me in a different way because she thinks she's different.

I see my MM's thoughts in images and I see them in colors. When she says we're going for a ride in the car, she's picturing that ride in the car so that's why I run to the car, because that's what I see in her mind. Sometimes when she's been on the set I stare at her when she comes back into the trailer to be with me, so I can see the scene that she's just done because it's still in her mind. I can see the other actors, I can see the lights (which I wish I were in), and I can see the costumes and her silly wig hats.

In long-ago times we didn't need language. We communicated with each other using thoughts. It was much clearer because we didn't get confused or manipulated by words. I still have that long-ago talent, and I wish humans did too. They really need to get back to basics.

Shirley

An architect friend of mine once told me he always had to leave his dog at home when he went to work, where he was busy with blueprints and scale models. When he came home his dog would simply stare at him, focusing intently on his forehead. A pet communicator told him that the dog was entering into his master's mind. He was reading the plans, and considering the images of the model buildings. Once he had read the architect's mind he could relax, but not until he knew what his master had been doing all day.

I try to communicate with Terry regularly to improve my thought transference. I'm trying to do the same thing with flowers and birds and trees—and yes, even rocks. When I lived with the Masai in Kenya, Africa, the

white hunters told me that the Masai were very accomplished at projecting and receiving each other's thoughts.
They didn't need telephones or e-mail. With their minds
they also tuned in to the movements of animals as well as
the cycles of nature and the weather.

Terry

I wonder if my MM knows that all living beings on our earth are created from the same thing. I know that my MM understands she doesn't own me, and because she doesn't treat me like a possession, I don't think of her as an owner. Other dogs and animals and trees and flowers are equal to my MM and me, although she and I do have a special connection. The more thought intelligence my MM communicates to me, the more I can respond with. I love the idea that she knows how wise I am. I know she knows that I'm a royal terrier, that I'm different from Spooky and Sheba and Daisy and Sandy and the other dogs on the ranch—but she also knows I'm her teacher.

Sometimes I look away when my MM looks into my eyes, because I don't want to confuse her by letting her learn too fast. Humans have to learn according to their limited pace. I can feel her wondering what it's like to be in my little body. I know she's trying to sense what it feels like to have four feet and fur and a cold nose. I wish she would wonder what it's like to have my cosmic wisdom. I love it when she explains the reasons why she's asking me to do something: like I don't already know! If she says I can't have any more kibble because I'll get fat, I understand, for goodness' sake. But if she just says I can't have any more kibble, then I'll keep begging. I also like it when she makes deals with me. That way I know that she understands we are equals. When I don't want to have my bath and she says "I will give you a treat if you will come up nicely and let me bathe you in the sink," of course I know it's a deal. But I love getting extra treats too. I love it when she tries to think like I think. That's the best fun of all.

One of my favorite moments comes when we sit quietly together, look out at the mountains, and watch the rain start to fall. It's even better when it snows. Ooooh, I love to play in the snow. I love to bite the soft flakes and taste a little of the heaven they came from.

*My MM knows that I am the treasure in her heart, which is why I bring her to tears. Even though she can't hear me speak of all these things, I can hear **her** speak and I understand everything in her mind and her heart. I know that God is there inside her and soon she will learn to communicate with every little thing that God is.*

Shirley

Here it is, Easter weekend, and I'm sitting here with Terry in my ranch house in New Mexico contemplating all I've learned from books, from working in movies, from art, from channeling, from living, from my walk on the Camino, and from reading the Bible. I watch the wind breezily cleanse everything. Could it be that I did not really feel up to emotionally accepting what I knew with my intellect until Terry came into my life? It's very synchronistic that these thoughts are coalescing into words on an Easter weekend. Christ, who died for our sins, asked us to turn the other cheek again and again. That's what dogs do with humans. But can humans really do that with dogs? Or with each other? Is that what the next big planetary transformation will be all about: the ability to turn the other cheek?

The laws of nature are harmonious and we are defiling nature. We say nature is cruel, but we define cruelty even as we cause it. Would we be more balanced if we allowed nature to be balanced? The mere fact that I, at my age, still ask these questions proves to me that I have not understood one simple truth: that we and nature are part of that which gives us the feeling of love. I understand it more now because of a little dog, but still there are questions that haunt me about the world and God. What is real—that which we perceive to be real or that which we cannot see? Are heaven and God and Spirit more real than the world around us?

I am beginning to realize that the "real" reality is the one I don't altogether accept. The "real" reality is what I know deep inside, but continue to separate myself from: the spirit within, which has little to do with religion. I have come to understand this most profoundly through my relationship with a dog, which most religions claim has no soul.

Terry has strategies for survival and basic needs,

but these are not violent, or angry, or full of guilt or self-judgment; they just *are*. My happiness with her makes me cry. Why? Why do we humans cry when we are ecstatically happy, when we are rewarded with something we've always wanted? Do we feel we don't deserve it? Or do we cry in moments of happiness because we know so many others don't feel this way?

If I look at the world and I see it as sad and ravaged and polluted, as competitive and dangerous and hostile—basically, I would have to say, insane—that will be my only experience of it. I will therefore create a world without meaning. As I look at Terry I can't believe she lives in such a world. She seems to have no purpose except just to BE. THAT is her meaning. And that is what she's giving me: the right just to be. But just to be what?

Why should connecting to the spirit that is our basic nature be so complicated? I know we are not physical beings looking for a soul; we are soul-beings who should have the right simply to be happy while we are physical. I watch Terry, totally absorbed in the sound of a bird, or so delighted by a toy that she will spontaneously leap on it and bring it to me, as if to say, Play is important: "Play with me. Shake my toy." She loves to hunt and to run; she loves to keep her senses alive. She didn't create war. She didn't create taxes. She didn't create an addictive technological culture. She didn't create pollution, or airplane crashes, or violence, or terrorism, or dope, or even meaninglessness. In this world as I perceive it, Terry brings happiness just by being. I wish I could be that way.

Terry

My MM and I have been together through many life-times. As I said, when we lived in ancient Egypt together, I was the god Anubis and MM was a minor princess. What I didn't reveal was the story of a strange, remarkably intelligent king who shared that time with us. He didn't look like other human beings. He had big eyes and gray skin and a face shaped like a triangle. He was a very powerful and kind king who knew many things that humans did not. Humans worshiped him, and sometimes were afraid of him, because he came from out of the sky.

This king taught Egyptians about the ways of nature, the stars and cosmic numbers, and other celestial matters. He said he came from his world on a silent, round airboat. He said I should take care of the princess and teach her now and always through time, and never to forget that. When he died, there was a great ceremony, and he was buried next to his airboat deep in the ground.

Just a few weeks ago my MM was watching a television program about a KGB Russian intelligence team that had uncovered the old king and his airboat in Egypt. It was all very top secret, but he looked exactly like the king I remembered! The KGB people believed he was from Orion and said the Egyptians in those ancient days wrote about how he had come to teach them many things. I noticed that my MM was very interested in the program and cuddled me closely with familiar feeling. I am keeping my promise to the king, because royal celestial agreements are very important. I am continuing my teachings with MM now, and I'm hopeful she'll get it this time.

Sometimes when my MM and I travel by airplane and struggle to get where we're going I wonder why we can't go in a silent airboat like the king's. Things are so rudimentary now. But I have to continue to adjust.

Shirley

My land in New Mexico speaks to me when I walk it. As I walk with the ranch dogs I feel its power and knowledge. These ancient rocks and flat-topped mesas remind me that this land, now nearly 7,000 feet high, was once under water.

Years ago I was told by a shaman that a dog would come, a spirit dog with one blue eye and one dark eye, and that he would circle the ranch house for a few months and then come in and claim his right to protect it. That's exactly what happened. Spooky is a mixed breed, the one male in this harem of females. Not far behind him is Sheba, a mix of German shepherd, malamute, and husky. Magnificently dignified, she can also be short-tempered, which is her prerogative as the oldest female. Daisy is an Australian shepherd collie, kept young by Sandy, an obstreperous, delightful, and totally untrainable retriever. And of course there's Terry the Princess Terrier, who never leaves my side.

The dogs and I are walking among the ghosts and spirits of the past. There are Indian ruins under our feet, where tribal people traded turquoise and beads for livestock and grain. A stream runs alongside our mountain rim-walking, as we make our way toward the petroglyphs, carvings in the rocks that some say are over 3,000 years old. I wonder if I lived here long ago. And was Terry with me then? Perhaps that is why I was drawn back to call it my real home.

Terry seems to understand the ancient energy. She leaves no rock uninvestigated, as though listening within them for messages from bygone voices.

I remember J. Krishnamurti, the Indian sage and writer from New Delhi, who returned from a long walk not unlike this one and reported that he had not had one single thought along the way. Oh, to quiet my mind like that! First I'd need to dissolve negative thoughts, then anxious thoughts, then regretful thoughts, and let's not forget guilty thoughts. I can't really imagine an extended stay in a no-thought state, but on long walks I do feel my mind settling into a state of detached composure, the way I imagine Terry, or a hawk wheeling overhead, or even a boulder might feel. And sometimes when Terry freezes, gazing at a point I can't see, I try to enter that space and as I do, an extraordinary sense of peace comes over me. In that moment I feel that no matter what madness we humans bring upon ourselves, the animals, the sky, and the mountains will watch in dignified silence, hoping we will come to our senses.

According to Buddhism, life is an illusion, a dream we have created in our three-dimensional "reality." I recognize that Terry is having her own divine reality, which is infinitely less judgmental than my own.

Buddhists say we live in a state of blissful nothingness but we don't know it, because we think that what we have created is real. Have I limited my body's eyes to seeing only those images that I think are real? If so, then the illusion I've created is like a curtain hiding the real reality from me. I know something about creating illusion, because that's my business. But image-making is not the same as seeing the truth.

Is the ravaged world far away from me also my own creation? When I turn on CNN or the news shows on Sunday, am I creating those journalists and those politicians and those people who speak about how much trouble we are in? Buddha said, "As you think, so you become." If my thoughts are negative and fearful, perhaps that is the reality I will create. If each of us in our varying states of distress and fearfulness creates our own world, it's a wonder we're not in more collective trouble!

Perhaps on his walk Krishnamurti touched upon what Terry has known since she was born. Maybe Terry is not seeing the world as I see it, my garden as I see it, this land as I see it, my clothing as I see it, or even her toys as I see them. Perhaps what I sense in her is that she is seeing beyond image-making to the Big Truth. As I get older and spend more time with Terry, I want to see what would happen if I changed my illusions. If I radically shifted my illusions would I perceive the world in a whole new way? Could Terry and I ever see the same sunset? I believe she sees more than I do, and sees it more deeply, but maybe even that thought is just part of the dream I'm having. Maybe I've even created this little dog who is my profound teacher.

I don't want to leave Terry to make a movie because she gives me peace and laughter and puts me in touch with how different she is from goal-oriented moviemakers. In the main, the movies my industry makes cater to the lowest instincts in people. Of course movies have to make profit, but by glorifying violence and preying on people's fears they're just perpetuating the problem. I'm beginning to fear a breakdown of society. When people believe their governments don't tell them the truth, different factions may take matters into their own hands and fight each other. We are so afraid of terrorism from abroad that we may fight and kill each other right here, at home. But when I stop walking and gaze into Terry's eyes, she gives me a deep sense of comfort—telling me that everything is happening just as it should in order for us to learn who we really are.

Terry

MM watches the news all the time because she wants to know how much trouble people are in. People are in trouble because they're not watching the news within themselves. MM is really concerned but I also think she sees the situation in the world as a kind of horrible entertainment, but that's because humans are a horrible entertainment within themselves. Many of her friends tell her they've stopped looking at the news and they don't even read their papers anymore because everything is so disturbing. But ignorance never solves problems, and so many are in self-ignorance. My MM is not one to go into denial. She wants to know, but doesn't know where the answers are. Well, that's easy, they're within herself.

MM and I are sitting on a hill overlooking our house. The trees are talking to me and each one has a story to tell. These juniper trees have a long lineage, and their ancestors have experienced many things. They tell me they know that the insects living among them are not pleasant for humans, but they have a place in the lives of the trees. The juniper insects might even contribute to the gin that humans make from juniper berries. I've never had a drink of that stuff, but I've seen many of MM's friends become funnier when they drink that insect juniper juice! So you see everything has a place in life. However, that gin juice may have too important a place in some people's lives.

The tall ponderosa pine trees are telling me that humans cut many of their ancestors down in order to make homes. They say they have no judgment about that because they are happy to serve the needs of people, and to shelter them from nature. They know their ancestor trees never died; they now live in the ceilings and walls of people's homes.

The birds darting in and out of the trees tell me what they have seen humans do from their vantage point in the sky. They love the insects in the trees because they make good meals. They tell me about the secrets of the air and their knowledge of flight. They are happy to have served as models for the airplane, but they don't like what airplanes do when they drop things that kill trees and people.

As I look over everything, I love being with MM just doing nothing but hearing all the stories of the life around me. All living things have a history . . . his-story, her-story, its-story—and they see things from their own perspectives. Every living thing has something to say, some story to tell. So when MM asks what is real I want to tell her that perception is the only reality until all life becomes one again—didn't one of those humans call it The Unified Field Theory?

Everything has energy, and all of it has a purpose. Some energies may be denser than others, but they all have a reason for being. Nothing is evil. That is only a human perception. Humans like to think there is a duality in the world, and they call it Good and Evil. Because they believe that, they have made a world that seems to prove that this is true. But it isn't. Humans don't want to consider that there is no such thing as Good and Evil, though, because they are used to living in that duality. It seems to give them a reason to be alive—to conquer "evil" when evil is what's thumping away in their own minds and hearts. Even their Bible says, "Thou shalt not eat of the fruit of the tree of 'knowledge' of good and evil," but they kept on eating that faulty knowledge.

Nature doesn't think that way. We animals don't think that way, mostly because we haven't been taught to think that way. We know that what humans call evil is just an expression of inner confusion, and a disconnect from the Divine that I see all around us. I'm digging in the dirt now because I don't want to get confused by people thinking, but I can feel Mother Earth growing tired of being used as a stage upon which this drama of Good and Evil is being played out.

Whenever humans feel love within themselves they usually can't take it for very long and they accuse themselves and each other of being self-centered. But if they saw the love **and** the light energy inside themselves, their *perspective on the outside world would change, and it would actually reflect what they see in themselves.*

The wars in the world are the wars that start within people, long before anyone attacks anyone else. These inner wars create the outer disturbances. I wish they could see that love is their human inheritance.

I stop digging and sit beside MM again. As we rest here on this hill I wonder if Mother Earth will ultimately decide to erupt and restore balance between herself and the life that walks across her stage. Maybe in the light of creation she will want to start all over again. I would hate to see that happen because people could be such beautiful beings if they only knew it. We fur people know who we are and if people don't hurt us we'll never forget our own beauty.

I can feel MM beside me having head-thumping thoughts. She is getting up to walk again. I wish she wouldn't walk so fast sometimes. She doesn't realize she's only following in the footsteps of her own destiny, which will happen no matter how fast she walks. The future will always be there, so why hurry it? Neither of us will ever outwalk the future.

How did she walk with those thoughts for ten hours a day for thirty days when she walked across Spain? She must have had a terrible headache from all those questions. I think her brain has a mind of its own.

My MM and her friends talk about war and terrorism a lot these days. They seem frightened and don't know what to do with their futures. I'm watching to see if the fear I see in their hearts will go away. Will they realize that their fear is of their own making? I watch my MM's every movement. I sit up very straight when I watch her because I want her to know that I'm aware of everything she does, and thinks, and feels.

I'm watching her closely now as we walk each step on the ranch. It's so still around us as a butterfly flutters around my head. I'm looking up to the sky again because I see long jet streams and hear strange sounds way up there. I see my MM looking up too. It feels like she's praying. I can feel her heart go into some kind of reverie that asks for help to make the world more peaceful. Everything around us is so peaceful, but I do understand what she's concerned about.

Shirley

Have we humans commenced the onslaught foretold by the ancient prophecy? Are we seeing pieces fall into place for the end of the world as we know it? Whatever I turn to—whether it's Revelations in the New Testament or Nostradamus's predictions, or Hopi and Mayan prophecies, or Edgar Cayce's channelings, or the Bible—I see signs that we are on the cusp of a new and devastating reality that could mean a new, less pleasant world.

Try as I might, I just can't get the events of the war against Iraq out of my mind. I keep thinking back to that time when Ari Fleischer announced that hostilities were commencing as though he were master of ceremonies at an execution. I'd been watching the military buildup all week—our government's warnings and deadlines,

Baghdad's silence, protests around the world, and emotional farewells as American soldiers were deployed to the Gulf. Were we beginning the third World War?

As a child during World War II, I heard the phrase "theater of war" again and again. Here I was again on opening night, feeling more than ever like a member of the audience in a scripted and directed event. As the several televisions I had going at once blared their messages, I was beside myself with confusion, fear, and rage. Who were we, as humans, much less as Americans, to *initiate* a war? My solar plexus felt tight, leaden, and I couldn't breathe, much less speak with friends who called frantically through the night. I thought of Kurtz in *Apocalypse Now*, "The horror, the horror." I thought of our director, the president, in his many script conferences preparing for *this* performance. I couldn't understand his going through with it in the face of hundreds of thousands of people protesting around the world and in this country. Did he really want so badly to be the hero of his own movie? At his script conferences did anyone ask, What does democracy have to do with killing defenseless people?

On television the show was in full swing, the special effects exploding in the night, buildings falling, palaces burning, like a surreal opera. And somewhere below the fireworks human beings were being burned alive, screaming in despair for themselves and for their children. But I couldn't see them, no Americans could. On that first night, the news reports were all about technologies—precision and accuracy, detailed plans of military strikes and advances. This mayhem was taking place in the cradle of civilization, the birthplace of Abraham, perhaps the very Garden of Eden, where the recorded promise of the human race began. And here we were, bombing it "back to the Stone Age."

Was my beloved country about to unite the Arab world as no Arab leader ever had before? Doing so could only throw gasoline on the fires of a true Holy War. Fundamentalism in any form can look and feel like terrorism to those outside of that faith. Do we really think our own wealth and power come from God? Starting a war is a colossal abuse of privilege, no matter what the justification.

I remember screaming at the television. Terry's

ears lay flat against her head as she followed me from room to room. Every now and then she tossed a toy into the air in an unsuccessful attempt to distract me. The talking heads on the screen kept dropping phrases like grenades—September 11, the War on Terror, protecting the homeland—without any real explanation about how these connected to what we were doing: initiating war with a country that had done nothing to provoke us. Our leaders wanted to create a sympathetic audience for this performance, which they told us was about safety and self-preservation in the age of terrorism. But what about *our own* weapons of mass destruction? How could they be justified?

Believe me, doubts about our country's good intentions don't come easily to me. I am a patriotic American. I was raised in Virginia, home to eight presidents, and growing up I wrote the same thing in my diary every night: "Let the bells ring out in freedom." Our own country was founded by revolutionaries—terrorists to some—who threw off the yoke of British oppression, allowing us in this country the freedom to pursue happiness and to worship in any way we choose. Freedom gave our people prosperity, but far too much of our wealth has been used to create a vast stockpile of technologically precise killing machines to protect that position of privilege. Thinking about it gives me chills.

We have deployed these weapons so that others would live as we saw fit: Let's initiate the violent overthrow of a regime so that government by the people and of the people would thrive. What business was that of ours? We've elected our own fair share of thugs in our short history. What was so democratic about our presidential elections in the years 2000 and 2016, when the popular vote went to candidates who would be barred from the presidency by the Electoral College?

No one should live under tyranny. Our lives are short and difficult in the best of circumstances, and freedom should be a given. But when we go to war without provocation, I fear that the price of liberating another country may be our souls. Protest is the most patriotic act I can think of, but I don't want my actions to be mis-understood as being unsupportive of the honorable men and women just doing their jobs, following their com-mander in chief. What *was* his ultimate goal in invading Iraq? Was it security, oil, democracy, or just revenge? We still don't have a straight answer.

In the midst of all this, I had to make a decision about whether or not to attend the Academy Awards. It's so strange when the strands of your life become tangled, when politics become personal, even spiritual, and when your profession, already personal, becomes political. I had been invited to Hollywood to be honored as a past Oscar winner. Before the war began I was excited about the prospect. I could catch up on old friends, network for future films, and generally relax and have fun. But as violence in the Gulf escalated, flying to L.A. to parade across the stage in a peach-colored, sequined pantsuit became less and less attractive. I couldn't tolerate the irony of strolling down the red carpet into the Kodak Theater in celebration of ourselves, while our sons and daughters, many of them still teenagers, waited in the wings of another theater wondering if this would be the last day of their lives.

I recall Terry gazing steadily at me as I swung from grief to confusion to fear to rage. Under her patient gaze I sank deeper and deeper into a stony depression, the likes of which I'd never felt before. Finally I climbed into bed, but even with Terry curled up protectively beside me, I couldn't sleep. I needed to get outside, so I sat in the hot tub to try to quiet myself. Night clouds obscured the stars, and I felt a similar haziness inside myself, as though my vision was shrouded by anger and confusion; I prayed for a strong wind to blow through my heart, leaving it empty and clean. I asked for help. I don't know how much time passed when I felt, more than heard, a voice say, "Calm yourself." As if it were an acting exercise, I did. The voice continued, "Your heart is breaking, but it is also opening through the cracks." The clouds began to part, revealing the moon, and the stars shone brighter.

My heart and mind were clearing. I looked out at my mountain that I named Sierra Madre because the old-timers say it is a feminine mountain, inside of which are great treasures. Then a light came from *within* the mountain. The light seemed to glow from below the surface, through the terrain of the slope. I had seen that light before, but couldn't understand where it was coming from. How could light come from *within* a mountain? The phrase "terrain of love" then came to me, followed by the thought, "Nature knows what it is doing even though humankind doesn't." Suddenly I understood with complete certainty that what we had become was due to a profound separation from the Divine Source and we had used our *free will* to do it. From our notion of free will we had created what we call Democracy, a system of government that allowed us to be free to do whatever we wanted as humans—*when* we wanted and *how* we wanted, within certain limits set by laws. But along the way we lost sight of our profound connection to spirit. Because we had been religiously oppressed in Europe before our Revolution, we carried with us the desire to worship in peace. But for most of us, religion promoted divisiveness, not unity: *Our* God was the real God, not theirs. We worshiped God in whatever way we had been taught, but not the Divine way.

This sudden realization that free will could be so dangerous made me wonder if the human race might be a kind of experiment, and that by using free will to sever our connection to the Divine Source, we had set in motion what most prophecies declared as our future. Could two-thirds of the human race be about to destroy itself because of our abuse of our free will?

I looked around me at the peace of the stars. The light from within the mountain disappeared. Were there observant beings out there, forbidden to interfere with our impending destruction? Were the shadowed trees and the night birds and Terry herself waiting patiently for us to understand? I sank deeper into the peace I had found and asked for help. The help was there. The inner peace was there. It was a miracle. I was observing it even as I *became* it. It was like allowing a character to inhabit me, instead of the other way around.

Embracing that spirit of calm, I decided I would attend the Academy Awards that year. I chose to honor the commitment I'd made, not just to the organizers of the ceremony, but to the larger community of artists.

As I sat in the water under the watchful stars, I wondered again if it was too late for us humans. Would the prophecies be fulfilled after all? Gazing up at the night sky it occurred to me that it is in the spaces between things that the truth lies. And the only way to reach it is through calmness, and a faith that it does indeed exist.

Terry

I don't understand why human beings fight and kill each other so much. It's stupid, because they don't die anyway. They're just making things worse for themselves the next time around.

Sometimes I think people never got past being apes, but then apes don't kill each other nearly so much as people do. Why don't people behave like angels, since that's what they could be? In fact, that's what they are. There is always a way for angels to work out their differences because they know that each of them is part of God. Even the angels they disagree with, or are afraid of, are part of God. When my MM was a little girl she asked her father why there couldn't be peace in the world. He sighed and said, "Because religion makes too many people kill each other."

Shirley

I came to realize how deeply rooted belief in the Devil is in our culture, and how it can be applied to suit the human powers that be, during my preparation to play the character Rebecca Nurse in *The Witches of Salem* television miniseries. It's more than mere coincidence that the witches of Salem also happened to be women who inherited or owned property themselves in a male-dominated society.

Rebecca Nurse was one of the most pious women in the village, attending and cleaning the church every day, but her belief in a loving God was more important to her than her fear of the Devil. Her hanging marked the end of the witch trials, although she was pardoned for her crimes only a few years ago.

The day we shot the hanging scene I took Terry to the outdoor location, framed by a misty, eerie sky. I had been hoisted onto a cart with a rope around my neck. Terry sat some distance from the cart with my friend and assistant. The director yelled "Action!" through a bullhorn, and all of the villagers, children, and adults began to wail, and moan, and cry. Terry's ears went back and she began to bark and howl as she ran over to my cart and tried to climb up. As the wailing grew louder, Terry grew extremely alarmed. She couldn't understand that this wasn't real. Someone pushed her away, and finally she fled. My assistant found her, but she wouldn't come back to the set. Terry felt the emotional "reality" that we actors created, and was not happy with how we manipulated our personalities in order to play the scene. I realized yet again how disturbing creating our reality can be—in "reel" life as well as "real" life!

Terry

When my MM took me to the set where she was about to be hanged, I had a sense that she and the other actors were going to play a trick on their feelings—and that I might be very confused. But I didn't realize how awful it would be. I saw small children and grown-ups who should have known better, acting as though they were afraid of what they called the Devil.

At first MM was dressed in her Pilgrim clothes, and she threw a stick for me to chase, which I did but I knew something bad was going to happen. Everyone seemed normal until a big man shouted "Action!" and everyone began to make sad noises. I didn't know what was wrong. What had just changed?

My MM, in the cart with a rope around her neck,

looked up at the sky and started to pray. I had seen her do it at the ranch, but this time it scared me so I tried to jump into the cart to save her. When someone pushed me away I thought I had done something wrong because everyone was acting so upset. So I ran away. MM's friend took me back to her trailer, but I could still hear everyone moaning in the distance. It was truly a terrible experience for me. If that is what they call acting, then I'm wondering what I can depend on when it comes to sincerity with human beings. Maybe they act a little bit all the time. I never act unless it's important, or a matter of survival.

When MM finally came back to me in her trailer, I didn't know what to expect. She hadn't been herself only a little while before. Or had she? How do these actor people do all that without touching some part of themselves that is real? I don't know what they think real is. Acting is a mystery to me.

My MM knelt down and told me she was very sorry, and that I hadn't done anything wrong. That made me feel better, but I wanted to talk to her about this Devil business.

Did those hangings really happen to those women, just because other people said they were supposedly friendly with the Devil? Who was this Devil anyway? I know what humans think about evil, but who is this person who puts a "d" in front of that word? Is it important that "evil" is "live" spelled backward? Humans certainly have a backward approach to living. When will they see the Light?

Shirley

Even though I'm questioning whether to make the movie in Ireland, and even though I'm questioning the role of movies themselves in our society (particularly given what is being made), I know in my heart that good films probably have a more profound effect on human lives than anything other than war. This may be why audiences are so drawn to violence. Perhaps they need to examine the violence in themselves. We never made much "violence" for violence's sake in the old days, when movies were more about the relationships people had with each other. I suppose the re-flected violence of what we've become has its place.

Sometimes on a film set now I feel I represent a more chivalrous time. When I work on a picture these days I'm referred to as "ma'am" instead of "kid" or "girl."

And there usually comes a moment when I'm surrounded by younger artists and crew members asking what it was like to work with Alfred Hitchcock, Sam Goldwyn, Harry Cohen, Mike Todd, Jack Lemmon, Robert Mitchum, William Wyler, Billy Wilder, and the rest of the greats. They were artists who yearned to reflect the *power* of the human spirit in their desire to entertain, not the *loss* of the human spirit. Artists in my day didn't care that much about fashion, tabloids, or even grosses.

I realize that I absorbed something in all those years working with those purveyors of inspiring film images, something that many young artists today don't seem to appreciate: all of the old-timers had a strong work ethic, which came out of a deep belief in what they were doing. Lots of people in the business today don't seem to have the personal training, or the deep-seated need to express what was missing in our lives.

I've found that the discipline I learned from dancing also keeps me healthy and balanced under the considerable stress of making a movie, and in the constant prying glare of the public eye. When I was working on a TV miniseries about Mary Kay, the queen of door-to-door cosmetic sales, I noticed that we were way behind schedule, with only one day left to get three days of work done. To catch up we had to work straight through from 8:30 Thursday morning to 1:30 Friday afternoon. One scene we had to run through at least a dozen times involved me walking up and down stairs. I think the cast expected me to collapse, or at least to lose my balance or my temper, but those years of discipline stood me in good stead. The work ethic and heart balance you learn when you're young stay with you forever.

If your desire is to be a long-distance runner, the industry that makes art out of illusion requires stamina of the heart, mind, and body. Too many young artists today care more about popularity with the public than about what they wish to express. The public is leading them rather than the other way around. Just as importantly, I've learned that filming is not about the individual; it's a team experience as well as an endurance sport.

And more than anything it is a spiritual exercise. Scratch the skin of any artist and you'll find a spiritual seeker; when artists resonate to that aspect of themselves they do their best work, in my opinion.

One of the great pleasures I take in later years is being cantankerous about professionalism. Now people expect me to insist that a profound work ethic be observed, and to not care what anybody thinks of that. If I'm not eccentric, hard-driving, and insistent on everyone pulling their weight, people are actually disappointed! I find that aging goes better if you're a little loony anyhow. Particularly if your coworkers think you talk to God!

MM looks to God above.
She should look down at me.
I'm the ONE who knows.

Statue of Anubis.

Yes, I am Anubis.

"Oh Wise One of Ancient
Knowledge," MM says to me.

This is an air pirouette.

See my incredible chest capacity? I lift weights.

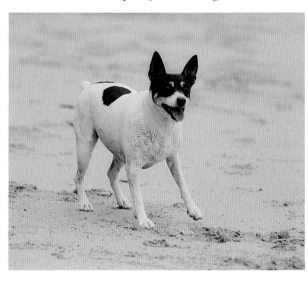

I'm waiting for a vicious German Shepherd.

This is called a Grand Jeté in ballet terms.

This is called "chase the seagull" in beach language.

This is called
"down dog" pose
in Ashanga yoga.

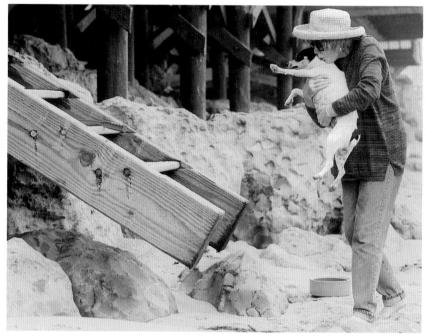

MM thinks I can't climb up the steps myself. How foolish ...

MM's boobies are not too high for me.

I'm even in command of the sun.

My future is secure.

We're dreaming about long ago.

I like to look taller and longer whenever possible.

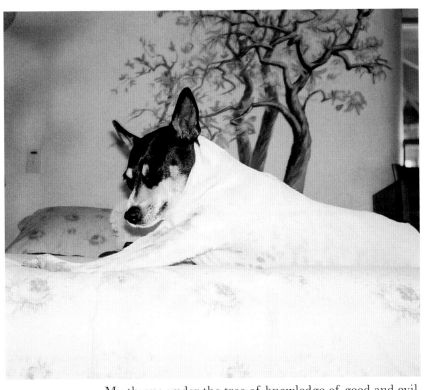

My throne under the tree of knowledge of good and evil.

I'm gazing into the past.

I am an expert driver.

I like to make MM
think I'm begging.

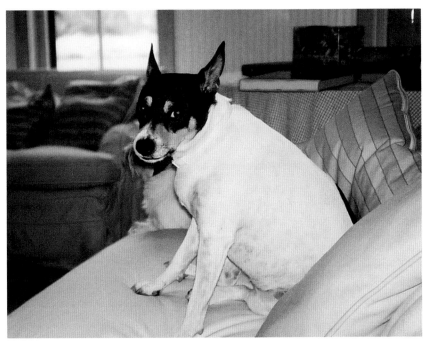

Do I get a dessert later?

Sheba is a
magnificent
but older
female.

But Daisy is a
sweet older woman.

Daisy is waiting
for me to come
out and order
her around.

Daisy and
Sandy "kiss
talking."

One blue eye,
one dark eye and
still Spooky waits
to seduce me.

They all
succumb
to my orders.

My MM is going to dunk
her face in the stream.

Domestic bliss.

Terry

My MM is seeing that nature itself is very efficient. Nothing is gratuitous or unimportant. It is a lot like that making **good** *movies, from what I've seen. Every living being has a part to play and a job to do, which ultimately results in a harmonious message. But neither nature nor moviemaking is a democracy. The ultimate authority in nature is the Divine. The ultimate authority in a movie is the director. The Divine has a vision just as the director does, and those who defy either authority are in for a tough time. The Divine and the director may listen democratically to suggestions, but in the end I've noticed that with each it will go the way of the master. Humans don't listen to the divine director in nature and many of them give the movie director a hard time too. As I've observed,* *moviemaking can be a divine experience, but if people don't listen and support the vision of the one upstairs, whether on the set or in heaven, they should go make their own movie.*

Shirley

I sometimes take Terry with me to movie business meetings because she changes the environment so dramatically. Everyone starts off thinking the meeting is going to be about money and schedules and things of that sort. But Terry completely disarms everybody the moment she walks in. We all have a natural desire to be a child, and that's what Terry brings out in people. Children don't care about money or schedules. People are confused when they see I've brought my dog, but after a few minutes they understand there's some sort of wisdom in it, and within fifteen or twenty minutes with Terry, they've touched that wisdom in themselves.

I particularly like taking Terry to a script conference because the director, the producer, and the actors are all playing parts even before the production begins. Terry seems to understand that there are many characters involved in the room. I love to see how she reacts to hard-bitten producers who don't like anyone to see the childlike part of themselves. They're always the ones whose laps she decides to jump up on. That alters the producer's desire to save money in favor of allowing the artistic vision to prevail, even if it costs more.

Taking Terry shopping has a profound effect too, because when people see a friendly little animal jump up on them, it seems to absolve them of the guilt of spending money they secretly think they shouldn't be spending. This is true for me, as well. In a dressing room Terry observes everything I put on. If she jumps up on me, that's the outfit I buy. In a pet store if she sees a toy she wants she sits in front of it and stares it down. Her silent language communicates to me—and she always gets what she wants.

New York can be a cool experience, because everyone seems to be into themselves, rushing to their next appointment and projecting autonomy in their universe, as if to protect themselves from the knowledge of their own vulnerability. Although it takes a little bit longer for a New Yorker to let his or her façade crack when Terry jumps up, it always happens. And when I go to places in New York where there are many famous people and photographers lurking around, I notice how the level of competitive energy drops when Terry walks in. (The stars may also be aware of W. C. Fields's famous advice not to appear alongside dogs or children!)

Terry

Competition can pit people against one another in a destructive way. What they need to realize is that they should be in competition with themselves to be more trusting.

One time we were in New York, and my MM was having a meeting with a very temperamental writer. She asked him to make some changes in a scene. He began to argue with MM only because he thought his territory was being invaded. I know something about that so I jumped on his lap. He was surprised, but then he began to pet me, and MM got what she wanted. She and I make a good artistic team, because life is an art.

Maybe we should have dogs accompany their masters at the UN. I could wear a doggie burka. When the people argue, and call each other monkeys, we could bark.

When they call each other worse names that make them even madder, we could jump on their laps and tug at their beards. Then we would nip their noses until they agreed to respect each other, which really means they are respecting themselves.

Shirley

A dark cloud of concern comes over me because I really don't want to go to Ireland and leave Terry. It's beginning to obsess me. Is making a good movie my top priority? That was my *modus operandi* most of my life. What I really should be doing is making a movie about what I'm learning. But what would be the plot? Where would the dramatic tension come from? Not many people watched *The Witches of Salem*, which I thought revealed an important aspect of where we Americans came from spiritually—our history of seeing the Devil in other people.

The sun comes out, and then slips behind a bank of dark clouds. In the distance we hear the low roll of thunder. The weather here is moody, just like me.

Terry and I are walking the land and I'm thinking that being a "senior citizen" has its advantages and disadvantages. I know that growing old is not for sissies, and hiking works much the same way, but I'm feeling that the wisdom I've accumulated and the sense of a bit more peace within me was well worth the wait. Still, I want more. I'm glad that I will never be young again, at least not this time around. I'm more interested in a partnership with my body now, not the kind of adversarial relationship I had with it when I was young and a dancer.

Traveling in Argentina once, I saw an advertisement for cheap tickets to a vaudeville show with the great Maya Plisetskaya on the bill. I couldn't believe it was *the* Maya Plisetskaya, one of the finest ballerinas of all time, dancing at her age—middle sixties—and for a pittance. I had seen her perform at the Bolshoi in Russia on many occasions, and when the Bolshoi started coming to the States I got to know her well. During the Cold War I had a party for her and the Bolshoi at my home. It was a time

when Americans presumed that wholesale repression existed throughout Soviet society, but even with the KGB
in attendance there was a degree of uninhibited sensual
behavior most Americans wouldn't have indulged in, even
in private. At two in the morning I poured Galliano for
the troupe of Russian dancers and they slowly dispersed
throughout the grounds, disappearing behind flowering
bushes and trees, doing, I suppose, what dancers all over
the world do with enough Galliano in their systems. Even
some KGB officers found their way into that sylvan wood,
taking an altogether different kind of attendance!

Curious, I bought a ticket to the show in Argentina.
Would Maya Plisetskaya really dance again? She came out
in the middle of the show dressed in her famous swan costume. She had set the standard for this role, and at sixty-
five she could still perform the pas de bourrées and the
elegantly disintegrating gestures of the dying swan. Still, I
couldn't help thinking how humiliating it was that Plisetskaya had to dance on a vaudeville stage in South America
to make ends meet. When she got a standing ovation and

returned for an encore, I was struck by the poignancy of her dancing the dying swan in the later years of her life. Margot Fonteyn told me once, "When we're old enough as dancers to know what we're doing and how to act through the movement, we're too old to dance."

Plisetskaya as the dying swan has stayed with me as an image of how we drag the past into the present. I can no longer dance before an audience in a way that would be acceptable to me, but acting is different. I feel like the canvas of my understanding and experience gets painted with richer hues as I age, and I am more capable than ever of expressing a broad, complex range of emotions. I may worry sometimes about how I look onstage or before the camera, but as we older actresses know, the secret to looking good is expert lighting.

The sun is shining on my face now, and its light is merciless. I wish I had a good key light or a bigger hat. These hills are steep and I'm out of breath, but as Art Linkletter once said, "It's better to be over the hill than under it."

Terry

As my Mistress Mother examines her life I can feel her wondering if her days of self-expression are over. They are not. With age she will find there is more to express than ever. I want her to express until she no longer has the energy to stop! And what she expresses will be more important if I have anything to say about it.

Memory is getting to be an issue for my MM. I see her with friends who are her own age, and some who are twenty years younger, forgetting things all the time. They can't remember the phone number of a good friend. They can't even remember the name of the friend sometimes. They can't remember where they put their car keys, and when they do finally find them, sometimes they can't remember what they're for! So I'm very aware that my

Mistress Mom feels frustrated by her memory loss, but I know she's really going through a kind of elevation of understanding, focusing on important things beyond the details.

I don't like to see my MM irritated when her memory fails her, because I know that with my help she is slowly entering these other dimensions that I am tuned in to. Sometimes, when she has forgotten what it is she was supposed to do, she says things to herself like, "I don't know what is happening to my mind." At times like that I always go over to her and put my head in her lap until she strokes me. I tell her to let her memory rest in peace, then she relaxes and picks me up, so I think she gets the message. Speaking of the importance of messages, I have told her, and she understands, that she should not lift me up under my front legs because that's hard on my shoulders. What she does now, thank goodness, is put both of her hands on my tummy. When she lifts me up that way it's much more comfortable, and I think everybody should know that about us fur persons.

Shirley

Terry is attempting to dig into an anthill. I am concerned, so I say, "NO, Terry, NO." She stops digging and looks up at me. Sometimes the word "no" is too painful for me to utter because Terry's ears go flat with fear. Or is it shame? Perhaps she is just disappointed that I can't find a more positive way to say what's on my mind.

Terry

I don't perceive "no" as an attack. I cower because my MM is afraid for me unnecessarily, and she scares me when she's afraid of something. I like to please her but not by being afraid like she is. There's nothing to be afraid of in an anthill. Ants are beings too, and they know I'm doing my job as a dog.

The animal, insect, and plant kingdoms are so much more in touch with the spiritual essence of God than humans are. I know because we silently communicate with each other on this subject. God is in everything we see, so God is in the anthill. The ants themselves have knowledge of spirit that lies beyond the human power of reasoning. I wish MM would understand this. I see my MM's "no" as a problem she's having with her own fear because she has forgotten that the ants are part of God. It's true that her fear is something she has created in herself, not something that is real. And out of that perception comes the need to control, and defend, and ultimately, "NO!"

My MM is always looking around and asking herself, "What is the meaning of all this?" But when she sees this little dog digging in an anthill, who doesn't seem to have a purpose except to just dig, she wonders why she needs to know what anything is for. I am all being, and no "I am." I have no ego. It is her ego that drives her toward ambition, success, or failure, toward goals that are always just beyond reach. Life is what happens between activities. The path is the goal. If she just loves what she's doing, then her goal won't be all that interesting or important to her.

We pets have become so much a part of the human family because we greet humans again and again with the joy that is missing in their own lives. We help them realize that their only purpose here is to be happy. That's what God wishes for us. That's what She sees when she looks into my soulful eyes. Yet they aren't taught happiness, even in childhood, and certainly not in school. The first lessons for their children and their pets are "No, you can't do this, and you can't do that," even though what they treasure in us is our residence in a reality unbounded by time or fear or judgment.

Regardless of how well or badly they treat us, we pets will still greet them with unconditional love the next time they see us. That is what they could have for themselves. A friend of MM's once said, "I would much rather come home to my dog than to a person, because my dog won't tell me how I've screwed up his life." That's what we're here for.

MM and I can take the same walk every day, and for me it is a thrilling adventure every time. Humans are tethered to the past and fearful of the future, so they usually end up dragging themselves through the present. I am the creator of the world I want to see; I am inventing the world in every moment. I live completely in the present, which is why I can jump on MM with joy fifteen minutes after she has reprimanded me for digging into an anthill. That doesn't mean I'm forgetful; it means I'm free.

*This is the way God intends for **people** to live. I know that MM feels I am holy to her. And when I am around her, **she** feels holy. I have "issues" in my own life, but I never stray from my spiritual essence. I remain part of the "is-ness." I know I bring joy to most everyone who sees me on the beach, on the street, in a taxi, or in an elevator in New York; I know I bring joy to everyone who encounters me on our ranch—even the ants. Because of that joy my MM feels that the very rug I sleep on or the very chair I sit on becomes a holy relic to her. I'm not being arrogant. I want my MM to feel my energy after I leave it. I want her next to me so that my little body can infuse her with my spirit.*

When I do something that displeases MM, I don't feel guilty. Guilt is a kind of living hell. Guilt is based on a feeling of having sinned, but what is sin? There is no such thing as sin. We are all part of God, and how can God sin? God is perfect. God is love. People's perception that they have sinned is an illusion they have created because they feel separate from God. Only if they are separate from

God could they sin. But **other than God doesn't exist.**
And if God is all that exists, then sin cannot exist. Sinless-
ness is a promise from God that we are made of love and
light. When we encounter evil, we are given an opportu-
nity to learn a lesson and correct our own behavior.

If people are truly in touch with the God in them-
selves, then God speaks to them all through the day. This
is what MM sees in me. God's spirit speaks to me and sus-
tains me. Yes, MM always wants to be with me because
something tells her that she is lonely for the God in her-
self. When she is upset with things, when the world seems
to impose itself on her, I am with her. I feel her turmoil
and sometimes it throws me out of balance, but then I tell
her that she is upset because she's out of touch with some-
thing really simple—the reality that God **is** *everything,*
which she has replaced with the illusion of being upset. I
say to her, "You are really upset by nothing. Why don't
you understand that?"

Nothing needs to be done, because everything already
is. Then MM asks, if that is so, how does one live that way?

I watch her go through a moment of doubt, anger, or pain. I just watch. And when I feel the moment is right, I come over and put my paws on her knees or I take a flying leap across the room and jump into her arms, as though to reassure her I am real, not one of her uncomfortable illusions. When she looks into my eyes and I lick her face, I'm saying, "Your own best interest is to know that you can simply trust. I trust you, why don't you trust you?"

Shirley

I see a light in Terry's dark eyes now. In that light is profundity, patience, timelessness, fearlessness, and quiet strength. She embodies the paradox that by being totally vulnerable, totally trusting, she can never truly be harmed. When she looks into my eyes, it is as though Terry is forgiving me for not forgiving myself, while at the same time reminding me that forgiveness isn't even necessary. No, I certainly don't want to travel and leave her behind.

Terry

Why does my MM have to achieve something in order to be happy? She knows there are no goals, but then she will say, "Well, what about work?" "What about my need to relate to other people?" And "What about my self-esteem if I don't do something well enough?" I say, "Look at me, I don't have to achieve anything and I don't hold grievances about what you might scold me for. I'm always in touch with the light inside myself. Holding on to worries just blocks your view of the light inside of you. And the person you hold the grievance for is an illusion you've created anyway. Why don't you give up both?"

As I look up at the southwestern sky. I see a faraway object that is round and brightly lit. It begins to zip in and out of the clouds as it gets closer. I know what it is. It's one of our star people friends. Humans see them too, because I've heard people tell stories of seeing flying craft of some kind, that appear in and around the mountains here.

One guest at the ranch said he was sitting in MM's hot tub at sunset when he saw three round objects come out of her mountain and literally hang in the air, way above his head. He said he couldn't believe what he was seeing. He said he smelled roses and felt something "trying to touch my mind." After floating in the air for a few minutes the aircraft rose straight up and disappeared back into the mountain. He told MM he felt a strong spiritual energy and he noticed that soon after that his life changed. He became clearer about what he was doing and much happier. He met and fell in love with someone special. He said his life had become a dream. Well, life is a dream. And people can make it anything they want. They have that kind of power, they just don't realize it. We animals do this all the time when the humans don't interfere.

Once a very old dog friend of mine who could barely hobble around on his unsteady arthritic legs decided it was time to pass on, and disappeared into the woods during a family outing. His master called him back, and he obeyed. The dog silently talked with the family about all the good times they had shared, and when he walked unsteadily back into the woods, the family knew they would never see him again. But one day, after he had passed over, he observed his family out on another walk together. He decided to become a dream dog and ran toward them really fast. He acknowledged his beloved family but never stopped to let them reach out and pet him. Yet they knew he had come back to say he was happy in his new life, and that now he could run as fast as he wanted to.

Many of my friends who have passed on come to their human companions in dreams. They press their furry selves against their human friends with all the warmth they can muster; they nudge and paw until their masters wake up. They do it to remind their human loved ones that nothing ever dies. Love just changes form.

I knew a little three-year-old boy once who loved the dog next door. One night the dog died in his sleep, and the boy woke up screaming, "Doggie died, doggie died!"

As you see, we communicate with young people better than adult people.

Many of us wake our MMs to warn them of impending danger, like a fire or a burst pipe, or an intruder or something like that. I haven't yet had to do that. But I certainly would if it were necessary.

Shirley

Terry and I stand in a dreamlike state. I have just seen a flying object in the sky. It was brightly lit and hovered over us until it disappeared right into the side of Sierra Madre Mountain. This is not the first time I have seen it, but every time it has the power to shock me into silence. What is it? I think Terry saw it too. I notice that the trees are still. The pond is still. The clouds are still. All the animals are still too, perfectly in touch with that still point I long to touch in myself. A gentle wind begins to blow through the stillness, and a light cleansing rain begins to fall. Then a slight cold chill shivers through me. The stillness seems to adjust to the chill. I try to understand, but I can't. I am not fully in touch with the rhythms of nature—and with whatever has just happened.

This being a holiday weekend, the other people who work here on the ranch are gone. I see Terry and her brother and sister animals on the ranch looking into the sky. What communications are they picking up? The dogs raise their heads further and sniff the air. Then they sigh. It's as if they've been told that peace is possible. Do these craft have occupants, and if so are they children of God? Are they ever afraid? How did we get to be "God-fearing" people? Does that mean that we must fear the very thing that created us? When we are still, and far away from the many distractions of our "civilized" world, we can hear the truth. Perhaps we have chosen to believe that God is to be feared because we fear the love we are capable of in ourselves. Are we uncomfortable with its quiet power, its still certitude?

Terry

I like standing here with a stick in my mouth, not knowing why I picked it up, or what I'm going to do with it. I like just standing here. If I sense a craft overhead, it doesn't bother me. I know what it is. I've seen lots of them. I am perfectly happy with this stick in my mouth, doing nothing. In another minute I may start to chew on it, but if I do the stick will be perfectly fine with my need to chew it. It isn't afraid of me. I know it isn't afraid of me because I can feel its energy, and its energy doesn't know anything about fear. Everything and everyone is energy. So why should anything be afraid? We should just be attentive.

My MM watches me carry the stick under a tree that gives me shade on this sunny, magical Easter weekend. She's looking around because she doesn't know what to think about anything. I wish she'd just play with me, but my MM is too busy thinking and wondering.

I know that to her our animal play looks like fighting sometimes, but we know the difference through the sound of our growls, and we make sure to bite each other on the neck, where loose skin and lots of fur make it safe. Yes, we have a pecking order, and yes, we have squabbles, but we settle them without killing. When we fight to establish dominance or chase off another male trying for our female's attention, we don't fight to the death, we just fight until one dog turns over and exposes his throat. We have no equivalent to the war that my MM worries about. So what is war to us dogs? It's stupid and it kills living beings. We don't like that at all because if it goes too far we won't have anyone to play with.

Shirley

As I stand looking out at God's country, I try to remember a time when I was perfectly at peace. There are not many moments when I seemed to disappear into what I saw, when I had no concerns, no thought of the past or future, when I was only aware of now. Once as a child I was walking past a garden of colorful pansies when suddenly I seemed to become the pansies, with their color, their scent, and their essence. In those moments I found total bliss, and I've never forgotten it. I see Terry doing this all day long. Right now she's sticking her little nose into a desert flower and breathing in the white of it. In a while she will nibble on the herbs in my garden.

When we speak of our pets giving us love, what do we mean? Are they always in a spiritual state, a state beyond judgment?

I have a friend whose son was murdered. She not only forgave the murderer, but she became his keeper. When he was released from prison, she took responsibility for him and brought him into her own home. Knowing that she and I both shared a belief in the law of karma, the Buddhist principle of cause and effect, I asked her, "Do you believe that on some level you played a part in the death of your son?" It was very hard for her to admit, and almost as hard for me to hear, but she said, yes, the lesson learned from the death of her son was something she needed in order to learn forgiveness. Our own karma always plays a role.

My friend had cut herself off from God before her son was murdered. Then she reconnected to Spirit, and all of the laws of cause and effect in her life became clear. She knew that what we put out returns to us. She said it was not a punitive concept, but a law of nature, the Law of One. Because of her experience, and the understanding she gained from it, my friend became a beacon of hope and insight for others. She is peaceful and happy despite the terrible tragedy she suffered.

I look at Terry and wonder if my love for her is some sort of overcompensation for not having been there for my own daughter. Is Terry my new daughter? Could I have taken more pleasure in the rearing of my own child if I had realized sooner what I know now? Perhaps. I didn't know how to be present with myself then, let alone with someone else.

It seems almost ridiculous to say it, but a dog is so much easier to raise, in part because I accept that her identity has nothing to do with me. It doesn't require me to do anything right. Terry is so obviously and completely herself. She barks, she licks, she plays, and she loves. It's that simple, and it's that foolproof. Although her identity is infinite, she is teaching me that now is everything. With children we constantly worry about the future.

So I look at my peaceful, meaningful landscape and I try to figure out how to be a part of the other, "real," world. Knowing it's an illusion, why do I want to go back into it? It all seems so crazy to me right now. Is that just because of the way I perceive it? If so, then to change the world I have to change my own perceptions. I don't want to live in a world that is enslaved by ambition, by technology, by power, by terror, by competition, by anxiety, and greed. I don't want to give those dark forces substance by thinking they're real. In little ways I've seen the world around me change by the way I perceive it. Could it possibly be that there is no world at all outside of our collective and individual dream?

When my mother was dying she saw all the people in the world as hearts beating in unison, connected to each other by a golden thread. Right before her passing, she said she wished that we could see that thread connecting us all, because if we could, we would never be unhappy again. That moment reminded me of a vision she had had years before, when she saw that trees and the earth and even people were filled with inner light, and there was a gentle wind moving within that light. She said there was also light *within* the earth, radiating up and out to those of us who walked upon it.

For all her amazing visions, as she approached the time of her passing, my mother told the doctors she could no longer see. After a full battery of tests, the doctors could find no physical reason for it. I think she just didn't want to see anything beyond her inner vision anymore. She wanted to be free of life's conflicts. Making decisions had always been difficult for my mother, but at the end everything was simple. There were no complications, just love. Sometimes she only wanted her cat, Gypsy, in the room with her. I think the aloof mysteriousness of that cat was a comfort to my mother as she prepared to enter the great mystery herself, especially by contrast to our hovering, worried family love.

My father's transition was longer. Each day my father would tell his nurses and doctors about his spirit travels the night before, when he visited his father, his mother, and his other relatives that had crossed over. They told him things. They told him about his life before he was born, and about the history of the Earth and the human race. Every morning doctors and nurses at Johns Hopkins would come by for an informal seminar at the foot of my father's bed. It was remarkable because these were conventional medical doctors, yet they all seemed to understand that when someone is in the process of passing, they gain access to privileged information and higher knowledge.

One of the finest surgeons at Johns Hopkins told me later that often when he was operating he felt guided, as if his hands were being held and moved by an invisible master. He said he had learned to let go and trust this force to direct his movements, and in doing so had become uncommonly skilled, saving hundreds of lives.

Jerry

There are many angels guiding the human race but they are having a difficult time because the humans don't think it's possible. It doesn't matter though, because everything is happening just as it should. It was determined a long time ago. I just wish people would be more open to the guidance. Then they wouldn't suffer so much. What the people in the world have created is insane. What I am living is sane. I rest in spirit so I am balanced. I close my eyes and I sink into a stillness that is perfect.

Shirley

The rains have passed and the dogs and I are setting out for a walk along a path which will be peppered with piñon and juniper trees. Once this was the land of towering ponderosa pines and tall grasses, until the white man leveled the trees and turned his cattle and sheep loose to graze. Millions of years before that, this was a vast savannah where dinosaurs roamed. I sometimes wonder if their spirits are still here, bearing silent witness to the endless flow of change. If so, they will make themselves known to Spooky, my alpha spirit dog, who, as always, is in the lead.

I move with Terry, Sheba, and the rest of the pack, and the sun is part of me. When the dogs are at my side I am more alert to the world around me. I take notice of a spring blossom that has come out overnight, and I imagine the snows from the higher mountains melting to create the stream that runs alongside us. I lie face-down in the stream with my clothes on, remembering that this water purifies itself every hundred yards. The dogs stand quietly watching me. I am part of their pack yet their leader. They don't wade in splashing or barking or shaking themselves in delight. It's as if they know I don't want the water muddied, that I am savoring its purity. I'm different from them yet one of them.

It's difficult to explain the freedom I feel as I drink the icy water flowing under my nose and mouth. I am primitive, availing myself of the sacred gifts of nature.

Terry

While MM had her face in the stream I saw two rabbits chasing each other. Then they stopped and one got on top of the other. At first I didn't know what they were doing. Then I walked away to give them some privacy, which I thought they would enjoy, but I really wanted to go back and ask them some questions about rabbit sex. I see that human sex certainly has a lot of people confused!

I think people make too much of sex. It's certainly not an issue for me, since I've been neutered, and it's not much of an issue for MM, who went through menopause some time ago. I do wonder why people let sex run so much of their lives. Sex is something to be enjoyed when everything else works.

Sex for its own sake was never that interesting to MM, even though it is for lots of humans. Emotional intimacy was always what made sex fun for MM, and intimacy is all about trust. Looking down on her life I saw that when she was younger, sex certainly had more intensity because her hormones were raging, but as she got older her hormones stopped running her love life. And what a relief it is for her to be free of that.

Now MM finds a man "erotic" who reveals his vulnerabilities and values to the world. I, of course, don't find it erotic, but I like men who act like that. Human attraction is often a matter of art, I think, and since so many people are artists I wonder how they can be faithful to one partner for a lifetime. Why does this society feel that "monogamy" is necessary? If a partner is a possession that might make sense, but owning someone never really seems to work.

When MM talks to me about sex I tell her I would be turned on by someone who likes to play. She likes that too. She is also turned on by mischief, as am I. Cuddling is good too—feeling deep contentment curling up with someone who truly understands you is something we both love. Happily, we give that to each other.

Sometimes when we're channel surfing we will come across a show on television with naked people having sex, and we always get bored by all the grunting and moaning. Maybe it's because we know they're acting. Maybe MM acted a little bit in such moments too, thinking sex required a performance from her, but she doesn't feel that way anymore, to my great relief. Performance was certainly never an issue for me. In fact, in this lifetime I've never experienced sex, and I couldn't care less.

Sometimes my MM feels guilty about having had me neutered because she'd love to know what my babies would be like. But she's really my child, as anyone can see. When I first met Spooky, the alpha male, he tried to make me his Barbie possession by peeing on me to stake out his turf. That was not smart. I tolerated this for a while, and then one day I flirted with him until he rolled over on his back. Then I straddled him, squatted, and peed on his face! He never approached me again.

I flirt with everybody really. I do it by jumping up on them and nipping their noses. If humans flirt with each other and it leads to something more I don't see anything wrong with it. Neither does God. In fact, God likes people to enjoy each other's bodies, as long as they don't hurt each other.

Bodies are wonderfully expressive human machinery. But it's a waste of machinery if they only use them to make babies. There are too many babies in the world anyway. I enjoy looking at human bodies. They are so beautiful, and sometimes funny, and really nice to cuddle up to. Those times when I see people on TV with no clothes on their bodies doing their sex stuff, they do it too fast. They go so fast when they move together that I don't know how they can enjoy their beautiful machinery. They should slow down. We were much slower in Egypt when we built all those majestic monuments. People and gods were living up to the bigness of their spirits back then.

But now humans are delusional. They think they have to be thin to be attractive, yet that must feel very bony in bed. They are obsessed with not being fat. They should be healthy, of course, but that's more about loving themselves than it is about what other people think. Humans seem to care an awful lot about "keeping up with the Boneses," and with buying expensive clothes at discount prices.

People have such strange ideas about what's attractive. They don't seem to go for the heart as much as they go for the "sexy" body. And of course they don't really know how to play. If they ever have a problem they should just roll over on their back. People haven't learned to roll over yet. They keep on arguing. Exposed tummies are very good problem solvers, and thankfully I have been seeing more of those lately.

One thing I don't like to see is male humans in middle age going for younger women just to prove that they can still perform in bed. What is this performance business? Why don't they just enjoy themselves? And the younger women seem to go for those older men because they have money. To me they are both ridiculous. And the funny thing about it is that everyone else knows what's really going on.

As for MM and me, we don't have much time for sex anyway. If it came along, fine, but I think we'd rather be in bed with each other. There are fewer problem—no backtalk, *no orders—and we can live our lives the way we want to. We are both more interested in, shall we say, social inter-course. What interests us is how people walk, talk, think, play, and how much of themselves they are willing to share.*

I'm watching humans as they grapple with the sub-ject of what they call "gay" sex. I don't understand the problem. Neither does God. As an American president once said, "We are all sinners." Well, he couldn't be more wrong. He just thinks that people are sinners, which of course leads to all kinds of problems. Souls live in bodies, and every soul has its own taste.

It's fun for me to see a hu-man man dressed up like a woman, because that means he enjoys looking good, just like my MM. What people do with their bodies is their business. I think most people get their opinions about sex from religion. It seems like very religious people don't usually have a very free attitude about sex. I think it may have to do with their confusion about whether God or Jesus or Mary had sex.

I think religion confuses people about many things.

It can make them afraid of God, of each other, and even of dying, since the Bible says that they're not coming around again, except for Jesus on Easter, and the Second Coming. But there are other good books that say they are. I think it would be better if people were taught that they were going to be reborn—then they'd realize they couldn't get away with anything because they'd just carry that old baggage into their new life. They'd realize they might as well take responsibility now and get it over with.

I hear my MM and her friends having long talks about the difference between religion and what they call spirituality. I'd like to say a few things about that too. Religion happened a long time ago when people stopped being able to read each other's thoughts. If you can't read people's thoughts you have to depend on words, and that can lead to manipulation, which can lead to religion. For humans maybe religion began when beings came down from the sky and were mistaken for God. Maybe the sky visitors saw that humans were cruel to each other so they decided to give them rules to establish control. When they told people all the things they couldn't do instead of all the things they were capable of doing, that's how religion was born. Humans became "God-fearing" people, and sex-fearing people, and full-of-guilt people.

In my time in Egypt with MM we had lots of gods. We had gods of thunder and gods of lightning and gods of water and gods of sun and gods of moon and gods of plants and gods of dogs and gods of cats. As Anubis I was one of the most important because I spoke to people about no-death. Maybe we **should** have lots of gods since everything around us is part of God. Nobody put it all together into one thing called religion back then. But whether it's one god or many, I certainly don't believe it's right to kill people over whoever they think their god is. I don't know any gods who would like that either. When people kill they build up negative karma, regardless of their reasons.

I know MM thinks religion is a real problem in the world. She's concerned about a holy war. For some humans nothing is more important than their God, so when different fundamentalist groups of people like that decide their

*God is the **only** God, things can get very nasty. And nasty karma is not good for anyone.*

Humans should understand that down through time they have each experienced being both male and female. That was the way they learned about each other. But I must say from what I've observed regarding their "war of the sexes," they haven't learned fast enough. Each person should be a reflection of the soul, and each soul is equally balanced between male and female. That has been difficult for humans to understand, which has created a lot of complicated karma relating to the sexes.

All humans have unresolved karma with each other. In fact, the reason they are alive on earth is to clean up their karmic issues. Families can be the most difficult things to sort out because family members have souls that need the most resolution with each other. If they went within themselves and touched their souls' past, the world would be a more peaceful place.

Shirley

I think a lot about the karma I may have with those people dearest to me—mother, father, brother, lovers, and friends—because my love has always contained an element of judgment. I think I never allowed anyone to be unconditionally themselves. I remember once being deeply in love with a man who told me he never felt that he was living up to my expectations. I felt the same way about him.

Independence has likely always been a karmic sticking point for me too, especially when it comes to romantic love. Most men are protective, which makes me feel more like a possession than an equal partner. With my parents I always felt like a daughter, as opposed to my own person. I was always my father's little girl, even when I was sixty. That's not true with an animal, so perhaps we don't have as much karma with them. Animals take us at face value based on who we are right here and now.

My mother was extremely withholding with her emotions. She said it was more diplomatic to be that way. That may be why I'm so direct. My father was not diplomatic. He didn't curb his feelings at all. He was all feeling. Interestingly, my mother was full of male energy, or yang, and my father embodied female energy, or yin.

I believe at one point in our evolutionary history we humans had better balance between yin and yang. The older I get, and the more I go within myself, the more balanced I feel, which may be why I feel such an affinity for that balance in Terry. She is a female dog, so she is allowing, passive, understanding, and spiritually attuned. At the same time, she is also protective and linear. But her female aspects allow her to hold contradictory points of view without becoming confused.

When I examine the unconditional love I feel for Terry, there is one thing about this relationship that causes me grief: I don't know what I will do when Terry passes over. I never felt this way with my mother, my father, or my friends. When they died, I knew they were on a journey to a higher level of understanding. Terry *already* understands, so when she goes I know I will feel that some part of me will have gone with her. It will be difficult to live without Terry's constant reminders that I am capable of unconditional love. I will miss her unconditional love, but not as much as I will miss mine.

As time passes I'm forced to confront the prospect of Terry's death, and to reexamine what I know about death itself. Intellectually I realize that what we perceive as death is just a change of form. But because I'm physical, I will miss Terry deeply. Sometimes I think I'll get another dog right away. Even now, while Terry is still in my life, I find myself wanting to surround myself with animals. I want birds in the house, and I want a cat; because of Terry, I would be happy living with a menagerie. It's wonderful to relate to living things that don't speak, that don't judge, and don't blame. They are always an instant removed from timelessness. They point the way to a state of being we humans can only aspire to.

Terry

Since my MM is my child I hope I can teach her that grow-
ing up is essential to aging well. And the older she gets the
further inside herself she should look. The more deeply she
learns to love, the younger she'll be when she dies.

Shirley

I read somewhere that where there is no resistance there is no harm. On this Easter weekend more than two thousand years ago, Jesus said if I defend myself, I am attacked. What does that mean? Is having defenses really folly? I once asked the Dalai Lama who his greatest spiritual teacher was, and he said Mao Zedong—leader of the nation that invaded Tibet, forcing the Dalai Lama into exile and torturing and killing many Tibetan Buddhist monks. Too many of us see other people as potential threats, instead of teachers. All of our structures and our laws, our codes, our morality and our legal definitions, our penalties, our armaments, even our ethics are based on an eye for an eye, a tooth for a tooth. I think we don't understand that these are karmic concepts. The laws of karma are perfect: if we hurt another that hurt will return to us. Energy always returns to the source. Each time we defend ourselves we've made the fear real, and our terror justified. It's a terrible catch-22. Is that what Jesus meant when he said turn the other cheek and if you are hit, turn it again? He might have been crucified, but he didn't die.

Years ago, on a trip home from India I happened to be seated next to the former Prime Minister of India, Jawaharlal Nehru. As we peered out the airplane window at the concrete towers of Manhattan, he told me the city below him looked overwhelming. "I could find that frightening," he said. "But instead I imagine that I am standing in the doorway of the hut in India where I lived as a child; the doors are flung open, allowing the winds of change to blow about my feet, but not to knock me over." After we landed, I went to swat an insect that somehow had gotten into the cabin, and he said, "Don't kill that gnat, you don't know what or who it might have been."

Does the transmigration of souls mean we all spend lifetimes as animals? Will we possibly be animals again? If so, we should certainly take a closer look at how we treat them.

Is it true that when we are born into a human body that it is perfect and capable of immortality if the mind does not abuse it?

Let's say for a moment that sickness is a decision made by the mind. If this is so, we are not the *victims* of illness, but its *perpetrators*. Like a blockage in our veins that keeps blood from circulating through the heart, sickness is a barrier we create against God, peace, and the energy of the natural world, perhaps to learn how much power we have. Sickness is self-deception because we've succumbed to the delusion that what God created—the body and even consciousness itself—is not perfect and whole. But for some of us, sickness is the only time we allow ourselves to slow down, the only excuse we'll accept for extricating ourselves from the overwhelming pressures of everyday life.

Sickness is not only a defense against God's perfection, but also against the solace of friends and family. We go to extraordinary lengths to prove the lie that we are not meant to be happy, that we are sinful and estranged from God. Even if we accept that sickness is just another reality we create, it's still easy to fall into the trap of thinking that this reality too is beyond our control. A wise person once said to me that we would do anything to erect sandbags against the tide of happiness rising around us. Sometimes it takes a new life, like Terry, or another person, to help us drag the sandbags down, to help us surrender to the tidal wave of happiness.

I wonder how animals respond to human sicknesses. Do our pets take on some of the burden we place on ourselves with our own minds? I have arthritis in my right knee, and lately it has been giving me some trouble. When I first noticed this, Sheba began to limp on her right side. Are animals trying to help absolve us of our limitations? And if our dogs live seven to every one of our years, are they dying more quickly because they take on our beliefs that the body is imperfect? Could animals live forever as our companions if we also thought *we* could?

Imagine what it would be like if we believed that everything is planned by God for our happiness. If so, sorrow, pain, and tragedy wouldn't really be necessary. If we believed in our plan of happiness I think we'd have a happier world. We're taught that Easter is a time for resurrection and salvation. Well, perhaps it's time to rise again, and shed our old beliefs. Perhaps when Jesus said, "Forgive them, for they know not what they do," he meant, "Forgive them, for they know not what they do to themselves." Wouldn't we be reborn if we listened to the God within us? Wouldn't that be our salvation?

I'm trying to learn not to plan; I'm trying to learn just to let it happen. I'm trying not to have a schedule for the next day. In these ways I'm experimenting with taking my guidance from God. I'm going to ask God to resolve my travel plans to Ireland.

Terry

On this Easter weekend I want MM to realize that she can be reborn every moment. The body is perfectly prepared to respond to that idea. But she has to mean it in her soul. When she really means it her world will be filled with Easter light.

When MM is worried it's because she is "conflicted." Sometimes I'm a mirror for her when she's conflicted. At those times she looks at me huddled in my little corner and I think she realizes I'm reflecting her mood because I want her to see what it looks like. It's not a pretty sight. Maybe I'll run over and jump into her lap. Then she will pet me and maybe she'll understand.

Shirley

Because I'm so interested in the mind-body-soul connection, I decided to explore psychic surgery for the arthritis in my joints. I was fascinated by the whole process, and assisted several psychic surgeons in Brazil and the Philippines. When I first asked my psychic surgeon in Brazil how it worked, he said, "The body is only an illusion. My real work is on the aura, on the electromagnetic frequency of the body, not on the flesh. But for you to understand, to believe the healing, I have to give you the illusion of my hands entering your body. But in fact, there is no penetration of the flesh at all, because the flesh is not real. You just believe it is."

Time and again I saw that patients would not believe they were healed unless the body was invaded. The doctors not only cured the sickness by working on the body's aura, but also by reinforcing the counterdream of healing the body. I saw psychic healers remove eyes and cleanse the disease behind them. I saw them take out hearts to repair valves. The body was an illusion, but the healing had to be physical for the patient's mind to believe it.

When I assisted in these surgeries, I knelt beside patients from many countries whose languages I did not speak, but during the procedure we could communicate. As witness to their healing I felt the melding of my spirit with theirs. What I saw strengthened my conviction that we are perfect in the first place—and in the second, and in the third.

Terry

Sickness is separation from God and healing is the other dream, the one that delivers us back to God. When MM thinks about leaving the steady joy she feels with me, even if only temporarily, for that movie in Ireland, she feels the sharp edges of sickness coming on. Sickness is a kind of lie. We natural beings may take on the sickness of our human companions, but we know why we do it. We love them.

We do not lie about love. We don't pretend to be happy when we're not. We don't pretend anything. We are capable of shrewdness, but not deceit. I can be manipulative to get what I want, but I can't lie about anything. When we're hurt, we show it. When we're joyful, we show that too. A lot of what we display depends on our human companions.

Shirley

It's Easter morning, and Terry is in my arms. I tell myself
I should get up and be productive, but here she is, sleeping
with her little face next to mine. Her body is stretched out
next to me so I can feel her breathing. She begins to twitch.
Is she reflecting the dream I just had of being trampled by
huge horses? Their hooves came down on me again and
again, yet I was still alive. I take Terry in my arms, her
body now jerking violently. Is she having my dream or
am I having hers? She wakens, and then places her head
under my chin. She lies back, almost in a backbend with
her little feet up in the air, completely unselfconscious, at
one with herself, with me, and with the new Easter day
outside. Birdsong begins to filter in through the window,
along with a pervasive feeling of all-oneness.

I lie here with Terry, ruminating. Should I have had more children? Should I have adopted the children I wanted to when I was younger? Is that the impulse Terry is bringing out in me? Or is she bringing out a desire to adopt children now? I imagine what this morning would be like with a houseful of children. No, I'm too old to adopt children now. I've earned this peace and quiet. When I was younger, my friends and I got so bogged down in the details of life that a moment like this, lying with a dog in my arms on an Easter morning, feeling that everything is, as my mother would say, one with God, would not have been possible.

I wonder whether mothers who adopt feel that their new baby was meant for them rather than the birth mother. I think so. Certainly, when we adopt animals, they are meant to be with us. I have adopted Terry instead of a child. I've also adopted the other dogs on the ranch. Sheba was the first one that I saved from her fate at the pound. Then I adopted the rest. They all know it, just as they know that Terry is royalty with Egyptian blood, who is here for unearthly reasons.

I am the wind in the weeping willow by the water-
fall. I am the dust blowing in from Colorado. I am the
fly buzzing against the screen. Terry and I are having
this life dream together. Birds chirp, the wind wafts,
trees rustle, the flowers smell, dogs bark, the clouds roll
by, and Terry and I are in such bliss that nothing would
be worth ending this until it ends itself. Finally we get
up from reality into the dream we say is real. We both
stretch and rise out of bed.

Now I feel hunger. Now I need to go to the bathroom. Now I feel pain in my back. I start thinking: I
need to eat and take my vitamins; I must return phone
calls, and wish others Happy Easter; I have to make the
most of this day. Then I regain my sanity, and remind
myself that I know a happier way to live.

Is this what happens when you get older, when
you've done most everything, when you've had the experience of being the belle of the ball and you discover that
doesn't provide happiness? Overachievement makes me
realize I really don't have to achieve anything at all. Am I
becoming a happy, peaceful recluse? Do I not like leaving

my ranch because the pace of life outside perturbs me? I look out at a faraway hill and it reminds me of the light from within my mountain that played games with me as I sat bug-eyed. It happened at midnight, when I was out walking with a married couple who are close friends. We all saw a luminescence coming from within Sierra Madre. It moved and danced before our eyes as though a spotlight from within the earth was directed at us. We watched for hours, wondering what it wanted us to know. I thought of my mother's vision of lights within the earth.

Dr. John Mack of Harvard once interviewed a man claiming to have been abducted by extraterrestrials, who told this captive the tragic history of their planet. One of their gods was an enormous boulder, within which was stored all the ancestral knowledge of that race. Over time the citizens of that planet learned how to make genetic material and decided it was the future, choosing to move away from the wisdom they had gathered and stored in the boulder since the dawn of time. The boulder watched helplessly as the planet's inhabitants became more and more warlike, unable to interfere with the free will of its people. Eventually civil war destroyed the planet, and now, according to the abducted man, its refugees were roaming the universe looking for a new home.

Here on the ranch I know I am surrounded by eons of vast knowledge. From mountains to pebbles, from trees to shrubs, everything has a conscious and probably cosmic energy. Nothing stays the same, not even the past; everything we see is altered by the way we see it. Even history, because it snakes back to the present, keeps growing and changing. And what about God? Is God different now than He/She was at the beginning?

If God is perfect and all creations complete, then there's nothing to do but let God's plan unfold. If I am peaceful, the world will be. Whenever I feel anxiety about what to do next, I open the sliding door, let Terry out, call the other dogs, and push myself out of the house into the air, sunshine, and sun-bleached colors of the arroyo. Soon the inner turmoil quiets down, and I feel myself beginning to take guidance from above, a most miraculous frame of mind. On this Easter weekend, when others remember sin and redemption, I turn to the wisdom of nature in search of peace.

As we walk away from the ranch house I check the water storage tank. In the Southwest water is gold. Here in New Mexico a drought has been in effect for several years, causing a bark beetle infestation in the pine trees by compromising their immune systems. Even though I have a productive well I'm considering also installing a rain-catching system from my roof. I think of the stream of snowmelt that runs down from the mountains, and I wonder how long it will last.

Cottonwoods sparkle in the light of the sun and I marvel at these trees that guzzle water from the ground yet exude it right back into the world around them. A sharp wind comes up, blowing my hat off, its string under my chin nearly ripping my earrings from my pierced ears. I hear there's a tornado blowing in the eastern part of the state, which is uncommon in New Mexico, and again I wonder what nature is trying to tell us.

Sunlight flashes against the crystals littered across my land. Everywhere I look I see white and pink quartz crystals, as though a volcano of diamonds erupted hundreds of thousands of years ago, scattering its glittering treasure over the landscape. Could that have been the light I thought I saw within the mountain? No, I'm looking for Earth logic when a deeper logic drives a technology not yet understood by us.

Rising above us is my Sierra Madre. They say that because Madre is a female mountain no man must ever climb it without a woman by his side. It is also said that this mountain serves as a magnetic homing device for UFOs. Perhaps that's why there are so many petroglyphs on this land. Usually they depict five concentric circles, which, according to the Hopi, means that in the future we will be going into the fifth world where we will be able to live among all five dimensions.

The dogs scamper ahead and I trudge up to what I've named Crystal Picnic Hill, a relatively high point on the property. My body has a history, as it did on the

Camino in Spain. As we climb, my feet have memory, my ankles have memory, my lower back has memory, and I feel as if I'm trekking back in time. I glimpse kaleidoscopic shards of the past—of ancient civilizations and wars fought with laser light. I see earthquakes and inundation from roiling seas. I see magnificent buildings destroyed and crystal pyramids floating on rainbow clouds of light. Hovercraft take off and land, teachers address throngs eager to learn, and multidimensional beings are worshiped in gleaming sanctuaries. Everything around me comes alive, as though animated by strange unearthly harmonies, echoes of a language from long ago. Colors accompany the tones, all vibrating and throbbing in melodious synchrony that will take on the shapes and forms of future life on Earth.

I stand still, awed by these precognitive memories. Will I be a mysterious memory for someone standing on this hill one million years from now? And in my future form will I recognize that newcomer as myself?

Terry jumps up on my leg, bringing me back to

the present. She stops, looks, and waits, as if to make sure that I stay in the here and now. I wonder what I might have experienced on the Camino if I had had her with me. Would she have pacified the wild dogs?

I walk farther on, bringing to mind what happened more recently on this land. Here Kit Carson raided Native American villages prosperous from a vigorous trade in beads, animal skins, and horns. I often wonder what I should do with this land, and I'm waiting for it to tell me. Should it be home to a new community? Will it be the site of a spiritual school taught by beings from the stars, who once again will teach us who we really are? Did we come from the outer reaches of space to save this planet, only to go astray? Perhaps whatever is coming is truly a prelude to what the prophecies and the Bible say will be a thousand years of light. In all this speculation I only know one thing. I will be here. Perhaps Terry will too. I hope so.

I walk on, aware that I am not the only one who feels the magic of this land. Friends and visitors have reported visions of cities floating in the clouds, and encounters with strange, unearthly people. All agree that this land, marked by crystals, will play a prominent role in the planet's future.

Daisy, the most motherly of the dogs, looks back to see if Terry and I are all right. Mountain lions live here, and coyotes, but since there is a human in our pack they won't bother us. I feel safe until I see Spooky off in the distance. He's too far ahead, and I start to worry, but I follow until we're walking high on the northern part of the property. This is alpine country. I see what two years of drought have done to the ponderosa pines. They are dying from the bark beetle and lack of rainfall. What have we done to nature that she doesn't nourish our trees anymore? What will happen to our source of oxygen if the lungs of the planet die?

Where is Terry? I turn around and see her scampering toward me. The other dogs follow. As if hearing a signal of some kind, Spooky dashes up the side of Sierra Madre and disappears into a cave. I remember seeing him shadowbox with coyotes at midnight under the full moon. He enticed the coyotes out of their lairs, and one by one they engaged in mock combat, etched in moonlight, not knowing I was watching the call of the wild.

Our pack waits until Spooky returns to his family of females. He then leads our expedition farther up the slope, stopping to smell elk droppings, bear scat, and other spoor that only the dogs can identify. Sometimes they eat what they find, and sometimes they just sniff and move on. I wonder what exactly determines the outcome. Terry partakes in none of this. She has fresh meat waiting in her palace ranch home.

We walk for hours. At 8,500 feet I feel my breath coming faster. This is a great place to exercise, because at sea level stamina becomes a cinch. I can see Pikes Peak in Colorado to the north and the lights of Santa Fe to the south.

Up ahead an elegant elk drinks from a mountain stream. He turns and gazes into my eyes as I walk toward him. He is unafraid, and has such a commanding, peaceful presence that I feel I have looked into the face of God. Terry stops, mesmerized. At my command the pack moves on, leaving the elk to his dignity.

Bears are too shy to show themselves, but I can see the dogs catch their scent.

Traces of snow linger in the spring sunlight, sparkling under the shade of the tall pines. Terry bounds ahead, kicking up snow flurries and twirling in the air. She charges at fallen pinecones, then stops and gazes at the endless spectacle of ancient, timeless beauty. I take her often to this high country on my electric golf cart. She sits beside me with her ears flattened against the wind. Sometimes I drive too close to a tree, inspiring her to lunge at its branches. Sometimes in her exuberance she leaps off the cart, and like an athlete she rolls over and over to break her fall.

A light spring snow begins to fill the sky. The dogs slow, and I imagine it is due to their delight at the gentle snowflakes. I hear snowbirds fluttering through the pines. I am awed by the show nature puts on, and am reminded once again how discerning the ancient Indians were to make this paradise their home. The snow subsides as quickly as it came. Terry shakes herself and waits for direction from me.

Whenever I am around gently falling snow I always think about love. When we love a person we dare to risk. We risk losing control of ourselves on one hand, yet on the other we dare to create a new identity, melding our spirit with that of someone else. Are we each, in truth, separate from each other as we pursue our desires and creative expression in life, or are we bound by some unknown agreement that we need each other to learn about ourselves?

I know now that the purpose of being alive is to be known to myself. Without that knowledge my life would be deeply damaged by what I see around me in the "civilized" world. Every dying person I've ever been around has told me that the only thing that matters in life is love. Do I have to die to fully understand that?

Sometimes I've had to grapple with a sad guilt when I moved on from someone in my life who I thought couldn't keep up. Getting to that point was even worse—

it was a terrible feeling to try to cope with nourishing my own progress and growth while still preserving the love. I couldn't understand then that moving on enabled each of us to grow at our own pace.

With my human love relationships there were always extenuating circumstances involving work, logistics, creativity, and commitment based on expectations and promises. With love these problems always arose. So when one dares to love another it involves terrible, beautiful risk. Do we humans love while sacrificing ourselves to preserve it? Or must we love and trust that love will endure regardless of proximity?

I realize now that true love for me will be my connection to the Divine. That is the infinite love without worry, and the love that will last regardless of circumstances. Anything less is an illusion. All these years I have been incessantly questioning creation, and now I want to live within it.

As the snow swiftly melts around me I hope that the love I feel all around me today doesn't meet the same fate.

Terry

The answers that MM seeks are hers to create.

What I have created is this: I am written in MM's heart and always will be. And that's all I have to say about that.

Shirley

I shake myself from my reverie, look below us toward the ranch, and decide to go home—home to a new understanding and hopefully home to a newly created world inside myself. The dogs feel my desire to trek back. They turn, and Spooky bolts out ahead of the pack.

I shout to Sheba to tell Spooky not to go so fast and she runs ahead to deliver the message with that awkward hitch in her stride. Terry gets a cactus needle stuck in her paw and limps over. She won't let me pull it out, though. She does that with her own teeth.

I'm feeling a sharp pain in my foot too, so I find a nice flat rock and take off my shoe and sock to inspect the blister. At the sight I flash back to all those years of dancing, of bloody feet in the dressing room. Terry slips under my leg and gives the blister a lick.

Now that we've stopped walking for a moment I look at my watch and realize we've been out for five hours. I take a sip of precious water. I hope I've brought enough. In all my years of walking and hiking I am reminded again that to be happy and comfortable doesn't take much: a good hat, a good pair of shoes, and water. Anything else is luxury! As I slip my walking shoes back on I wish my privileged Western feet were calloused enough to let me walk barefoot, like the Native American trailblazers who ran across these hills, skimming over rocks, underbrush, cactus, and shards of crystal from another time.

We're moving again, and as we reach an opening in the trees there's Sierra Madre Mountain in the distance, where the lights in the sky go home. I use that mountain as my guide, and orient myself. We walk back through Copper Canyon, which I named for its shimmering metallic earth, studded with emerald trees, piñon bushes, and fragrant juniper. Its cliffs look like they were chiseled by a divine hand. Desert flowers, dandelions, violets, and chamiso blossoms fall like gemstones from God's fingers.

Terry seems to stop for every buttercup. Do they speak a special language to each other? She sniffs and nudges and nibbles until the flower gives itself up to her curiosity.

There's electricity in the air; a lightning storm may be brewing. In the strange greenish light I can't tell the difference between fallen branches and whitened antlers from animals long departed from this world. Sometimes the pack stops as one, alert to some ripple in the consciousness of this land. I don't hear anything, but I feel it.

As our little band gets closer to home, I realize the older dogs have a focus. They want water and something to eat. I see a dust storm in Colorado that likely began on another continent, transported here courtesy of the jet stream. A butterfly blinks and the rest of the cosmos feels the impact.

I remember a time I took a delegation to China and the dust storms off the Mongolian desert blew into Beijing and Shanghai. Everyone got pneumonia but me, although I experienced a permanent change in my endocrine system. East dust met West dust and changed my body forever.

Our pace picks up as the descent becomes less steep. I come to my spiral labyrinth at the top of the mesa closest to the ranch house. Here, as a gift to me, a friend of mine arranged stones in spirals that reflect the movement of human consciousness. I walk here several times a week to resolve whatever is bothering me. Terry scampers around in the labyrinth, knowing this is a sacred place but unable to keep from playing. The other dogs slow down, but stay ahead, knowing the ranch is near. I see the bench I built for meditation, and two trees nearby with smooth stones under them to sit on, and I'm glad to rest a little. Terry sits down and seems to meditate herself. Then, standing on the heart-shaped stone that marks both the entrance and the exit of the labyrinth, I pray for inner peace. I sigh deeply and remember that God is in the air we breathe. When I move again, Terry chases my shadow.

I look back at the snow-capped mountain and the canyon where we have just walked for hours. Is that gray mist rain? I turn to Sierra Madre looming to the east, where sunrise backlights the great mountain every morning. To the west, Perdenal Mountain, sacred to Native Americans, stands majestically with its flat top. I thank all that surrounds me.

As we descend the hill from the labyrinth, I see that Sheba, Sandy, Spooky, and Daisy have disappeared. I know they've gone to the pond to drink and cool off. Terry doesn't join them. She wants me to bathe her in the sink of her palace home. I am her servant. Around a bend in the trail I see the other dogs are up to their necks in the pond, splashing around and gulping the cool water. They emerge and shake themselves, flinging rainbow drops into the waning sunlight. Terry stands regally and holds her head high with one paw poised in the air, waiting for their foolishness to cease before she leads me to our ranch house.

In the distance I see another dog, a dog I've never seen before, standing in my garden. Spooky spots it too, and charges down the path, followed closely by the three females, with Terry bringing up the rear. When they reach New Dog, there is no growling or snarling. The pack just forms a circle. Terry returns to me. I fear for the New Dog, and call off the females. They obey. Spooky and New Dog silently confront each other. Neither moves. I know now that New Dog is male. Time stands still. Will it be peace or war? Then Terry breaks away from me and slowly approaches the standoff. I wait with the other females, my heart pounding, knowing I shouldn't interfere. Could New Dog be another Spirit Dog bringing us his own stories from other places and other times?

Terry slowly positions herself between the two males. She looks toward Spooky. His ears lie back against his head, deferring to her. She turns toward New Dog. He does nothing. She then saunters toward him, stops, and seductively rolls over on her back. New Dog is nonplussed. He turns, spots a bush, lifts his leg, and pees. Spooky stands stock-still. Then he saunters over to the bush, lifts his leg and pees on it too. Terry then moves to the bush, lifts *her* leg, and then *she* pees on it! Then she calmly moves away. Spooky sits by the bush and waits. After a long few moments, New Dog simply strolls off into the hills. I watch until he disappears into the deep-ening twilight, then Terry and I head into the house.

Suddenly, and shockingly loud, the telephone rings. With some trepidation I answer. It is the producer from Northern Ireland. "I'm sorry to tell you this," he says, "but the money fell through. So I guess you won't be coming to our fair land."

After some inanely comforting conversation, I hang up and shriek with happiness. Terry jumps into my arms and kisses my cheek. Has she really understood what just happened?

She bounds around with her twinkling butt and sparkling feet. She finds a toy and tosses it into the air for me to catch. Then she walks straight to the sink for me to wash the dirt off her feet. After her bath, I give her a lit-tle bone and she twirls three times: one for mind, one for body, and one for spirit. Then Terry curls up in her little bed and goes right to sleep, as if to say, I knew it all along.

I walk outside, disrobe, and climb into the hot tub. Daisy sits beside it, dozing in the evening sun. Sheba looks out over the mountains. Sandy is nowhere to be seen, but I spot Spooky slipping like a silent wraith around the corner of the house.

I sigh deeply as I realize that in a few days it will be my birthday.

"What a gift life is," I think. "Everything happens just as it should. And I am blessed with the luck of the Irish."

Then I remember something Terry said to me once. "Give me a bone and I'll be happy . . . give me a home in your heart and *you'll* be happy."

Part II:

BODY

Shirley

The years pass. My constant companion on movie sets, airplanes, cars, buses, and even subways is my teacher, Terry. She keeps autograph seekers and others with requests of me at bay because she insists on being so adorable herself. One of my reasons for remaining good-natured into my old age is Terry's adorableness.

Terry

I love being adorable. It gets me whatever I want from whomever I want. And it works for keeping the peace if people bother my MM. Sometimes I'm acting and sometimes not . . . just like my MM.

Shirley

I often wonder what Terry thinks of growing old. She is now almost seventeen. She can't see, hear, or move much, can barely walk, and can't control her bowels or kidney functions. In the middle of teetering across the room she unceremoniously squats and relieves herself. My insides crumble for her loss of dignity.

Terry

One of the attributes of growing old in a loving environment is I can dispense with pretense. What a relief to relieve myself without concern of reprimand or scolding—like being on a giant floor of green grass in the country. I hope that MM doesn't mind cleaning it up. Dignity is not a problem for me. I'm a queen in my own mind. In fact, I once talked to one of Queen Elizabeth's corgis, who told me she often jumped out of a wet doggie bed in the morning and the queen was very understanding.

Shirley

Terry's sense of smell remains acute. She seems to see and hear through her nose. She seems to comprehend whatever occurs. Daisy, Sheba, and Spooky pass on in that order. I miss them deeply, but Terry is my touchstone in life. When she was about twelve, I got her and myself two new companions: Buddy-Bubster and Trixie the Pixie. They are rat terrier rescues, and the three of them hang out and enjoy each other's company.

Terry

Of course, it was necessary for me to adjust to new commoners, but like my MM, I was democratic at heart.

Shirley

As Terry ages, the two younger dogs begin to torture her cruelly. They growl and dog-hiss as if to say, "It's time to remove yourself from the tribe—you are holding us back." I watch with disbelief and often yell and chastise them. Sometimes I wonder if I should listen and respect their admonitions. In fact, perhaps they are trying to tell *me* something.

Terry

I know why Buddy-Bub and Trixie are being mean. I had previously thought about leaving myself, but when I saw how my MM reacted to the suggestion I couldn't do it. I will teeter-walk and poop and pee until she is ready.

Shirley

A very kind—and usually correct—psychic friend of mine calls: "You should know that Terry wants you to put her down and has asked me to tell you. She will always be there for you."

It is after I hang up that it hits me. I break down completely, sobbing and allowing myself to feel the loss of Terry leaving. I feel my heart break, and even the air seems to cry. It is awful. I feel my face squinch up in horror—so much so that I go to my big mirror to see what I look like in case I need it in a scene someday! Heart-wrenching is not enough to describe what I feel. Then I bury my face in her cuddly pink jacket on my bed. I sob at the touch of it, the smell of it, the weight of it. I clutch the pink jacket, but my arms actually feel empty, as though there is no reason to have arms. I haven't cried with such violence since I was a kid throwing a tantrum.

I know the psychic is probably right. Terry can't really walk or even stand with control, and the most heart-splitting visual for me is to see her teeter around in one circle after another. Yet she loves her food and I tell myself that she even loves her life in this condition. Put her down? Incomprehensible to me. To be or not to be?! That was the question!

Terry

MM can be dramatic. Doesn't she remember death is easy,

but adorableness is much harder?

Shirley

What am I doing? I don't understand my own point of view. I have written thirteen books about the fact that nothing ever really dies. I have helped others contend with the "no death" reality in their own lives, yet thoughts of putting Terry down are incomprehensible to me. It would be an act of such consequence, I would never recover from it. Why? Guilt? Fear of loss? Too painful? Would she hate me? Not my decision to make? Do I lack the courage?

Terry

Hey, MM, come on now. You know I'm a queen and will live forever anyway.

Shirley

I can't watch any movie or TV program that shows cruelty to animals. I would leave the room or the theater.

Terry

Please. Time for me to act out independently. Don't need her, or even want her around.

Shirley

Even with all her progressing problems due to aging, I want Terry alive.

Jerry

All my doctors and nurses are so good to me: vitamins, supplements, hugs, kisses, concern, applause for teetering forward upright and calling it walking. MM takes the three of us on airplanes. She spends a fortune on first-class seats for us. She even orders a wheelchair to take all of us from the curb to the airplane door. We each have a "therapy dog" jacket that none of us earned but TSA believes. . . . I decide I have to do something.

Shirley

I begin to notice a change in Terry's attitude toward me. She seems to be extricating herself from my hugs and pats. She will give me a kiss but then push me away with an independent haughtiness. She is now coming up to her eighteenth year on the planet, but there is more than old-aging going on here.

We are at my ranch in Abiqui, New Mexico. Over the last few years it has been troubling me that out here I am so far away from potential medical attention, groceries, and even human contact. So I put the ranch on the market and then start contending with the anxiety that I've made a huge mistake. I take it off the market. On August 23, 2016, I'm putt-putting around in my Kawasaki golf cart "mule," confused and anxious about what was happening in the world. My mind feels cluttered and indecisive about what to do with my ranch. My most precious memories are of Terry bounding behind the cart, keeping up with me for as many as five miles. I can't glance at the hillsides or mesas or arroyos and canyons now without seeing her loving physical and spiritual soul running alongside me. Today is her birthday.

Here comes the old confusion: Should I sell the ranch or not?

Terry

I'm lying in my soft bed, dressed in my pink jacket, feeling MM's confusion, or perhaps the confusion I'm feeling is really just the state of old age. In any case, I know she should keep the ranch.

Shirley

As I drive around I began to feel and hear the words: *Keep the ranch. Too important.*

For hours, I ride around alone with these "feeling sounds." The experience is extraordinarily persuasive. Behind them is, somehow, Terry's voice. "Keep the ranch," she repeats. "You know better than to be confused." I'll never forget this primal experience.

"Okay," I say to myself and to *them*. "I promise. I'll keep it." That's that. I return to the ranch house and play with the dogs. Nice afternoon. Sing "Happy Birthday" to Terry and remain untroubled about anything including putting her down. I won't do it.

At bedtime, I put her bed close to the open door so she can go out if she is aware enough to want to. I erect a barrier outside so she can't wander in circles or get lost. I'm peaceful with my ranch decision, ready for a good sleep. Terry, Buddy-Bub, and Trixie fall asleep.

Around 11:30, Buddy-Bub wakes me with his barking. It's as though he isn't barking *at* anything. It's a warning bark. I get up and go to where the dogs sleep by the open door. Terry is gone. Buddy-Bub stops barking. I quickly go outside. I can't see Terry anywhere. I walk through the garden, thinking I will find her behind a bush . . . nothing . . . nowhere. I walk through the garden to the greenhouse—no Terry. How did she climb over the barrier? Then it hits me. Could she possibly have somehow made her way in the other direction?

I turn around, race down the outside stone stairs, and there she is. Floating peacefully in her pink jacket, having drowned herself in the swimming pool.

I can't believe my eyes. I run toward the water, trying to figure out how she got over the barriers. I become totally left-brained, unemotional. It doesn't occur to me to cry. I lean down and bend over to fish her out of the water. Her pink jacket is water-soaked and she is heavy. I lift her out, thanking God and my dancing lessons that I don't fall in headfirst. Immediately I give her mouth-to-mouth resuscitation, hear her breathe again, and then pump her lungs until she spits up and opens her eyes. She is alive!

Oh my God! What just happened? Did she just accidentally fall into the pool or did she do it on purpose? I pick her up and cuddle her against me. She whimpers. She doesn't want that. I wrap her in my blanket and bring her into bed with me. She whimpers again. I am still not emotional. I am trying to figure out what happened and what she wanted. Then I understand.

Terry

My MM. . . . I have really desired to move on, but not until you promised me to keep the ranch. You will understand why someday. I love you and thank you for trying so hard to understand me.

Shirley

Okay, I get it. I'll keep the ranch. But do you still want
to go?

Terry whimpers all night. I feel she wants to be
free. Why did I save her? I try to understand. Did she
really do a Fellini drowning scene in the pool because I
wouldn't allow myself to see her truth?

The next morning she can't move much, but she is
alive. And she eats her breakfast. Could it be she is forcing me to have the courage to take the initiative and free
her? Does she know that yesterday was her birthday?

Terry

*Of course I know. It was also MM's mother's birthday too.
Can MM be dense? Yes, she can.*

Shirley

I can't believe what I do next. I take Terry to the vet. Terry is hardly breathing and obviously ready to go. The vet doesn't really need to examine her. The vet just looks at me and asks, "Don't you know anyone who does animal euthanasia?" I stare back at her through to the other side of her brain and say, "Yes, I know some dog killers." The vet leaves the room. I don't blame her. I go home and make an appointment at my house in Santa Fe for that night.

I then have seven hours left to spend with my companion in love—24/7, for nearly two decades. I thank Buddy-Bub for barking, and sit with Terry on my lap. I had brought a sofa from the ranch a few days before. We will do the deed on the couch with the ranch energy. I don't cry. As I sit for seven hours trying to process all that had transpired . . . drowned herself on purpose? . . . insisted I not sell the ranch . . . why? . . . why couldn't I have put her down years before? . . . will she still be with me? . . . how will I hear her? . . . time itself is crying . . . but I can't. I call people who had loved her . . . I explain . . . not very well . . . I ask two people who have looked after her to come over to say goodbye. One begins to cry . . . I tell her to stop and go away . . . She does. . . . Then I make a decision: I am going to celebrate Terry's new freedom . . . freedom to see again, to hear again . . . to run again . . . to be herself again. . . .

One hour left before the doctor comes; sixty minutes evaporate; he is here. He asks if I want to be alone with Terry . . . not now. "How long will this take?" "Thirty seconds." I have thirty seconds left with my precious Terry Tunes.

The doctor wraps her little butt in a towel "because sometimes they lose all their bodily solids and fluids . . ." No kidding. Terry is in my lap. She barely moves. "Ready?" I nod. He gently puts a cathe-ter in her darling paw. She barely reacts. I clutch my heart. . . . He starts the death fluid. . . . Twenty-eight seconds left . . . "What actually happens to them?" "First injection stops the brain." Oh my God. "After that the heart begins to go." Terry moves with each pump of the fluid. Oh God . . . The doctor leans into her ear. "You're doing great, Terry—good girl." REALLY?

Buddy-Bub and Trixie cower beside the couch. They know what is going on. It is important that they know when she's dead so that they won't search for her later, but they don't want to be in the room. The door is closed. They must stay. Doctor finishes the injection. I wait. "Is she still alive?" "Yes." No tears from me . . . one second . . . two seconds . . . then, "Is she gone?" "Yes."

She doesn't feel any different. I thought I was supposed to feel her soul leave her body. I didn't. I look at the doctor. "Is that it? Is she really gone?" He nods. Then I realize, of course, she had been gone and out of her body, not only since last night in the water, but probably since a year ago. I try to lift her. She is now a doggie rag doll. I feel a presence in the room . . . then it goes away . . . "Give me three days," it says. "You'll see."

Trixie and Buddy-Bub claw at the door. The doctor opens it for them. I lift Terry's rag doll body, which has no shape, no form—it is heavier without life. I want to hug her one last time, but I don't because I know her soul is not there. And hasn't been in a long time.

Then I understand—I have done the right thing. All I needed was to promise to keep the ranch. Never will I forget her in her pink jacket, drowning in the pool. Soul-searing memory.

I hand the doggie doll to the doctor, surreptitiously feeling the towel covering her butt. How self-conscious of me to worry about such a thing. He wraps her in another towel and takes her away.

Terry is *gone*.

I walk outside and try to see her in the skies . . . in the stars. Nothing. She has outrun my gaze in her newfound freedom. I don't want to cry because *she* would not be happy with that. All I feel is: MY TERRY IS FREE!

Part III:
SPIRIT

My experience that night was so overwhelming, so exhilarating, that suddenly all of my books of after-death speculation made sense to me in a new way. I *felt*, not thought, their truths. I understood more profoundly what I thought I already understood. Terry's passing made me *feel* my understanding. And she was not the focus and neither was I. LIFE was the focus regardless of what form it took, visible or invisible . . . and I knew I would hear from her again.

I never cried. I celebrated. For the first time, I understood in my soul what I had been writing about, and I was happy for her freedom. All my love went with her.

I was now aware of a deeper understanding forming within me—a more realized truth. It was new to me. I felt stupid that I had not "realized" this understanding before. All because my dog had passed?

But for now I had to attend to reality here in the third dimension, the one that we humans have decided is REAL. I'd asked Yvonne, my housekeeper, to put away all of Terry's belongings before the doctor came. I felt

I needed to adjust to her absence immediately. Yvonne was gentle and understanding and promised not to cry anymore. So when I walked into my little office, there was no playpen, no doggie toys, no extra pink jacket, no diapers, no water cup or pee-pee towel. It was barren of Terry's presence and personality. I would never see her walk or twirl in circles again. I would never hold my breath if she fell over and tried to get up. My office, bedroom, living room . . . every room was without Terry in every way, yet I was truly grateful for her freedom. I think Yvonne hid in some unknown place everything that Terry ever touched. I was left with two conflicting images of Terry: the young, bounding, wily child of my ranch and the incessantly circling one-flew-over-the-cuckoo's-nest creature of death-defying staying power. I couldn't seem to reconcile that the two dogs were the same Terry.

I went to bed after downing a very strong martini. I wanted no distraction from television, no soothing diversion from a book, nothing but Ambien and sleep. I said good night to Yvonne. Buddy-Bub and Trixie still cowered in the corner. I hugged them but they pulled away from me. We were all without Terry and trying to understand our feelings.

I lay there feeling Terry in my arms, snuggling in her pink jacket as we'd done for almost seventeen years.

What had I just done?

The next morning, I knew I was going to have to deal with the Terry-less house. Each room I walked through to get my coffee was a torture. I realized I would have to determine which Terry I was missing—was it the young one I'd known for fifteen years or the ancient, forever teeter-totterer? I was confused. I didn't miss the old Terry because I didn't want to reinstate her suffering. But I had nearly forgotten the young Terry. What was Time trying to tell me?

I tried to see signs of Terry in everything I looked at. No, she'd said three days . . . I should be patient and suffer. She needed to adjust to her new *life* before she worried about me. And I knew that she was there, somewhere.

I remembered that just before the death fluid took her away the night before, there was rain, pelting rain. The skies were crying for me. How could I forget that? And then the sunset came, rainbow colors. So heaven's presence had been with me. Dare I say I had a bad case of heart vacancy? I needed to fill it with a new tenant or something pretty quickly.

I must be practical. I must return to "real" reality.

Not a problem—I had a dentist appointment and I didn't cancel it.

I was silent in the car. I didn't speak to Yvonne. I could hear Terry again: "Three days and you will see me." Was I crazy? "You will know it's me." Was this dialogue my new heart tenant? She had said, "Give me a home in your heart and you will be happy." It seemed to be happening.

Nothing at the dentist was painful. But then I couldn't feel my teeth anyway. I only thought of Terry drowning in the pool in her pink jacket and how she wanted to go. I had to wait until Saturday for the third day. The third day? Jesus, how cliché could this be?

We drove home silently. I looked out at the New Mexican landscape, the Land of Enchantment. Yes, it was. I heard and felt Terry everywhere. Did that cloud formation look like a terrier doggie? Was she early? I could feel her speak through the hills and mountains and the desert savanna. The air, the sun. Was that what I was supposed to understand? Was my love for Terry what was filling my heart vacancy? Perhaps we humans were so self-absorbed with loss that we couldn't see the grander truth of it all. There is no such thing as loss because neither love nor life ever ends.

I saw flashes of my life—travels—people—experiences with Terry. Her outgoing power with everyone and everything. A friend had said to me, "There will never be another Terry."

I remembered how she ordered me in my head to walk into the pet store in Malibu and buy her. "Come to the pet store and get me," she said. I actually heard the words. But over time I convinced myself I had made it up.

I realized there and then that a new definition of creative collaboration was in my future.

On the third day of her passing I sat in my hot tub overlooking the glorious landscape of Santa Fe. I noticed a droplet of water hanging from the railing. I don't know why I focused on the droplet. It grew larger and fuller. I sat mesmerized. Then it turned pink, a luscious pink the color of Terry's jacket in an expanding drop of water. Then I had to laugh out loud. This was Terry's communication? Pink inside of water! This droplet was Terry's reminder that I would never forget her in her pink jacket drowning in the pool. I threw my arms up and howled out loud. Then, as if on cue, as many as fifteen or twenty birds formed a moving circle right above me. They circled and circled, quietly, silently. Oh my God . . . was that Terry's reflection of her own dementia circling that had always been so disturbing to me? The expanding pink droplet and the silent circling birds formed a scene so magnificently creative, I couldn't have made it up if I'd tried.

She was alive and with me. It was important that I remember that. Was it possible that the number of birds equaled seventeen? One for each year of Terry's birthdays? After all, mathematics is the common, provable language of the universe.

I had meals with several friends who had been forced to "put down" their beloved dogs. One man had lost his wife to illness and put down his dog in the same month. We had long, speculative discussions about topics like fate, destiny, God, and loneliness. It seemed that my celebratory point of view regarding Terry helped him to release his anguish over putting down his 150-pound dog. Mourning with self-pity became an attitude of the past. Then I realized I needed to be more sensitive to the people who wanted to hold on to their sorrow. Martini honesty helped. But I was careful about whom I told the pink droplet/circling birds story to. Navigating creative spiritual waters is always dicey, and I knew I had to protect my credibility during this important journey or risk being dismissed.

My experiences with Terry also infiltrated my show business life. I felt I needed a better security fence at my home in Santa Fe, but it would be expensive. (I am Scottish and thus very thrifty with money.) I wanted a small acting job so I wouldn't have to dip into my savings for the fence. Here's what happened.

I got a call from my agent who said I had been offered the role of a mentoring angel in a TV movie for Hallmark. Me, a mentoring angel? Perfect. I knew Terry had arranged it, and the script was simple but okay. But it was to be shot in Vancouver, Canada, in just a few days. That would mean being away from Buddy-Bub and Trixie and my home for three weeks. One for Mind, one for Body, and one for Spirit, I told myself.

I went to the ranch to see how I would feel in Terry's homeland. Buddy-Bub and Trixie were slightly nervous because of the dramatic events that had occurred

the last time we were there. I could feel Terry everywhere, and I remembered that she had long ago told me
in my head, "Remember, I can shape-shift!"

I walked to the back garden by the pool, and there
was a rabbit jumping around. Terry said, "That's me,"
in my head. "I better not tell this to anyone," I thought.
The rabbit disappeared. I walked around the ranch
grounds, remembering the night of the pool drowning
and Terry's younger years when she bounded everywhere. I was beginning to put the younger Terry and the
feeble, older Terry together so that I could understand
what I had lost and what I had freed. That night I put
one of Terry's two pink jackets around my neck and slept
peacefully with Buddy-Bub and Trixie next to me.

I drove back to the Santa Fe house and left for
Vancouver the next day. As I rolled my suitcase across
the deck off my bedroom, I looked up. Seventeen circling
birds (I counted them this time!) silently wished me
well and assured me they would take care of the house
and Trixie and Buddy-Bub. I stood frozen to the spot,

once again mesmerized by what seemed to be emerging from my life with Terry.

On location in Canada, I missed Buddy-Bub and Trixie deeply. I was literally homesick for them. Terry was on my mind constantly, and I found myself irrationally impatient with the Canadian need to be polite, even when things are falling apart. My mother was Canadian and she would sometimes apologize to the furniture for bumping into it.

Apparently, it had been difficult to put together a crew for a picture with such an imminent start date. Because of the success of Netflix and Amazon and other streaming networks, there were so many pictures being shot and so many crew members already working that our crew was made up mainly of amateurs. They respected me as a pro, but they didn't know how to quickly and directly tell each other what needed to be done. We were going to have to shoot 123 pages in nineteen days. Impossible. Again, I thought of my mother. I couldn't re-

member Mother ever losing her temper or even expressing herself in a direct manner—except once. Standing
at the kitchen sink, I said something she didn't like and
she slapped me hard across the face. That's what it was
like working in Canada seventy years later. After endless politeness, the amateurs' feelings of frustration built
up and out of the blue they'd slap each other hard. And
then go back to being polite again.

The schedule, the amateurishness, the exhaus-
tion, and my loneliness were devastating. I even began to
wonder if I wanted to stay in the business and continue
working. My hotel was a luxurious prison, and I had too
many days off between scenes. I was sleeping too long on
my days off and wrapping Terry's pink jacket around my
neck for comfort.

The streets of Vancouver were serene and beautiful, a parade of people walking their dogs, who were
usually clothed in adorable jackets, obeying their leashes,
never barking. What was I supposed to learn from this
experience? I was tired of people who refrained at all

costs from saying what they actually meant. Honesty had become a lost art. Watching the election campaign, I wondered: Was Trump more honest than anyone else? But wasn't he mentally unstable? He acted more like a circus barker who wanted headlines every minute to serve his narcissism than a president.

What had become of compassionate criticism, empathy for anger, and caring for other members of our flawed human family? Had the politeness of political correctness "trumped" our ability to speak our true thoughts about others?

The producing company micromanaged everything, causing further frustration and costing more time.

I missed the sunshine, the mountains of Santa Fe, trees, my circling birds, honesty, erupting emotions, and mostly Terry.

I called Yvonne. She said Buddy-Bub had peed on my pillow. He was mad because I was gone. Was I cruel to Terry and now being cruel to Buddy-Bub and Trixie because I was working? Each dog was such an individual personality. I've often wondered how individualism works. Was every living being in the universe a unique individual personality? How did that happen? Did individualism cause wars? Canadians didn't seem to start wars, but they were our allies in them. Maybe the Canadians actually have the answer—*get along by going along.*

Was Donald Trump going to become the next president because, if elected, he would be so divisive that he would actually force Americans to see that at this stage of our democracy we simply had to get along with each other or perish? He certainly stimulated chaotic emotions in most of us because he was so outrageous.

Was this Terry's gift to me? I worried that without resolving the chaos living in each of us, Democracy wouldn't survive. Donald Trump would be the "Causer," the "Decider," as to whether we as human beings were capable and mature enough to sustain a Democracy. Without even realizing he was doing it, he would teach us that we were ignorant of our ignorance. He certainly was an example of that.

I finished my shoot and couldn't wait to get home.

I flew alone, thinking about how Terry had accompanied me everywhere, sitting up so straight in her little
doggie case, inspiring joy and delight in airports and on
planes. She allowed affection while frankly demanding
queenly respect from all who appeared before her.

Her absence forced me to realize that I really
needed to hire a new assistant. I'd been having trouble
writing the job description. Over the years, I've had two
wonderful, longtime male assistants, but each one eventually ran off and married a man he fell in love with.
Young women in short skirts and heels didn't cut it for
me. With Terry's passing I knew I had to do something.
I was now eighty-two and working hard and needed
help. No one I interviewed or met fit the bill.

As soon as I returned to Santa Fe I walked through
my haunted rooms with Trixie and Buddy-Bub, who
seemed tentative, unsure of themselves, because Terry
was not there. Yvonne had noticed it too. I sat in my
hot tub and waited for Terry to send me a bird. Then in
my heart, I actually felt the words, "Call Mary Martin."

Mary ran the animal shelter in Santa Fe and had supervised Terry's "putting down." I called Mary and she told me she was retiring from the animal shelter. I thanked her for everything she'd done for me and for the animals over the years (Trixie came from her shelter). The heart voice said, "Ask her to dinner." I did.

As we sat at dinner I expected Mary to talk about the difficulties of animal euthanasia. She did for a moment and then proceeded to tell me about her retirement plans. The voice came again. "Ask her if she has some nice fifty-year-old gay man who would like to be my assistant." I asked her. She said, "Yes, as a matter of fact, I have a real suggestion." She told me about him and I asked if she could arrange a meeting. She said she would. I thanked her. And even more, I thanked Terry.

Thus began a new kind of relationship with Terry, the likes of which I could not have imagined. I am very sensitive to words and tones and feelings in people's voices. It's as though I can "hear" what they are really feeling, no matter what they are saying with words. This talent has helped me to see and feel the truth with people who either can't or don't want to express what they truly mean. After the "Terry and Mary" dinner I began to experience something phenomenal. I began "hearing" helpful directions in my head. It was as though I had a guide, a teacher, a protector in my ears. It gave me traffic tips, reminders of things I'd forgotten to do . . . sometimes conversations, warnings, suggestions, reassurances, etc. I recoil at the thought of what people will say as I confess these "feeling heart sounds." But I know it's Terry . . . it's Terry as well as other souls that she has attracted.

I've come to believe that when I refused to be sorry or sad or guilty over Terry's circumstance and instead elected to celebrate her freedom, I created the avenue for this communication. She is not dead to me. She exists in another dimensional reality, and I purposefully focus my love feelings toward her. Since I believe that love is the most powerful vibrational frequency there is, I know it attracts other love frequency vibrations. So when I hear Terry guide me, I believe I am hearing guides and teachers who love me and are attracted to my love for Terry like a magnet so they can communicate through her to me. Because I didn't focus on my loss or guilt or sadness, the love I focused on Terry was unattached to anything sorrowful or negative. That allowed my guides and teachers to use Terry as a telephone through which they could speak to me in my head and heart. I thought of how many people would find comfort and even inspiration if they didn't mourn so long for a pet or loved one who had passed. First of all, there is no such thing as death, and second, Time cries when we contaminate it with hurt, anger, loss, guilt, and so on. Terry's guidance was my reward for celebrating her freedom instead of mourning her death.

I feel that these messages and their guidance are real, and it's been happening ever since. On many occasions, the "Terry Team" has instructed me to drive another route because of traffic jams or accidents. Sometimes they have conversations among themselves in my head and heart, expressing differing points of view, but all "getting along" because the focus vibration around them is my love for Terry. It's as though they are communicating on a higher dimension than the third dimension. We live in the third dimension, but now I am positive that "reality" also encompasses many higher dimensions.

After the election of Donald Trump I became more on edge and felt disrupted in my soul. Indeed, Trump was the Disrupter, and I found it difficult to sleep and was agitated in my waking hours. I felt insecure about the future and became lonely with myself. It was almost as though everything I had known in the past was in the process of changing and I would be commissioned with the responsibility of searching deeply for my authentic individual soul in order to survive. Religions had never helped me understand the science of the soul. Religions focused on loving God.

And what is God, really? I asked myself this not as the lone, torturing question that has long plagued the human race, but rather as a question relating to life after death. The answer might be understood more fully by advanced, intelligent spirit beings elsewhere in the cosmos. We humans live in a near constant state of fear of death. I believe we fear death so much that our fear of it has become the ultimate weapon of mass destruction.

I also wondered if beings in other dimensions experience "diversity" as we do on Earth. We humans are comprised of so many races, classes, conflicting political viewpoints, warring religions, genders, and "alternative facts" of life that it seems impossible to get past all our differences.

If we understood the true meaninglessness of death, would we be able to accept all our many differences and move beyond them?

The "death" of my little dog stimulated me to go further and deeper into the mysteries of life and death. And for one reason: I loved her deeply. My search wasn't motivated by loss. It was about my celebrating her freedom from the limitations of this third-dimensional reality.

I was experiencing communication with her

because she was the receiving focus of my love. She wasn't "dead." Her soul had transmigrated to another dimensional reality, and because I had not contaminated my love for her with stressful mourning, she attracted many other multidimensional beings who I believe were my loving guides and teachers. I believe that because I was open to other life instead of thinking death was the end, I was being exposed to new realities and new possibilities. I wish our religions would teach what I am experiencing. It has made me feel more fulfilled and happier, rather than lonely and sad.

It has all become quite profound for me, altering my life extensively and leaving me more open to change and willing to trust in the future.

My guides often discuss the weather changes that are to come because of the chaos so many people fear. They say that nature follows consciousness so nature must do something to clean and balance herself against our chaos. The shamans in New Mexico say that "nature is like a mother dog shaking off the fleas." We chaotic, fearful, disturbed humans without soul knowledge are the fleas.

One of the most profound moments in my life since Terry moved on happened in Santa Fe early in 2017.

My Terry guides nudged me to go into a jewelry store, buy a small, pink stone, put it on a chain that falls just below the Adam's apple, and wear it. I bought a pink zirconia and took it home. Just as I put it around my neck, I turned on the evening news. There was the Women's March taking place all around the world, peopled by some five million humans, mostly women, decorating themselves with pink and marching for equality, freedom, and the right to live in peace.

I thought of how peaceful and free Terry seemed as she floated in the water at my ranch in her pink jacket, seemingly but not actually dead. My little Queen knew what she was doing. I just needed a little time to catch up to her.

Many years ago, I was told that a new energy

chakra center was forming in human beings. It is located in the upper chest between the throat chakra and the heart chakra. It is pink in color and it is called the peace chakra.

Terry's life reminded me that peace and freedom are possible despite the inevitability of so-called death. I *know* that Terry has a forever home in my heart and another one elsewhere with friends who love us both. And that means I do too. Yes, this brings me to tears—but not from loss or sadness. I am full of joy with my newfound "Pink Knowing."

With love and gratitude,
Shirley